MANHUNTER

Keller thought he saw movement at the single window that faced him, so he stopped about a hundred feet from the front door. "Hello the shack. Smith, come outside. I want to talk to you."

The door slowly creaked open an inch and a voice answered from the dark interior of the shack, "Whaddya want? Who are ya?"

"Name's Keller. You're coming back to Santa Fe with me. Sheriff Bushrod wants to talk to you about what happened up in Cimarron. Now come on out with your hands up."

Keller saw the rifle poke out of the doorway and immediately spurred Pacer toward a slight fold in the ground toward the left side of the cabin. A bullet hummed by his head as he pulled up his horse and swung off the saddle in a fluid leap, taking the Winchester rifle with him. He moved to the top of the rise and sighted the weapon at the cabin. For the moment, it was quiet. . . .

Ride the
Red Sun Down

Thom Nicholson

A SIGNET BOOK

SIGNET
Published by New American Library, a division of
Penguin Group (USA) Inc., 375 Hudson Street,
New York, New York 10014, USA
Penguin Group (Canada), 10 Alcorn Avenue, Toronto,
Ontario M4V 3B2, Canada (a division of Pearson Penguin Canada Inc.)
Penguin Books Ltd., 80 Strand, London WC2R 0RL, England
Penguin Ireland, 25 St. Stephen's Green, Dublin 2,
Ireland (a division of Penguin Books Ltd.)
Penguin Group (Australia), 250 Camberwell Road, Camberwell, Victoria 3124,
Australia (a division of Pearson Australia Group Pty. Ltd.)
Penguin Books India Pvt. Ltd., 11 Community Centre, Panchsheel Park,
New Delhi - 110 017, India
Penguin Group (NZ), cnr Airborne and Rosedale Roads, Albany,
Auckland 1310, New Zealand (a division of Pearson New Zealand Ltd.)
Penguin Books (South Africa) (Pty.) Ltd., 24 Sturdee Avenue,
Rosebank, Johannesburg 2196, South Africa

Penguin Books Ltd., Registered Offices:
80 Strand, London WC2R 0RL, England

First published by Signet, an imprint of New American Library,
a division of Penguin Group (USA) Inc.

First Printing, May 2005
10   9   8   7   6   5   4   3   2   1

Chapter 1

The Stranger

"Gawd Almighty, it's hot." The lounging, shabbily dressed old-timer spit a brown stream of tobacco juice at a persistent horsefly that was buzzing the toe of his right boot. His spit missed everything but the stained floorboards of the hotel veranda. "By Gawd, it's hotter 'n a branding iron on a calf's rump," he grumbled. The scorching sun stood high in the cloudless blue sky over the western Colorado town of Cimarron this last day of June 1875. Shimmering waves of heat rose up from the flat ground, blurring the high mountain peaks on the far horizon. A solitary hawk circled high overhead, riding the thermals while listlessly looking for lunch.

Shorty Rogers was lazing in the guest rocker outside the Foothills Hotel, sharing the shade of the veranda with a spotted mongrel dog that lived off the scraps from the slop barrel behind the Two Aces Café. Stretching his extremely bowed legs, the by-product of many years as an itinerant cowpuncher, he settled deeper into the familiar contours of the old rocker. The unwashed odor from his faded and patched shirt discouraged any passersby from lingering to gossip. Shorty's worn, muck-stained boots were years beyond their last shine and the visible remains from a dirty horse stall still caked the sides. Absentmindedly he scratched his beard with a dirt-incrusted finger as he halfheartedly tried to make out the tinny tune being played by the new piano pounder over at the Foothills Saloon. The melody was almost imperceptible over the noise of the panting mutt at his feet.

Shorty had a dilemma. It was hotter than Hell's doorstep, he needed a cool beer, and he didn't have any money. He wouldn't have any until Friday at the earliest, when he swamped out the stables for Heck Pearly. "Damn, pup," he mumbled to the dog at his feet. "I gotta figure out some way to convince someone over to the saloon to buy me a cool glass of beer right soon now. My tongue's turnin' to dust as I sit here." The mental effort of trying to find a solution to this problem consumed his mental process.

He shifted the worn toothpick in his mouth as he spotted a lone rider emerging from the shade of the Aspen trees surrounding the ford across the Gunnison River a quarter mile south of town. With the influx of prospectors flooding the region since old Rafe McQuinn found traces of silver on his claim last March, another rider coming to town was nothing to arouse anyone's notice. Still, something about the way the rider sat on his horse kept the old cowhand's attention focused on him.

Shorty followed the slow journey of the rider up the long slope from the river bottom toward him. The stranger was leading two horses; canvass-wrapped bundles were slung across the animals' backs. As the dusty rider drew closer, he saw Shorty in the dim shade and turned his mud-spattered gray toward him. Shorty and his canine companion watched him in practiced indifference.

The grizzled ex-cowpuncher looked past the rider and

sat up straighter in his rocker. A pair of boots stuck out from one of the folded bundles while long, greasy blond hair dangled from under the other. *Men, by gum,* he concluded, *and deader than doornails if I'm any judge.* Muddy rain slickers were wrapped around the limp bodies like slabs of beef ready for market.

"Howdy, stranger," Shorty greeted the weary-looking rider. His eye caught the dried blood, which had soaked the rider's left sleeve. Shorty looked more intently at the grim, unshaven countenance of the wounded man. Deep blue eyes, clouded in pain, weariness, or both, peered intently at him. Sun-chapped lips, a straight nose with a strong, bronzed jaw that needed a razor's attention, all covered by a thin veneer of trail dust. Long legs gripped the saddle. High-topped Texas-style boots that looked trail-worn and dusty were jammed into the stirrups. "Looks like you've run into some trouble, Mr. . . ."

The stranger answered in a low, deep voice cracked with fatigue and thirst. "Howdy. Would you direct me to the sheriff's office, please?" The stranger carefully shifted in his saddle causing the leather to creak. A faded blue shirt stretched across broad shoulders. The dark stains on the left arm could only be blood—some were shiny and new, some dark and dry. "Also need to see the local sawbones, if you've got one. Even a horse doctor or anybody who can get a bullet outta my shoulder will do."

Shorty answered eagerly, his interest piqued. "Happy to, mister. Sheriff's office is down to the crossroads, turn left, next to the feed store. I don't know about a doctor though. Doc Evans is the only doc in town and he's over to Grand Junction, a-visitin' his daughter and grandkids. Be back Monday a week, I heered."

"Thanks," the man grunted, as he tugged the reins, urging his horse and pack animals down the street. The wrapped bundles bobbed with every step of the tired horses. Shorty evaluated the stranger with keen interest. The stranger's face bore the bronze cast of long hours in the sun, while the wrinkles around the eyes dated him in his thirties. Shorty's eyes dropped to the black twin-gun holster wrapped around the rider's lean middle. Brass .45 cartridges gleamed in the afternoon sun. The pearl-handled grips on the pistols stood out in sharp contrast to the black leather and blue steel. Silver initials, MK, were inlayed into the white mother-of-pearl handles. "Gawd Almighty," Shorty muttered to himself. "It's Marty Keller, the Mankiller, sure as I'm sittin' here. Hot damn, wait till I tell the boys over to the saloon."

Fairly dancing with impatience to spread his tale of discovery, he waited until the stranger turned toward the sheriff's office, then scooted across the dusty street, kicking up little puffs of powder with every step.

Bursting through the bat-winged doors and into the stale air of the saloon, he hurried to the bar and looked around importantly. "Vince, gimme a beer. Fellas, guess who just rode into town?" The bartender halted his idle conversation with a customer and eyed Shorty warily. He had fallen for the old man's ploy of cadging free drinks for tidbits of fresh gossip in the past. Finally, Vince sighed. The day was slow and maybe Shorty did have a story worth hearing. He drew a small brew and slid it down the scarred bar to Shorty's eager grasp.

Shorty gulped down a long swallow from the foam-topped glass. Casually wiping the white residue from his upper lip, he looked at his attentive audience. "Marty Keller, the Mankiller. He just now rode into town leadin' two horses with dead bodies lashed to 'em. He's all shot up to boot."

A sudden outburst erupted as the drinkers gathered closer, peppering questions at the smug center of their attention. Shorty finished his beer and pushed the empty glass toward Vince, who filled it quickly and slid it down the wet top toward Shorty. The bartender leaned his elbows on the wooden bar and waited for the rest of the story.

Shorty took another long swig, again wiping the foam off his lips with the back of a dirty hand. "Yep, it was him, sure as shootin'. I directed him over to the sheriff's office and came right over here. I knowed it was him all right. I seen them pearl-handled six-guns he wears—you know, the ones he got fer cleaning up Bixley, Kansas. He was also a-carryin' two fancy rifles in scabbards on his saddle. Yep, it was the Mankiller all right." He finished the second glass of beer and looked over the men who crowded around him. "Wounded too. A bad one, I calculate. Asked fer a doctor, he did."

"Come on," someone hollered above the din of conversation. "Let's git over to the sheriff's office and see what's goin' on."

His thirst momentarily satisfied and not anxious to lose his audience, Shorty led the way through the batwinged doors of the Foothills Saloon, followed by a crowd of curious men. *By damn, two beers and I didn't pay for neither,* he gleefully thought. His short legs moving much faster than his normal shuffle, he led the small throng to the corner and turned past the feed store, the sweet smell of grain hardly registering on the crowd as they rushed past.

At the hitching post in front of the sheriff's office, the three horses stood patiently. The grisly cargo still lay strapped over the backs of two, while the sweat-streaked gray chewed at the bit in its mouth and stoically awaited its rider.

The crowd stopped and looked in awed silence at the closed door of the jail, awaiting the outcome of the confrontation between their deputy sheriff and the notorious bounty hunter. Those closest to the door strained to hear the muffled voices through the wooden barrier.

The young lawman—name of Morg Simmons, if the sign on the desk was right—had been dozing when the wounded stranger stepped into his office. Keller suppressed a smile as the startled man dropped his feet to the floor with a thump, glaring crossly at the interruption of his little nap. Keller quickly scanned the office for any hidden surprises before moving toward the desk, where the young deputy rubbed the sleep from his eyes. Since going on the bounty trail, he had never felt completely comfortable inside any lawman's office.

"Sheriff . . . ?" he courteously asked as he took off his sweat-stained Stetson, wincing at the renewed shock of pain the movement caused to his wounded shoulder.

"I'm Deputy Sheriff Simmons. The regular sheriff was kilt six months back, and I'm holdin' the job until the elections in November. What can I do fer ya?"

Marty carefully eased the wounded arm against his side and reached into his shirt pocket with his other hand. "Name's Keller. I've got Faro Carson and Ira Whitedog outside, both dead. They're wanted in Nevada on bank robbery and murder charges. Here's the warrants for them." He dropped the folded papers onto the cluttered desktop. He looked at the deputy sheriff. "Would you wire the authorities in Elko, Nevada, for me and tell them to send the reward here as soon as possible?"

Morg Simmons felt the blood rise up in his throat. He knew that he disliked bounty hunters, even though this was the first he'd ever met. He got forty-two dollars a month and a cot in the back room, while killers like this man got hundreds, even thousands, of dollars for taking the same risks. It wasn't fair and he wasn't gonna take any guff from some backshooting bounty hunter, especially one as beat down as the man in front of him.

"Well, Mr. Keller," Morg sneered, "first off, let's make sure they're who you say they are. You better be able to prove all you're claimin'. And the bullet wounds better be in front of them jaspers and not in their backs."

Pushing back from the desk, Morg stood and started toward the door. "Come along. Let's mosey outside and have a looksee at yur dead outlaws."

Martin Keller swallowed his anger as the young deputy stood. It wasn't the first time he'd run up against instant hostility from a local lawman. He needed this man's help, so he bit off any harsh words and simply nodded his agreement.

"I trailed 'em out of Grand Junction last week and caught up with them about thirty miles north of here. They set up a little ambush and knocked me out of the saddle before I knew they were there. I played dead and let 'em come up to finish me off before I cut loose." Wearily, he concluded, "You'll find the bullet holes are in the fronts of both of 'em."

The deputy carefully opened the wrapped slickers and checked the stiff bodies. A quick probe of their pockets provided enough proof of identity to satisfy the young lawman. "All right, Keller," Simmons spoke with contempt dripping from his voice, "appears you have who you say you have. Shot in front too. Harry," he called out to a man in the gawking crowd, "take these jaspers to the undertaker. They're starting to stink up the street. As for you bounty hunter, I'll send the telegram, but you ain't welcome in Cimarron. This is too good a town fer the likes of you. You camp out in the trees yonder. I'll send you word when your blood money gets here. Then I want you gone fer good."

Keller bit down on his tongue as the deputy deliberately turned his back on him and stalked back into his office, obviously pleased that so many townsfolk had heard him ride hard on the famous bounty hunter. The man was talking for the November elections, Keller knew full well. He spoke just loud enough for Morg to hear him. "Whatever you say, Deputy. Just get my money and I'll happily eat trail dust outta your town."

Marty Keller watched the deputy shut the door before turning to face the people surrounding him. He didn't see any friendly faces. Some were just curious, while some were downright unfriendly. As the crowd realized he was taking an interest in them, most followed the men carrying the bodies over to the small building where a sign proclaimed a friendly undertaker was in residence.

The others drifted back toward the saloon to discuss what they had just witnessed. Only Shorty Rogers stayed close, giving the bounty hunter a sincere smile. Maybe he'd get enough new information to finagle another free beer or two from curious drinkers at the saloon.

"Want me to take care of yur horse fer ya, Mr. Keller?" he inquired. "It'd sure be my pleasure."

Marty dug into his vest pocket and pulled out a silver dollar, which he flipped to the old rummy. "I need to find a place to stay and get this shoulder looked at. What do you suggest?"

Shorty scratched his dirty chin. "Well, I don't rightly know. The hotel's full 'cause there's been talk of the silver strike up in the foothills. All the rooms in town are full, for a fact—even if the deputy said you could stay in town." He paused and mumbled to himself for a second. "Ya know, I recollect hearing Sheriff Thompson once say that his missus was a nurse at a Reb hospital durin' the war. The sheriff was kilt about six months ago, shot in the back during a robbery. His widder is a-tryin' to keep their ranch goin' by herself."

Shorty paused and nodded his head in agreement with himself. "Yep, I reckon your best bet is to ride out to Mrs. Thompson's place and see if'n she'll fix yur arm and put ya up. Most of her ranch hands has drifted on since the sheriff was kilt. She oughta have plenty o' room and she probably won't mind that yur a boun—er, excuse me, Mr. Keller. You try her. That's my best suggestion."

Marty nodded, fighting to stay on his feet. "That's it then. How do I find this Thompson place?"

"Just foller the east fork out of town. It's about an hour's ride right past the ford over Swift Creek. You'll see the turnoff with a sign by it. Box T ranch. Tell Mrs. Thompson that Shorty Rogers sent ya." Shorty puffed out his scrawny chest. "Me and the sheriff was close while he was alive."

With an audible grunt, Marty mounted the dusty horse, taking up the reins of the other two horses. "Let me know when the deputy has my money, Shorty. I'll make it right by you. If the deputy wants to know where the horses are, tell him those two backshooters willed them to me before they departed this life." Marty touched the brim of his hat with his forefinger. "Thanks for your help." He chucked the reins. "Get going, Pacer. I'm about done in and we're still a long way from rest."

Shorty watched the slumped rider leave by the east road, then strode back to the saloon. He had more news to share with gossipy drinkers. He was certain to get all the free beer he wanted. Wait until the guys at the saloon heard that he'd advised Marty Keller and given him help.

By the third beer, he'd told several different accounts of the day's activities, but nobody seemed to mind. Vince, the bartender, came over and wiped the bar before asking, "Shorty, what all do you know about this Keller fella anyway?"

Shorty Rogers knew something about everything. If a

body didn't believe it, just ask him. Actually, he had been sitting with a drummer one afternoon a couple of years earlier, listening while the man read a story about Keller from a newspaper the drummer had picked up someplace. Shorty looked around at his attentive audience before commencing his tale.

"Well, I read about him in a Dallas newspaper a while back." Everyone knew that Shorty couldn't read the label on a whiskey bottle, but no matter. "Seems that Keller was the son of a rich Mississippi plantation owner afore the war. He was commander of scouts fer the Reb gen'l Nathan Bedford Forrest durin' the war. After he got back home, he found his place burned out by the Union Army and his land seized by carpetbaggers. Him and his new bride went to Texas, where he started a small ranch. He worked off and on as a Texas Ranger fer spendin' money."

Shorty paused and took a long swallow of his beer. Wiping the foam off his upper lip, this time with his shirt-sleeve, he pushed the empty glass over to Vince, who immediately filled it. Satisfied, Shorty continued. "Some two years later, it seems Keller was out tracking Co-mancheros fer the Rangers when three men robbed the bank in the town close by Keller's place. They must have stopped off at Keller's ranch on the way out of town. They kilt his Mex hand and took their pleasure with Keller's wife afore slitting her throat. One of 'em bashed the brains out of Keller's little boy as well."

Shorty looked around at the silent faces staring in fascination at him, every man hanging on every word of the story. Sipping the fresh beer, he continued. "Well, when Keller came home and found out what happened, he cracked wide-open. He quit the Rangers, sold his place, and started hunting the men who done it. That's how he became a bounty hunter. He hunts outlaws to git money to hunt his family's killers. When he runs out o' money, he bounty hunts agin. Them pistols I was a-tellin' you about was gave to him fer bringin' in the Carter gang after they sacked Bixley. Six men, all dead, like most of his prey. He only goes after 'em if the reward is dead or alive. Handmade Colt .45s with pearl handles and hair triggers. Even got silver writin' on the barrels, I hear. And his initials writ on the grips in silver."

Shorty finished and spoke with more insight than he knew he possessed. "I reckon Keller is a-lookin' fer the man mean enough and quick enough to kill 'em. Only then will he ever find peace of mind." Shorty licked his lips. All the talking had made him thirsty again. He pushed the empty glass toward the bartender. "Vince, how 'bout freshinin' up this here beer? Hell, ya know what I reckon? We'll find him dead on the road tomorrie, shot up as bad as he is. Yep, he'll never git to the widder's place, if'n ya ask me."

Chapter 2

A Hard Ride

The ride to the Box T ranch was about as difficult as any Marty Keller had ever experienced. The only thing that kept him from collapsing out of his saddle was the wave of pain in his shoulder that followed each step of his horse. Waves of intense nausea surged through his belly, like he had swallowed alkali water. Blackness drifted across his brain, in and out. Time became meaningless to the weary rider. He was fortunate to be riding Pacer, the big Thoroughbred he'd purchased four years ago in Kentucky. The smooth even gait of the animal was a blessing to the suffering rider.

"Come on, old fellow," he whispered to the animal. "Get us there. I'm about done in."

The faithful horse wiggled its ears, as if in agreement and splashed across the ford of a small creek. Keller forced himself to watch for a turnoff with a sign nearby. There it was, just ahead. The sign proclaimed BAR T BAR RANCH painted in faded, blue letters on weather-beaten wood. R. THOMPSON, PROPRIETOR in smaller letters beneath framed a block -T- brand in the center. It was a welcome sight for the wounded and weakened rider.

"Come on, Pacer. Find the ranch house for me." Clutching the reins, Keller slumped over the saddle horn and touched Pacer's ribs with his spurs. The smooth gait acted like a sop to his weariness and he dozed off. The abrupt stop of the horse jarred him awake. He was there, facing the pillared front porch of a rock-walled ranch house. Patting the loyal animal's neck in appreciation, Marty called out, his voice cracking with pain and exhaustion, "Hello the house. Anybody home?"

The front door opened and a tall woman in a worn gray cotton dress, with a ruffled white apron around her narrow waist, stepped out on to the porch. Light brown hair framed a face of beauty and strength. The wear and tear of life had not eroded her looks, as far as the weary Keller could tell. Shading her eyes from the low-lying sun, she looked up at the man and horse silhouetted against the bright glare. Marty was slipping away from consciousness, but he could still marvel at the grace of the delicate hand that seemed to fill his vision: long fingers, with shaped nails, clean and smooth. They showed little of the ravages that farm life usually played on the female hand. *Too pretty for a working girl's hands.* She stepped off the porch and walked up to the horse.

"May I help you?" Her voice resonated with the lowlilting drawl that affirmed her Southern roots.

"Yes'm," Keller mumbled as she started to fade from his vision. "Shorty Rogers said you might help me." With that, he slid off Pacer and passed into unconsciousness, falling into the arms of his surprised hostess.

Caroline Thompson tried to hold the stranger up while she shouted for Mose, her elderly black employee, who was forking hay in the stable. "Mose, come quick. Mose, can you hear me? Come quick!" She eased the limp form

down against the steps leading from the porch to the front
yard.

Fresh blood from a wound glistened red against the
dark black of dried blood on the man's left shirtsleeve.
He'd been shot, apparently some time ago. *He's probably
lost a lot of blood,* she thought as she ripped the sleeve
and inspected the ugly red hole in the muscled shoulder
of the unconscious stranger.

Mose came running around the side of the house, a
pitchfork still in his dark-skinned hand. "Yas'm, Miz
Caroline. What's you want from me?" His eyes widened
at the sight of the bloody stranger.

"Help me get this fellow into the house, Mose. Carry
him to the downstairs bedroom." Hurrying inside with
Mose behind her carrying Keller in his arms like a little
child, she led the way to the small guestroom off the
kitchen. Turning down the bed's coverlet, she watched
Mose lay his burden on the clean linens. "What a waste
of clean linens," she murmured to herself. They would
have to be boiled and washed in lye soap to remove the
dirt and blood. For an instant, she returned to those dreadful days back in Charleston during the war. The relentless
monotony of pain-ravaged men—boys actually—and
the pitiful little she could do to help them. No wonder the
offer from the Yankee officer had seemed so wonderful
afterward. Shaking her head to rid herself of the memory,
she returned to the task at hand.

"Mary, where are you?" she called in a loud voice.
"Mose, get the medical bag from the cupboard in the hall.
Mary, I'm calling you. Come here at once."

A miniature version of Caroline poked her head
around the corner with a second still younger copy right
behind. The two little girls looked with wide eyes at the
scene before them. A dirty stranger lay quietly on the

guest bed, while their mother cut his shirtsleeve away from a bloody arm.

"Girls, you'll have to help me. Mary, get some water and put it in the white pitcher. Rose honey, get Mommy some clean rags and towels from the closet in the washroom. Hurry now."

She watched the two dash away to do her bidding. Quickly, she pressed her hankie against the puckered hole and with her other hand started to unbutton the vest and shirt. Mose rushed back with the bag of medical supplies and stood watching until she instructed him to help. "Mose, hold him up while I get this shirt off him. Now you press this hankie against the wound like this while I get the medical supplies ready."

She gazed with detached interest at the person on her bed. Like most men of the day, his bronzed cast stopped at the base of his neck. His chest was alabaster white and showed the signs of several days' sweat and dirt. He had an impressive layering of muscle in his chest, with a satisfactory flatness to his stomach. He did not show any flab to mar the cut of his muscles. *This is a fine-looking man,* she thought. *But if I don't stop that bleeding, he'll be dead in an hour.* Unexpectedly, her thoughts turned to Ray and the never-ending pain of his loss. Angrily, she shook off the feeling and focused on treating the stranger's wound.

As she dabbed at the puckered hole, wiping away clotting blood, the memory of those tragic men in the Charleston hospital flooded her mind, unbidden and unwanted. She counted the signs of previous wounds on the desperately injured stranger. Three other pink scars of healed bullet holes and eight inches of jagged scarring from a knife along the ribs. *This fellow has been in a few scrapes in his life, for a fact.* "God, I hope he's not some outlaw on the run," she muttered to herself.

The red stains gave way to the wet rag and warm water. The two little girls watched subdued as their mother swiftly cleaned around the blackened hole. With Mose's help, she turned him on his right side so she could inspect the exit hole. All she saw was an angry lump pushing against the skin. "The bullet hasn't gone clear through. We'll have to cut it out. Mose, pour some whiskey over the scalpel and give it to me."

She took the sharp knife and carefully cut through the skin at the point of the lump. It only took a shallow cut before a misshapen lead ball popped out on the pillow.

Putting the bloody missile on the bedside table, she pressed a rag against the bleeding before lowering the man back down on the bed. The pressure of his body would hold the rag hard against the new incision until she was ready to sew it closed.

"Good. Now I'm going to clean out the bullet hole while he's unconscious. A wonderful Southern doctor once told me it would help hold down infections from pieces of shirt and dirt that get pushed into the wound. Pour some whiskey on the bullet probe. That one there. And the clamps, yes, that one."

Using the clamp and clean rags, Caroline swabbed the wound. She picked out several small bits of linen and some flesh that was torn free from the muscle of the shoulder. Ignoring a hiss of pain from the unconscious man, she poured some of the whiskey right in the hole, then checked her cut into his back. The blood that trickled out was red and clean. "Well, that's the best we can do, I suppose." She smiled at the wide-eyed faces of her two daughters, who were intently watching the proceedings. "Now I'll show you girls how you sew up a bullet hole. She how small I make the stitches? I'll put a small strip of rag in the hole to drain any puss that forms. Watch, this is how you pull the skin together."

The two young little girls stared intently. Caroline smiled at their fascination. Caroline finished the grisly chore of sewing the skin together, then started to wash the arms and chest of the unconscious man. As it came time to pull the pants off their new houseguest, Caroline ordered the girls out of the room, and they cried in frustration. After their mother finished, they both crept back in and stared in awed silence at the sleeping form until it was time for them to help with·supper.

"Ma," little Rose asked while they ate, "can we keep the hurted man with us for a while?"

Caroline choked back the lump that rose in her throat. She knew how much her daughters missed their father. *Damn the dirty bastard that backshot him.* "We'll have him for a while I suppose, honey. I'll need help taking care of him while he gets well. Would you like that?"

"Oh, yes," the young girl replied. "I think he looks very nice. Don't you, Mary?"

"Ma, who do you think he is?" Mary asked, ignoring her little sister's question, as she often did. "Why did he come here for help instead of to Doc Evans? Why was he leading two horses? Do you think he's a horse thief being chased by Deputy Simmons?"

"I doubt that Shorty Rogers would have sent us a horse thief, Mary. Probably Doc Evans is away to see his daughter and grandchildren. That's why Shorty sent him out here. Your father may have told Shorty that I worked in a hospital during the war." Caroline paused at the thought of her husband. The girls grew silent, awaiting her return to the present. The rest of the meal was restrained, the girls eating perfunctorily, with none of the usual banter among the three of them.

After they had cleaned the dinner table and checked on their sleeping visitor, Caroline walked over to the bunkhouse to speak with John Black Crow, the elderly

Ottawa half-breed who was the ranch's chief horse wrangler. He had worked for her husband since the late sheriff had bought the place, fifteen years earlier. JB, which
is what everyone called him, sat on the ground, leaning
against the log wall of the bunkhouse. He was carefully
weaving a bridle strap out of horse-tail hairs. Wiry, his
black hair heavily streaked with silver and his bronzed
face creased from thousands of hours in the sun, the old
Indian still looked fit enough to break a wild mustang.
His legs were bowed and his fingers gnarled and bent, yet
he still projected a fitness of one much younger.

Caroline spoke with the formal courtesy the old Indian
liked. "John Black Crow, ride into town and see Shorty
Rogers for me. Find out who this stranger is. We also
need a gallon of coal oil, some coffee and ten pounds of
flour. Tell Mr. Potter to put it on my bill." She nodded
slightly and turned to leave. "Find out if Deputy Simmons knows anything about our visitor," she instructed
over her shoulder.

JB responded with a guttural utterance and headed for
the corral. Caroline knew he could speak English when
he wanted to, but he was a principled person of few
words whenever possible. She stood on the porch to
watch the old half-breed ride down the road toward the
turnoff to Cimarron. After going back inside the house,
she read to Mary and Rose until their bedtime. The man
in the guest bed slept soundly, undisturbed by their
voices. The wound seemed clear when she checked it
after tucking her daughters into their little beds. Except
for some fever, he appeared to be recovering as well as
could be expected.

Afterward, Caroline sat in her favorite chair on the
porch, enjoying the cool darkness and drinking the last of
the coffee until JB returned from town. He rode in slowly,
nearly invisible in the night, until he stopped at the porch.

Even though it was a black night, he had seen Caroline awaiting his return.

The old Indian handed over the supplies and a piece of paper. "Potter say you pay bill next time in town." JB paused, collecting his thoughts. "I find Shorty. Him plenty drunk, but tell me about stranger. Some may be whiskey talk. Some talk may be true." The half-breed scout repeated what he'd heard from the drunken Shorty. Caroline shivered at the description of the bounty hunter in her house. Like most lawmen, Ray had disliked bounty hunters, so she had acquired his prejudice against them. Well, she'd fix the stranger up and send him on his way quick enough. *What would make a man want to hunt others for money?* she wondered as she climbed the stairs to the lonely bed that she had once shared with her husband.

Marty Keller opened his eyes to find himself in a soft bed smelling of clean sheets. He looked up at the sweet face of a little girl, about four, who was solemnly staring at him. Even though he felt like he'd been trampled by a stampede, he smiled and spoke.

"Hello. Who are you? Are you an angel? Did I find my way to Heaven?"

The little girl shyly grinned and spoke swiftly. "My name is Rose Ann Thompson." She turned and shouted loudly, "Ma, he's awake." With a tentative smile at the stranger, she dashed from the room.

Marty's eyes explored the room. His gun belt hung from a hook next to the door. He saw his pocket goods piled on a sturdy wooden dresser along with his hat. His boots were placed next to a wooden rocker; they had been brushed free of trail dust. Judging from the sunlight streaming through the window, he must have slept nearly twenty-four hours or more. He realized he was undressed and clean. Carefully he reached for a glass of water on the stand next to his bed, gratefully washing out some of the dryness in his mouth. He awaited the little one's ma, who should be arriving shortly. He tensed his shoulder. Except for some stiffness and a throbbing pain, it didn't feel too bad. Apparently the sheriff's widow did have some experience in treating gunshot wounds.

He snuggled down in the softness, suddenly aware that he was plenty hungry. That was a good sign; it looked as if he was going to live. He spoke out loud. "If she can cook as good as she doctors, well . . ." Just then a tall woman hurried into the room, the little girl right behind her.

"See, Ma," the little one almost shouted, she was so excited. "He's awake. You made him well."

The woman smiled at her daughter and moved to the side of the bed. All business, she felt his brow and his arm just below the bandages. "Don't worry, Mr. Keller. You'll not starve with my cooking. How do you feel?"

Marty started at the sound of his name. "Sorry, Mrs., er, Thompson, isn't it? I don't remember much of my trip out here from town. I feel pretty good, considerin'. Shoulder's a little tender, but a lot better than yesterday. It was yesterday, wasn't it?"

The woman gave Marty a smile that would have stopped a mountain man in his tracks. "Yes, it was yesterday. You've slept like you were half dead."

His memory stirred at the soft drawl in her voice. "Do I hear some of the South in you, ma'am?"

"Why, yes, you do indeed. I was Caroline Gilliard before I married. Raised at Beaufort Plantation, Charleston, South Carolina." She looked at him inquisitively. "I take it there's some in you as well."

Marty nodded and smiled. "Yep, raised in Mississip, educated at VMI, class of sixty-two." He paused, then continued. "I don't know what I said to you yesterday, but I'm looking for a place to stay while I recover from this." He pointed at his shoulder with his right thumb.

"Mr. Keller, I . . . I . . ." Caroline stumbled for the words to tell this man he was not exactly a welcome guest in her home.

Marty misunderstood her hesitation. "Don't worry, Mrs. Thompson. I'm prepared to pay you well for your hospitality. There's three double eagles in my pants pocket. I'll have more coming shortly."

Caroline flushed at the idea that this bounty killer would think she was trying to weasel money from him. Unfortunately, she did need the money, desperately. "Really, sir, I wasn't concerned about any payment for my hospitality. I'm sure you can afford it. Unfortunately, it is the reputation that had preceded you which worries me. It's your status as a kil—I mean . . . what I mean is . . ." Gamely, she pushed on. "It is your profession. I cannot abide a bounty hunter in my home."

Marty realized this beautiful widow knew what he was and didn't like his career or him. More reserved, he replied, "Of course, my apologies. I'll remove myself as soon as I can travel, I assure you. Until then, may I impose on you? I'll take the greatest of pain to be on my best behavior."

He looked at the beautiful Caroline with regret. Her long, wavy brown hair was still shiny and free of gray. A green silk ribbon held it away from her remarkably youthful face. This woman obviously took care of herself. Her figure was firm and shapely with none of the excess roundness that some women accepted with childbirth. Her intelligent brown eyes showed a strength and maturity that comes with the pain of a hard life.

"Very well, Mr. Keller. I'm confident you will be a gentleman while my guest. Please understand I appreciate your offer to pay. I do need the money right now, but

I'm somewhat uncomfortable with a . . . a man of your reputation in my home. What if you are the cause of some harm to my daughters? I trust you understand."

Marty nodded. "I understand completely, Mrs. Thompson. I will be most careful around your girls and will be gone as soon as I am on my feet." He felt the harsh gore in his throat as he fought back the words he wanted to say: *I'm a person like anyone else, dammit. No need to be afraid of me. If you only knew why I bounty hunt.* But he didn't and the moment passed.

Day by day he slowly recovered. The food and companionship of Caroline and her daughters were a welcome balm to his weary spirit. His relationship with the widow remained detached and proper, but Marty let down his reserve with the two girls. The little tykes were soon spending much of their free time with their new friend. His cold heart grew soft when they scampered into his room.

Keller tried not to become too attached to the two little girls, but he could not resist them. He knew it would make his leaving all the more difficult when the time came, and that time was fast approaching.

Chapter 3

Awakened Feelings

"Mr. Marty! Mr. Marty! Are you awake?"

A small, determined voice nudged Keller out of his deep slumber. Groaning softly, he sleepily opened his eyes and saw little Rose standing beside his bed, still in her flannel nightie, her blond pigtails stuffed into a sleeping cap. The little tyke was tightly clutching a ceramic-faced doll and insistently pushing against the feather pillow cradling his head.

"Good morning, Princess Rose," he responded. "Yes, I'm awake now. What are you up to so early in the day?"

"I've come to see if you are all well yet." Rose scrambled on the bed, daintily tucking the long folds of her flannel nightie under her legs. Marty could just see the tiny toes peeking out from under the hem, trimmed in the same lace as her skullcap. "Martha Beth and me are here to visit with you," she said as she settled the little doll in her arms. "She wants to know if you are well yet."

"I'm getting there, little princess. As much as I hate to admit it, I should be out of this bed and about my business. Thanks to you and your mommy. Hello, here comes

Mary. Good morning to you, Mary. Have you come to see how I am too?"

The older daughter nodded and reprimanded her little sister. "Rose Ann Thompson, did you wake up Mr. Keller again? You know what Mommy said."

"I didn't either," little Rose protested. "He was awake when I got here. Ain't that so, Mr. Marty?" She stuck her tongue out at her bossy big sister.

"That's right, Mary. Rose and I were just talking about how much better I'm feeling. Here, jump up here next to your sister and feel my brow. See, no fever at all. Tell me, why are you two up so early?"

"We're going into town," Mary said excitedly. "Ole JB is drivin' us in on our wagon. Mr. Marty, what would a fairy princess wear? Do you think a dragon would have scales just like a rock lizard?" The two girls had thoroughly enjoyed the fairy tale Marty had spun for them the night before. They had been cuddled up on either side of him, deeply engrossed in the story when Caroline walked into his room. She had waited patiently until the story was complete before shooing them off to bed, ignoring their vocal protestations. After a hurried check of his brow and a quick glance at his healing wound, she had left him with nothing more than an impersonal good night.

Once again, Caroline stopped at the doorway and watched with loving amusement the scene on the bed. She worried a little at the way the girls had taken up with the stranger. Of course, it was because they missed their father so much and Keller was good for the girls. He listened to them and was never impatient with their request for stories. It was hard for her to be cool and formal with someone who received so much affection from her girls. She mentally collected herself. She owed it to Ray's memory not to grow too fond nor trusting of the bounty hunter.

"Girls," she scolded as she came into the room, "haven't I told you not to bother Mr. Keller so much? I swear, what am I gonna do with you two?" She smiled at them and leaned over the bed to feel Keller's forehead. "Good morning. Umm. Not a bit of fever that I can tell. How do you feel today?"

"I feel good, thank you. There's still a little pain and stiffness but not much. And the girls don't bother me, honest. They're a fine pair and I enjoy their company." He watched his nurse for her reaction, but she just nodded her head in response, her face impassive and noncommittal.

Caroline gently commanded the two little females scattered on the bed, "Girls, go get dressed and then eat your cornmeal. Mary, don't use too much syrup. We're almost out until I can buy more in Cimarron." She and Marty watched the two scramble out the door, their tiny bare feet slapping on the wooden floor of the hallway. "Mr. Keller, I'm going into town this morning. Do you need anything from the general store?"

Marty nodded, "Yes'm, I do. I need a new shirt and two boxes of forty-four-forty shells. Also, if you don't mind, please stop by the deputy sheriff's office and ask if he's heard anything from Nevada yet."

Caroline gave Marty a calculating look. "Of course, your bounty money. You're thinking about moving on again, I suppose."

Marty nodded his head. "I think I'd better get started, before I grow fat from all your fine cooking."

Caroline looked at the bewhiskered face of her patient. The man was healing quickly. He would soon be able to withstand the rigors of the trail without difficulty.

Keller lay quietly, admiring the way Caroline cocked

her head as she gazed down at him. Suddenly, she surprised him. "You know what, Mr. Keller? You could stand a shave. When I was a nurse in Charleston, I became quite good at shaving my patients. Would you mind?"

"Mrs. Thompson, you don't have to do that. I'll do it myself if you'll supply the hot water."

"I don't mind. In fact, I enjoy shaving a man's face," Caroline replied. She raised an eyebrow at Keller. "It's a pleasure to have a sharp razor in my hand when I tell a man to hold still. You rest and I'll be back in a few minutes as soon as I feed the girls their breakfast." She walked out to the satisfying sound of a chuckle issuing from her patient.

Soon, all three were back in Keller's room. The two girls solemnly stared in fascination as their mother lathered and shaved their new friend. They giggled at the contorted faces Marty made as Caroline maneuvered the razor around his nose and ears. The job was completed without bloodshed, to Keller's relief, and a week's growth of beard was quickly dispatched under Caroline's gentle hand.

"You rest up while we're gone, Mr. Keller. I'll cook up some more elk stew when I get back."

Marty rubbed his hand over his smooth cheek. "Mighty fine job, Mrs. Thompson. There's a couple of silver dollars in my pants. Take 'em and buy the girls a treat from me."

With the pronouncement, the two little ones rushed out to finish their morning chores and to get dressed. They were doubly anxious to go into town now that they would be shopping for themselves. Caroline grinned at Marty. "You'll have those two spoiled rotten before long, Mr. Keller."

Marty returned Caroline's infectious grin with one of

his own. "Please, Mrs. Thompson, call me Marty or Martin. After nursing a fellow like you have, it's your right."

"Perhaps, Mr. Keller, someday I will." She frowned ever so slightly, uncomfortable with the growing familiarity and left the room.

Keller leaned back against the pillows. "Dag gummit, when it comes to being nice to me, that woman is as resistant as a cat next to water," he grumbled softly. He vowed an oath to himself. *By damn, she'll call me Marty before I leave or I'll eat my hat.*

Cimarron was quiet in the hot afternoon sun when JB drove the wagon up to the town's only general store. Caroline and the girls went inside while the old Indian dozed in the shade, leaning against one of the pillars that supported the upper balcony of the living quarters occupied by the store's owner and his plump, rosy-cheeked wife.

Caroline felt a quiet sense of freedom, having some spending money in her pocket again. Quickly, she finished her shopping and paid the outstanding bill to the shopkeeper's delight. Finally, she gave the owner, Seth Potter, the two silver dollars Marty had given her and turned to Mary and Rose. "Girls, Mr. Potter has the money for your treats. You all shop around and make your choices. I'm going over to the dress shop to look at the new styles. Mary, be sure Rose spends half the money now." She smiled at Mr. Potter, knowing he would watch the two as they made their choices.

The two girls swooped toward the candy and toys excitedly debating what they were going to buy, with the old shopkeeper right behind. *That should keep them out of my hair for a few minutes,* Caroline chuckled to herself. She stepped out in the bright sunlight and walked toward the little dress shop down the street. She bought a couple of new ready-made dresses for herself and some fabric for the girls, then again paid her outstanding bill.

Now there was only one last chore to complete. With a shiver of trepidation, she turned toward the sheriff's office, icicles forming in her heart. This would be the first time she had been past the place where Ray died. Almost blindly she walked the familiar route. She stopped and looked at the corner of the building beside the alley next to the feed store. This was where he hid, in the darkness, to shoot her husband in the back as he walked toward Main Street. The townsmen had found Ray facedown right here the next morning, dead. White-hot rage flowed again in her veins. *Somehow, I'll see the murdering bastard brought to justice if it is the last thing I ever do.* It was a vow she had made countless times before. She straightened her back and composed herself.

With her head held high, she opened the door and walked into the little office, where her beloved husband had served the law for twenty years. Morg Simmons was dozing again, his booted feet up on the desk, his hat pulled down over his eyes. Ray had once told her that Morg could sleep standing up. The noise of her arrival jolted him awake and he stood with a sheepish smile on his boyish face.

"Why, Mrs. Thompson, it's a real treat to see you again. Come in, come in." His eyes narrowed. "Is everything all right out at the ranch?"

"Of course, Morg. I just wanted to see you and say hello. I did promise to give you a message from Mr. Keller. He would like to know if you've received any word from Nevada?"

"The marshal in Elko wired that he'd send the money by wire express as soon as the town council released the funds. I suspect it'll be here most any day now. Now you take care, Mrs. Thompson. That Keller is a cold-blooded killer. Don't give him any opportunity to be alone with you or the girls. If you want, I'll come and run him off your place right away." Morg paused and preened his thinning hair with his hand. "I guess you heard I tied a can to his tail when he tried to stay here in town."

"Really, Morg," Caroline protested. "The poor man was half dead. You're probably fortunate he didn't collapse right on your doorstep. I wouldn't talk too strongly about tying any cans. I want you to be sheriff a long time." She smiled to take some of the sting out of the rebuke, but her tone of voice remained serious. "Things are just fine. He's getting better and will probably be on his way very shortly."

"Well, Mrs. Thompson," Morg blustered, "you just take care and call fer me if you need any help sending him on his way. I'll deliver his blood money and make sure he knows he's not wanted around decent folks."

Caroline sighed at the blind stubbornness of some men. She bade goodbye to the young deputy, hurrying back to the general store. She'd have to stay close when Morg came to the ranch, or Keller would have the overconfident deputy for breakfast. She gathered the girls and settled them in the back of the wagon, then joined JB on the front seat for the journey back to the ranch.

The girls played with their new purchases until they fell asleep on the sacks of flour and cornmeal. As they bounced along the road, Caroline went over in her mind for the thousandth time any plan, no matter how impractical, that would ensure her husband's killer faced justice.

"It just isn't fair," she argued aloud, more to herself than JB. "I'm a woman and stuck at the ranch with the girls. I don't have the ability Keller has, nor the freedom to take off and find the bastard. Keller is lucky. He can come and go, no ties, no responsibilities. If only I had the same choices." Her eyes narrowed at the image her mind projected. Ray's killer begging for his life, kneeling in the dirt of some street. It was a satisfying picture. A savage grin crossed her face as she savored the image.

The bounce of the wagon as it rolled across the rocky ford of Swift Creek aroused her from her musings. "Why not use Keller?" she asked herself out loud. "He is an experienced bounty hunter. The town has put up five hundred dollars as reward for the killers. It's not much, but it is something. Maybe I can add a little more to the reward. Heavens knows the ranch is nearly broke, but maybe I can find something. What do you think, JB? Should I try?"

JB merely grunted and continued to drive toward the house. Caroline gave him an exasperated glance and continued voicing her mental deliberations. "There has to be some way of convincing Keller to go after Ray's killer. There has to be a way. I'll pick a good time and bring it up. After all, he's accepted my hospitality and care. He owes me something for saving his life."

They rode into the ranch yard to find the invalid sitting in the porch swing, enjoying the warm afternoon sun on his bare chest and feet. The two girls dashed off the wagon to show him their treats, excitedly describing each one. Caroline instructed Mose to unload the wagon around in back. After a quick inspection of Keller's nearly healed shoulder, she helped him into one of the new shirts she had purchased. She decided to make a fine meal as the first step in her scheme.

"It appears, Mr. Keller, that you can start taking your meals with the girls and me in the dining room. I'll call as soon as it's time to wash up. Girls, finish up telling him about town and come help me get supper ready." She smiled somewhat tentatively at her unsuspecting target before moving inside. The first step in her plan was already under way.

Marty leaned back in his rocker, satisfied. It appeared that the widow Thompson was suddenly becoming much friendlier. That suited him just fine. He watched the evening sun slip behind the far horizon, content for the moment.

Chapter 4

Caroline's Story

The next three days saw continued improvement in both Keller's shoulder and in Caroline's attitude toward him. He was certain she was treating him more like a human being and less like a skunk at a picnic. She had made it clear from the very first that she didn't care for him, and he had accepted that. Not many decent folks wanted anything to do with bounty hunters. Her new attitude was a welcome change.

When Marty chose to track human prey for money, he quickly learned that his only company was likely to be saloon dregs and whores. Most other folks either feared him or scorned him. He had convinced himself long ago that was all right with him. He had a job to do and the folks who felt he was beneath them because of it could be hanged.

The only trouble was he needed the company of those very same people now and then. One winter he'd stayed four months helping an old rancher who'd lost his herd to rustlers. The old man didn't have money to pay working cowhands and would have lost the ranch except for

Marty. That stop had cost him time and money he needed for his search, but it had to be done to salve his troubled soul.

Keller wasn't as hardened as he wanted folks to believe. Now, in the clean and cheerful ranch house of Caroline Thompson, he began to yearn for the things he'd lived without most of the last seven years. The two little girls had brightened his spirit with their animated visits. Mrs. Thompson, whose tragedy closely matched his, was kind and gentle as she treated his wound. Even if she discouraged familiarity, he enjoyed her company and only wanted her to feel friendlier toward him. Although he knew it was better to remain aloof, he needed her friendship. He relished the warmth he felt in his insides when she was close, or gently changing the dressing on his shoulder.

As his health improved, he became restless and walked around the yard of the ranch several times a day. He began to exercise his arm to regain strength and flexibility. Late one afternoon, while carefully pushing against a fence post of the corral with his injured arm, he answered a call to supper from Mary.

Marty washed up and joined the family at the dinner table. "Mrs. Thompson," he began as soon as everyone had filled their plate, "I'd like to take a ride tomorrow morning. Pacer needs the exercise. Where do you suggest I go?"

Caroline looked up from cutting Rose's portion of meat. "Well, if you're feeling up to it, why don't you ride with me to the upper meadow?" She finished cutting the seared steak. "I need to check on the condition of the grass up there. I plan to cut it this fall and use it for my winter feed." She paused and continued in a friendly tone. "We'll survey the ranch while we're out. You've never seen it, have you?"

"Mommy, can I go too?" Mary quickly interjected. "I want to ride with you and Mr. Marty."

"No, honey," Caroline replied. "You'll have to stay here and help Mose watch after Rose. We'll go for a ride some other time, I promise."

"Oh, Mommy," Mary sighed in exasperation, "you always say that when I want to do something. When will Rose be able to take care of herself? It's not fair, is it, Marty?"

Marty shook his head. "No, princess, I suppose it isn't entirely fair. However, you must remember, you're the oldest and your mommy depends on you to help her. You should be very proud that she trusts you with so important a job. I know it makes me proud of you. I promise to let you ride Pacer around the yard when we get back. Is it a deal?"

"Oh yes," the appeased Mary cried. "I get to ride Pacer, all by myself." She stuck up her nose at her little sister, who couldn't have cared less.

"Marty," Rose beseeched her tall friend, "will you bring me a present for staying home with Mary?"

"Sure thing, little princess," Marty agreed. "I'll bring you a bouquet of wildflowers from the high meadow, if I can find some."

Marty turned toward Caroline and caught her looking at him with more appreciation on her face than she'd ever shown before. Caroline quickly dropped her gaze, and when she raised her head, the look was gone. Marty smiled at the lovely woman. He had seen the look, no matter how hard she tried to conceal it now. He felt a small warming at the chunk of ice that had once been his heart. His sleep that night was sound and free of the familiar dream of bitter loss and loneliness.

The next morning foretold a pleasant day. A gentle breeze from the west cooled the dried slopes of the western Colorado foothills. The azure blue sky was filled with scattered clouds, which soared white and fluffy high overhead.

Pacer had been saddled by the old Indian, along with a calico mare for Caroline. Both horses were waiting when the two stepped outside around midmorning. Caroline packed her saddlebags with sandwiches and some sliced candied apples in a wax-sealed glass jar. She told Keller that there would be several streams of water where they were riding, but Marty carried a filled canteen. "Old habits," he muttered to Caroline as they mounted their horses.

They rode a circular route away from the ranch house, down rolling meadows toward the creek that formed the southern boundary of the ranch. Marty appraised the landscape. Caroline's husband had chosen his land well. The ranch was at the highest point of a gentle plateau, sloping down from the higher hills to the east of the ranch. Several meadows spread east and north from the plateau, like fingers from a hand. The flat meadows reached back into the protective mass of the mountains, giving range grass and prairie wheat room to grow. The winter winds would be shielded by the steep hills and if the back end were blocked, the meadows could be natural corrals for stock.

At the small creek that marked the south boundary, they turned east and started a gentle climb into one of the fingerlike meadows off the central plateau. The slough grass of the lower creek bottomland was replaced by heartier switch grass and prairie wheat. Purple coneflowers and mountain daisies were in abundance, their bright colors a contrast to the green of the grasses.

Marty finally spoke. "You must have underground water up here, Mrs. Thompson. There's no evidence of dry land like I encountered riding south from Grand Junction."

Caroline shifted in her saddle, stretching the muscles in her back. "Yes, Ray said we'd never be affected by the ordinary summer dryness here. Swift Creek has never run dry in the nine years I've lived here."

"What sort of stock did your husband run?" Marty swung his head in an arc but saw no animals.

"We have a few head of cattle, of course," Caroline answered. "Mostly Ray wanted to raise good horses. We were slowly building up the bloodlines, buying good stock when we could afford it, but not rushing to put just any animal in our herd." She paused, then pointed toward the north. "I suppose most of the horses we have left are grazing in the north pasture. We graze them from the north to the south as the summer progresses and the higher streams start to dry out."

Caroline led the way up a cutbank and on toward the dark mountain to their front. "All our men left when Ray was killed, except for Mose and JB. I'll have to sell the rest of the herd next summer, I guess, to pay the taxes and put food on the table. We don't need many hands to keep going, but Mose and JB can't do it alone." Bitterness crept into her voice. "I haven't found any wranglers who will work for a woman. Most men are too proud."

Marty nodded his head in sympathy. "Mose and John Black Crow been here a long time?"

"Yes, they have. JB has worked for Ray and now me for nearly twenty years. Mose has been with me since St. Louis, before I married Ray. He was an ex-slave looking for work when I hired him to be my servant. He's been a loyal friend, although he can't do much more than gardening or fix-up work around the ranch house. He can barely ride a horse, certainly not enough to handle a half-wild herd. JB is a wonderful breaker of horses, but is well past sixty, so he's limited as well."

They rode on in silence. Marty flexed his left arm. It was still stiff, but he had regained most of his full range of motion with very little pain, no matter how hard he flexed it. He wanted to shoot his pistols with his left hand. If he was able to handle his weapons, he could be on the trail soon. Somehow the trail didn't have the appeal it once did. He shook his head at the momentary weakness. *The job isn't done,* he reminded himself angrily.

They reached a narrow opening into a wide, grass-filled meadow. "Here we are." She waved her arm in a broad, sweeping motion. "This is my winter feed. I'll cut enough here for all my horses this winter." The wild prairie wheat was belly-high to their horses as they rode farther into the protected meadow. High, steep, rocky hillsides rose from the green basin of the valley floor. The meadow could easily furnish an ample supply of winter hay.

"There's enough grass here to build a mighty big haystack," he observed to Caroline. "Who you gonna get to cut and stack it for you?"

"Ray thought of that when he decided to save this meadow for winter feed," Caroline answered. "He sold a broodmare and bought one of those horse-drawn cutting sickles last fall. It came by freight wagon about three months ago. JB, Mose, and I will stack it, unless someone in Cimarron is willing to work for day wages. It means the horse herd can winter here, protected from the worst of the wind and with plenty of food until the snows melt."

The open meadow pinched down to a narrow pass as they moved closer to the rear. A rock-choked opening in the hill led to a small stream that fed a meandering creek. Marty followed Caroline as they entered the narrow val-

ley between the two sides of the cut. About one hundred
feet beyond, the cut opened onto a wide meadow with a
serene pool of water in the very center.

Caroline stopped her pony and climbed off. "Ready
for some food?" she asked as she tied her reins to a small
bush.

"Yep," Marty answered. "My stomach's as empty as a
rain barrel in the desert."

The lovely widow swiftly set up a cozy little banquet
on the red-checkered oilcloth she threw over a flat rock
beside the burbling water. Marty ate the hearty sandwich
and candied apples with relish. "Mighty fine vittles so far
from home," he remarked. "This is a fine spot to picnic.
You must have been up here before."

"Feel the water," Caroline suggested. It was warmer
than Marty had imagined. "This pool is fed by a hot
spring. I used to bring the girls up here to swim. It also
means the horses have a spring that doesn't freeze in winter, so they have water, as well as hay."

Marty smiled at his hostess. "Planning on swimming
today?" he asked.

Caroline laughed out loud for the first time since
Marty arrived. "Not likely, Mr. Keller. But you are welcome to come up by yourself anytime and use it while
you're here."

The silvery laughter struck a responsive chord deep in
Keller's soul. He wanted to hear it again, but Caroline
grew quiet and spoke softly. "This is the first time I've
been here since Ray was killed." She stared at the water
for a few quiet moments and then abruptly began packing
the tablecloth and empty jar back into her saddlebags.
"We better be riding on back. I want to show you the
north range, and you must be tired from all the exercise."

"I'm fine, really," Marty protested but he couldn't
think of any reason to stay longer. He followed Caroline

out of the valley, back on to the flat meadow. Their horses walked side by side as they moved toward the wide opening and the plateau beyond. The only sounds were the footfalls of their horses and the swish of the windblown grass.

Finally, Marty broke the silence between them. "I really don't know much about what happened to your husband, Mrs. Thompson. Do you feel like telling me?"

"Why not?" she answered. With a bitter laugh, she continued. "I've thought about little else myself for these last six months." She composed her thoughts and looked toward the dark mountaintops to the north.

"Ray had picked up a fellow for a disturbance in the saloon, just a couple of weeks before Christmas last. The next few days he let him stay at the jail on account of the cold. The man was a drifter, Ray said, down on his luck. The night after Christmas, the fellow broke out of jail, shot Ray in the back and broke into the Wells Fargo office. He stole three hundred and some dollars from the safe and lit out to the south. Ray was dead when they found him. The town raised a posse and started after the killer but came back that same day, because a big snowstorm hit unexpectedly."

Caroline paused and looked at Marty bitterly, her lips quivering, dark clouds of sorrow evident in the depths of her brown eyes. "By the time the weather cleared enough to resume hunting the killer, the townsmen had given up. They told me the killer was long gone and couldn't be tracked. They did send out a wanted circular, but nothing ever came of it. The reward was only five hundred dollars, so I suppose it's not worth the effort of men like you." She glared at Keller.

Keller remained silent He wasn't about to fall into the trap set for him by the angry widow.

"I don't suppose you can appreciate just what a good

man. my husband was," Caroline continued. "He gave Cimarron twenty years of peace and protection, often alone, against more than one bad man. I don't think the town gave him the respect he deserved." She sighed and looked at Keller defiantly. "I've never told anyone this before, but I'm going to tell you, Mr. Keller. Ray saved me from Hell."

Caroline stopped her horse and let the mare drop her head to the lush green grass. In a few minutes they'd be out on the plateau, where the graze wasn't as sweet. Marty did the same, throwing his leg over the saddle horn, relaxing in the saddle while Pacer nibbled at the green stems growing around them.

"You know how the war was," Caroline continued. "I was married and widowed in my eighteenth year. My pa died of the flux in sixty-one and both brothers were gone to the war. I never saw them again. My younger brother was killed at Gettysburg and my older lost at sea on a blockade runner. To stay alive, I worked as a nurse for the rest of the war. The suffering and agony I saw nearly drove me insane."

Caroline paused again. "When the war ended, I didn't know what to do. The South was in ruins, my home destroyed, and the field hands run off to the North. Desperate, I swallowed my pride and took up with a Yankee officer. He said he would marry me and I wanted to believe him. He was transferred to St. Louis in August of sixty-five. I went along, still believing in him. That winter, he got his orders to return home to New York. Only then did he tell me that he was married and I was on my own. He gave me some money, so I hired Mose to be my manservant and went to Kansas City, looking for work.

"I could only find work as a bargirl in a fancy saloon. My job was to drink with the customers and sing during the evening shows. Most of the girls working there were taking men upstairs for money." She paused and glanced at Marty, her face crimson with shame. "You know what I mean. Before long, so was I. I was drinking too much and slipping fast into ruin and dissipation."

Caroline raised her downcast eyes. "I know this must sound terrible to you."

All Marty could do was keep his gaze averted, trying hard not to show his shock at her confession.

"By spring I was about out of hope and self-respect when Ray came to KC to buy a stallion. He came in to the Golden Pheasant, where I worked, and saw me sing. After I was through, he introduced himself and bought me a drink. After I was through with my next song, he talked with me some more, until one of the men I was . . . you know, seeing regularly, came up to us, quite drunk, and demanded I go upstairs with him immediately."

Caroline's cheeks flushed with embarrassment as she recounted the story. She was a brave woman to bare her soul to another; Marty admired her grit. He forced himself to look directly at her, keeping a neutral expression on his face.

"Ray knocked the man flat on his back. One thing led to another and I was fired. Ray and I were married soon afterward and on our way back here to Colorado. He restored my pride and dignity, as well as giving me a home and two beautiful daughters. Never in all our years together did he throw up my past to me. He always treated me like a lady, bless him forever. He gave me hope and respectability when I'd given up ever having it again. I was happy for nine wonderful years, and then some back-shooting bastard took him away from me and his children. I mean to bring that man to justice, Mr. Keller, if it's the last thing I ever do."

She jerked up her horse's head. "Now come on. We've got to finish up this ride and check your shoulder before dinner." She spurred her horse, which galloped off, leaving Marty and Pacer trotting after her. Marty spent the rest of the ride back to the ranch house thinking of what she said, his mind whirling.

Chapter 5

The Big Rifle

Marty walked outside the next morning and greeted old Mose, who was standing on the front porch, watching the approach of a distant rider. "Good morning, Mose," Marty gingerly stretched his shoulder. "It looks like it's going to be a hot day, doesn't it?"

"Yes, sir, Mr. Keller, that it does," the old black agreed. "'Pears like we gots us a visitor a-comin'."

As the rider grew closer, Marty recognized the young deputy from Cimarron. The sobering thought that the bounty money had arrived and his excuse for staying was gone flashed through his mind. Before he'd come to this ranch, reward money meant freedom and the means to continue his search for Meg and Bobby's killers. Now, since meeting Caroline and her daughters, it meant separation and loneliness.

"Howdy, Deputy Simmons," Marty politely greeted the man as he pulled up his horse in front of the porch. Mose moved to take the reins, while the young peace officer swung off his horse, scowling at Marty.

"I've brought you your blood money, bounty hunter.

Now there's no reason why you can't be away from here pronto, is there?"

"Good morning, Morg," Caroline said before Marty could reply. Neither man had heard her open the front door. "Mr. Keller is still recovering from his wound. I'll not have him gone before it's well and he can take care of himself. Now, come on in and I'll get you some coffee. You must have missed your breakfast to be clear out here so early."

Grabbing Deputy Simmons by the arm, she guided him into the house, leaving a disturbed Marty standing in the yard. "Excuse us, Marty. Morg and I have some visiting to do. Go on about your morning's business, please."

Marty bit his tongue as the two entered the house. He turned back to Mose, who was still holding the deputy's horse. "I swear, Mose, that youngster's not gonna live to see many more summers unless he learns to walk a little softer around his betters. He acts like that badge makes his skin bullet-proof."

Mose chuckled as he tied the reins of the deputy's horse to the hitching post next to the front porch. "Mr. Ray said that boy had a head stuffed with rocks. I reckon that just about sums him up, Mr. Keller."

"Well," Marty grumbled, "he needs to have a few knocked out so he has room to think about what he says. Tell Mrs. Thompson that if she wants me, I'll be in the barn, giving Pacer a currycomb brushing."

Caroline poured Morg a cup of coffee before putting some raisin cookies on a plate in front of him. "Really, Morg," she chided the young deputy, "Mr. Keller has been a perfect gentleman while he's been here. You shouldn't be coming around telling him to leave. That's up to me."

"I'm sorry, Mrs. Thompson. It's just I know that Ray,

er, Sheriff Thompson wouldn't want you putting up with some killer like him. I just want him away from you and the girls afore he causes you any trouble." Simmons bit into one of the cookies and looked up at Caroline with a sheepish but somewhat defiant expression. "I'm sort of responsible for your safety now. I'm just trying to do what's best."

Caroline patted his arm. "Thank you for that, Morg. I appreciate your concern. Truly, Mr. Keller has been no trouble to me or the girls. I'm certain he'll be on his way as soon as he has fully recovered. Don't forget, he was gravely wounded."

"Well, it won't be any too soon for me. I'll leave his blood money with you. You give it to him and run him off. Believe me, Mrs. Thompson, it's for the best."

Simmons passed over an envelope stuffed with twenty-dollar greenbacks. "There's four thousand here," he remarked with a sneer. "That's five year's salary for a decent man. Now that he's got it, he'll be able to pay you well for your care and hospitality. Charge him plenty for his stay. That'll get him on his way quick enough."

Caroline took the bulging envelope of blood money with a grimace of distaste. Quickly she put it on the shelf of the hutch, as if its contents were loathsome. "Thanks, Morg. I'll see that Mr. Keller gets it. Now tell me what's going on in town."

Keller brushed Pacer hard, trying to work off the anger Simmons' visit had caused him. "Pacer, old friend, you've had it soft these last few days. It's time to hit the trail again." Marty swept the stiff brush across the loyal animal's flanks. The horse snorted and contentedly chewed his mouthful of hay. It seemed to Marty as if the animal was questioning his common sense, wanting to leave such an ideal place for the hardships of the trail.

Marty laughed at such perfect logic coming from the dependable animal and finished his chore, reflecting on the past week. He had known more peace and happiness than at any time since Meg's death. It would be difficult to leave all this behind to ride down the lonely trail again.

Marty walked out of the barn, brushing the horsehair off his arms as Morg and Caroline came out onto the front porch. He watched them bid their farewells while the young deputy climbed into his saddle. As Simmons swung his horse away from the hitching post, he saw Marty standing by the barn door and rode over to him. Keller tensed as the brash lawman approached.

"Keller, I gave your blood money to Mrs. Thompson. I suggest you take it and get going. You're fair game for any gun-crazy bum who happens by. The widow or her girls might get in the way and be hurt. Think about it." Simmons spun his horse and galloped out of the yard toward the town road.

Nodding his head in agreement, as much as he hated to, Marty walked toward the main house. Caroline was still on the porch, observing the exchange between the two men.

"Did Morg tell you that he brought your money?" she inquired. "I've got it inside, if you want it."

"Yes'm," Marty replied. "Just hang on to it for now." Marty hesitated, looking hopefully at Caroline. "I think I'll go out and shoot my guns this afternoon, Mrs. Thompson. Would the place where we ate yesterday be all right?"

She shook her head. "Ray had a better place fixed up for target practice over in the east meadow. I'll take you there after lunch, if you don't mind company while you practice." She turned back into the house without waiting for Marty's reply. His look of anticipation would have made her smile.

As they leisurely rode to the target range after a light lunch, Caroline thanked Marty. "I'm glad you didn't react to Morg's insensitivity, Mr. Keller. He thinks he's got a special mandate to take care of me and the girls for Ray's sake. I know you could chew him up and spit out the splinters if you really wanted to. I appreciate your patience with him. Ray had high hopes for him as a peace officer." She smiled. "That is, in time."

Marty chuckled. "I sure hope he grows up fast then. He seems bent on getting his head busted, the way he reacts to strangers." He looked at his riding companion. To him, she was a vision of beauty. Her maroon leather riding skirt and long-sleeved white shirt contrasted with the sweat-stained Stetson on her head and her work-roughened boots. He observed to himself, *"This woman has done her share around the ranch."* Marty tuned back in to what she was saying.

"Not all strangers, Mr. Keller. It's just what you happen to do for a living. Ray didn't have much good to say about bounty hunters. I suppose Morg picked up his attitude."

"And you too, Mrs. Thompson?"

"Well, I must admit," Caroline replied, "it took me a while to get over my prejudice. However, you've been a gentleman and welcome guest. The girls have thoroughly enjoyed your visit and the money you paid me came in handy."

"Maybe then, Mrs. Thompson, you would now do me the honor of calling me Marty or Martin. I'm plumb uncomfortable hearing Mr. Keller all the time. Toadies at the bar call me that, not my friends." He smiled warmly at the tall, lovely woman riding beside him. "Please."

Caroline looked at him solemnly. "All right, Martin, I will. You may call me Caroline. Look, there's the place I was telling you about." She pointed to her right.

The late Sheriff Thompson had laid out a nice target range fronting a high valley wall, which caught stray bullets. Tying the horses to a gnarled cottonwood, Marty took his rifles and extra ammunition to the firing area. Caroline walked with him, noting the professional skill he exhibited as he prepared his weapons for use.

Keller slid the Winchester rifle out of its saddle scabbard and ejected all the cartridges inside. He reloaded and began firing at objects on the hillside, moving from one to another at various distances, out to two hundred yards and more. Caroline was impressed that he hit just about everything he shot at, dead center. After three quick blasts that splattered on a flat, man-sized rock over two hundred yards to the front, she interjected.

"That's some shooting, Martin. And what a handsome rifle. Is it something special?"

Blam! Blam! Marty fired twice more and ejected the last empty shell from the smoking weapon. "Yep, it's called a Winchester 73. One in a thousand." He turned the rifle in his hands, looking fondly at the workmanship. "I went back to New Haven, Connecticut, a year ago and bought it directly from the factory. The name means it has been put together by the best craftsmen in the factory. Out of the ten thousand rifles in the production run only about a hundred were good enough to be so designated. This rifle cost as much as a good horse but it has saved my life more than once, so it was worth it." He laid it down on the blanket he'd placed next to the stump upon which Caroline was sitting.

Stepping again to the firing line, he pulled out the pearl-handled pistol from his right holster. *Pow! Pow! Pow!* He deftly put three .45 bullets into a lightning-shattered tree trunk about sixty feet to the left front. The impacts appeared to be almost on top of one another. He fired his final two shots at a small black rock about sixty

feet to the right. The rock dissolved in a cloud of darkened dust. As Marty holstered the gun with his right hand,
he pulled the left gun free and pumped five quick shots at
a large rock about one hundred feet to the front. It seemed
to Caroline that every bullet hit the rock, busting off dust
and chips, but Keller was frowning as he slid the gun
back into its holster.

"Still having trouble with your left arm, Martin?" she
inquired.

Marty made a couple of fists with his left hand and
shook his arm. "It seems a little shaky," he muttered.

"Well, I shouldn't wonder. You nearly died from the
wound you had. However, it seems to me that you did
pretty good." Caroline watched him reload the two pistols with gleaming .44 cartridges.

"Pretty good won't slice the bacon in my business. To
stay alive, I have to be the best, anytime and every time."
He filled the air with gunshots, until both pistols were
empty and smoking in his hands. Nodding his head in satisfaction, he reloaded one pistol and put it in his holster.
He put the empty one next to the Winchester. "I never feel
comfortable with all my weapons empty at the same
time." He smiled, yet his eyes were sad, she observed.

Finally, he removed the last rifle from its saddle scabbard. Digging into the leather pocket sewn on the scabbard, he withdrew six massive bullets.

"My goodness, Martin!" Caroline exclaimed. "What
on earth is that? I suspect that's about the biggest gun I
ever saw."

Marty smiled, holding the rifle up for her to see. "It's
a Spencer .52 caliber, breech-loaded, single-shot, heavy-
barreled buffalo gun with a four-power scope on it. That's
what this long brass tube is on top of the barrel. You can
see four times better than with your eye alone. They were
used during the war to shoot at enemy officers from ex-

tremely long range." He pointed way up the canyon wall. "See that rock just to the left of that cedar tree?"

Caroline shaded her eyes with her hat. "Why, that rock must be half a mile away. I can barely see it."

"Look through the scope in my rifle," Keller told her. "It's just like seeing with a sea captain's telescope."

She looked, then turned to Marty. "I can see it easily. Amazing." She remarked as she handed the rifle back, "Mercy, but your rifle is heavy." She admired how effortlessly Marty held the heavy weapon.

"Yep," Marty replied. "Weighs about twelve and a half pounds, but it will knock down a buffalo at better than half a mile. When bushwhackers get me pinned down, it sure kills their appetite for shooting it out."

Marty took a thin, steel forklike object from the scabbard and pushed the long leg into the ground. Then he rested the octagon-shaped barrel in the twin forks. "This helps me to hold it up while I aim," he explained. He sat Indian fashion and peered through the scope. Caroline walked over to stand beside him while he aimed the rifle. "Watch your ears," he told her.

Boom! In spite of his warning, the loud explosion startled her. Looking toward the rock, she saw a huge puff of dust rise up from the middle of it. "What a shot!" she cried out in amazement. Marty cocked the trigger housing, ejecting the smoking-hot, empty brass casing and slipped in another round.

He fired four more rounds, two holding the rifle without the fork, hitting the rock every time. "Would you like to try it, Caroline?"

She hesitated only an instant. She really didn't want to shoot the massive gun, but she knew it would please Keller and she wanted to do that. Sitting as he had, cross-legged behind the steel fork, she allowed Keller to settle the rifle into the pocket of her shoulder. "Now put the

crosshairs of the scope dead center on the rock. See it?"
Caroline grunted her affirmation. "Now squeeze slowly,
holding your breath. Try to make the firing a surprise to
your finger."

Caroline had fired with Ray before, so she knew how
to shoot. Slowly she increased the pressure on the trigger.
"It's hard to keep the crosshairs centered," she murmured. *Boom!* The big rifle went off with a shock against
her shoulder that hurt more than the recoil from any shotgun ever had. She didn't see the target at all through the
gun smoke and dust raised by the explosion of the cartridge.

"Did I hit it?" she inquired anxiously.

Marty grinned broadly. "You sure did, it was a grand
shot. Not many women could've done it. I'm impressed."

Caroline felt a twinge of embarrassment at her pride in
handling the deadly weapon. "I suppose it has killed its
share of men, hasn't it?" she remarked as she handed the
rifle to Keller.

"Only outlaws who were trying to kill me, I promise
you." Marty carried the rifle over to the other weapons
and got out his cleaning tools. "I learned to use a gun like
this during the war and realized how useful it would be
against bushwhackers." He looked hard at Caroline. "I
hope you believe me when I tell you that I don't sneak up
on men and shoot them in the back, like what's been said
about me. I've brought in many men alive and even
wounded. I only kill those that don't let me take them any
other way."

Caroline sat on the stump and watched as Marty
started to strip and clean the tools of his trade. Keller
sneaked a quick glance at her. Her hat hung loose off the
back of her neck and her shiny brown hair was glistening
in the sunlight, highlights of red teasing his eye.

Marty continued. "Even the two who jumped me ten

days ago. I'd have just as soon brought them in alive. I needed the reward money to continue my search, not just a way of making so-called easy cash."

Caroline jumped on his statement. "What search are you talking about, Martin? Can you tell me? Please, I'd like to hear your story."

Keller's eyes narrowed. His countenance grew grim. His mind retreated to the past, even while his hands continued the familiar routine of cleaning and oiling the stripped guns. His distress was clearly visible and he was tense, as if facing an angry rattlesnake.

Chapter 6

Marty's Story

Keller spoke slowly, as if the telling itself was physically painful. "You know how it was after the war. Ruin and destruction everywhere. I returned to my home to find it gone, burned and looted by soldiers from both sides. The only friendly face I found from the old days was Meg's. She was the daughter of one of our neighbors, Margaret Sue Lyman. She'd been just a little girl when I left for college. She was a full-grown woman when I returned; beautiful as a new day, with light blond hair and deep blue eyes that would draw you down like sinking into a clear pool of water. Why, when she smiled, a cloudless sky seemed drab in comparison."

While he talked, Keller continued to wipe an oily rag over the dirty pistol. "I haven't told a soul on this earth what I'm tellin' you now, Caroline. Mainly, I suppose, because nobody's ever cared to ask. Anyway, Meg and I had no choice but to leave Mississippi and strike out for a new place to put down our roots. The tax assessors were selling out the old plantations as fast as they could fore- close on them. We had each other and two good horses her pa had hidden from the Confederate confiscators. After he died, Meg hung on to them even though she had to go hungry and could have sold them for eatin' money. I still had a good horse I'd taken from a raid up in Kentucky, so we sold one of her two and bought a small place in east Texas."

Marty fussed with his pistols, working the action as he continued. "It was hard going the first few months and money was short. Luckily, I was able to join the Ranger Company over in Dallas. It was a way to make extra cash money. A couple of the rangers had ridden with me in the Army. With their help, I didn't have any problem getting a commission." Keller paused as he continued wiping the burned powder from the barrel of the weapon. "Most of our trouble was with Comancheros and Indians. I was gone a lot it seemed, but Meg never complained. We kept on working our place and raising cows. Money I made in the Rangers went right back into the ranch. Meg did without a lot, but she kept saying that we'd have it all someday, if we just kept at it."

Keller glanced at Caroline. She was picking at some small spatters of mud on her skirt. He would have quit talking if he'd seen a look of pity from her. He certainly didn't want that. Her face was gentle and concerned, but there was no pity there. Carefully, Marty started to reassemble his pistol as he continued.

"The second year, Matthew was born with Meg's blue eyes and curly blond hair. I was so happy, I nearly wanted to bust. We had a hundred head of prime cattle and a few dollars in our pockets. I was just about free from having to ride with the Rangers anymore. One Sunday, in June of sixty-eight, they called for me to help track a raiding party of Comancheros who'd killed some settlers over by Abilene." Marty slid the cleaned pistol in its holster and started working on the Winchester rifle.

"I really didn't want to go. Two of my hands had taken some cows to San Antonio to a buyer and Meg would be at the ranch with only one Mex hand to watch over her. She insisted I go on, that it would be all right. My vaqueros would be home in three days and we could use the fifty dollars I'd get for the posse. The Rangers were anxious to get started, so I got my goods and kissed her and little Matt goodbye. We chased those raiders clear down to the Rio Grande River before we caught up with them. We shot a few, but most escaped over into Mexico."

His voice tightened as he continued. "I was anxious to get back home. You know, I just seemed to feel Meg needed me." His voice caught as he went on. "I knew something was wrong as soon as I rode into the yard. My two hands and my next-door neighbors were waiting for me with the news."

Keller savagely brushed at his eyes, then proceeded. "They'd returned from San Antone about a week after I left. They'd been held up waiting for the buyer to come up with the money for the cattle." Marty sighed, bitter pain in his voice. "It seems that five men had held up the bank in Brownwood—that's the town we lived nearby. They had come to the ranch, probably to steal fresh horses. They shot my Mexican hand right off, then proceeded to have their way with Meg for some time before they cut her throat."

Caroline gasped at the killer's viciousness. "What about your son?" she demanded.

With hate in his voice, Keller replied, "One of them bashed his head against the fireplace hearth and dumped him on her body. My men were in tears when they told me. The Mex had lived for a few hours after they found him and told them what he could. Five men: one a Mex half-breed, one with a scar above his right eye and maybe only three fingers on his left hand. Two who must have been brothers: short, blond, gaps between their front teeth. And one gray-haired older man with sleeve garters on that had Injun hair—you know, scalps—hanging from them."

Marty finished the rifle and slid it back into the saddle scabbard. "Come on," he abruptly announced. "We need to be getting back. I promised Mary a ride on Pacer before supper." He moved toward the horses, a subdued Caroline behind him. Softly, he continued his story. "I went to the little graveyard where they'd buried my wife and son and swore I'd find the men who had killed them and have my revenge."

Swinging up on Pacer's back, he led the way out of the canyon. Now that he had started the grim story, he couldn't stop. "I tried to find them with the Rangers, but the trail led out of Texas. They'd headed north, into the Indian Territories and the Rangers couldn't leave the state. So I resigned, went back, sold my place, and took up the trail after 'em. I hunt them until I'm out of money, then bring in a bounty outlaw, then hunt 'em again. I've been doing it for better than seven years now."

Caroline spoke for the first time since he had started. "And you never found any of them in all this time?"

"One. I did find Richland, the fella with the sleeve garters, about a year later up in Kansas. I caught up with him in a saloon. When he realized who I was, he drew on me and I had to shoot him. Before he died, he told me the others were named Sanchez, Al Hulett, and Andy and Bob Swain. I got them in Bixsley, Kansas, a year later. The one named Hulett did have three fingers on his left hand. A grape shot took off the other two during the war." Keller slammed his palm against the pommel of his saddle in frustration, as he continued.

"They'd split up six months earlier because Hulett and Sanchez wanted to ride west, robbing gold prospectors, while Richland wanted to stay in Kansas and work as a card sharp. I've not heard a word about the others in all that time. That's what I was doing out in California, before I came to Cimarron. I didn't find any leads out there, so I was working my way east, when I got on the trail of the two bank robbers outside Elko, Nevada. They weren't the men I wanted, even if they near finished me off."

At the top of a small rise, they spotted a small herd of horses grazing on the sweetgrass. "There are our horses!" Caroline exclaimed with pride. "I was hoping you'd get a chance to see them today."

To Marty's experienced eye, it was a fine-looking bunch of horseflesh. The leader was a magnificent Black, an Arabian, from his looks. "'Pears like you've got better than thirty head there," Marty observed. "Fine-lookin' animals too. You've got the makings of a great breeding herd."

Caroline nodded proudly. "Ray put a lot of work into this herd. He was determined to upgrade our strain to the best horses this side of the mountains."

She pointed at the dark stallion. "Ray spent a bundle on the Black. He's a registered Arabian. Put him in with Morgan mares or some good quarter horses and you'd get a good mix for this area." His voice was upbeat, as he drove the demons of his past back to the hidden recesses of his mind. Caroline looked at Keller with empathy drawn from shared grief. She understood the fire that burned in his belly. She had the same feeling in hers.

Biting off any statement, Caroline spurred her mare on. Keller rode beside her as they crossed the grassy slopes of the plateau toward the ranch below them. "Now you're about ready to start again, aren't you?"

Keller shifted in his saddle, as he answered, "Yep, I guess I am. I'm filled with hate and revenge like dirt in a grave. Until I find the men who did it, I'm not fit for anything else." His eyes demanded that she agree. "You understand now, I reckon, what it is that drives me."

For a few moments they rode silently, each engrossed in their own personal loss. Finally, Caroline answered, "I do, Martin. I wish I could go out and find Ray's killer. My daughters and this ranch make me stay here, unable to find my own revenge." She turned to look at him as they rode together and finally said what had been on her mind for some time. The words tumbled out in a rush. If she paused, her courage might fail her.

"You could do it for me, Martin. You could find the man who killed Ray. There's five hundred reward money on them and it wouldn't hold you up much at all in your search."

Keller was jolted by the impassioned plea from his riding companion. "Whoa now, Caroline. You know I can't do that. Why, I don't need your money, and besides, my fight is with the men who killed Meg. You mustn't even think of it. I'm not a hired gun. I bounty hunt only to make enough money to continue my search. No, don't even consider it. It's not possible. I will not do this for you." He spurred Pacer to a lope to get away from Caroline and her demanding eyes.

A short time later, as he led Pacer around the ranch yard, a proud Mary perched on the animal's back, he felt Caroline's accusing eyes burning holes in his back. He tried to get involved in Mary's conversation, but wasn't very successful. His mind was elsewhere.

"Marty, you sure aren't much fun today," the little girl exclaimed with some exasperation.

"Sorry, princess," he confessed. "I've been thinking about something else. Now what was it you were telling me?"

Dinner was strained and silent. Caroline excluded him from her attention, while the two little ones were busy jabbering about sewing a new dress with their mother after the meal. Marty glumly ate in silence.

After supper he went outside and sat morosely in the rocker on the porch. He watched the old Indian currycombing the horses in the corral and inhaled the cooling air of the evening. The sun painted the western horizon shades of red and orange as the burning orb dipped behind a dark cloudbank lying low.

The gentle pastoral scene held little comfort for him. He didn't notice Caroline's approach until she was beside him. Gracefully, she slipped into the matching rocker and breathed deeply.

"The breeze feels good, doesn't it?" she remarked. She stretched her booted feet out in front of her, crossing them while she slowly rocked back and forth. "Martin, please reconsider. You admit you've been looking for these men for years and only found one. You may not need the reward for Ray's killers, but you do need this place."

Marty frowned. "Now look here, Caroline—"

She held up her hand. "Hear me out, please. You're going to need a place to come back to. A place to rest, one that's safe from men who might want to try their skill with a gun against yours. If you'll find Ray's killer for me, I'll have a place for you here, as long and as often as you want it. This will be your home and you'll be welcome anytime."

"Dammit, Caroline. You don't know what you're saying. I'm considered scum, not fit for decent folks' company. No, it would never work."

"Yes, it would work, Martin, because I'll make it work. The girls and I are your friends now and we'll always be your friends, no matter what."

She was both defiant and determined. "All I ask is that you find my husband's killer. If you do, you'll be a part-

ner with me and the girls in this ranch, no questions
asked. Now think about that before you go to bed."
Swishing her dress, she rose from the chair and walked
back inside. Marty could hear her preparing the girls for
bed.

They burst outside with their nighties on, to give
Marty good night hugs and kisses, and then left him alone
on the porch, slowly rocking and considering Caroline's
offer. *Damned if Caroline isn't as stubborn as I am,* he
chuckled. *If she can't hunt down her man's killer herself,
then she'll have me do it for her.* He admired her spunk
and determination. He owed her and the girls a lot. They
had restored more than his physical health. They had restored some of his humanity—something he thought was
long gone. The very thought of going back on the
hunter's trail was becoming difficult to confront. He lay
awake for long hours that night, mulling over her offer.

The next morning, he walked into the kitchen to find
Caroline making biscuits, her arms white to the elbows
with flour. Her greeting was as warm as the oven behind
her. "Good morning, Martin. I hope you slept well. And I
hope you considered my offer."

"Dammit, Caroline," Keller grumbled. "You're making a serious mistake, offering me a part of this place and
for all the wrong reasons. Besides, I have my own men to
hunt. I don't need to take on yours too."

Tears of frustration suddenly dripped from Caroline's
eyes. "Damn you, Martin Keller. If I was a man, I'd do it
myself. But I'm not, so you have to do it for me. You owe
me. I kept you alive. Without me, you wouldn't be able
to go on hunting your killers."

Keller sighed. She was right. He quit fighting her. "All
right, Caroline, you win. I'll track your killer, at least for
a while. Now stop crying, please."

Caroline wiped her eyes with the corner of her apron.

"Thank you, Marty. What I offered last night still goes. There's only one other condition."

Marty groaned. "I knew it. Well, what is it?"

"I want you to take John Black Crow with you," she replied, beating the roll of white dough with her fist, sending up a small cloud of white dust.

"What on earth for?" Marty exclaimed. "He'll be no help and may even slow me down. Besides, don't you need him here?"

Caroline shook her head, her brown hair flying across her cheeks. Carefully she pushed a wisp away with her arm, trying not to get flour on the shiny brown strands. "No, I want him to go with you. One, he's an excellent tracker. Ray said he was the best he'd ever seen. Two, he's wanted to go after Ray's killer from the first. Three, he'll remind you of your agreement, when it gets hard to go on. There may come a time when you'll want to say to hell with your promise."

She smiled and blew hair away from her cheek. "You may as well say yes. My mind's made up."

"All right," Keller capitulated. "But if he holds me up, I'm sending him back to you. Tell him we leave tomorrow morning. Today, I'm riding in to talk with Deputy Simmons. I need to get an idea of the direction your husband's killer took when he left town. Fix up some supplies for us and tell JB that we'll take one of the horses I brought in as a packhorse. He can have the other for his own, unless he has a better one."

Keller paused as he started out the door. "I'll buy your half-breed a new rifle in town. You tell him to pack enough for a week on the trail."

As he trotted Pacer past the house toward the town road, Caroline stood in the doorway, her hands tucked in her apron, watching him. The image stayed with him all the way to Cimarron.

Deputy Simmons was more agreeable when Keller told him he was leaving to take up the hunt for Sheriff Thompson's killers. Marty got all the information the deputy had of the earlier chase, bought supplies for the trail, then returned to the ranch late in the afternoon. The old Indian's eyes lit up when Marty gave him the new Winchester rifle. He bobbed his head in quiet gratitude, then hurried out to finish his preparation for the trail. Caroline was in her kitchen, busy packing slices of bacon, dried beans, and flat bread into bags for the pack horse.

"Don't forget the coffee beans," Keller reminded her. "I'd not be worth much if I missed too many mornings without my coffee."

"I put in two pounds already," Caroline reassured him. "Did you find out anything from Morg?"

Keller nodded. "Yep, he's certain the drifter rode south toward Durango. By the time Simmons got word to the sheriff there, he'd already gone on, probably to Santa Fe or into Arizona Territory. I'll check around in Durango. Somebody may give me some solid information. Morg also told me about your husband's pistol with the two twenty-dollar gold pieces mounted in the grips."

Caroline nodded and continued to pack the supplies for Keller. "Yes, I forgot about that. The town gave him the gun when he reached his twenty-year anniversary as sheriff. Ray was mighty proud of that pistol." Elation swirled through her. Finally, someone was going after Ray's killer—someone she could depend on. Yet she knew she would miss the quiet presence of Keller, and so would the girls. "You sure your arm's fit and ready to travel?"

Keller moved it in a quick circle. "Yep, feels just fine. You're a good nurse." He smiled at her.

A grave expression crossed her face, then she returned to her packing. Marty went to tell the girls that he was leaving in the morning. He found them playing on the front porch, where he distracted their disappointment by playing with them until supper.

The sun was just a pink promise of light when he slipped out of the house the next morning. JB waited patiently as Marty inspected the goods strapped on the packhorse. Caroline entered the barn with a cup of coffee and some cookies on a plate just as he finished tugging on the main lashing.

Smiling at the tall man standing beside her, she offered him the food. "Here's your start-up coffee, Martin. You seem about ready to go."

Marty glanced at JB and nodded. "Yep, we'll be off in a few minutes." He sipped the hot fluid for a moment and handed her the empty cup. He reached into his pocket and pulled out some of the reward money. "This is for you."

Caroline waved her hand. "No, you keep it. We can manage. You don't owe me anything more than you've already given me."

Keller put the roll in her hand and closed her fingers over it. "Believe me, a man on the trail as long as me pays his way. You've earned it and I got full value for the money. Use it to keep the ranch going. It may be a while before I come back this way again."

He swung into the saddle, then looked down at the woman. "I will be back, Caroline. After I've done what has to be done, I'll be back."

"I pray you will, Martin. Take care of yourself, you hear?" As he led JB and the packhorse out of the yard, she muttered softly, "Kill the bastard for me, Martin. Kill him." She continued to watch the two riders until they faded in the haze of morning, whispering softly, as if the wind would carry it to him, "Get him Martin. Then come back safe. Get him for me. Please, God, let Marty get him."

As the riders merged into the shimmering distance, she brushed aside a drooping wisp of light brown hair and turned to go inside. The girls would be up soon and wanting their breakfast. She looked one last time to the south, but there was nothing to see. With a heavy heart, she shut the door on the quiet morning.

Chapter 7

The Outlaw's Deal

Alva Hulett stirred on the filthy bed, then suddenly jolted wide-awake. He looked up at the darkened ceiling. Sometimes at night, the uncanny ache of his missing fingers would wake him, as if they were still there on his hand instead of fertilizing the wildflowers outside Shiloh Church, back in south Tennessee. But that wasn't it this particular time. He shivered, as if a chill had swept over him. When he was a barefoot brat in Tennessee, his gran'mammy had said a sudden awakening at night was a sign. "A cat's walked over yur grave, sonny boy." Then she would nod wisely, puff on her old corncob pipe, and look at him with her head cocked, as if waiting for him to thank her for scaring him.

Was someone peering at him from the edge of the bed? No, there was nobody in the dingy room but him and Rosa, the fat whore who lay snoring softly beside him. The eerie chill slowly passed and Al settled his head back against the grimy pillow.

The past year had been his best one since the war started. Not that he didn't deserve it, after the five miser-

able years locked up in that hellhole of a prison in
Sonora, Mexico. He yawned and stretched his long, lean
arms. Al was well over six feet tall, taking up the full
length of the bed. Like most Tennessee hill boys, he was
as slender and sinewy as a green willow branch. He had
come a long way since he'd marched off to war in sixty-
two, only sixteen years old and already meaner than a
timber rattler at shedding time. The war had only refined
his innate cruelty. Now he killed easily, man or woman,
child or granny, with neither remorse nor hesitation.
Nowadays he took what he wanted and the devil with
right or wrong. He and Sanchez had ridden with the Comancheros right after the war and planned to do a bit of
business with them again, real soon now.

When his longtime partner Sanchez and he were released from the Mexican prison along with Lute Payson,
who had shared a cell with them for the last three years,
their fortune seemed to change. The five long years of
busting rocks in the broiling sun had made him viciously
thirsty for some quick money. First, the stage in Arizona
and then the bank in Nevada had filled their pockets the
easy way. They had ridden into Santa Fe completely free
of pursuit.

Except for having to shoot a damned smart-assed cowboy who had caught him cheating at cards, the time had
passed peaceably. Without evidence, the local sheriff had
called the shootout self-defense and let Al go free with a
stern warning that he would be banned from Santa Fe if
it happened again. Smugly, Al snorted to himself.

As luck would have it, shortly thereafter he hit a hot
streak at the tables in the Red Garter Saloon, It wasn't
long before he had better than a thousand dollars stashed
in the old pinon tree south of town. He also had the rifles
that Lute and Sanchez had robbed from the freight wagon
last month. Twenty brand-new Winchesters and five

thousand rounds of ammunition coming on consignment to the hardware store in town. Sanchez had killed the teamsters driving the wagon, so their trail was still clear.

Sanchez had met up with Al when the pair had ridden with Comanchero raiders right after the end of the war. They were two of a kind. Sanchez had drifted into the work of killing and stealing as if he were born to it. The vicious Mexican peasant had developed a strong feeling of loyalty for Al and had followed him when Al decided to strike out on his own. Al was cunning enough to always make the split of their stolen gains as fair as possible. For reason's inexplicable even to himself, he had stayed in contact with the Comanchero leader, a ruthless killer named Muley Hawkins. The pair had done just fine on their own until he had decided to try the banks in Mexico.

He had even laboriously scrawled a few lines to the one man he felt kinship toward while in the prison, hoping it might stir Muley into bringing the whole gang down to Sonora to bust him out of the hellhole. While he had not even received a reply, now his connection with the outlaw was going to bring him a tidy profit. Four days ago, he had received a wire in response to his offer to sell Muley the new Winchesters. They had a deal with the outlaws for four thousand in gold for the rifles.

As soon as the Comancheros arrived with the gold dollars promised for the rifles, he, Sanchez, and Payson would be off to Mexico to buy his dream: a grand hacienda on prime cattle land far away from U.S. marshals. Then they'd live like the kings his mama had read about to him when he was a young'un. He felt Rosa stir against him, and the urge to have her struck him. Rolling over on her warm brown flesh, he soon forgot all about cats and graves. Shortly thereafter he was snoring away, not to wake until the heat of the day drove him from the bed.

He dressed hurriedly, avoiding any conversation with the talkative brown whore who shared his bed. "I'm gonna git a shave an' haircut," he declared. He wanted to go over to Pedro's to let the half-breed Indian girl shave him and cut his hair. She aroused his blood to the boiling point when she lathered his face and combed his hair. It was almost as good as having Rosa in bed. He had tried more than once to buy a night in bed with the shapely young female, but old Pedro knew a good thing when he had it. He never allowed the girl he had purchased from a destitute Indian father to spend the night with anyone. As a result, Pedro's barber business had boomed.

Looking into the spotted mirror over Rosa's vanity, Al ran lean fingers through his dirty hair. He could hear Lute Payson's raucous snore in the adjoining whore's bedroom. Scowling, he shook his head. He was completely disgusted with the third member of his little gang. The black-bearded Lute was drunk most of the time. He stank like a wet pig and was hardly worth the effort that Al had spent keeping him out of trouble.

To make it worse, during the war, Lute had deserted from the Confederate Army, which was as close to sacrilege as Al could imagine. Only the fact that the bearlike Lute was a cold-blooded killer, always willing to do what Al didn't want to do himself, made Lute's presence tolerable. Al smiled at his reflection. For sure ole Lute would get a bullet in his back before they reached their final destination in Mexico, he decided. Satisfied at his decision, he walked out of the room into the street, where the morning sunshine warmed his face.

As on most summer mornings in the capital of New Mexico Territory, it was hot and dry. Santa Fe bustled with cowboys, trappers, prospectors, teamsters, and cold-eyed human predators. The pickings at the card table made the time spent here as lucrative as Al had ever known. He had money, girls, and sippin' whiskey available for the taking and not a hint of any lawman hunting them.

Al walked briskly toward the edge of town and Pedro's barbershop. His pulse quickened at the thought of the soft fingers against his face and scalp. Stepping off the boardwalk to cross the rutted street, he spotted a grimy rider with greasy buckskin trousers riding toward him. Pale blue eyes shifted from side to side as the rider rode down the street. Al grinned. Muley Hawkins, sure as shooting. The man hadn't changed a bit in the last six years. His cold eyes never stopped searching for trouble as he approached Al. He turned his horse to pass close by Al.

Muley's presence in town meant the Comancheros and the gold had arrived. He talked softly as they casually passed each other. "Howdy, Muley. Meet you two miles south of town around two o'clock. There's a cutoff into a grove of cottonwoods. Be waiting in 'em."

The shifty-eyed rider barely nodded and continued on toward the center of town and its numerous saloons. With greedy anticipation of the coming meeting, Al turned into the barbershop. The soothing effect of the shave calmed the rushing blood coursing through his body. As soon as his shave was over, he hurried back to the rooms above the saloon. Pounding on the connecting door, he stepped inside and shouted at Lute, who was still snoring like a drunken hog, "Git up, you drunken bastard. Ya hear me? Wake up."

Lute groggily raised his head and peered bleary-eyed at Al. Mumbling a soft oath, he looked around for a bottle that still had some whiskey in it. "Yeh, I hear ya."

"Well, git up and make it quick," Hulett ordered. "Then find Sanchez and git back here. I just saw our friend from the Comancheros ride in. Now git on up and move yur ass."

Payson groaned again. His head was about to burst, as were his kidneys. He needed a drink bad and there didn't seem to be any whiskey in the room. The old acne-scarred whore he'd been shacking up with was gone, so he would have to take care of both problems himself. He headed for the outhouse, scratching his belly and unbuttoning the filthy shirt he had worn for the past week.

Sanchez saw Lute enter the Mexican cantina. He watched with detached indifference as the heavily bearded outlaw moved over to the bar and had a quick shot of tequila before making his way to the table where the husky Mexican was sitting with two young bargirls. As Lute shuffled up, Sanchez motioned them away. The Mexican member of the unholy threesome was short and squat, cruel as a mountain lion, with eyes the color of obsidian. He pushed an empty chair out for Lute to plop in.

"Alva wants us to get over to his room right away," the foul-smelling Payson whispered in a conspiratorial manner. "Says the contact is here fer our meetin'." He took a quick gulp from the half-empty tequila glass in front of Sanchez.

Sanchez immediately stood and, after throwing a couple of silver dollars on the table, strode from the cantina, Payson scurrying after him. Turning down the alley, they went up the back stairs to the Red Garter and to the room where Hulett impatiently awaited.

"Christ, Lute," Al complained. "How long does it take fer ya to do a simple chore? I've been waiting fer the better part of an hour."

"Sorry, boss," Lute whined. "I had to go to the outhouse first and it took a little longer than I figgered."

Al glared at Lute's pathetic face. "Don't give me none of yer stupid excuses. When I tell you to hurry, ya damn well better do it. I'll kick yer dirty ass out of our party if'n ya don't get crackin'—ya hear me?"

Lute nodded and mumbled an abject apology, which Al ignored. Instead, he turned to Sanchez and reported his conversation with the Comancheros leader. "Met Muley Hawkins outside 'bout two hours ago. Told 'im to meet us down by the cottonwood grove south of town at two."

Al paused and collected his thoughts. "Sanchez, rent us a wagon from the Mexican livery and pick up the rifles and ammo. I'll go on ahead and cut the deal. You take Lute with you." Sanchez nodded and slipped out the back way, followed by Lute.

Al smiled contentedly to himself. Soon they could get on the trail to Albuquerque and then on to El Paso. After that, Mexico and freedom. They'd overstayed their time in Santa Fe. Al liked to keep moving and he couldn't shake the feeling that they hadn't got away as clean as it seemed from that killing of the bankteller in Nevada. Al rubbed his hands together in anticipation of the cash soon to cross his palms. He decided to take a few bottles of whiskey with him to smooth the negotiations with the hard cases he was meeting.

When Al turned his rented horse into the grove of Cottonwoods, a red-bearded man with a beaded buckskin jacket stood before him. The sentry scanned Al carefully. The rifle he held never wavered from Alva's stomach.

"Howdy," Alva greeted him, "I'm Alva Hulett. Lookin' fer Muley Hawkins. Where 'bouts is he?"

The red-bearded man answered in a raspy voice, as if his throat had been injured with a club or bullet at one time, "Back that a-way bout three hundert yards." He pointed downstream with a horny thumb and spit a glob of brown fluid into the dust. Shifting some chew to the other side of his mouth, he wiped his lips and pointedly asked, "Got any terbacca on ya?"

Hulett reached into his saddlebags and pulled out a fresh-bought twist and a pint bottle of liquor. "Here's some on me, friend. The wagon with our goods'll be along right shortly. Guide 'em on back to yer camp, whilst I go on and palaver a spell with Muley." He rode deeper into the grove, feeling the cold eyes of the lookout boring into his vulnerable backside.

Muley Hawkins sat waiting for him at the edge of the small clearing along with several other white men, a couple of Mexicans, and about a dozen Indians, mostly Comanche, but a couple of half-breed Apaches as well. The Indians were dressed in a motley assortment of garb, with only the feathers in their long black hair to identify them as Indian. One Indian wore a faded red shirt over a breechcloth. His high-topped moccasins came to just below the knees. He carried himself with the proud carriage of a leader. Al had never seen him before, but several of the others looked familiar.

"Howdy, Muley," Hulett greeted the ex-muleskinner, who was the leader of the gang. Muley had been a teamster hauling freight until he saw how easy it was to steal what he once carried for others. "Here's some tobacco and whiskey fer the boys. My wagon's on the way, with the goods I promised. Ya bring the gold?"

Muley grabbed a bottle and tore off the cork top, taking a long swig before answering, "Yep, four thousand, just like I said in the telegram." He passed out the bottles to the eager crowd of foul-smelling men. They scattered to different places in the clearing, nursing the amber fluid, or gulping it down, as was their inclination. Muley motioned to the tall Indian wearing the faded red shirt. "This here's Red Shirt, the war chief of my Comanche warriors. Red Shirt, this here's Alva Hulett, who used to ride with us Comancheros."

"Howdy, Red Shirt," Hulett solemnly intoned. He pointed to his eyes and then his heart. "I'm pleased to greet the great war chief of my Comanche friends." The tall Indian stared at Hulett with expressionless eyes, then grabbed the whiskey bottle from Muley. He moved away and sat alone and drank greedily.

"Friendly bastard, ain't he?" Hulett whispered to Muley. The ex-teamster just grinned and nodded, taking a sip of his whiskey. Al tried to strike up a civil conversation with the outlaw until Sanchez arrived, but it was pointless. Muley preferred the whiskey to talking. Hulett sat morosely beside the surly outlaw leader. He was glad he'd left riding with men such as this. He was meant for better things.

Finally, the wagon appeared, clattering through the rocky streambed, driven by Payson and followed by the red-bearded guide and Sanchez, both on horseback. The new rifles were unloaded and passed around to outstretched hands anxious to get a new killing toy. The money was passed over and packed into the saddlebags carried by Sanchez. Finally, Hulett and his two henchmen prepared to leave. Muley Hawkins looked up at the mounted Hulett, wiping his lips with his sleeve.

"Where you boys off to now?" The pale-eyed outlaw inquired in a most civil tone, softly stroking the wood stock of his new rifle.

With a flash of intuition, Alva answered smoothly, "Hell, we're gonna spend this here money in Santa Fe, at the card tables and whore houses, until we're plumb busted. Where you and the others a-going?"

Masking his disappointment over the fact that he wouldn't have a chance to steal back the gold, Muley pointed with his thumb. "We're gonna move west a spell.

A couple of the half-breeds have family up around Shiprock Reservation. We'll stay there awhile, maybe pick up some new recruits and then swing south back toward Texas way." He slapped the stock of his new rifle. "With this here Winchester, I reckon we'll have no trouble gettin' what we want, when we want it."

Hulett nodded and led the way back toward the road. He knew that he was fortunate that the Comancheros' sense of honor wouldn't allow them to rob or kill in their camp or he would be buzzard meat right now. Back on the main road, Hulett urged his horse toward the adobe buildings of Santa Fe. A cold feeling nestled hard in his back until he was safely surrounded by townsfolk going about their business blissfully, unaware that cold-blooded killers were only a couple miles away.

As the safety of others surrounded him, Al relaxed and made his decision. "Sanchez, you and Lute be ready to travel at daybreak tomorrow. Meet me at the O'Brian Stables. We're gonna git on down to Albuquerque before those Comancheros raise some hell around here and draw attention to this area. We'll pick up the money on the way outta town." Taking the saddlebags full of gold with him, he left the other two at the Mexican livery and returned to his meager room.

The livery stable still needed a light from a soot-covered coal-oil lantern when they assembled the appointed morning, ready for the trail. Al had lost nearly five hundred dollars in the past twenty-four hours, a sure sign that it was indeed time to travel. They loaded the last of the supplies on the pack mule that Sanchez had purchased with some of the newly acquired gold.

"I'm sure ready to light outta here, boss," Lute Payson announced. "That whore I'm shackin' up with is startin' to talk about settlin' down." He gave a loud, irritating laugh. Looking around the dimly lit barn, he spotted a wagon sitting in the far corner. PROFESSOR SEAN MCNULTY'S MAGIC POTION AND ELIXIR was brightly painted in red on its clean white side.

"Hey." Lute pointed. "There's the wagon that there patent-medicine man was sellin' from. Did you guys taste his elixir? Man alive, it was good. Had the taste of peppermint and the kick of a mule. I wouldn't mind havin' some to drink whilst we're on the road to Albuquerk."

"Well, hurry up and grab a few bottles," Al snarled. "It's time we was outta here." He watched Payson break the simple latch off the back of the wagon and rummage around inside. He emerged with an armload of pint-sized bottles of the brown liquid, which he hurriedly stuffed into his saddlebags.

Unknown to the three men below, the stable boy was up in the hayloft, sleeping away the last of his night shift. Hearing the commotion, he peered over the edge of the rafter, a frown on his face, as he watched the three men break into the McNulty wagon. He knew that Fionna McNulty, who was the singer and entertainment draw for the professor's sales pitch, was staying with the livery stable owner's daughter.

The livery owner wouldn't be happy to hear that his friend's wagon had been looted in his stable, but the young man wasn't foolish enough to say anything to the hard cases below. He just watched sleepy-eyed the theft of the elixir.

After the three men rode out of the barnyard and down the street toward the south way out of town, the young man climbed down from the hayloft to survey the damage to the wagon. When the livery owner showed up, he explained what had happened. "It was the three-fingered man from the saloon and his cutthroats. He killed a man who accused him of cheating at cards last April. I saw him and he was for certain a deadly killer if ever there was one."

The professor was enraged at the wanton theft, but shrugged his shoulders philosophically. "It'll give Fionna a chance to finish her dress and I'll mix up some more elixir before we go. Damn the scurvy bastards. I wanted to get over to Durango sooner not later." He sighed as he surveyed the damage.

Chapter 8

Durango Bound

Keller and John Black Crow's first day on the trail was warm and cloudless. At noon they stopped by a small stream found by JB under the canopy of several tall cottonwood trees. There were both water and sweet grass for the horses, as well as shade for the tired riders. Marty was quick to praise the choice. "A good spot, JB. Plenty of shade for us and green grass for the horses. You hungry?"

Without awaiting an answer, Marty got Caroline's dried beef jerky and passed some over to his taciturn half-breed companion. JB had barely spoken since they left the ranch. After receiving only grunts in response to his statements, Keller quit trying to start a conversation and instead concentrated on his plan for tracking the killer of Sheriff Thompson.

He would have to visit the saloons in Durango and all the general stores on the outside chance that someone might remember a man who had ridden in ahead of a storm last December. He prayed they would also know where the same man had headed. If not, he'd have to make a fifty-mile circle around the town, searching for some lucky sign that would put him on the trail.

Marty had passed the long miles thinking of Caroline and the ranch where she waited with her daughters. She had willingly offered part of her ranch and all her reputation for his stalking skills, and he was determined to succeed. Demanding half the ranch as payment was ludicrous to him, but considering it as a safe haven, a respite whenever he needed one, was somehow comforting. He knew he was working for an extraordinary woman. The picture of her standing in the yard as he rode out remained clear in his memory.

The old man sat silently beside him, his aged, weathered face inscrutable and calm. The old Indian seemed to be making the ride just fine. He showed no sign of fatigue. His gray-streaked hair was tucked under a ragged beaver top hat with an eagle feather in it. His high-topped moccasins were in good condition, as were his checkered shirt and canvas pants. JB carried a knife sheathed to the belt around his waist. Only the worn coat he had tied behind his saddle pommel seemed insufficient for any long track. *Never mind,* Keller thought. *I'll get him a new one when we reach Durango.*

After a restful noon hour stretched out under the shade of a tall cottonwood, Martin got to his feet. "Time we pushed on. You ready to ride?"

The old breed merely grunted and swung into his saddle with a fluid movement of one many years younger. As the pair left the streambed, JB spoke for the first time.

"I go up into hills. You ride on. JB find where you stop for camp." Without another word, he turned his pony left toward the wooded foothills and trotted off. Keller watched him until he entered the trees, then continued on down the trail toward Durango.

"Well, all right, old-timer," Keller spoke to the retreating figure. "Go off into the hills and smell the wildflowers. See if I care. Come on, Pacer, we'll make better time without the old codger."

From a great distance, he heard a faint rifle shot. Several hours later, he heard another. *If he's in trouble, he'll have to get out of it by himself,* Keller decided. *I'm headed to Durango, not to round up some lost half-breed.*

The afternoon sun was touching the western horizon when he stopped by another small stream and hobbled Pacer. As he wiped down the big horse with his saddle blanket, JB rode in, a fresh haunch of venison strung over the pinto's rump. The half-breed swung off his panting horse and carried the meat to a branch, where he hung it. Turning to Keller, he smiled and pointed to the venison.

"JB try new rifle. Good weapon. I shoot very straight. Kill young doe. Now we have fresh meat tonight." With that, he unsaddled his paint and hobbled the tough little range horse next to Pacer.

The venison steak JB cooked that evening was delicious. After eating the meat, some beans, and bacon-fat biscuits, Keller was satisfyingly stuffed. He stretched out on the soft grass and relaxed. Giving a mighty yawn, he was fast asleep before the moon had risen a quarter of the way up the sky.

As he drifted off, he vaguely sensed JB prowling around for a few minutes, before settling in across the campfire. Keller didn't stir until the morning showed pink in the eastern sky above the high mountains.

JB had smoked some of the venison all night over the banked campfire and Keller ate a fair-sized hunk with his morning coffee and dried biscuit. They were on the trail before the sun fully cleared the eastern mountaintops, reaching Durango after a hard day's ride. As they rode down the dusty street, Keller scanned the small weather-beaten town, which was as raw as any he had seen in

some time. At the far end of the street he spotted a livery
stable and he pointed Pacer that way. "We might as well
spend the night here. I'll ask around about our man as
soon as we take care of the horses." Keller paid to stable
the horses and got permission for him and JB to sleep in
the hayloft from the livery owner.

"Rub the hosses down good," he told the stable hand.
"They've been ridden hard these last two days. Also feed
both animals nothing but oats before you turn 'em out for
the night." He left the stable hand and JB busy rubbing
the horses with rags from an old burlap bag and walked
toward the nearest saloon. Pushing open the glass door,
Keller strolled in and walked slowly to the bar.

The High Mountain Saloon was almost full. Keller
had to shoulder his way up to the scarred bar that
stretched along one wall. The husky barkeep was polish-
ing shot glasses with a soiled rag, while steadily chewing
on a well-worn toothpick. The barkeeper kept a careful
eye on the activity at the numerous tables while expertly
refilling his customers' empty glasses.

Keller put a five-dollar greenback on the bar. "Give
me a beer." He put his left arm on the bar and leaned over
a bit so the barkeep could hear him above the babble of
voices and a tinkling piano. As the barkeep delivered the
foam-topped glass, Keller said, "Looking for a man,
young, blond hair, and carrying a fancy ivory-handled
.44. Came from the north last December, just about the
time you had the big snowstorm. There's ten more where
this came from for the right information." He pointed his
thumb at the greenback on the bar.

The bartender scratched his gray-flecked mustache
and thought a few seconds. "Sorry, bud, can't help you.
There's been a bunch of fellas driftin' through the territory, with all the gold and silver strikes, ya know. Why
not try the Hungry Man Café? It's the best spot in town

fer food. He mighta stopped there and et." Scooping up the bill, the bartender walked back to his glasses.

Keller sipped the cool beer, then left the noisy saloon. Nothing was ever easy, it seemed. He spotted the café across the dusty street. Avoiding the numerous horse piles on the dirt thoroughfare, he crossed over. A good meal would be welcome, even if nothing else came of his visit to the café.

After a hearty steak-and-potato dinner, with lots of black coffee to wash it down, Marty tarried while the plump-cheeked waitress cleared the table. "How 'bout some dried-apple pie?" she inquired.

"Fine by me," Keller replied. "A slice would strike my fancy if it's as good as the vittles I just had."

When the friendly waitress put a large piece of the warm pie in front of him, Keller smiled and asked, "I'm looking for a fellow came through town last December, just about the time of the big storm." He described the drifter to her and looked hopefully at the flush-faced woman.

She furrowed her brows, then suddenly smiled in satisfaction. "I do remember a stranger, now that you mention it. Rode in covered with snow. Another hour and he'd have froze to death out there. He smelled." She pinched her nose at the memory. "You know, bad, like it'd been a year since he took a bath. Tall and skinny, with a mean look about him. Acted nervous the whole time he was here. I don't remember much else, just that he ate and left, like he was in a hurry. Friend of yours?"

Keller shook his head decisively. "Nope, just the opposite, although I aim to find him. Do you have any idea where he went after eating?"

The waitress wiped her hands on her soiled apron. "It seems to me that he asked where he could buy horses and supplies. I directed him over to Mr. Logan at the livery stable. I don't know if he went or not, though. More coffee?"

"No, thanks, but thanks for your information. I appreciate it."

Keller finished and left a sizable tip on the table. He walked out and turned toward the stable, where he had left JB and the horses. As he walked past the general store, a coat hanging in the window caught his eye. It was sheepskin, with the fur side in. It would replace the worn thing the half-breed scout was now wearing. He turned into the store.

A slight clerk with sleeve garters on his shirt moved to his side. "Yes, sir, what can I do for ya?"

Keller nodded toward the sheepskin coat. "I'll take that coat and some coffee and some canned peaches, if you have any." He scanned the shelves, picking up another pair of cord pants and a blue denim shirt for himself. As he prepared to pay, he spotted a leather-bound writing tablet with paper and envelopes inside. He had promised Mary he would write her while he was gone, so he bought it as well. After receiving a few coins in change from the solicitous clerk, he walked out of the twin doors with their wavy glass inserts distorting the view and returned to the stable.

JB was already up in the hayloft, getting settled in for the night. He climbed the wooden ladder to the loft, carrying the coat draped over his arm. "I figger you'll be needing this," he told the kneeling Indian, handing him the coat.

With solemn formality, JB took the offering and nodded his head. "JB thanks Keller." Slipping his arms into the sleeves to see how it fit, he asked, "We leave tomorrow?"

Marty nodded. "I reckon so, if I can find out a bit more

from the livery owner." He stepped back to the ladder and headed down. "I'll be back in a few minutes."

Marty knocked on the open door of the livery where the owner, a Mr. Silas Logan, sat at his paper-stuffed roll-top desk, writing numbers in a journal.

"Come in," the balding owner commanded. "What can I do fer ya?" He pushed back from the desk. Keller could smell the odor of the barn floor rising from his work-stained boots.

Keller eased into a rickety old chair next to the desk. "Mr. Logan, the waitress over at the Hungry Man said she sent a man over to see you last December. Just about the time of the big storm. He was a stranger, tall and mean looking, and smelly as an old goat. Did he get some horses from you?"

Logan leaned back in his chair and looked at Keller. "I sort of do recollect the person in question. Why d'ya wanta know?"

Keller looked hard at the livery owner. "He killed the sheriff over in Cimarron during a robbery, and I aim to catch him."

Logan nodded his head. "I heered about that. So he's the one, huh? I sold him two of my best stock. He'd about rode his hoss to death, gettin' into town ahead of the storm. A barrel-chested sorrel. I hardly got nothin' fer him when I resold him last spring. Yep, a tall, skinny fella, and a mean looker fer sure. Took off the next day, I 'spect, over to Santa Fe, in New Mex Territory."

"What makes you think he went to Santa Fe?"

"He took four days' rations of grain fer the horses," Logan replied. "You wouldn't figger he'd go back to the north, seeing as how that's where he came from. Nothing to the west fer two weeks and only Farmington to the south. That's a no-place town to go to, filled with tame

Injuns and busted ranchers. Nope, I'd have to figger on Santa Fe, if'n ya was to ask."

Marty nodded. "I suspect you're right at that. Well, I'll head on over that way and look around a bit. Why don't you wrap up four days' worth of grain for me and my companion? We'll be on our way come sunup. And thank you for your help, Mr. Logan. I sure appreciate it." Keller offered his hand to the older man.

"My pleasure, son," Logan quietly replied. "You take care and watch yourself. That fella was plumb mean, no doubt about it. I wish I hadn't sold him such good horse-flesh." He sighed and turned back to the mound of papers on the desk.

Keller exited the small office and returned to the sweet smelling hayloft, where he swiftly fell asleep next to a softly snoring JB.

By the time Marty had finished washing and shaving the next morning, JB had the packhorses loaded and Pacer saddled for him. The two of them rode out of town accompanied by the yapping of a local dog declaring to the world that he feared no strangers. Marty set a steady pace as the pair of riders followed the rough road to the east. JB rode easily beside him, proudly wearing the sheepskin coat in spite of the warm morning sun.

The old Indian seemed more open to conversation, so carefully, Keller drew him out. He needed to learn the half-breed's history. Would he be a help or hindrance?

"How long you worked at the Thompson ranch?" Marty asked when the time seemed most appropriate.

JB glanced over at the white man. "Many years I ride with Thompson, even before the white man's war. My père a French Canadian trapper. Jean Valose come to Mississip in 1815. Take my ma, who Ottawa Indian princess, for wife. He bring us to Great Mountains when

JB a small boy. We hunt and trap, all alone except for animals and other mountain men.

"When Père and Ma die, JB hunt and trap alone until I go live with Blackfeet. Soon I have fine squaw and fat papoose. Then they die of white man's fever, so JB live near fort at Leavenworth and scout for Army. Get drunk every payday. Not happy time. Sheriff Thompson come to fort and meet JB. Hire JB as scout and tracker. When I get older, he make me head horse wrangler. Now I stay to help Thompson's woman. Her life sad and hard. Maybe change when we find Thompson's killer."

The old breed pulled out his new Winchester rifle. "Now I go ahead and scout for camp. You ride easy, Keller. JB take care of you." The pinto loped off, the wiry Indian scanning the country to the front.

Keller smiled. He had gotten more information than he had bargained for. JB was determined to be an asset again, just like in the old days with Sheriff Thompson. Well, it was obvious the scout had some good experience. If he didn't give out, he would probably earn his keep. Keller kept Pacer moving along, eating up the miles toward Santa Fe and what he hoped would be a deadly, yet final, encounter.

Chapter 9

Comancheros Attack

John Black Crow, called JB by most white men, the son of a French trapper and an Ottowa Princess, once the chief scout for the long-knife soldiers at Fort Leavenworth, sat easily on Wind Walker, his best Pinto pony. He watched as the manhunter Keller rode across the valley floor, his horse splashing through a stream swollen with runoff from a late-summer rain. John Black Crow still had the keen eyesight of his father and could easily see the white man patting his horse's neck, while talking to the big animal. John Black Crow instinctively respected any man who liked horses.

He had picked a good place for the evening's camp site, then ridden back to the little hillock where he now sat. He knew Keller was famous among the whites as a hunter of bad men. However, the bounty hunter had still to prove to the stoic half-breed that he was worthy of his loyalty, just as Thompson had earned it before Keller, and Colonel Watters, commander of the long-knife soldiers, had before Thompson. He did not easily commit his friendship to any white man. They had to earn it.

The manhunter had given him a fine new rifle and a warm coat, so Keller was far ahead in the respect JB held for most white men. JB softly caressed the warm sheepskin lining of his jacket as he pondered his thoughts. He knew he was destined to spend the rest of his days in the company of the white eyes, yet he held the majority of them in low esteem. Only a very few had ever earned his loyalty or friendship.

He sensed that Keller saw him sitting in the shade of the tall pine tree. The hunter angled his direction slightly, trotting his horse directly toward him. The tall white man gave a slight nod of his head, but patiently waited for JB to speak first.

"I find good camp back there." JB motioned to the rear with his thumb toward a copse of trees as he turned Wind Walker's head. Without waiting to see if Keller was following, he rode back toward the tree-shaded grove.

Riding into the thick cover of pines and aspen trees, they soon came upon a small clearing protected by a bare rock hill on one side and thick cedars on the other. A tiny fire was already burning beside a bubbling stream and the smell of burning pine boughs filled the air. Quickly, JB unloaded the packhorses and set about cooking some red beans and bacon. Marty took the saddle off Pacer and rubbed the gray horse with some moss he found growing along the rocky hillside. By the time he had finished and washed away the trail dust from his face and hands in the cool water, the meal was ready.

They ate in silence, as they had every meal. Marty wiped the last of the bacon fat up with his last bite of biscuit. He sipped the scalding coffee gingerly, then sighed contentedly. "Good grub, JB. Hit the spot. I thought I'd go over how I think we should proceed once we reach Santa Fe. The man who killed Sheriff Thompson will think no one's on his trail after so long. He's bound to get a little careless. We'll ease into the town and ask around. We might get lucky and find him still there. Thompson's gun will help. Not many .44s around with twenty-dollar gold pieces worked into the grips, I reckon."

Keller paused to pour another cup of coffee before leaning back against his saddle and continuing. "If he's gone on from Santa Fe, we'll just hope someone can point us in the right direction until we catch up with him." Keller turned to look at JB, hoping for some response.

John Black Crow merely grunted his agreement and laid his blanket on the pine needles he'd raked up for a bed. "We catch him for sure, Keller. We catch." With that statement of assurance, JB put his hands behind his neck and looked at the black sky filled with twinkling dots of light. Campgrounds for the dead ones on their long journey to the Great Spirit's world, as he had been taught by his mère, so long ago.

The old half-breed lay beside the small fire, suddenly thinking about Thompson's woman and daughters. The old Indian felt a special responsibility for them, yet he knew his limits. He must put another white man into their lodge. The women needed a man to help them run the ranch and protect them. The white eyes would never allow it to be an Indian or, for that matter, a half-breed. Was the man with him, the hunter with the determined eyes, the one?

Keller's value would be tested and JB would consider the results. If he were the one, then JB would take him back to the ranch after the killing of Thompson was avenged. JB glanced over at Keller. The man wasn't bothered by the silence, JB was pleased to note in his favor. Many whites talked just to hear noise pass by their ears. JB saw the eyes of the hunter ease open and probe the darkness for signs of danger. Satisfied, the white man closed them again and settled deeper into his bedroll. JB closed his as well, content that he had a good plan.

They were under way at first light, and as on the previous day, JB left Marty as soon as they broke their noontime camp to ride ahead and he would be waiting at day's end with a campsite chosen, a fire started, and their meal almost done. A comfortable rhythm developed between the two men, as they developed each other's roles in their common quest.

After a supper of beans and pan cornbread, JB took his rifle and walked around the camp, peering into the darkness and checking the horses, just as he did every night before settling down to sleep. When he'd finished and lain down on his bedroll, he looked over at Keller, whose head was cradled on the smooth leather seat of his saddle.

JB abruptly spoke in the still darkness. "Where Keller's woman?"

Marty was half asleep, recalling the compelling brown eyes of Caroline with their depth and warmth, as well as their buried pain. "Dead, many years ago. Killed by outlaws. Cowards, like the one who killed your friend, Thompson," Keller replied, hoping that would be enough for the half-breed.

JB grunted and shifted in his blankets. "That is why Keller hunt bad men now? You hunt your woman's killers?"

"Yep," Marty replied somewhat defensively. "I've been looking for them for nearly seven years now. Someday I'll find them, just like we're gonna find Sheriff Thompson's killer."

"Will Keller kill them when he find? Will this make Keller happy again?"

The question hung empty in the still night air. The soft crackle of the fire was the only answer the old Indian got. Keller was silent, staring at the flickering yellow flames of the campfire until his eyes closed and sleep overtook him. JB understood Keller's struggle with his dark memories and pondered again. *Was this the man for Thompson's woman and her little ones?*

The next morning a moist fog warned of approaching rain. JB put on his new coat and rode beside the tall white man, savoring the growing sense of kinship. The old halfbreed felt that his heart was lighter now that he was in search of the killer of his friend. He believed the Great Spirit guided and blessed their quest. They would find Thompson's killer and destroy him. It was good. The old Indian was satisfied and slouched more comfortably in his saddle.

JB moved on ahead as soon as the noon meal was over, scouting for game and a suitable spot for the night's camp, when he heard shots from beyond the hill to his front. He spurred Wind Walker into a steady lope toward the sounds until he came to a small hilltop. He slid off the pinto, and carefully crawled to the crest of the hill and looked over a shallow but wide valley between wooded hills and a dry plateau. Both white eyes and Indians were firing at a small wagon, brightly painted, with one of its lead mules down in the traces.

JB turned toward the sound of a galloping horse and saw Keller racing over the top of the hill behind him. As the white manhunter slid off his horse and ran toward him, JB pointed. "Indians and white men ahead, shooting at wagon, kill a mule. Now sneak up in brush. Come, I show." JB led Marty to a spot where they had a clear view of the ambush in progress.

Marty questioned JB. "White men and Indians together, you say? Are you sure?"

JB grunted. "Together, all attack wagon."

"Damnation," Keller complained. "It must be Comancheros. I never knew 'em to get this far north. What the hell are they doing so far from their regular raiding area?"

Together they peered over the wide valley, cut by several erosions from the spring melts of a thousand snowfalls. In its center, about five hundred yards away, Keller saw the small, brightly painted wagon surrounded on two sides by several men hiding behind brush and rocks. The ambushers fired a steady stream of bullets in the direction of the wagon. Keller assumed no one was alive in the wagon, until a puff of smoke billowed from the wagon's rear door. Someone was firing a shotgun toward the outlaws.

About a hundred feet to their left, a fifty-foot-high outcropping on the hillside had a sheer dropoff in the direction of the ambush. "JB." Keller pointed at the ledge. "If we can get up there, we'll have a clear field of fire at the backs of those bushwhackers. They'll never be able to rush us. Grab your rifle and come with me."

Quickly, Marty rode Pacer into the cover of some trees and tied him and the packhorse securely. Grabbing his Winchester and the heavy Spencer, still in its scabbard with the bag of heavy bullets attached, he ran toward the base of the outcrop, JB close on his heels. Scrambling to the top, Marty looked out over the valley. He had an unobstructed view of the entire ambush. He quickly pushed several loose rocks into a small barricade for cover.

JB grumbled, "Too far Keller. Cannot hit man from this distance."

Marty pointed with a finger. "You build a spot over yonder where you can cover the approach to this place. I'll reach them. Don't worry." He unwrapped the heavy buffalo gun with its attached sniper scope. John Black Crow had never seen such a rifle in his life. Quickly Marty pushed the fork into the ground and laid the heavy barrel of the rifle in the crook. Estimating the range to the fighting below, he set the necessary adjustments to the scope. Looking into the brass tube toward the scene below, he chose his first target. One of the Indians was rapidly closing in on the wagon from a blind spot to the wagon's defenders.

Placing the crosshairs of the scope in the center of the Indian's fringed buckskin coat, he slowly squeezed the double trigger of the heavy rifle. The first trigger released the safety of the gun and the second released the hammer.

A massive *boom* rent the air and an instant later the creeping Indian pitched forward on his face. Smoothly Keller pushed down on the trigger guard of the Spencer, throwing open the breech, flipping out the empty shell. He inserted another as he chose his next target. JB watched with admiration at the smooth and highly practiced motions of Keller with his rifle.

One of the Indians held the outlaws' assembled horses in a draw several hundred feet behind the action. Keller's heavy bullet took the unsuspecting Indian in the stomach, throwing him back against the startled horses, prompting them to gallop away in terror. Keller's lips curled back, the cold look of death was upon his handsome face. JB watched as the manhunter swung to his next target. Keller was killing enemies at a distance never dreamed possible by the old half-breed. In thirty seconds, Marty had hit four of the attackers.

A red-bearded man turned his head toward Keller and opened his mouth to shout a warning when the heavy 450-grain bullet, still hot from its explosion out of the rifle, flew in like a deadly horsefly. The gut-wrenching sight of exploding blood and brains caught the pale blue eyes of the skinny man crouched by a small boulder beside him. Muley gulped in sudden terror. Someone was ambushing them and doing a damn good job of it.

The Comanchero leader rose to run to a safer location

and took a bullet in the ribs. It passed through the slender body, shredding both lungs. Muley's cry of agony was drowned in a bright fountain of fresh blood. JB had to resist his impulse to scream out the Ottowa war cry. The enemies were falling as fast as Keller could load, aim, and shoot. He hoped some would remain for him to fight.

Several of the remaining Comancheros tried to put some cover between themselves and the deadly gunman. Three of the braver ones started to ease their way along a ravine toward the outcropping, but JB patiently waited until they came within range, then calmly picked them off one by one with his new rifle. The satisfying buck of the stock into his shoulder and the *crack* was a welcome intrusion into his battle-flamed brain. The three outlaw Indians never got within two hundred yards of the two rescuers.

Marty took his time, his concentration focused on the familiar business of killing. When he found a target in his scope crosshairs, he shot it. The heavy bullet paid no mind to brush or a hastily-scooped sand berm as protection for the unlucky recipient.

Only half a dozen outlaws were left before a red-shirted Indian waved his arms and led the survivors down a ravine to where they had left their horses. Keller waited until they burst out of cover to find their horses gone. Then he hit the leader squarely in the middle of his chest, knocking him into a limp ball in front of the others. Their courage completely dissolved by the incessant slaughter of their ranks, the others ran toward the distant mountains to the south. Marty methodically dropped each in turn, until no movement could be seen across the battlefield. Carefully, he rested the stock of the Spencer on the ground and turned to JB.

"You all right?" he asked. A sudden weariness washed

over him as the adrenaline quit coursing through his tense body.

JB grunted with pride. "JB good. We kill all outlaws. This a great day, Keller. I never see such shooting, ever. I sing of this day the rest of my life. I will sing it at the campfire of the Great Spirit when it is my time."

Keller nodded. "We were lucky, you know. This ledge gave us the view and the protection we needed. If we'd had to rush them, it would have been a different deck of cards to play." Keller knelt, and started picking up the spent cartridges, stuffing them into a small bag. At JB's inquisitive look, he explained. "I save the spent brass to make reloads. It's hard to find this size shell in most towns."

JB nodded, then scanned the now quiet scene before them. A white-haired man and a girl were cautiously climbing out of the wagon, shotguns at the ready. "We may as well go on down and introduce ourselves." Keller stood and started back to the horses.

JB noted the lack of animation in Keller's voice. He had just achieved a mighty victory and yet wasn't rejoicing. *A strange sign,* JB thought, *a mankiller who doesn't like to kill his enemies.*

They returned to their horses and rode to the disabled wagon. "JB," Keller said, "gather as many of the outlaws' horses as you can and bring them back to the wagon. Be careful around any of those." He pointed toward the sprawled bodies. "One of them may be playing possum. I'll check the folks in the wagon."

JB willingly galloped off in the direction of the spooked horses. His black eyes swept from side to side, willing any outlaw still alive to show himself. "I slay you good, bad ones, if Keller not kill you. Show yourself to me if you dare." He sang his fighting song, but no enemy answered his challenge. The mighty gun had done its deadly work. "Too bad, evil ones. JB cannot take your hair. Another owns it." John Black Crow was filled with fighting blood, and he had not cooled off yet, not by a long shot.

Keller rode up to the wagon, leading the suddenly skit-tish packhorse who was upset at the smell of the dead mule's blood. "Howdy, folks," he said to the man and the auburn-haired girl standing beside the wagon, shotguns warily cradled in their arms. "Name's Marty Keller. Any-body hurt?"

"Me nephew's inside, with his arm busted. Fionna's tied it up so he won't be bleeding to death. Saints be praised. You came only in the nick of time, sir. I, Profes-sor Sean McNulty, and me family give you our most sin-cere thanks."

Keller swung off his horse and smiled at the freckled face of the young woman, whose green eyes reflected in-stant adoration. "My pleasure. I hate Comancheros like the plague. Let's take a look at the wounded man. What's your name, miss?"

The girl blushed fiery red on every inch of her pale freckled face and giggled. Then she gushed, "Fionna Mc-Nulty. Here's Patrick now. I tied a bandage to his arm straight off. Patrick, this is Mr. Keller. He ran off the hea-thens who were attacking us."

An ashened-faced, younger version of Professor Mc-Nulty was biting his lip in pain as Marty scrambled into the back of the wagon. Swiftly, he examined the angry red wound on the man's right arm. The arm was obvi-ously broken, but it didn't appear that any arteries were severed. Looking at Fionna, he nodded. "You did an ex-ceptionally good job of stopping the bleeding, Miss Mc-Nulty. Now do you have any whiskey? We have to set his arm and clean the wound."

The young lady laughed, "Faith, sir, look about ye.

We've spirits to spare. Take any bottle. They'll have you drunk faster'n any whiskey money can buy."

Keller laughed. "Not for me, but for Patrick here. Lend me a hand and we'll have him up and about in jig time, mark my words."

By the time they had dressed and set the wounded man's arm, JB was driving a dozen horses to their location. He announced to Keller, "All enemy dead. What we do with them?"

Marty rubbed his eyes with the heel of his left hand. "Load the horses with the bodies. There's a standing reward for Comancheros. We'll take 'em to Santa Fe with us. And I reckon the professor and his kin had better go as well. That means two days on the trail, so wrap 'em good in their blankets. They'll be getting ripe before we arrive."

He introduced JB to the professor and Fionna, saying his full name, John Black Crow, and calling him "My friend." JB's pride swelled upon hearing the words from such a powerful fighting man.

Marty walked over to the dead mule. "Leave one of the horses with me, JB. I'll hook it up to replace this poor critter." He watched JB return to the dead men and start the grisly task of wrapping the corpses. "Don't forget their weapons," he shouted at the scout. JB held up his hand in acknowledgment.

"Come on, Professor. Help me get this dead mule out of harness and the horse hooked up. We need to find a quiet campsite so Patrick can get some rest."

JB rolled over the first dead man he came to. *What a heroic story to tell the little ones when I get back,* he thought to himself. He was already framing the saga in an Ottowa chant as he went through the dead man's pockets.

Chapter 10

Fionna's Story

JB chose a secluded campsite, tucked back in a cluster of big rocks and hidden from view of any passersby on the road. After starting a small fire, he surrendered it to auburn-haired Fionna. In short time she was busy stirring a savory-smelling stew in a blackened iron kettle. Keller stopped beside her and appreciatively sniffed air filled with the aromatic scent of spices and meat. He was ravenous and eagerly awaited her announcement of supper. "If you hear a rumble loud enough to wake a dead man," he announced to her, "it's my stomach a-growlin'."

Professor McNulty sat inside the wagon with his nephew, who had fallen asleep, thanks to the liberal application of the professor's elixir as a painkiller. JB was sorting through the pile of weapons and treasures he'd take from the dead Comancheros, now securely wrapped in their ponchos for the trip back to Santa Fe.

"Look, Keller," the old scout suddenly broke in. "All have new rifles, never used before."

Keller walked over to the blanket, where JB had piled the booty. He picked up one of the new Winchesters.

"You're right, sure enough. Now where would these scum get new rifles like this?" he mused. "Pack 'em up good, JB. We'll turn 'em over to the law in Santa Fe." He glanced over the rest of the items: knives, rings, watches—all probably taken from unfortunate victims, he surmised. There was also more than a thousand in gold double eagles hidden in the saddlebags of one of the outlaws. "Give half that to the professor," he instructed JB. "It'll pay him for the loss of the mule and the expense of healing Patrick."

JB held up a silver pocket watch with a linked chain. "JB take this. All right with Keller?"

The old scout addressed Marty with uncommon respect. Marty repressed a grin. They had now become bonded friends instead of just traveling companions. Marty welcomed the eager look on the lined face of the half-breed. *Like a kid on his birthday,* he thought.

"Sure, JB. It's little enough reward for the three you killed." Marty glanced over at the ten horses, double laden with their graveyard burdens. "We've done the country a service, ridding it of skunks like this." He picked up a beautifully inlayed .32 caliber five-shot pocket pistol from the pile. It would be a fine handgun for Caroline. "Put the rest of this stuff in one of the extra bedrolls and tie it on the packhorse. The sheriff in Santa Fe can sell it at auction, to cover the burial expenses for these jaspers."

"Come and get it," Fionna called, ending the men's conversation until all the delicious lamb stew was consumed. To the amazement of both the professor and Fionna, their saviors gulped down what was to them ordinary fare as if it were the best meal the men had ever eaten.

Marty sipped the hot coffee and leaned back contentedly against a cottonwood stump. Stretching his legs toward the fire, he praised the cook. "Mighty fine food, Miss Fionna. What was it anyway?" JB belched his satisfaction to underscore the compliment.

"'Tis what we call Irish stew, Mr. Keller," Fionna answered, her voice showing satisfaction at the unexpected praise. Seldom did her uncle or cousin ever praise her cooking. She smiled brightly as she looked directly into Marty's dark blue eyes. "'Tis a happy thing when someone saves me life and raves about me cooking in the same day. Thank you for your gallantry."

As if anxious not to be upstaged, the old professor harrumphed, "Yes, my dear. That was quite tasty. Be so good as to take a wee bit to Patrick. He'll need to eat if he's to regain his strength."

Professor McNulty pulled a small silver flask out of his coat pocket and offered it to Keller. "A wee dram o' whiskey to ward off the evening chills, me boy?"

"Thanks, Professor." Marty sipped the mellow-tasting liquor and passed the flask back to its owner. "Mighty smooth stuff. Thank you."

"Me very own private stock." The professor savored his drink and returned the flask to its accustomed place next to his heart. "What 'tis your plans for us now that you've saved us?"

Marty rubbed his hands and stretched his arms toward the fire. "Well, I reckon you'd better come back to Santa Fe with JB and me. You'll need to replace your mule, and there may be more of these outlaws around. With Patrick hurt, you don't want to risk more trouble right now."

Professor McNulty nodded his white-haired head. "'Tis odd that outlaws such as these would strike at a small wagon such as mine, don't you think?"

Keller shrugged. "Hard to say. They're worse than a pack of wolves. They may have seen Fionna or they may have wanted your medicine, to drink like whiskey. I'm just grateful we came along in time to stop 'em."

"Aye," the older man agreed. "'Tis the blessing of St. Michael that you were close enough to intercede on our behalf. Where have I heard your name? Keller, Martin Keller. Yes, I remember now. You're the famous bounty hunter, right? You're called the—what is it?—oh, yes, the Mankiller."

"Some call me that," Keller admitted, his voice growing stiff. "I don't particularly care for it though."

"Of course, my boy. Gruesome name at that." The professor quickly backtracked, "Forgive me." He rubbed his hands in front of the fire, even though the night was pleasantly mild. "Would it be impolite for me to ask what brings you to this spot so fortuitously for me and mine?"

"John Black Crow and I are looking for a man who killed the sheriff in Cimarron, up Grand Junction way, and we think he may have headed this way."

"'Tis the devil himself that lives in some of these men here in the West. I pray you find him and strike him down without harm to yourself or the red Indian." They both glanced over at JB, who was swinging his new silver watch back and forth on its chain. McNulty got to his feet and brushed off his pants. "If you'll excuse me, Mr. Keller, I suppose I should relieve Fionna at Patrick's bedside. Have a good night." He walked over to the wagon and climbed into the back.

Keller stood and pulled his Winchester from its scabbard. He strolled over to the bed JB had made near the picketed horses. "I'll stand first guard, JB. We'll switch around midnight. I don't want to take any chances that some more Comancheros are around." The old Indian grunted and rolled even tighter in his bedroll. Keller walked out of the light of the campfire to check the picket rope of the horses. It had been strung between two juniper trees and was secure. He didn't want to lose any of the animals, along with the valuable cargo of corpses lashed on them.

Fionna climbed out of the wagon, a wool shawl over her arm. As she walked away from the glow of the campfire, Keller moved over to her.

"Taking a little stroll, Miss McNulty?" he inquired as he walked up behind the unsuspecting girl.

"Aye," she answered as she adjusted the shawl around her shoulders. "'Tis all right I hope? 'Tis such a grand night and all."

Keller smiled at the freckled nose and green eyes that looked up at him in frank admiration. "Of course, if you don't mind some company. I wouldn't want to take any chances that some others like those we just met are out about."

Nodding her head in understanding, the young girl swung around and continued to walk away from the camp. The night was cooler now, and scattered against the black velvet darkness, thousands of stars twinkled brightly. "Oh, 'tis a lovely night to be alive," she whispered aloud, for Marty's benefit.

"Yes, Miss McNulty, I couldn't agree more."

"Please, Mr. Keller, call me Fionna. 'Tis an old woman you make me feel, with that Miss McNulty talk."

"I will if you'll call me Marty."

"With pleasure, Marty."

The pair reached an opening in the trees that revealed a breathtaking view of the rolling plains brushed by the silver light of the moon. Fionna sat down on a small boulder and inhaled deeply. Keller stood beside her, his rifle cradled in the crook of his left arm. The country seemed still and safe, with no sign of danger.

The young woman sighed and cupped her chin in her

hand. "'Twould be grand to have a home somewhere that one could sit such as this every night," she sighed.

"You must tire of all the traveling," Keller offered. "I suppose it must be wearisome after a while."

"Aye, that it 'tis," Fionna agreed. "Me uncle needs me, and I'm grateful to be away from Ireland and the dreadful famine there. It's just that I'd hoped to find a nice man to settle down with when I came to America. I want to raise a family, not traipse about selling syrup mixed with raw whiskey to old men and women."

Keller chuckled. "Well, there's nothing wrong with that idea. You've plenty of time. A beautiful young woman such as you will have no trouble once the right man comes along."

Fionna beamed. "Well, I'm almost eighteen," she asserted. "I'm not anxious to become an old maid. You can be certain of that." She looked up at Keller, so tall and strong, beside her. "What about you? Do you have a wife and home to go back to?"

"No, not really," Keller admitted. "But I have to agree, on a night like this, the idea becomes especially appealing."

"Well, see then," she blurted out. "'Tis a grand opportunity for the both of us. That is, if it appeals to you as much as it does to me."

Keller startled at the unexpected proposal. He finally responded with a small chuckle. "No, my sweet Irish lass, I'm not the one for you. That lucky fellow is out there somewhere, maybe just over those hills yonder." He pointed with his finger. "My trail and yours crossed too late, I'm sorry to say. Come on now. Let's walk and you can tell me all about Ireland. I've never been across the sea. What is it like?"

Shrugging her shoulders in disappointment, Fionna thought for an instant. "Oh, 'tis a lovely land, me Ireland.

Lovely to see, with the green of her fields and the blue of her skies. But ugly, too, for there's hunger afoot and the cries of children with empty bellies. That's why I came to America. No man for me, and me father's land is too poor to feed all the hungry mouths of his family."

Keller listened sympathetically as Fionna continued to describe her childhood in Ireland. He shared a little of his own life before he rode the bounty trail, hunting his personal demons. Finally, he spoke of Caroline, her daughters, and his growing affection for them. The moon was high in the sky and coyotes were howling their nighttime lullabies before the two new friends ran out of words.

"Mrs. Caroline sounds just grand, Mr. Keller," Fionna announced. "If me uncle takes us to Cimarron, I'll visit her and tell them all the grand tale of how you saved us from the savage outlaws."

"Come on now," Marty finally commanded. "We'll have a long day on the trail tomorrow. It's time we got some shuteye." He took her arm and turned toward the camp.

"Marty," she whispered, "you may kiss me if you'd like. 'Tis something I would like, for certain. 'Twould be a thing I can always remember about this day."

Keller knew he was on thin ice. If he made a joke of her innocent offer, she'd be hurt and embarrassed. If he went too far, it wouldn't be fair to her. Carefully, he raised her chin with his hand. He bent toward her. She closed her eyes and puckered her lips expectantly. Gently, he touched his firm lips to hers and then pulled back, looking down at her freckled face. Her eyes fluttered open and she smiled at him, a smile as sweet as her unspoiled soul.

"Good night, Marty, me darlin'." Swiftly, she ran back to the wagon.

Keller woke JB before crawling into his own bedroll,

and soon was dreaming of Caroline, her sweet brown eyes smiling at him and her windblown hair teasing his cheek.

By morning two more horses had wandered close enough for JB to gather, so they now had recaptured fourteen animals. Marty and JB loaded three of the horses with the guns and booty taken from the dead renegades. Before midmorning, they were on the trail to Santa Fe. The day slowly passed, but to the wounded man in the bouncing wagon, it was relentless pain from his wounded arm. Only the continual sips of elixir given him by Fionna made the trip bearable. Before nightfall of the second day, the city of Santa Fe, nestled in the foothills of the San Mateo Mountains, appeared before them. Patrick's arm showed no sign of infection and the trip had passed without incident.

Their entrance into the town created quite a commotion. Keller rode Pacer in front of the wagon, while Patrick, his arm in a sling, sat on the wagon seat between Fionna and the professor. JB brought up the rear, leading the string of horses with the draped cargo swaying with every step. Keller pulled up in front of the sheriff's office, a buzzing crowd of spectators gathering behind them. A weatherbeaten man, his bow legs and stooped shoulders speaking of a vigorous past, stepped out, his graystreaked handlebar mustache curled at the corners. The crowd grew quiet.

"What the hell you got here, whoever you are?" the old lawman asked as he eyed the packhorses.

"Name's Keller, Sheriff. Came upon a pack of renegade Comancheros attacking these folks' wagon. Me and my friend here were able to get some of 'em." He nodded toward JB. "These"—he jerked a thumb at the bodies— "are worth five hundred apiece in bounty. We're here to collect."

The sheriff walked to the load of bodies and grabbed several by the hair, lifting their heads so he could look at their faces. "Got to admit these yahoos look the part. Whatever, ya'll have to wait until I get the marshal's okay afore ya get yer blood money. My name's Bushrod by the way." He looked at the old professor. "Howdy, Professor. This yahoo giving the whole of it?"

"Absolutely, Sheriff. He saved our lives, for a fact. We're indebted to Mr. Keller and his Indian friend."

The sheriff looked up at the professor standing between the two younger McNultys. "Perfesser, come on inside and give me yer statement. The Injun can take the bodies down to the undertaker, there at the end of that street." He pointed down a side street. As JB led the horses away, the old sheriff complained to Marty, "How do you suggest the county pay fer all these funerals anyway?"

Keller stretched his stiff muscles. "I've got an idea you'll figure out some way," he said, smiling at the crusty lawman. "There's enough goods on the packhorses to pay for the best services available, not that these scum deserve it."

Keller pulled a wrapped pile of rifles off one of the horses and walked into the sheriff's office. He laid one of the rifles on the sheriff's desk. "They all had new Winchester rifles, Sheriff. I imagine you might find that interesting."

Bushrod grabbed up the weapon. "Damn right, Keller. The freight company had two dozen stole a couple a months ago. I reckon these are them." He paused. "Strange fer Comancheros to be this far north. And whatta they been doin' since they hit the freight shipment?" Bushrod scratched the full mustache on his lip. "Cain't imagine these boys staying quiet fer so long, can you?"

Keller shook his head. "Nope, sure can't. Notice these rifles haven't been out of the packing case more'n a week. You can see there's not a speck of rust or dirt on any of them."

Bushrod picked up the rifle. "Yer plum right, Keller. Someone has just delivered 'em lately. I'll be lookin' into that right off." The sheriff pulled some paper and pencils out of his desk drawer and handed Marty a sheet. "Here, write down yer story, and don't leave nuthin' out." He turned to Professor McNulty, who was standing patiently beside his desk. "Professer, I'll start with you. Gimme the whole story jus' as ya remember it."

Marty walked outside. JB, back from delivering his cargo to the undertaker, was patiently waiting for him. The string of horses was tied in a line behind him.

"Let's get these horses to the livery, then find us a clean room, partner," Marty told the old scout.

Fionna ran out just as Marty climbed on Pacer's back. "Oh, Mr. Keller," she called sweetly, "I'll be staying with Rose O'Brian. Her papa owns the livery stable. You will come by and see me before you leave, won't ye?"

"Of course, Miss Fionna. Tell your uncle that I'll come by tomorrow night and take all of you to supper. Will that be all right?"

"'Twould be grand, Mr. Keller. I'll have him and Patrick ready by six o'clock." She waved as Marty rode down the street, but he never turned back. Sighing at what might have been, she returned to the sheriff's office.

Chapter 11

JB's Revenge

The livery owner eagerly accepted all the horses into his care. "I'll give you a special price: only ten dollars a day, feed and brushing included for the lot of 'em. Say!" the chubby owner exclaimed. "Are you the feller what brought in all them dead Comancheros?"

"Yep, my friend and I." Marty's tone discouraged any further discussion of the subject.

"Well . . . er . . . Mr. Keller, was it? Well, Mr. Keller, Perfesser McNulty is a friend of mine. In fact, my daughter, Rose, and Fionna McNulty share a room whenever the perfesser's in town. What I mean to say is, you're on my list of good folks now. Anything I kin do to help, you just say."

"Thanks, Mr. O'Brian. I appreciate your offer. Most folks would just as soon stay out of the same room I'm in, if you get my meaning." Marty handed over a fifty-dollar gold piece that JB had taken from one of the dead renegades. "Here's stable money for my string. Where do you suggest I stay while I'm in town?"

O'Brian pointed across the street. "I happen to own the

hotel over there. I'd be mighty proud if you'd stay there. You kin have the best room I got. I'll even let the Injun stay in the room with you, although it's really against the house rules."

Keller looked across at the small hotel. It was adobe, two stories high, with reddish-brown stucco over mud bricks. Wooden beams protruded from the upper walls and green shutters flanked the upper windows. "Looks just fine. Thanks." He paused as he started out of the office. "I'll take care of the room for the professor and his boy as well. Tell 'em that it's on me. I suppose Miss Fionna will be staying with you?"

O'Brian nodded cheerfully. Another paying guest for his place was always welcome. "She will fer a fact, Mr. Keller. My Rose wouldn't have it otherwise."

"One last thing, Mr. O'Brian. Did you happen to notice a tall, dark-haired man ride through here last December? In a hurry, probably pushin' hard. He might have purchased a horse from you. He carried a six-gun with twenty-dollar gold pieces worked into the handgrips."

O'Brian scratched his ear. "I don't recollect, right off. Let me think on it a bit. I'll review my records fer last December tonight. Check with me tomorrow."

Marty signed in himself and JB as instructed by Mr. O'Brian, and scrubbed the trail dust from his face and upper body before easing onto the only bed in the room. He sighed as the soft mattress accepted his weary body. He'd been sleeping on the ground for too long. He was snoring before JB had finished his evening meditations. After a good night's sleep, a hot bath, a shave, and a change of clothes, Marty felt like he was fit to be among the townsfolk again. He walked out of the hotel lobby adjusting his weatherstained Stetson. JB was already at the livery, carefully evaluating the horses they now owned, since nobody had come forward to dispute their claim for the animals. The horses' most likely disputants were being readied for permanent planting on the town's boothill.

Keller walked casually down the sidewalk toward the sheriff's office. He carried the big Spencer rifle in its leather saddle scabbard along with the small bag containing the empty brass cartridge cases from the fight with the Comancheros. In his wake, he could hear the whispers. "There's Keller. There he is, the Mankiller. That's him. That's Keller." Marty was sick to his soul of hearing the whispers behind his back. He muttered a vow: "If I ever find the bastards who killed Meg, I swear I'll get so far away from bounty huntin' that folks will forget I ever existed."

Sheriff Bushrod was scanning some papers when Keller walked in his office. "Mornin', Sheriff," Keller greeted the lawman.

"Howdy, Keller," the sheriff grunted back. "Come fer your money already? Well, I was over to the attorney's office this morning and he agreed with ya. There'll be ten thousand fer ya to bank, probably by Friday. In the meantime—"

Keller interrupted. "In the meantime, I'll stay out of trouble and not get too close to any townsfolk. I know, Sheriff. What I do want, however, is to get some information you might have on a stranger. Came here last December. He killed the sheriff of Cimarron, up near Grand Junction. I'm lookin' for him. Tracked him to Durango and heard that he was heading your way. Do you have any memory of a stranger passin' through about then?"

Bushrod frowned. "I don't know why I'm helping some bounty killer, but I reckon I'll bend a little backward this time, since you done rid my territory of them damned Comancheros. What else can you tell me about him?"

"Not too much," Keller answered ruefully. "He was a

drifter who backshot the sheriff, then robbed the Wells
Fargo office. He took the sheriff's fancy gun, which had
two double eagle gold pieces fitted into the handle."

"Say!" Bushrod exclaimed. "Damned if'n I don't
know about jus' such a pistol. The Bar J east of here hired
a man carryin' the very same. One of the regular hands
was a-tellin' me about the fancy six-gun with double eagles in the handgrips. Belonged to some jasper they hired
to ride line over the winter. He may still be there."

"Thanks, Sheriff. Me and JB'll ride out there right
away. Who knows? We might get lucky this time."

Bushrod only grunted. "If you bring the backshootin'
bastard in dead, Keller, he'd better be drilled in the front.
You savvy?"

"I wouldn't have it any other way, Sheriff," Keller
replied as he left the office. "I want this fellow to know
what he's paying for."

JB and Keller galloped out of town toward the Bar J
ranch, following Mr. O'Brian's directions. The ranch was
about a twelve-mile ride west of town. It was early afternoon before the two manhunters arrived at the main ranch
house. The owner, a ruddy-faced man of middle age
named Jake Aikens, stepped out onto the front porch at
the summons of a hired hand. He warily eyed his uninvited guests, his thumbs hooked in the risers of his sus-
penders.

"Yep, I did hire such a man, name o' Smith," he said.
"I have him up at my north range line shack, riding line.
Been working fer me nigh on to six months now. What
you want him for?"

"We believe he shot the sheriff of Cimarron in the
back and robbed the local Wells Fargo office."

Aikens shook his head. "Well, I don't want no killer on
my payroll. But I got to tell you, he's been a good hand
ever since I hired him." He jerked his thumb to the north.

"Follow the treeline there till you get to a small stream. Then turn east past a bare-faced hill to a meadow. The line shack's at the far end of the meadow. No way out the back. It dead ends into a canyon, so he won't be able to run, but he'll most likely see you comin'. Well, I guess that's your worry."

Aikens turned away from the two and went back inside. He felt a little twinge of guilt for not sticking up for his employee, but a backshootin' sheriff killer was not worthy of any loyalty. If Sheriff Bushrod had sent the men out, their story must be true. He watched the two men ride away, then returned to his desk, a worried frown on his face.

It did not take Marty and JB long to make the trip. They looked across the grassy meadow toward the little shack barely visible against the far treeline. "What do you think, JB?" Keller asked. "Do we ride up bold as brass or circle in on him?"

"You cannot ride up on the coyote," JB answered, his eyes never leaving the cabin. A wisp of white smoke curled from the chimney.

"All right," Keller decided. "You swing around through the trees and come in from the rear. I'll wait ten minutes and then come up from the front. If he's there and starts shooting, you bust in behind him." Keller smiled at the old half-breed. "Take care, my friend. We don't want him to escape us this time."

"This one not get away, Keller. I know this. We avenge Thompson. I go now." JB trotted his pinto away to the left and soon was hidden in the trees.

The front door abruptly opened and a single man stepped outside, throwing a pan of water in a feathery plume. It had to be the man they were seeking. The man slowly moved back inside. He had not seen them.

Keller patiently waited the full ten minutes and then gently spurred Pacer on. The gray trotted out onto the dried yellow grass of the meadow toward the ramshackle line shack. Keller thought he saw movement at the single window that faced him, so he stopped about a hundred feet from the front door. "Hello the shack. Smith, come outside. I want to talk to you."

The door slowly creaked open an inch and a voice answered from the dark interior of the shack, "Whaddya want? Who are ya?"

"Name's Keller, Smith. You're coming back to Santa Fe with me. Sheriff Bushrod wants to talk to you about what happened up in Cimarron. Now come on out with your hands up."

Keller saw the rifle barrel poke out of the doorway and immediately spurred Pacer toward a slight fold in the ground toward the left side of the cabin. A bullet hummed by his head as he pulled up his horse and swung off the saddle in a fluid leap, taking the Winchester rifle with him. He moved to the top of the rise and sighted the weapon at the cabin. For the moment, it was quiet. The door was closed. Marty could see no movement.

He held his fire and wondered about JB. He carefully started to move toward the shack, keeping his eyes on the door and the side window, watching for movement. He spotted JB silently closing in on the rear of the cabin. There must have been a door or window there as well. Keller moved faster, JB was going in, without waiting for him to get in position to back him up. Keller started to shout, but it was too late.

The old scout hit the rear door with his shoulder, his rifle ready and promptly tumbled into a trap. The wily outlaw Smith had dug a two-foot hole right in front of the doorjamb. He'd been on the outlaw trail too long not to cover his back from a surprise assault. JB lay sprawled on the dirt floor of the cabin, stunned by the fall. The smug face of the man who had killed his friend and benefactor looked down at him and a handgun was pointing at his head. Silently, JB chanted his death song. Now the woman and her little ones would have no one to keep them safe. He had failed his holy vow. A bitter taste followed the saliva he hastily swallowed. JB watched helplessly as the grinning man cocked the hammer of his pistol.

Outside, Keller saw faint movement through the window, but was it JB or Smith? He couldn't understand what had happened to JB and he dared not wait. He had to shoot—something was wrong. He aimed at the blurred figure and pulled the trigger. The window shattered in a shower of sparkling slivers as the bullet broke through the glass pane.

Inside, the killer staggered and lurched to the side as the window shattered. Keller had hit the man and JB knew he had to move quickly. The old half-breed rolled off his rifle and snapped a quick shot at the falling figure. The crack of the weapon was amplified in the small space of the cabin. Smith banged against the wall next to the door, then sat down hard, the pistol dropping from hands that grabbed at the stain spreading across the front of his threadbare shirt.

Keller burst through the door, confused as he saw JB still lying on the floor, the smoking rifle poked out in front of him like an iron cigarette. "JB, you hit?" Only then did he see Smith sitting on the floor, his face slack and pasty white, with a crimson stain pooling between the outstretched legs. The man was gasping hard, dying by the second.

"JB fine. I kill the one who murder Thompson. Thank you, Keller." JB got to his feet and moved to the side of the man he had shot. Pulling out his sharp knife, he slashed the right forearm of the dying man, who was so far gone he was oblivious to the Indian insult.

Martin squatted next to the wounded killer. "Smith, you're hit bad. Time to make your peace with the Almighty. You shot Sheriff Thompson in the back, didn't you?"

"God," the man groaned, "I'm hurtin' bad. Get me to a doctor quick." He moaned again and a fresh flow of blood slipped between his fingers.

"Sure, pard, just as soon as you answer my question. You did shoot Sheriff Thompson, didn't you?"

The man groaned softly, "Yeah, I shot 'im. He came down the street while I was breakin' into the freight office. I didn't think no one was still after me fer that. Oh, God, it hurts." The dying man's chin slumped to his chest and he moaned softly.

JB pulled the worn pistol out of Smith's holster. "Where Thompson's gun? Where gun with golden coin in handle."

Keller gently shook Smith's shoulder. "Where's the fancy pistol you took from Sheriff Thompson?" The eyes were glazing over and Keller knew his time with the dying killer was short. "Where's the pistol, Smith?"

The answer was faint but clear. "Lost it in a card game a couple of weeks ago. Damn that three-fingered card shark. I sure liked that gun." His body sagged and air rushed out of his lungs, relaxing in death. Smith had uttered his last statement in this world.

"Tell it to the devil," Keller whispered to the corpse. A thrill coursed through him. *A three-fingered man had the gun. Could it be the one he had looked for for so long?* Excitement washed over him. At last, he had a solid lead. He wanted to dash to Pacer and race back to Santa Fe. With enormous effort, he restrained his impatience as JB loaded the body of the killer on his horse and they rode

back to the Bar J. No way would they get back to Santa
Fe before late at night, so he would have to wait until tomorrow to ask about the three-fingered man.

They arrived at Aikens' headquarters just as the sun
was setting, tinting the clouds soft shades of red and gold.
Aiken walked out of the main house as Marty and JB
guided their horses to the water trough by the corral. He
was barely civil as they described the gunfight. "I don't
cotton to bounty hunters gangin' up on a fellow, even one
as deserving as Smith. Why don't you two ride on out of
here as soon as yer horses git their water?" He turned his
back again on JB and Keller and walked inside the ranch
house.

Marty shrugged off the unhappy rancher's bad manners and followed JB and the horse carrying Smith's body
back to Santa Fe. His mind couldn't rest repeating over
and over what he had heard: *A three-fingered card player.
Could he be the one? Let him be the one I've been seeking for so very long.* "Hurry up, Pacer. This time maybe
I've found 'im."

Chapter 12

Another Reward

Once again Marty Keller led a grisly convoy into Santa Fe. Even though the hour was late, people gathered on the wooden sidewalks of the main street and whispered in awe as the tall rider, with the silent Indian and a dead man strapped to a horse, pulled up in front of the sheriff's office.

"Well, fer sure, you make it easy fer me, Keller." Bushrod checked the back of the corpse as he spoke. Satisfied, he instructed, "Harry, take this fella over to the undertaker's and tell him to prepare the newly departed fer plantin'." He glanced at Keller. "I suppose you want the bounty fer this one, too, huh?"

"Nope," Keller answered. "Tell the deputy in Cimarron to deliver it to the sheriff's widow, if you don't mind." For the first time, Keller saw something besides cool contempt in Bushrod's eyes.

"Fella, that's one message I'm proud to send. Come on in and I'll pour ya a drink to wash the trail dust outta yer throat." He held the door for Keller while Marty instructed JB, "Take the horses to the livery and bed them down. I'll catch up with you at the hotel." He knew the Indian would rub and brush both animals carefully before cleaning himself.

Keller quickly outlined what the dying Smith had said about a three-fingered gambler. The sheriff scratched his left ear and replied, "Has to be the fella that kilt the Russell kid from Taos about two months ago. The boy drew first, even though he probably had reason enough. Didn't have enough to hold the shooter. Called hisself—what was it? Al somethin'. Anyhow, I hadda let him go. Bad sort, I could tell that easy enough. No doubt 'bout it."

Bushrod frowned. "Seems there was a dark-bearded jasper hanging around with the man. Let's see, he called hisself Luther somethin'—that's it. Anyhows, the two of 'em stayed pretty close to the Red Garter. That's a saloon and gambling house over to the east end o' town. They run whores upstairs and it seems to me that pock-faced Opal was sleepin' regular like with that Luther fella." The old sheriff paused. "Haven't seen 'em around fer a few days, now that I think on it. Tell ya what. Much as I don't want it around that I'm a-helpin' a bounty hunter, I'll stop by there on my rounds tomorrow morning and tell the owner, Russ Gibbons, that ya want to talk to his gals, and he's to let ya. Otherwise you'd jus' run into a stone wall." The sheriff busied himself with the stack of papers on his desk. Looking up at the still present Keller, he blustered. "Go on now. Go clean yerself up and git some sleep. Nothin's gonna happen tonight that can't be cared fer tomorry."

Swallowing his impatience, and knowing he needed the goodwill and help of Bushrod, Keller reluctantly left the office. As he walked by the closed café, he suddenly remembered he had promised to treat Fionna to supper. "Damnation," he muttered to himself. "I forgot about it. Hope she's of a forgiving nature."

Keller slept very little that night, and was at Bushrod's office early the next morning.

"Don't worry," the old sheriff reassured him. "I'll stop by around lunchtime. Gibbons or his gals ain't up much before then. You go in around two. They'll know you're a-comin' and that they'd best speak plain with ya."

The sheriff pointed across the street. "By the way, those rifles ya found did belong to Mr. Zollicoffer, over to the gun shop there. I done turned 'em over to 'im. Stop by. He'll be wantin' to thank ya personal-like." The old sheriffs eyes grew crafty. "Whatta ya plan to do with them horses ya took offa the lately departed? The Montoya ranch is always interested in good horseflesh. I could set up a meetin' with their head vaquero. They'd give ya a good price fer 'em."

And give yourself a nice commission, Marty thought. *Well, what was he going to do with the stock? One thing for sure, the Comancheros had all been riding good horseflesh. Their lives depended on it.* Suddenly, an idea occurred to him.

"Sorry, Sheriff. I'm going to send 'em to the widow Thompson I was telling you about. She's trying to keep a small horse ranch going and it hasn't been easy for her. The stock will give her some new blood to breed."

Disappointment crossed Bushrod's face. "Well, all right, if'n ya say so. Leave me know if'n ya have a change of mind. Where ya stayin', anyway? I'll want to get aholt of ya when yer money's ready."

"I'm bunked at Mr. O'Brian's hotel, across from his livery stable at the west end of St. Mary's Street." He touched the brim of his hat with a forefinger. "Be seein' you as soon as I talk with those whores at the Red Garter." Then he crossed the dusty street to the wooded sidewalk on the far side, where he saw the gunsmith shop sign: FRANK ZOLLICOFFER, MASTER GUNSMITH was painted in flecked gold script on the wavy glass. Ducking two hefty matrons with packages in hand, he tipped his hat and went inside.

The smell of gun oil and black powder filled the clean interior of the shop. The walls and display cases were filled with all types of firearms. Keller saw a white-bearded man bent over the stripped-down parts of a rifle, filing away at a steel piece of the breech. His head was shiny bald and reddened from the sun. Square-shaped bifocals were perched precariously on the end of a large nose. Lively blue eyes were nearly covered by bushy white eyebrows.

"Good morning, *mein herr*." The man looked up. "Vat may I do fer ya?"

Marty nodded. "Mr. Zollicoffer?" At the old man's bob of assent, he continued. "I'm Martin Keller. Sheriff Bushrod said you wanted to talk to me."

"Ja, ja." The shop owner's face beamed with pleasure. "My t'anks for getting back my rifles from dose outlaws. May I buy for you a drink?"

"Thanks, but not right now, sir," Keller replied. "I do need to reload some rounds if you don't mind. I'll pay for some lead and rifle powder and the use of your heating furnace." Keller pulled a bullet mold and the empty brass cartridges for his big Spencer from the bag he was holding.

The gunsmith held out his hand and Keller dropped one of the empty cartridges in it. "Mmm, .52 Spencer, center fire. Dis is a big bullet, Mr. Keller. Made fer hunting der buffalo, I suspect." He looked sagely at Keller. "May I see der rifle?"

Keller handed over the rifle, still in its leather scabbard, for the elderly gunsmith's careful inspection. The weapon was a masterpiece of workmanship and the gunsmith appreciated it. For a few minutes, the two men

talked on the merits of the deadly sniper rifle. Zollicoffer
picked up the mold for the lead bullets. "How big?" he
questioned Keller.

"I use a 455-grain bullet with 110 grains of double-
base powder. Gives me better'n two thousand feet a second and hits like a mule kick."

The gunsmith nodded. "Das is good. I vill start de lead
to melt. Vould ya like to look at any of my guns till is
melted?"

Keller wandered around with the friendly gunsmith,
who eagerly described the many weapons he had on display. In his gruff manner, Zollicoffer asked to inspect the
famous .45s that Marty carried, praising the intricate silver inlay carved on the barrels and handles.

Keller stopped at a case where a compact little .41 caliber Remington derringer was displayed. *A perfect fit for
the professor's coat pocket. I'll get a couple of rifles as
well. They need more protection than that old scattergun.*
He bought the derringer as well as two new Winchester
rifles. One for Patrick, a .44-40 like his, only not as carefully made, and the other a smaller .32-30 for Fionna. He
decided he'd offer to show Fionna how to use her new
rifle the next day—Patrick, too, if he didn't already
know how to shoot. Maybe the gifts would make up some
for his forgetting the supper he had promised her.

The lead had melted, so Keller and the gunsmith carefully made twenty-four new bullets for his Spencer rifle.
Zollicoffer held the bullet mold while Marty poured the
molten lead with an iron dipper. After the lead cooled,
Marty trimmed off any flashing and smoothed any rough
edges of each bullet. Finally, Zollicoffer used a tiny silver
measuring cup to weigh out the powder for each round,
then poured it into the cartridges sitting upright on the
desk. He let Marty squeeze the brass edge of the cartridge

around the lead bullet with the grip swedger. Marty had done the job so often it was second nature to him.

Keller paid Zollicoffer with one of the gold coins found in the Comancheros' pockets. The old gunsmith was profuse in his thanks for recovering the rifles; then he walked Keller out to the sidewalk, shaking Keller's hand and patting him on the shoulder.

At least I've got a couple of friends in this town, Marty thought, as he walked back to his hotel.

Keller knocked on the door to the professor's room. "Come in, come in," the patent-medicine husker called out. "Ah, Mr. Keller. Top o' the morning to ye." The professor was combing the white fluff on his round head while looking critically into a tiny mirror held by Fionna.

Patrick lay in the bed, while the local doctor stood on the far side wrapping the wounded shoulder. Fionna smiled brightly at the tall bounty hunter.

"Morning, Patrick," Keller greeted the young man. "Morning, Miss Fionna. How's the patient?"

"I'm fine," Patrick announced before anyone else could speak. "I'll be up and about in a couple of days— just you see."

Keller laughed. "No need to hurry. Get all the bedrest you can. You know what it's like sleeping on the ground. By the way, Miss Fionna, I'm sorry about last night. JB and I—"

"We heard the news this morning, Mr. Keller," she interrupted. "I forgive ye." Her expression was still warm and caring as she looked at him.

He turned around to the door. "I've got something for you all. Wait here, and I'll be right back."

He quickly got the new weapons, then returned to their room. "I figured you folks better get properly armed if you're gonna be wandering around in this part of the West. Miss Fionna, I'd be happy to take you out tomorrow morning and show you how to use that rifle, if you'd like." Her quick acceptance was eager and excited.

With appreciation, the professor put his new derringer in his pocket, then looked with interest at Fionna's small rifle.

"Praise the saints, Mr. Keller, but why did you get this child a rifle?"

"Hush, Uncle Sean," Fionna admonished. "Of course I need to be able to shoot, just in case something happens to you or Patrick. Thanks to ye, Mr. Keller. I'd be happy to take your lessons, but won't I be keeping you from more important matters?"

"Not at all," Keller assured her. "I've got to wait until the reward money is released before I can continue looking for my bad men. We'll have plenty of time to get some lessons in."

"Well then," she beamed, "I'll be ready tomorrow morning."

"Excellent. Come to the stables about ten. Now I need to see some people who may have some information I need about my killers." Keller picked up his hat and headed for the door. "See you around suppertime tonight? I guess I still owe you a dinner to make up for last night."

"My pleasure, sir. I'll be ready."

Their excited talk followed him as he walked down the bare steps to the lobby. First he stopped by the livery to tell Mr. O'Brian to have his horse saddled early the next morning. Walking with the livery owner to the corral, they looked over the stock he now possessed. Pointing at a small-sized bay mare, with white stockings on three hooves, Keller instructed, "Put a woman's saddle on that blaze-nosed bay as well. If she rides as good as she looks, I'm going to give her to Fionna as a present."

O'Brian cast an experienced eye at the animal. The horse was about fourteen hands high and had good lines.

"'Pears to be a good choice, Mr. Keller. I'll have John Black Crow work her some this afternoon. He'll be able to say fer sure. That Injun sure knows his horseflesh."

Keller nodded in agreement. "Where is he anyway?"

O'Brian laughed. "He rode out about an hour ago. Said he was gonna do some scoutin' and would be back before supper. I don't know what he expects to find, but out there he is, scouting his red-hide heart out."

"Just keeping his hand in, I reckon," Keller replied. "He takes pride in his ability. He was scouting for the army years ago, then worked for a sheriff up in Colorado Territory for many more years."

Keller paused. "Mr. O'Brian, do you know a good man who would be willing to take those horses up to a ranch near Grand Junction? Maybe someone out of work who might stay on and help around the place. I'd pay top dollar to the right fellow."

O'Brian thought a minute. "Why, I sure do fer a fact. Bob Layden and his nephew Joe have been working fer the Montoya spread, up till last week. Joe and one of the younger Montoya gals got too chummy, so he and his uncle was let go. The old don wasn't having no gringo fer a son-in-law. Bob is a top hand—knows his horses better'n most. Joe is a fine young man. I wish he'd git eyes fer Rose. I'll put the word out fer 'em to come see me and let ya know."

"That'll be just fine, sir. Now, if you'll excuse me, I have to get over to the Red Garter and talk to someone."

"You be careful, Mr. Keller. That's a tough place, and the customers there'll be just as bad." O'Brian grabbed a lariat and crawled between two of the rails of the corral. "I'll get that filly hitched up right now."

Keller walked out of the livery, toward the center of Santa Fe. The tension he had suppressed began to flood his senses and his stride quickened.

Chapter 13

The Whore's Story

Marty pushed through the bat-winged doors of the Red Garter Saloon. Standing just inside the entrance, he slowly looked around the dim interior. The atmosphere stank of stale beer and staler tobacco smoke. Two soiled doves, standing on either side of a solitary drinker at the long wooden bar, listlessly plied their trade. Their eyes swiveled to Marty as he entered, sizing him up as a potential customer. Only two tables were filled with afternoon low-stakes gamblers trying their luck. A black-frocked gambler wearing a vest of brazen gold lamé, his expression one of sullen indifference, manned the faro table, idly spinning the big wheel. The gambler's gaze tracked Marty as he approached the bar.

Marty motioned to the muscular whiskey pourer, who was busy wiping shot glasses with a dirty rag. The man's nose had been broken so many times it looked like a mashed red turnip. "Draw me a beer, please."

"Buy me a drink, cowboy?" the younger of the two working girls inquired. The harsh reality of her profession was clearly imprinted on her young but rapidly aging

face. Marty had spent time with more than one bargirl
after he had lost Meg, but now Caroline filled his memory with her courage, strength, and beauty, and he had no
desire for the working girl's company.

"Sure," he replied. "Barkeep, bring the young lady her
choice."

Moving closer to him, she whispered in a seductive
voice, "My name's Annie, honey. What's yers?"

The drinks arrived swiftly, and the two silently toasted
each other. Marty wiped the foam from his upper lip with
his left hand before replying. "Name's Keller." He saw
the recognition flash in the young whore's eyes.

"Well, nice to meet ya, honey. Thanks for the drink."
Annie looked up at Keller with a practiced smile of false
affection. "Would ya like to accompany me upstairs? I'll
show ya some special things, seeing how yer a famous
man in these parts." She moved the tip of her pink tongue
around her brightly painted lips.

Marty slowly shook his head. "Sorry, Annie, but I'm
here on business. Would you tell me where I can find
Russ Gibbons?"

Annie gestured with her head toward the man standing
at the Chuck-a-luck table. "That's him right there. Want
me to introduce ya?" For an instant Annie hoped that this
famous killer held a grudge against her mean-tempered
boss. Maybe he'd shoot Gibbons full of holes. She
wouldn't shed a tear if Keller did.

Tipping his hat, Marty declined. "No, thanks, Annie. I
hope you'll excuse me." He moved over to the flashy-
looking saloon owner. The expressionless eyes of the
gambler never left him as he approached. Gibbons ignored Keller until Marty spoke. "Gibbons? Did Sheriff
Bushrod speak to you about what I want?"

The gambler sullenly eyed the tall bounty hunter
standing before him. Distaste was evident in his voice as

he answered, "Yep, he told me, mankiller." He saw the tightening in Keller's eyes. *Careful*, he cautioned himself. Flashing a weak smile that never reached his eyes, he answered with forced bravado. "So talk. Just don't take up all her time. She's busy and time's money in her business. She's in her room upstairs, number twenty-six, at the end of the hall." He angrily spun the faro wheel.

Marty set his jaw, staring the gambler down. The gambler dropped his gaze, surrendering in the contest of wills. "I might have a few things to discuss with you afterward. Don't make me have to find you." Marty turned on his heel and strode toward the stairs. He paused, turning back before climbing the scarred wooden steps. Gibbons' face was red with embarrassment and anger. Keller deliberately turned his back on the man and started up the stairs. Annie took some solace in what she witnessed from her spot at the bar. As Gibbons hurriedly shifted his gaze to scan the room, his cruel face flushed with chagrin. Annie prudently returned her attention to the drunken cowboy beside her.

Marty walked down the dimly lit hall. Behind the closed doors, the sounds of the activity within easily penetrated the thin wood. The door to number twenty-six was open. A hefty woman sat in front of a dressing table peering into a spotted mirror, idly brushing dull henna-dyed hair. Scars from the pox dimpled her sagging cheeks in spite of a thick layer of rice powder and rouge. She wore a gauzy robe, loosely tied at her waist, offering a free view of fat thigh to any passerby. A half-smoked cigarette smoldered in a glass ashtray. She put down her brush as Keller knocked and stepped into the room.

The woman was already half drunk, although it was still early in the afternoon. "Opal, my name's Keller. I'd like to ask you a few questions. Answer me straight and

I'll not take up much of your time. Play crooked with me and we'll have a long afternoon at it."

Her bleary eyes were weary and unfocused. "Well, what's yer problem, big guy? Russ says I'm to tell ya what I know. So ask away. Say, would ya like to get a little action before we start to converse?"

Marty sat down on the edge of the sour-smelling bed. "No, thanks. Just tell me what you can about a big fellow with a dark bushy beard. You were seeing a lot of him, Sheriff Bushrod tells me."

Opal talked to Marty's reflection in the mirror while she continued to brush her coarse hair. "Ya mean Luther. The bastard done run out on me last week. He said we was gonna git married. Now he's gone and didn't even say goodbye or nothin' 'bout where he was a-goin'." She sighed and picked up the cigarette, sucking a deep drag into her lungs. After coughing out a stream of smoke, she continued. "I was good to 'im, too. It was that bastard sidekick of his, Alva. I jest knowed it was him what convinced Luther to leave me here."

"What do you mean, it was Alva's fault?" Keller asked.

"That Alva was mean, clear through. He was the boss and treated Luther plumb awful. Him and that nasty Mex, Sanchez. Luther jumped when they was around, fer sure."

Marty's blood ran cold. Sanchez, the name Richland had uttered back in Kansas, just before he died. Marty's voice was hard as iron when he spoke again. "Opal, did Alva have some fingers missing on his left hand? Was he tall and lanky, with dark hair? Tennessee mountain twang to his voice?"

"Why, sure, that's him. He done lied to Rosa, same as Lute did to me. She cried her eyes out all day after he run off. Didn't tell her nuttin'. Just shucked out one morning and didn't come back." Opal continued her brushing. "That's all I know, 'cept if'n you find Lute, you tell him he's a lying bastard, but come back to me anyway."

Marty stood and snarled as he left the room. "He won't be alive two minutes after I find him." He ducked out of the door just ahead of the brush thrown by the enraged Opal. It hit the wall and clattered to the floor. Keller stepped over it and headed back to the saloon below, Opal's curses ringing in his ears.

The fire of revenge burned in his gut, like in the old days when he had first started his quest. It felt good. The fire was burning away the years of failure. He was ready to do some killing. He questioned Gibbons, the bartender, and Rosa, the girl who had taken up with that Alva, but none knew the outlaws' destination after they had left Santa Fe. Rosa wiped away tears as she told what she could about Hulett, whom she called Hawkins. Keller's hopes faded as he listened to their denial of any knowledge of the killer's destination. His face reflected the fury he was barely restraining.

Keller pressed every shopkeeper up and down the street for information, including Mr. O'Brian at the stables. The livery owner remembered the men, once they were described to him. "They hightailed it outta here before daylight last week. Put the money fer the bill on my desk. They were the ones who busted up Professor Mc-Nulty's wagon before they left. A bad pair. I never saw Sanchez—that what you called him? He musta kept his horse down at Gomez' livery, over in Chilitown."

Keller ended up at Sheriff Bushrod's office. "I need to get going, Sheriff. When do you expect the reward money will be released?"

The old lawman shook his head. "I can't say fer certain. I'll go over to the territorial building in the morning and try and push 'em along. I'd figger in a day or two fer sure."

Marty stomped out of the office, frustration darkening his mood. It seemed that he was no closer to the end of his search than when he had started. He had missed his quarry by less than a week. The men could have gone in nearly any direction. He would have to make a wide sweep around Santa Fe, and he would fall many days more behind his quarry. He stomped back to this hotel room, punishing the wooden slats of the sidewalk with every step.

He knocked on the McNultys' door at suppertime, but his mood wasn't any better. Only Fionna stepped out at his first knock on her uncle's door. She looked quite striking in a light green taffeta dress, probably her Sunday best. "Patrick's asleep and says he's not ready yet to go about. Uncle Sean had a headache this afternoon and drank too much of his medicine, so he's asleep in the chair. I'm afraid I'll be your only companion this evening, if that's agreeable with you."

Her bright smile and innocence broke through Marty's dark mood. He grinned at her with genuine warmth. "Certainly, Miss Fionna," he answered. "I'm most happy to have the pleasure of your company."

Over supper, he told her the news about his elusive prey. "I'm sure they don't know I'm on their trail, so they're probably not trying to hide their tracks. If I only knew which way they headed, chances are I could get close real quick." Looking at his pretty young guest's worried expression, he relented. "Hell, enough of this sort of gloomy talk. Tell me about your day."

Fionna happily obliged, chattering for many minutes about her errands and a visit to a dressmaker, and her care of Patrick. At the end of the meal, Keller walked Fionna back to O'Brian's house. Mr. O'Brian was on the porch, rocking in his favorite chair, talking with his plump daughter, Rose, as Marty and Fionna walked in the gate. Marty accepted O'Brian's invitation to sit and talk a while.

The two girls soon left the men alone, but only after Fionna had done her very best to bid Keller a grown-up good night. After formally thanking him for the wonderful meal and interesting conversation, she stood on tiptoes and kissed his cheek. With a swing of her long red tresses, she whirled and dashed inside, Rose chasing after her.

O'Brian chuckled. "I do believe you've made a conquest of that gal, Mr. Keller."

"She's a fine young lady," Keller admitted. "I don't want her getting hung up on me, though. She needs to find a good man her age. It's hard for her, I imagine, traveling all the time with her uncle." He shifted in his chair, causing it to squeak in loud protest. "She's like your Rose. They're about the age where they are starting to think real serious like about marriage and family." He smiled at O'Brian. "Right?"

O'Brian laughed. "That's all Rose seems to be talking about lately, fer a fact. By the way, I got aholt of Bob Layden. He'n Joe'll be here tomorrow morning about eight, if you want to talk to 'em. I reckon they're interested in hearing what you have to offer."

With a promise to be at the livery early the next morning, Keller returned to the hotel. JB was already in his bedroll, lying on the floor next to the open window. The Indian opened his eyes and sat up when Keller walked in.

"We'll be getting the reward money in a day or two, JB. Make certain the horses are ready to travel."

"What we do with the Comanchero ponies?"

"I'm gonna send them back to Caroline," Marty replied.

The old half-breed grunted and dropped back down on his bed. He was pleased with the gift. He decided to accompany them back to Cimarron. The only problem would be telling Keller that he was leaving him. He would think about it as sleep came, he decided.

Keller took off his gun belt and shirt, then got out the writing kit. He wrote a long letter to Caroline, describing the discovery and death of her husband's murderer. Then he wrote to the girls, telling them about the many horses he had taken for the ranch. When his eyes grew heavy, he blew out the oil lamp and settled in for the night.

When Marty and John Black Crow strode into the livery barn the next morning, two cowboys were waiting in the office with Mr. O'Brian. Bob Layden and his nephew looked like cowboys. Both were wearing faded work shirts, red bandannas around sun-bronzed necks, work-worn jeans, and Texas-style riding boots. Lean and lanky, they greeted Marty and JB politely, then waited for someone to speak. Keller liked what he saw. He read honesty and integrity in the two faces and both men looked him square in the eye when they spoke with him.

"I want to hire someone to drive a string of twelve horses over to the Box T ranch in Cimarron, up near Grand Junction." He pointed to the location on the map tacked to O'Brian's wall. "It's about a week's hard travel from here. Mr. O'Brian has spoken highly of you fellows. He says you might be interested in taking on the job. I can't guarantee it, but I would also write the owner, a widow named Thompson, and recommend that she take you on as permanent hands. If you're interested and willing to take the job, I'd pay each of you a hundred dollars, fifty now and fifty upon arrival."

Bob Layden paused for a moment and then nodded. "Sounds great, Mr. Keller. Me and Joe are on short rations right now. We need the work and that's a fact. If you take us on, I promise you we'll git them critters there. You won't have to worry about nuthin'."

Keller smiled. "Bob, I don't have any doubt at all. The next question is, would you have a problem working for Mrs. Thompson? She really needs the help."

Layden rubbed his heel on the floor. "Well, me'n Joe never worked for no female before, but I don't see why not. Do you, Joe?"

Joe shook his head. He was twenty years Bob's junior, but looked just like him. "No, sir. I don't see why not. You can count on Uncle Bob and me, Mr. Keller."

Marty looked closely at the young man. He had dark blue eyes and tousled brown hair. He was tall and lanky, but his muscles were well defined on his thin frame. He had the look of an intelligent and mature youngster.

"All right." Marty counted out five gold double eagles and handed them to Bob. "That's it. From now on, you're on the payroll. Bob, you and John Black Crow check all the horses this morning. Make sure they're all properly shoed and ready for the trip. Joe, I'm gonna take a young female friend of mine out to the hills and show her how to use a rifle. I'd like you to come along and help me." He instinctively guessed Fionna would like the young cowboy.

Both men nodded, slapped stained Stetsons on their heads and followed JB to the outside corral. "Please saddle up the bay mare for Miss Fionna, Joe," Marty instructed. He went to saddle Pacer, with O'Brian as company.

As he finished tightening the cinch strap, Joe led the saddled mare into the barn. "Here she is, sir. All ready to ride. Seems to be a right good animal." He tied the horse next to his, a rangy dun with the look of a working cow horse.

Marty noticed that the young man's saddle was old

and worn, with numerous repairs. "Joe, I'd be proud to have you check out those saddles over there. If you see one you like, take it with my compliments. I don't have any use for 'em." Keller pointed to the pile of gear he'd taken off the outlaw's horses.

Joe eagerly began sorting through the pile and presently let out a yell of discovery. "Gosh, would you look at this!" He pulled out a Mexican-style saddle, with silver inlay on the wide saddle horn and covered stirrups. "Do you mean it, Mr. Keller? I can have this saddle?"

Marty nodded his agreement. "Take it and welcome to it, son. Tell your uncle the same. If he wants any of the gear here, he can have it." He looked at O'Brian. "The rest of the stuff is for you to sell Mr. O'Brian. Sell it or trade it, whatever you want. I told the sheriff he could plant the dead Comancheros with the proceeds. After you deduct your commission, of course."

O'Brian beamed his appreciation. "Thanks, Mr. Keller." He walked over to survey the stacked saddles and bridles. Joe swiftly replaced his old saddle with the new one. He took his used but well-maintained Model 1866 Henry .44 repeating rifle and slid it into his new saddle scabbard. The pride of owning such a fine saddle was written on his wide grin as he leaped on his horse and rode outside to show his uncle.

When they returned, Bob Layden approached Keller. "Mr. Keller, I sure appreciate that fine saddle you gave Joe. Mighty nice of you."

"My pleasure, Bob. The last owner probably stole it from some wealthy Mexican after he bushwhacked him. Joe'll put it to a more honorable use. How about you? Do you need anything from the pile?"

Bob shook his head. "No, thanks. I'm just fine. I want you to know I'm proud to be a-workin' fer you."

About then, Fionna appeared in the doorway, carrying her new rifle awkwardly in her arms.

Marty greeted her. "Hello, here's our student. Good morning, Miss Fionna. This here is Joe Layden and his uncle Bob. They're going to work for me. Joe'll be going out to shoot with us. Joe, please get her horse for her."

Joe Layden staggered as if he'd been hit with a pick handle when he first laid eyes on Fionna. He stammered out a gasp of greeting to the pretty young redhead, then immediately hurried off to secure her pony.

Fionna barely noticed the other two men as she watched the young cowboy lead the new pinto mare to her side. Shyly, he took her rifle and placed it into the saddle scabbard. "My gracious, Mr. Keller," she finally remarked, "what a beautiful animal this is. Did ye rent her for me to ride?"

"Nope," Marty answered. "This is your horse now, Fionna, compliments of JB and me. You can take her with you when you and your uncle leave."

"Oh, Marty," she gushed, clapping her hands together. "What a grand surprise. Oh, thank you. Thank ye to the heavens. What's the wee lassie's name?"

"You'll have to name her, since the previous owner forgot to tell me." Keller chuckled as Fionna rubbed the mare's black-and-white nose while whispering endearments in the pony's ear.

"Then I shall call her Fila, after me sweet auntie back in Ireland. Fila, I love you." She patted the animal's neck and smiled sweetly at Joe. "Isn't she grand, Joe? What a beauty, she is. Come on, let's go ride." She gracefully climbed on Fila's back, assisted by Marty's boost up.

Joe was right behind her. Keller laughed before climbing more sedately on Pacer's back. "Bob, I'd better shake a leg or those two will be out of sight."

Marty trotted out of town after the two youngsters,

whose youthful laughter and conversation never abated until they reached the hills, where Marty felt it safe to shoot their rifles.

Fionna was a naturally coordinated young woman. Under the tutelage of Marty and Joe, who was quick to help, she soon mastered the concept of firing the weapon. Before much longer, she and Joe were shooting up every rock and cactus in sight. Marty was satisfied when the young girl could hit most things she aimed at. After they finished, he showed her how to clean the rifle and cautioned her in its use.

"My gosh, Miss Fionna," Joe exclaimed, "I never saw a gal who could shoot as good as you after only one lesson."

"'Tis your patient teaching, Joe." Fionna's eyes danced with amusement and fire, her natural exuberance intensified by the chemistry growing between her and the young cowboy. On the way back to town, perhaps to make up for the attention she had been giving to Joe, Fionna chose to ride beside Marty. His thoughts were focused on his search, and that dominated his conservation. "If I can't find out which way they went, I'll have to swing a fifty-mile loop around Santa Fe and hope I pick up a clue."

"Well, Mr. Marty Keller," she proclaimed, "I'll pray to St. Thomas that your search is successful. Don't you worry. Something good will surely happen." She glanced at the young cowboy behind them. "Isn't he the grandest thing now? Ye do like him, don't ye? I know I do. Would you mind if I saw more of him?"

Unexpectedly, Keller suddenly felt very old.

Chapter 14

Fionna's Clue

Marty spent the rest of the afternoon in a futile attempt to glean any tidbit of information from various people who might have some information on the three outlaws. By suppertime, it became obvious that nobody in Santa Fe had any idea where his quarry had gone. He had apparently reached a dead end in his investigation.

His mood sour, Marty headed for the café, where he had promised to dine with JB. The old scout rarely initiated conversation with Marty, yet out of the blue had requested that Marty dine with him and Keller happily agreed. He figured JB wanted to thank him for saving his life at the cabin. As he walked down the wooden sidewalk, jostling shoulders with other pedestrians, his thoughts were on his search. He fiercely told himself, *I'm closer now than I've been in seven years, thank God. I must find their trail and finish what I started. If JB and I have to stop in every town and trading post within a hundred miles, we will.*

JB was waiting for him in La Casa Café. "Tacos and beans," Marty ordered from the tired waitress. The café was crowded with loud and hungry men. Normal conversation was almost impossible, so once again, he and JB ate in silence. As they finished their second cup of coffee, the café slowly cleared of customers. Marty brought JB up-to-date on the failure of his inquiries.

"We'll have to circle the town and cut their trail." Keller brought the cup of hot coffee to his lips. "But we'll find it. I'm certain of that. Those types of men can't go unnoticed for long."

"JB go back to Cimarron," the old scout abruptly announced. "Thompson is avenged. His women need JB. I must go back now."

Marty choked on the hot liquid. "But, JB—that is, I . . . I thought you'd stay with me, at least for a while longer." Marty thought fast. Not once had he wanted companionship on the trail during the last seven years, but now he needed the old scout. Not only as companion, but because JB was a first-rate tracker. "JB, I was . . ."

His argument was interrupted by the sudden arrival of Fionna, who walked up to their table. "Gentlemen, may I join you for a piece of apple pie?"

Grateful for her timely interruption, Marty jumped up and offered her a chair. "It will be our pleasure, Miss Fionna," he answered. "What are you doing out so close to dark?"

"Praise the saints that I found ye. Come with me to see my uncle Sean. Mr. O'Brian told him about your looking for three men. Me uncle has talked with Sam Daffer, the night boy at the stable. He told him something about the men who broke up our wagon. I think he has something ye may want to hear."

Marty quickly dropped some money on the table. "Come on, JB. This may be the break we needed." The two men escorted the young redhead back to her uncle's room at the hotel.

The old professor, his eyes twinkling in excitement, started talking the moment they entered the room. "My Fionna says ye are looking for Hawkins, Sanchez, and one named Lute. Bad eggs, each o' them. 'Tis the very same men who busted into me wagon and stole my medicine. Well, while they were helping themselves, the night boy, name o' Daffer, saw 'em. He said to me that he heard the black-bearded one say they were goin' to Albuquerque. Then they rode away, on the south road out of town. 'Tis to Albuquerque they went, for a fact." He beamed at Marty in satisfaction.

Marty shook the older man's hand in gratitude. "Thank you, Professor, for that piece of info. It's the break we needed. That'll save John and me a heap of time and trouble trying to cut their trail. We'll be leaving tomorrow, I reckon." He smiled at his new friends, shaking the happy professor's hand.

"It was me good fortune to meet ye lads, and I'm happy I could help," the older man proclaimed. "Anything you ever need from Sean McNulty or his kin, ye have but to ask."

"Do me a favor then," Marty said, while the promise was still warm on McNulty's lips. "Accompany my men and horses to Cimarron. That way you can add support to their number, in case any more outlaws are about." *And,* he thought, *that will give Joe and Fionna some time together.*

"Consider it done," the professor grandly proclaimed. "As soon as Patrick can travel, we'll add our numbers to your men with pleasure."

Marty took his leave, offering heartfelt wishes of good fortune to the professor and Patrick. "Miss Fionna, would you allow me the pleasure of escorting you over to the O'Brian house?" At her nod, they left the hotel together.

"Fionna, I asked you and your uncle to ride with Joe

and Bob back to Cimarron for two reasons. First, is to provide you with more protection, and frankly, the second is to give you a chance to get to know Joe better. Please excuse my boldness, but if you like Joe, make sure he knows it before you get to Mrs. Thompson's ranch. Help him to say the right things, if he's the man you want." Keller gave the young woman a small roll of bills. "Here's two hundred dollars, just for you. Keep it for your dowry and my wedding gift in case I don't meet up with you again. You're a fine gal, Miss Fionna. I envy the man who marries you."

At the porch, he hugged Fionna and kissed her lovingly on her forehead. As he turned to leave, the wet-eyed girl softly called after him, "Oh, Marty Keller, thank ye, now and for always." Then brushing away the tears that sparkled in her eyes, she rushed inside the house.

Marty quickly walked to the hotel, his mind like that of a predator closing in on its prey. *Now, to convince JB to stay with me, at the very least until we're closer to the end of my hunt.*

He entered the room and sat on the edge of the four-poster bed. JB was lying in his bedroll under the open window, his dark eyes following Marty's every movement. *The old Indian knows how much I want him with me,* he thought.

Carefully, he chose his words. "JB, I need you to ride with me for a ways yet. We still have to get Sheriff Thompson's pistol back. Bob and Joe Layden will stay at the ranch after delivering the horses we're sending to Mrs. Thompson. She'll be all right, at least until the snow comes." He looked intently at the silent half-breed. "Will you come along with me, for a while?"

Silence filled the room. Marty heard the sound of a rider galloping out of town, the beat of his horse's hooves fading away. Finally JB answered, "JB go with Keller for

now. JB must go back to ranch before the first snow
comes." Then he turned on his side and said no more.

"Thanks, JB," Marty spoke to the silent form. "We'll
both go back before the first snow. I know it." He grimaced. He knew nothing was ever certain. After a moment, sitting quietly on the bed, thinking, he undressed
and finally fell into a fitful, restless sleep.

Marty and JB were at the livery the next morning right
at sunup. As they finished packing their animals for the
trip south, Bob and Joe walked in with O'Brian. Marty
swiftly explained that he wanted Joe and Bob to accompany the McNulty wagon to Cimarron. Then he gave two
hundred dollars to Mr. O'Brian. "This is for the bill I'm
running up and to pay for a good mule to replace the one
the professor lost. Bob, I want you to go with me to the
bank. I'll be sending a bank draft back to Mrs. Thompson
and a letter. I want you to personally deliver them for
me."

"Be my pleasure," the older Layden replied. "And
me'n Joe'll take good care of them folks in the wagon,
won't we, Joe?"

"Yes, sir, Mr. Keller. We sure will."

Marty motioned Joe to his side and spoke softly, just
for the younger man. "Joe, I'm counting on you to watch
over Miss Fionna for me. Get to know her good. If you
feel it's right, don't let her get away. No tellin' when you
might see her again. Do what your heart tells you, pard,
and best of luck." He walked over to Pacer and led the animal out of the barn. "Come on, JB, Bob. Let's get the
business out of the way so we can hit the trail." He shook
hands with the livery owner. "Goodbye Mr. O'Brian. It's
been a pleasure meeting you."

He rode to the sheriff's office, located just off Governor's Square. Sheriff Bushrod nodded at him as he entered the office. "Morning, Keller. Got your money."

On the sheriff's desk was a ten-thousand-dollar payment note from the Territory of New Mexico. Handing it to Marty, he sighed. "I figgered you'd be by early today. Well, here it is. More'n an honest man'll see in a lifetime. Take care of how you flash it around. I'd hate to find you with yer throat and pockets cut, even a no-good rascal like you. Now you would pleasure me to no end if you was to hightail it outta town pronto like."

Marty put the note in his shirt pocket. "Thanks, Sheriff. Me and JB will be gone before the hour is out. Headin' south for Albuquerque—just as soon as we stop by the bank, that is." He signed the necessary papers and took his leave of the old lawman. With Bob and JB following, he walked into the bank up the street.

At the door marked BANK MANAGER, Marty knocked and went in, motioning JB and Bob to follow. "Howdy," he drawled to the muttonchopped man who looked up. "I need to get a bank draft made out."

"Of course, sir," the manager replied. "Just tell me for whom and how much."

Marty turned to JB. "John Black Crow, two thousand of the reward is yours. What do you want to do with your share?"

JB looked thoughtful. "What Keller do with his share?" The old scout glared with distrust at the soft-looking banker in his fancy suit and clean white shirt. JB's every expression displayed the unease he felt in the bank of the white man. It was quite evident he had no intention of putting his money into a bank.

"I'm gonna send most of my share to Mrs. Thompson with Bob here. I'll keep a little for our expenses. So, Mr. Banker, I'll need a six-thousand-dollar bank draft made out to Mrs. Caroline Thompson, care of the Box T ranch, in Cimarron, Territory of Colorado." The eyes of the banker opened wide, and he became quite solicitous of his new customers.

JB grunted, "Good. JB send his share to the little ones. I can do?"

Marty nodded. "Good idea, JB. They'll have quite a pleasant surprise in store for them when Bob and Joe arrive."

The two money drafts were quickly prepared, and Marty returned to give Joe his final instructions. Marty handed him the bank drafts and his letter for Caroline and the girls. It felt strange, since it was the first letter he'd sent to anyone since the war. He had every confidence that Bob and Joe would get them both delivered safely. Before midmorning, he led JB and their packhorse out of Santa Fe, down the dusty rutted road toward Albuquerque, sixty miles to the south.

Marty wanted to reach a trading post Sheriff Bushrod had mentioned about thirty miles south of Santa Fe before camping. It was late in the afternoon when they rode up to the hitching post in front of the log-and-sod building. To the side was a small grove of cottonwood trees clustered near a tiny stream. As the two men climbed down, stretching their weary muscles, Marty craved a cool beer. "I'll treat you to a beer before we set up camp if you want one." He walked inside the dim interior, with JB right behind him.

The dirt floor was smooth-packed from years of use; beer and alcohol permeated the air with their dank odors. It was cooler inside than out, thanks to the thick sod walls. The owner stood behind a small bar, idly wiping its rough wood surface. Two cowboys sat at a corner table, nursing a nearly empty whiskey bottle and conversing in low tones. They grew silent and watched Keller and JB approach the bar.

Marty took off his hat and nodded. "Howdy. Would

you pour my friend and me a couple of glasses of beer, please."

The unshaven owner, his eyes small and bunched close to his puffy nose, squinted at JB. "That an Injun with ya?"

Marty answered carefully, hoping to defuse what he sensed was coming. "This is the son of a French trapper and an Ottawa Indian princess and a particular friend of mine."

The owner of the bar snarled, "We don't serve Injuns in here." Pointing his finger at JB he ordered, "You, redskin, git outta here, pronto."

JB's face darkened in anger, but he started to turn and leave. Keller put a restraining hand on his arm. Then he turned to face the tavern owner and said politely, "All right, mister, it's your place, so we'll both go. How about a small bucket of beer to take to our camp?" He flipped a half-dollar coin on the scarred bar.

The scraping of a chair echoed in the room. One of the half-drunk cowboys stood up and called out, "Ya don't git it, stranger. That Injun with you doesn't git any beer, period. And that goes fer a Injun lover, too. Now both of you git." He swaggered toward Marty, his companion right behind him.

Marty started to comply, since he had nothing to gain by arguing with a drunk, but it was too late. The cowboy grabbed his shoulder and growled, "Ya crawled in here with yer Injun friend, so crawl out. Ya heer me, Injun lover? Crawl like the snake ya are."

Sighing in frustration, Marty slipped his shoulder away from the cowboy and turned to face him. The punch he knew was coming was already en route, and he barely ducked under it. Swinging with his left, he hit the man hard in the stomach, then followed with a vicious right uppercut. The drunk knew some about fighting; he jerked his head aside so Keller's fist only grazed his cheek. Had it connected, the man would have been knocked out cold. Even so, the force of the blow sent the cowboy tumbling backward over the nearest table, upsetting chairs and poker chips in all directions.

The second drinker, a stockier man, with more meat on his bones than his friend, lowered his head and drove hard into Keller's midsection, pinning him up against the bar. Keller sensed movement behind him, but was too busy to take notice. Gripping both hands together, he came down hard on his opponent's neck, knocking him to the ground at his feet.

Stepping over the stunned cowboy, Marty met the first man just as the enraged drunk threw aside the offending table he had rolled across. The two men traded quick blows, Keller's head snapping at the solid impact of the fist against his jaw. His second blow hit the taller cowboy squarely on his bony chin, and the cowboy's eyes rolled back in their sockets. The man fell, as if he'd been pole-axed, blood trickling out of his open mouth. Marty turned, but the second drunk was still down by the bar, too woozy or drunk to get to his feet.

JB was behind the bar, his knife pressed against the barkeep's rib cage. Both silently watched the action. The owner had a big wooden hammer, a bung starter, in his hairy hand. When he saw Keller's hard glance, he hastily dropped it.

Marty nodded at the Indian scout. "Thanks, partner. You"—he pointed his finger in the owner's face—"give me a bucket—no, two buckets—of beer and make it quick." While the cowed man was drawing the beer, Marty demanded, "Did three men come through here last week? One a Mexican, one a fellow with a dark bushy beard, and a third man who's tall and skinny, missin' two fingers on his left hand. Answer me straight and quick."

The tavern owner put the two buckets on the bar. "I reckon they might. Didn't stay long. Just wet their whistles and rode on."

Marty paid for the beer and paused at the door after JB had walked out carrying the foam-topped buckets. "We'll be staying over in the cottonwoods. I suggest nobody comes around tonight or my friend'll have 'em for breakfast." With one last look at the unconscious cowboys, he ducked through the low-hanging door into the fading twilight. The glare of the setting sun framed the manhunter in a halo of red. The outline of his body disappeared into the fiery orb as he walked away.

As they sipped their hard-earned beer and cooked their evening meal of biscuits, beans, and bacon, JB chuckled. "Keller hits hard. Thompson would want you for friend, I know. JB happy that Keller his friend. We find Keller's killers and whip them, too. Now tonight is JB's guard. Keller sleep and get strong again." He chuckled again, then turned his attention to the frying bacon.

Marty's jaw ached with every bite, but he finished his meal and soon was sleeping soundly. The old scout stood guard and mused over the fight in his honor. The half-breed hummed a song of the fight under his breath while he watched the darkness and planned Keller's future. *Keller is good man, like my friend Thompson. I must take him to Thompson's woman when this hunt finished.*

Marty did not wake until a tinge of pink was peeking over the Sangre de Cristo Mountains above them. They were under way shortly after they finished their morning coffee, headed south toward the anticipated showdown with their elusive foes.

Chapter 15

A Careless Blunder

On the same afternoon that Marty Keller led the McNultys and twenty draped bodies into Santa Fe, Alva Hulett entered Albuquerque with his two desperado friends. The small city, named after a duke in Spain, was a dry spot sitting on the east bank of the Rio Grande River. That day, Albuquerque was taut with tension. The Ninth Colored Cavalry, posted across the shallow ford of the river, was engaged in a fierce fight to contain the latest Indian trouble. An ongoing war between Apache Indians and the ever-growing numbers of farmers, ranchers, and prospectors lured by the wealth of the region was suddenly hot again.

The most precious resource of the area, water, was being diverted or claimed by whites, isolating the warlike Apaches ever deeper in their mountain strongholds. A succession of great war chiefs had allowed the fearsome Indian nation to maintain a foothold on the land of their ancestors, but had not succeeded in permanently driving the white man from the land.

The vicious fighting had stagnated into a series of

raids against isolated ranches, wagon trains, stagecoaches, or individual travelers unlucky enough to be
spotted by the merciless Indian warriors. Currently,
Hulett quickly learned, the road to El Paso was considered too dangerous to travel without a military escort. On
Monday of every week, a stage, along with any other
wagons or riders that cared to join, departed under military escort to head south to El Paso, while another departed from El Paso north. Otherwise, travelers were not
allowed to leave the city for any destination south or
west. To do so, in disobedience of the army directive,
meant instant arrest if caught by the Army and unpleasant
death if discovered by the Apache.

Hulett checked himself and Lute into a cheap hotel
near the main plaza, leaving Sanchez to find a place on
his own somewhere on the Mexican side of town, where
the large Hispanic population all resided. "We'll hang
around fer a spell and then join the next convoy to El
Paso." He paused for a second. "Maybe I'll try my hand
at cards while we wait. I'd like to make up fer what I lost
that last night in Santa Fe." Looking around to make sure
nobody was paying any attention to them, he dismissed
his Mexican accomplice. "Sanchez, I'll see ya tomorry.
Let me know where yer a-stayin'. Come on, Lute, let's
clean up and git some vittles."

He paused and glared at his bearded companion. "I
mean it, Lute. You smell worse than a skunk in a pig
sty. Git yourself a bath. Put on some lilac water, too You
need it."

"Aw, boss" was all the chagrined Lute could come up
with as he tagged after his leader.

The two Anglo killers looked the town over the next
morning before putting their aliases on the listing for the
next convoy south. Al's nasty mood had returned. Once
again he had suffered through a terrifying nightmare. A

stranger, shrouded in black and cold as death, had stood at the foot of his bed. A grim angel of doom was watching him sleep. He'd awakened, drenched in sweat, to find the room empty and still. He felt certain however, that someone was on his trail. He prided himself on his inborn sixth sense about such things. More than once he'd made a sudden decision to move on, fortuitously staying a step ahead of any pursuers.

Only once had Al failed to foresee a problem, the day in Mexico when the federales arrived just as he and Sanchez walked out of that fleabitten bank, their hands filled with bags of silver pesos. He had almost died in that sweat hole prison in Sonora. *I'll go down shootin',* he swore to himself, *before I let another man put me back in prison.*

"Lute," he snarled back at the crude henchman dogging his footsteps. "I'm gonna git in a game of cards. Ya come in after me, like we was strangers, and play to my hand. I'll make back what I lost before we git gone from this dust wallow. Also, I've had a certain feelin' someone's after us fer quite a spell now. So keep yer eyes peeled."

Lute looked around apprehensively. "You bet, boss. If I catch anyone paying us too much mind, I'll let you know pronto."

"Ya jus keep yer mind on the cards and ya know what to do if anything happens—jus like ya did last spring in Santa Fe."

"I gotcha, boss. You can count on me." Lute dropped back a few steps from his boss, his dark piggy eyes shifting nervously from side to side as he scanned the dusty street for danger.

Alva turned into the biggest saloon in sight. He glanced around for a moment, looking the place over. Several tables with green felt tops were available for the

card players. A gambler was spinning the Chuck-a-luck
wheel for two dirty cowboys. Several girls in low-cut,
frilly dresses were scurrying about with drinks on their
trays. Slowly, he made his way to a table where three
cowboys and a house gambler were playing cards.
"Howdy," he offered to the players in false friendliness.
"Can a feller sit in on yer game?"

"Sure can, mister," the older cowboy replied. "Pull up
a chair." Like his two younger companions, he was in
faded pants and a calico shirt. He had a blue bandanna
tied around his neck, and a weather-beaten Stetson lay on
the table beside him. The older cowhand was browned
like a dried berry from his eyebrows down to his neck,
but his forehead was as pale as a baby's bottom. Gray
streaks were evident in his uncut hair and bushy mustache. "Name's Frank Tucker. This here's Bobby Akins
and Cabe McKeon, who work with me on the D Bar. The
house man's named Whitey Slater. What we gonna call
you?"

Alva sat down next to the house shill and put his
bankroll on the table. "I'm Al Hawkins, from Tennessee.
Visitin' my sister until I can git on to El Paso." He played
a few hands to get the feel of the game. It was for low
stakes, but the cowboys drank straight whiskey while
they gambled, so he took every opportunity to slowly
raise the stakes as the alcohol dulled their senses. Lute
waited at the bar, nursing a beer, watching for the signal
to join the group. He had learned the hard way not to
drink too much while working for Al. The slapping
around he'd received the one time he'd messed up by
being drunk was lesson enough even for his limited brain
to absorb.

The saloon began to fill as the evening approached. Al
carefully began to push the pots, winning just often
enough to stay even. The house gambler was no threat to

him, apparently concerned only with drawing out the house cut. The cowboys were becoming more intoxicated with each hand played. Al smugly surveyed the pot on the table. He had pushed the stakes high enough to make it interesting. He had folded to an obvious bluff from one of the players, then signaled to Lute. It was time to make some money.

Lute shuffled over and asked for permission to join the game. "Why, sure," Al quickly replied. He pushed out a chair to his left, where Lute could bump his raises, and shuffled the deck. "Always happy to git new money into the game, right, boys?" He chuckled as he shuffled the cards.

The cowboys cheerfully agreed and the quiet house gambler simply nodded. It did not matter to him. The more players, the more the house cut would be. Play resumed and gradually, Al began to push the stakes ever higher. Lute did his job, bumping the pot every time Al nudged his boot with his foot. By ten o'clock, Al was more than a hundred dollars ahead. The whiskey was flowing freely, and the time was ripe to spring his little trap on the inebriated cowboys. Better than two hundred dollars was scattered around the table and Al had the deal. He planned to palm a couple of aces, then get all the money with one hand. He would up and leave before the drunken cowboys fully realized what had happened. He dealt himself a pair of aces and made sure all the players had good cards for themselves. When he palmed his two other aces, he would have four of them and win the pot, hands down.

Just as he was making the switch, a stranger dressed in dark clothing walked through the swinging doors. The sight of the man startled Al. He looked like the demon in Al's dreams, sure as shooting. His concentration interrupted, Al awkwardly palmed the two aces. His sleight of hand did not completely escape the sharp eyes of the player across from him.

Frank Tucker's eyes narrowed and he sat up straight in his chair. The cowboy wasn't sure, but it appeared that the skinny stranger had just palmed some cards. Frowning, he folded his cards and watched the play. Alva raised and nudged Lute's foot with the toe of his boot, who promptly did the same. The other two cowboys stayed in and called. The house gambler hesitated, but he was holding a full house, jacks high. Since Al had dealt him the hand, Al knew he was in to stay.

After the gambler raised, Alva bumped the pot one more time. "Looks like we're all a bunch of winners this hand," he remarked. Pushing across the fifty dollars' worth of chips he had in front of him, he raised for the last time. "Fifty to you, boys. Who's man enough to stay with me?"

Lute swiftly called and both Cabe and Akins pushed in the last of their pile of chips. Bobby Akins slurred softly, barely able to speak coherently. "I'll take your money, thank ya kindly. What about you, Whitey?" He looked greedily at the house gambler. Whitey was a little hesitant, but his hand was a good one, so he added his money to the pot. The gambler was cursing himself for not paying more attention to the deal. He suddenly had a very uncomfortable feeling about the game.

Al smirked as he laid down the winning cards. "Four aces, boys. I win the prize." He reached to rake in the pile of chips. Frank, who had sat out the hand, spoke up in a soft, menacing voice. "Hold it. I think you've been pullin' a fast one on us." He pushed back his chair and stood, a pistol in his callused hand. He never took his eyes from Al. "Boys, I'm certain I saw this jasper palm some cards, sure as I'm standin' here. Git yer money and let's go."

Al curled his lip and scornfully responded, his voice as cold as death as he glared up at the standing Frank. "Yer wrong, cowboy, and yer wrong to pull down on me. Now I'm gonna have ta show ya just how wrong." He nudged Lute's foot and the burly man swiftly pushed back from the table, drawing everyone's eyes to him for a decisive instant. Al took the opportunity to swiftly draw and shoot Frank, knocking him back against a neighboring table, sending beer glasses, chairs, and occupants in all directions.

Leveling his gun at the shocked cowboys still seated around his table, he motioned with the barrel. "Keep yer hands on the table and don't move. I reckon I'll cash in now and take my leave."

Nodding at Lute to pick up the chips, he was backing toward the door when he felt a gun in his back. "Don't make no foolish moves, stranger. I'm Sheriff Lowrey, and you'd best come with me until we clear this up."

Lowering his gun, Al saw it was the dark stranger he'd seen entering earlier. *A dad-blamed sheriff, damn the luck. What a rotten break.*

The sheriff reached around and took Al's six-gun, which he pushed in his own holster. Sputtering in indignation, Al was marched out of the saloon to the city jail, where the sheriff locked him up with a sleeping drunk. The lawman looked frostily at his new tenant.

"Well, card shark, you jus cool off a spell while I go back over to the saloon and git the boys' statements." He closed the door between his office and the cells, before Al could say a word.

"Hey," Al shouted in anger at the closed door of the jail. "Ya ain't gonna keep me in here, are ya? This cot stinks like a bar rag in summer." Silence was the only reply. Cursing a blue streak, Alva settled back on the hard cot to await the lawman's return.

When the sheriff entered the office two hours later, Al hollered for him to come back into the jail. Finally, the sheriff appeared. "What'd ya want, fella? You make enough racket to wake up Charlie there and he's passed out."

"What about me?" Al complained. "How long you gonna hold me in this flea pot?"

"Mister, you're plum lucky. Your shot hit Frank Tucker in the short ribs and bounced off. He's laid up fer a few days with a cracked rib. I reckon to keep you in jail that long. I couldn't get any of the other players to back up his claim that you was cheatin', but I reckon it's a fact. I gave 'em back their money and they agreed not to press charges. If you'd have kilt Frank, I reckon I'd have the pleasure of hangin' ya from a cottonwood down by the river."

"Wait a minute," Al whined. "I was plannin' to leave on the next escort to El Paso." With a false smile and feigned sincerity, he pleaded, "If'n ya let me go, I'll promise to stay away from here, permanent like."

Sheriff Lowrey grunted. "Sounds like the best news I've heerd tonight. I'll let you out just afore they leave. You be gone and don't come back." He turned and left the room, ignoring Alva's sputtering complaints.

Alva and his two cronies joined the thirty men and two women who assembled in the plaza the next day. The Army patrol consisted of a dozen black cavalrymen commanded by a young white lieutenant. They patiently waited for everyone to get ready to depart, then led the convoy across the Rio Grande toward the El Paso road.

Al rode beside Lute, viciously cursing his poor luck, Sheriff Lowrey, and life in general. His disposition only improved when they crossed the last hill before El Paso, six days later. Nearly every night Al dreamed the same dreaded nightmare. He hadn't the sense to realize that the more he dwelled on it during the day, the more likely he was to dream about it again that night.

Their convoy was just too large for the angry Apaches to tangle with, although they did see numerous sign of Indians tracking their progress south from Albuquerque. The young officer had learned his job well, and the night stops and long days on the road passed without incident.

A dusty twin city to Albuquerque, El Paso sat on the north bank of the same muddy Rio Grande River. Across the shallow water, the small Mexican village of El Paso del Norte served as the gateway into the barren desert of northern Mexico. Al wasted no time crossing the boundary between Mexico and the United States. Only then did he feel certain the unknown tracker would be stopped at the border. No lawman could legally operate in Mexico, and no Mexican would help a gringo lawman look for a Mex outlaw. He pulled up at the first cantina they saw and turned to Sanchez. "Yer the man now, amigo. Get us some provisions and some idea what's happenin' to the south. Ya know about where I want to go."

Sanchez' obsidian eyes glittered in anticipation as he nodded. The crafty mind of Al saw the gleam and surmised the reason. He had better watch how he treated the Mex. Now they were in his country and his word carried weight. No more pushing him off to the flea-ridden Mex hotels at the edge of town. Sanchez' knowledge of the language and people now made him the most valuable member of the gang. "Yer the man, Sanchez," Al repeated again. He watched the short, dark Mexican ride off, humming a peasant melody.

Al and Sanchez had ridden over much of northern Mexico before they were captured six years earlier. They had lived in the mountains southwest of Chihuahua, the nearest big city. There were mountains with thick forests, lakes, green grass, lush valleys among high peaks—all a person could want in a place to settle down and live well. Al had already picked out the place he wanted and he meant to get it, even if he had to buy it legal. Sanchez had the connections he needed, with relatives all over the area.

Al grimaced in pleasure as he sipped the fiery tequila and greedily sucked the green wedge of lime. Things were looking up for this son of Tennessee.

Chapter 16

Down Mexico Way

Two mornings later, the sun was just a tiny sliver of red on the east Texas plains when Al and his two sidekicks rode out of El Paso del Norte. Sullen Al suffered from too much tequila and cursed every jarring step his horse took. He viciously berated Lute for asking a simple question. The tirade seemed to help Al's pounding headache more than anything else. Al was certain they were at least five days ahead of any pursuer and that meant a hundred miles into the wild country of Mexico. He was well hidden now. As the miles passed, he relaxed and began to breathe easier.

The three outlaws reached Chihuahua in a week of hard, dawn-to-dusk riding. The dark demon no longer haunted his dreams each night. By the third day he was talking with Sanchez about the grand ranch they would soon own. The high desert country of northern Mexico was a balm to his ragged nerves.

Chihuahua was the provincial capital, a thriving town compared to El Paso del Norte. The outlaws took rooms in the town's finest hotel and relaxed. The next morning

Sanchez left to visit his relatives and Lute crawled into a whore's bed in a dingy room over a decrepit cantina on the edge of town. For three days Al enjoyed his leisure and indulged in the excitement of Chihuahua's night life. His money would stretch a long way south of the border providing him with the good life he believed he had earned.

On the morning of the fourth day, Sanchez returned, a satisfied grin on his face. "Senor Al, what are your plans? Do you still want to go now for the ranchero grande near the blue lake to the west?"

Al licked his lips hungrily. Ever since he and Sanchez had run across the spot, nestled in a green valley next to a pristine blue lake high in the mountains to the southwest, he had dreamed of it. "Yep, partner," he answered. "I aim to get me that ranch, find a woman or two, and raise cattle like a grand jefe the rest of my days." He desperately wanted the ranch and the power it represented.

Al gave a bemused smile to his Mexican sidekick. In Mexico the cruel ex-peon was an invaluable asset. Al needed to treat him right. At least until his usefulness was over. "That is, you and me will, right, partner?"

Sanchez nodded happily and rubbed his hands together in excitement. Al could see the effect of his carefully planned inclusion of the Mexican into all Al's schemes for the future. The swarthy ex-peon was already dreaming of the fine lifestyle Al was always describing. His evil little brain grew more desirous of such a fine life each day.

As far as Al was concerned, it was time for him to get off of the owlhoot trail. The hard rides, cold food, and miserable nights of sleepless tension were wearing him down. A fine ranchero with pretty women at his disposal and many cattle suited him perfectly. Having Sanchez and his many relatives to protect him, the past would never interfere with his future.

Sanchez broke into his reverie. "I asked my uncle Jésus about the place you seek, Senor Al. It is part of a big ranchero owned by a Don José del Vargas. For many generations his family has lived there. He is now here, in Chihuahua, with his daughter and son-in-law for the governor's monthly fiesta."

"The shindig tomorry night, over to the governor's hacienda?" Al queried. At Sanchez' nod, he thoughtfully rubbed the stubble on his chin. "Reckon I might just pay a visit to the party, amigo. May be possible I'd git a chance to ask this here Don José if he might be willin' to sell us a piece of land fer our ranch." The smile on his face would have made an honest man shudder.

"While I was drinking at the hotel bar last, I met a cattle buyer from San Antonio who mentioned that he was a-goin' to the party. It won't take much effort to convince him that I'd be a perfect guest to take along. A few free drinks and a line of bull manure about me being in the land business should do the trick. I reckon I'll jist mosey over to the cantina right now and set it up. You check with me first thing tomorry morning, amigo."

The next evening, Sanchez drove up to the massive double doors to the governor's hacienda in the finest buggy Al could rent. Sitting on the leather seats were Al and Hec Billows, the Texas cattle buyer. The Texan wore a rumpled brown tweed suit that he'd brought in from Texas, but Al was agleam in a newly purchased Mexican vaquero suit. He sported tight black pants and an elaborate waist coat with silver piping at the seams and silver embroidery at the cuffs. A crisp white silk shirt, for which he'd paid an outrageous price, was buttoned to the neck, and a red silk bandanna was carefully tied around his neck. He'd had a bath, a shave, and a haircut, paying extra for a heavy splash of bay rum. His new boots gleamed from the hog fat Sanchez had carefully rubbed on them.

Hec Billows sniffed the air and rumbled something about Al smelling like a New Orleans whore in summertime, but Al didn't care. He meant to show Don José del Vargas what a gentleman he truly was. Al disguised his disfigured hand with a pair of black kid gloves, wearing the left glove while holding the right one in his left hand.

The two Anglos easily passed between the two armed sentries at the front door and soon were mingling with the crowd of wealthy Mexicans and numerous military officers in their bemedaled uniforms. The women were dressed in their finest gowns of colorful silk and taffeta, billowing over numerous petticoats. They had lace fans and mother-of-pearl combs securing shiny dark hair, coiled in the latest fashions. Colors swirled as the couples danced in the glow of the racks of candles ensconced on the walls and hanging from twinkling chandeliers above. Al's imagination stirred at the scene. He lusted for just such a life. It was a tonic to the greedy outlaw's eyes. He deserved this kind of life, and now he was about to have it.

He immediately dumped Billows with a couple of older Mexican ranchers. They were already immersed in discussing cattle prices in Texas. They paid no attention to Al's abrupt departure.

He stopped a waiter hurrying past with a tray of drinks and whispered. *"Savvy ingles, por favor?"*

"Sí, senor," the polite waiter replied. "I can speek a little."

Al bent over until his mouth was level with the waiter's head. "Which one is Don José del Vargas?"

The waiter gazed around the huge room. "There, senor, by the columns. That is the don with his family."

Alva looked across the room. A slender white-haired man with a trim goatee was talking to a young couple seated in chairs along the wall. His white ruffled shirt sewn with silver thread gleamed in the candlelight. His narrow face bore the refined countenance of one born to wealth and power.

The woman was definitely the man's daughter; she was as tall and slender as her father. Her dress was light blue, shiny as satin, with lace at the bodice and cuffs. Her hair was as black as new coal. A diamond tiara gleamed in the candlelight. *Not truly beautiful,* Hulett thought, *but regal, haughty, unapproachable in her gentility.* She glanced around the room, her gaze flicking over Hulett as if he did not exist.

Next to them stood a young man with a thin, dark mustache, which he carefully brushed from time to time. He looked as if he were bored to death.

Al confidently began to work his way toward the del Vargas family. He waited impatiently until the two younger people left for the dance floor. At last the family patriarch was alone. Standing so close that the man couldn't ignore him, Al bowed slightly and spoke. "Good evenin', Don José. Permit me to introduce myself. I'm Alva Hulett from Tennessee, just visitin' yer beautiful country fer a few weeks. Nice party, ain't it?"

Don José acknowledged Hulett's presence and responded in a cool but civil tone. "My pleasure, Senor Hulett. *Sí,* it is a fine fiesta indeed." He started to turn away from the intrusive gringo, forcing Al to gently restrain his arm. The brown eyes narrowed and the voice became frosty as he faced the Yankee. "What is it?"

Al flashed his most sincere smile. "Don José, I've been lookin' around this part of the country and I'd like to start a small ranch where I can raise some cattle. I'd like to buy a thousand acres of land across the blue lake from you. I'd gladly pay you five thousand in gold for the land. Whatta ya say?" Al thought, *First a thousand acres and then all your land, you stuck-up old Spic*. He looked expectantly at the grandee, awaiting his reply.

The coldness in the don's eyes matched the chill in his voice. "I am afraid you have asked for the impossible, senor. My land has been in my family for over one hundred years. I would not sell it for ten times that amount. And"—he paused to underscore his meaning—"I would never sell my land to you. Now, senor, I must bid you *buenos noches*." The old man turned his back on Al and moved toward a portly merchant and his young wife.

Blood rushed to Al's face, enflamed by the insult. If there hadn't been a hundred witnesses in the room, he'd have shot the rude Spic in the back where he stood. Instead, he had to settle for a threat to the don's retreating back. "Ya jist signed death warrants fer you and all yer snooty family. Jist ya wait." The humiliated outlaw glared defiantly, then spun on his heel and stomped from the room.

Outside, he hurried to his buggy and climbed in before snarling at Sanchez, who was dozing on the driver's seat, "Let's git to some cantina quick. I've got a bad taste to wash outta my mouth."

Al did a slow burn the entire ride back into the heart of town. "Find a place with women and loud music," he ordered Sanchez. "I gotta have some tequilla bad and some lovin' woman to enjoy. I jus' wish it were that upitty daughter of Don José I had under me."

They left the cattle buyer to find his own way home and soon were surrounded by cheap whores and cheaper tequila. Al told Sanchez that the old don had refused to sell any of his land. "We'll jus' have to figger a way to take it. But by damn, take it I will," Al grumbled between drinks and sucks of lime.

Sanchez' lips curled in a vicious grin. "Don't worry, Senor Alva. I've been thinking on this and have a plan." He shooed the girls away and lowered his voice. "My cousins Ignacio and Pepe are now here in Chihuahua. They are riding with a band of men under one who calls himself General Morales. The general has over fifty men and a hideout in the mountains near Matamoros. This night they are only a few miles south of here. The general plans to strike the federal bank in Delicias next Friday." He paused and glanced around suspiciously.

"My cousins are in town now, buying supplies for General Morales. They say we should join with them. The general is getting careless about his drinking. They say a smart hombre like me could soon become the leader. With your help, I will take over the general's army. Then we can use them to strike the don's hacienda. As soon as he is dead, you can register a bill of sale with the federales and we'll have the land."

"Damn, Sanchez," Al spoke admiringly. "That's a hell of a good plan. Yer sure the general will let us in his army?" He chuckled, thinking of what sort of army it was.

Sanchez nodded eagerly. "*Sí*, my cousins say he needs good men to replace those who fell in their last raid. They ran into a strong patrol of federales and many were killed before they escaped. Also the general was drunk and led them badly, so the men are ready for a new leader. My cousins will argue that we should be allowed to join the army. I think it will work. Have no fear."

Al sipped his drink and sank his stained teeth into a lime wedge. This was more like it. Just when one trail petered out, another one opened up. "Tell yer cousins that we're new recruits fer their general. Now let's git them gals back here. I've got a itch what needs scratching mighty bad."

The next day, Sanchez and his two cousins escorted Al and Lute to the hideout where the outlaw General Morales had bivouacked the motley band of cutthroats he called his army. The men were poorly equipped, wearing ragged clothing and carrying dirty, rusted weapons. All wore trinkets taken in encounters with federal army soldiers or hapless villagers. The general was a squat, gray-headed man with a gold tooth and a potbelly. He had a fondness for knee-high boots with silver conchos inlayed around the tops. Like most of his men, he wore crossed bandoleers of bullets and carried a silver-inlaid pistol in a hand-tooled leather holster. Pushing the wide-brimmed sombrero back on his head, he welcomed his visitors with a hearty guffaw, nearly sickening them with his foul breath. "Well, well, amigos, what have we here?"

Sanchez' cousin Ignacio spoke first. Then Morales spoke to Sanchez, listening carefully to the answer. From Hulett's limited knowledge of the language, he knew Sanchez was telling General Morales about Hulett's career in the Confederate Army.

Finally, the general seemed to agree. He stared hard at Hulett and Lute for a few moments, then nodded his shaggy head. "Gringos in my army? *Sí*, I like that. You will show my men how the gringo army fights, *sí*?" The old outlaw scratched the sweat-stained shirt under the fold of his big belly. "You can start with my new recruits. They are dumb as the pigs who live in their villages. Make them soldiers, gringo, and I will make you a sergeant someday." His booming laugh echoed around the camp.

Al and Lute assembled the hapless peons recently recruited from some peasant village. The first lesson was how to aim and fire single-shot carbines. The better weapons were reserved for the more experienced men. The camp was poorly deployed for self-defense and revealed just how inept their commander really was. A tall hill towered over the campfires and bedrolls. There was very little cover if they were attacked by federal soldiers. No outposts were manned to watch for any stranger's approach.

"Hell," Al muttered to Lute. "Any decent sheriff's posse back in Texas would clean 'em like plucked chickens." Lute's quick laugh pleased him. He continued, satisfied with his wit. "Helpless villagers are about all this bunch can handle. They'll be so grateful fer the experience I got durin' the war that I'll be able to git 'em to do anything I ask."

Al's scheme called for the general not to survive long as commander, but the Friday raid on the bank did not allow him an opportunity. The general ordered Lute and Sanchez to ride with the group robbing the bank, while Al was sent with half the men to attack the federal soldiers at their barracks, just outside the small town.

As they took their positions in the dull gray dimness of dawn, Al scoffed at the idea that the bank held any appreciable sums of money. The only two buildings of any size were the church on one end of town and the bank on the corner of the plaza. The rest of the town consisted of small adobe huts and clapboard stores.

Al's men were the new recruits, along with a few experienced outlaws sent along to ensure they didn't run away at the first gunshot. Al carefully placed his men in the cover of some trees just outside the barracks. Warning them not to fire until he did, he settled down behind a tree trunk to wait for the main body of bandits to ride into the town. He hoped when the action started the soldiers were as poorly trained as his band of cutthroats.

The racket of the general's army as it rode into the small town roused him from his musings. A head stuck out of the door and then three men ran out, clutching their rifles and throwing on clothes. Al's shot dropped the first soldier in the dirt, while the third sprawled back in the doorway, hit by one of the newer recruit's lucky shot. The second hesitated, then turned to run back inside, but he'd waited too long. Lute dropped him on top of the third. After that, it was a matter of firing at the windows and keeping the soldiers inside pinned down. Al had two men standing by with six sticks of dynamite wrapped together with a short fuse.

At his signal, they began creeping around the far side of the barracks. The two men lit their fuses from the small cigars in their mouths and then threw the dynamite into the open window. Only one soldier ran out of the building before it blew up and the massed fire from Al's men cut him down. The rest were obliterated within the building as the dynamite exploded in a shower of brown dust and red fire. None of the doomed soldiers had a chance.

Al and his men were poking through the wreckage when Morales rode up with the rest of the gang. Several had small sacks of loot from the bank and others had whatever they could grab from the stores or houses they had invaded. The old general beamed at the men standing before him.

"Come, we must ride. This town will long remember the raid led by General Morales." He glanced at the wreckage of the barracks, pride in his beady eyes. The excited men proudly waved new clothes and weapons picked from the rubble. After taking a long swig from a bottle grabbed from the town's only cantina, Morales threw the bottle against the adobe wall of the ruined barracks. With a cry of victory, he spurred on his white horse and thundered out of town. Al and his men scrambled to the ravine where their horses were hidden, then rode hard to catch up with the retreating outlaw band.

Just as Al had surmised, the loot from the bank was

pitifully small. The raid yielded only a few bags of silver
pesos and a couple of stacks of paper money. Al had as
much in his pocket and vastly more in the saddlebags he
and Sanchez carried. The men he now rode with would
have cut their mothers' throats for a fraction of what he
had.

After four days of hard riding, they finally arrived at
the outlaw's mountain hideout. It was well situated for
defense, with a narrow pass leading up into the small cul-
de-sac where the camp was located. The high ground surrounding three sides was impossible to traverse and a
couple of guards at the neck of the pass could hold off an
army of men. Somehow, the outlaws had chosen their
hideaway well.

Some women maintained the camp for the men and
provided for their physical and sexual comfort. A small
village of mud huts and adobe shacks was scattered along
the narrow creek that traversed the valley. Al and Lute
moved in with Sanchez and his cousins and made themselves comfortable. The general split up the loot, allowing several men time off to visit their families. He took
Sanchez and his cousins to guard him while he went into
Monterrey, four days travel to the east.

Al cursed his luck, but settled in to await the next raid.
He knew his chance would come. Morales would eventually turn his back and get a bullet in it for his careless-
ness. With the general dead, Sanchez would assume
leadership of the band of outlaws. He would help Al finish what Don José had started. And best of all, Al would
have his ranch and maybe a slender Mexican widow to
keep his back warm at night as well. It would be extra satisfying to force the haughty young woman he'd seen at
the ball to share his bed for a while. Then, maybe, he
would give her to the outlaw army for sport.

Chapter 17

A Near Miss

Martin Keller was bone-weary with fatigue as he and JB rode into Albuquerque. He felt as if he had spent the day astride a wooden beer barrel. His thighs ached and his butt was numb. The strain of worrying about both the men he was chasing and the possible loss of John Black Crow took its toll on him. He was asleep almost before his head hit the thin pillow in his hotel room.

The next morning he would have sworn that he had passed out from too much drink if it had not been for a half-remembered dream about Caroline and the girls. He ignored a nagging headache, dressed, shaved, then followed JB back to the stables to check on the horses. The night man had promised to currycomb and feed the tired, mud-splattered animals, but Marty wanted to make certain. To his satisfaction, the liveryman had kept his word. He found his clean horses standing on fresh straw, oats in their feed buckets, and water buckets filled to the brim.

As he and JB drained their breakfast coffee mugs, Keller spoke first. "Let's go over and check in with the

local sheriff, JB. I learned a long time ago that it saves
trouble if he knows I'm in his town.

"What you mean?"

"In most every town I come to, there's some fool who
is anxious to see if he's just a little faster than me. Or
there's some law-abiding citizen who thinks bounty
hunters offend their pristine community. It's a good idea
to assure the local law I aim to cause no trouble and that
my business has official sanction by the federal govern-
ment."

JB scratched his head, not quite certain he understood
Keller's message. "JB go with Keller. That all JB know."

Marty knocked at the sturdy wooden door of the sheriff's office, entering upon command. A gray-headed man
with deep lines creasing his ruddy cheeks raised his head
from a pile of paperwork on a cluttered desk. "Howdy.
What can I do fer ya, stranger?"

Marty moved up to the edge of the desk, removing his
hat. The sheriff was older than most lawmen he had met,
but still looked hard and fit. The austere interior of the
office was clean, with a rack of rifles and two double-
barrel shotguns hanging from one of the whitewashed
stucco walls. Another wall was covered with wanted
posters, easily visible to anyone in the room.

"Howdy. You the sheriff?" Marty kept his voice neutral, with no threatening tone.

"Yep. Name's Ben Lowrey. What might yours be?"
The sheriff's quick appraisal took in Marty's twin hol-
sters and pearl-handled six-guns tied low on the tall
man's hips. He glanced at the other man, an old half-
breed Indian who stood by the door, his dark, age-lined
face impassive. Sheriff Lowery sat up straighter in his
chair. *Hard men, the pair of them, and on the prod.*

The tall stranger answered in a low, even voice. "I'm
Marty Keller, Sheriff. My friend and I have trailed some

wanted killers down from Santa Fe." Keller motioned back at JB. "JB and I were just stopping by to pay our respects before lookin' around."

Sheriff Lowrey raised his bushy eyebrows. "What do ya know? Marty Keller, the Mankiller. Ain't that what they call ya?" He paused, seeing the look of discomfort on Marty's face. The basic fairness of the old lawman softened his next words. "Well, Mr. Keller, I sure don't need yer presence here in my town. Ya git in any trouble, no matter who starts it, and out you and yer friend go. Savvy? That's the way it's gotta be." Shifting the subject, he continued, without awaiting Marty's reply. "I noticed them six-guns you is a-wearin'. Read all about 'em in the *Police Gazette*."

The old lawman abruptly stood and held out his hand for a friendly handshake. "I usually don't cotton to bounty hunters or gunslingers, but I reckon ya got a better reason than most." He nodded at a straight-backed chair, next to his desk. "Since yer here, sit down and tell me yer story. Got any papers on the men yer a-huntin'?"

Keller pulled up the chair and sat down, reaching for the oilskin pouch in his shirt pocket. He passed over the old warrants for Lowrey's inspection. "I cut their trail up in Santa Fe last week. They left just before I arrived. Should have arrived here last Thursday or Friday, I reckon, if they didn't stop somewhere along the way."

Lowrey inspected the warrants. "Doesn't say much, 'cept that one has a left hand short some fingers. What else do ya know about 'em?" He frowned in concentration as he passed the warrants back to Keller. A thought nagged at him, but he could not put it in focus.

"The leader is a tall, skinny fella named Alva Hulett. He's the one with only three fingers on his left hand. Another is a Mex name of Sanchez. I'm certain these two were part of the gang that raided my home and killed my wife and son several years ago. The third is a bushy-bearded lout, real stupid, if my info is correct."

Lowrey sat up straight in his chair. "The hell, ya say. Ain't it always the case?" He slapped his meaty hand on the desktop. "I had a skinny fella in jail last Saturday fer cheatin' at cards and shootin' one of the local cowpunchers who caught him. Said his name was Hawkins, but he was short the fingers just like yer description. I ran 'em outta town the following Monday, on the convoy to El Paso. I watched 'em leave, so I reckon they're outta here, fer a fact. I sure wish I'd have known about all this. I'd have him in jail till time stops."

Disappointment deflated Marty's face, another dashed hope. "You didn't know, Sheriff. I doubt if any current wanted bills are out on the three of 'em. Hell, it's only Thursday. I'll head right out for El Paso. I'm only four days behind 'em."

Lowrey shook his gray-haired head. "Bad luck, son. Ya can't leave fer El Paso till next Monday. Army's orders. Lots o' Injun trouble with the Apaches right now. The way south 'tween here and El Paso is closed tighter than a tick's mouth, 'cept fer the weekly convoys. Anyone who wants to go south has to go with the Army convoy." He quickly filled in Marty and JB on the latest problems with the unruly Apache tribes roaming the area south of the city.

"Damn the luck," Marty groused. "I'll just sneak out after dark tonight. JB and I will be miles from here before the Army even knows we're gone."

Sheriff Lowrey shook his head again. "Don't try it, pard. If the Army catches ya, they'll bring ya back here in chains fer breakin' military law. If the Army don't catch ya, them Apaches will. That'll be even worse. Losin' your hair would be the painless part of it. Take a break, rest up, and leave with the Army come Monday. Ya'll still be only a week behind your men and will live to catch 'em. Don't get too anxious this close to 'em and blow yer chance."

Marty was bitterly disappointed, but reluctantly agreed with the old lawman's counsel. "I've never been this close before," he complained. "I sure hate falling behind, even a day, no matter what the reason. But I guess you're right, Sheriff. It'll be hard to wait, but I don't have many options at this moment." Keller paused. "I think I'll mosey over and speak to some of the fellows Hulett played cards with. He may have said what his plans were, once he reached El Paso."

"Good ideer. I'll walk ya over to Doc Gibson's and ya kin talk with Frank Tucker. He's laid up fer a week, with a busted short rib. He'll tell ya somthin' if anyone can. The other cowboys was so drunk, they can't even remember what happened durin' the shootout. Whitey Slater was the house gambler at the table, but he wouldn't tell a lawman the truth if his ma's heart depended on it."

JB spoke up. "JB go to fort. Talk with Injun scouts. Maybe find out news 'bout Apaches."

Marty nodded. "Good idea, JB. I'll meet you later, at the hotel." He knew the old scout was sure to find out more than anyone from the Army scouts, who were Pimas from the northern reservation near the Colorado line. He watched JB leave the room. JB had opened up since they left Santa Fe. He had even begun to initiate conversation with Marty. Marty believed they were strong friends. JB had told Marty the story of his adventurous life, including his days as a scout at Fort Leavenworth and later for Sheriff Thompson. *At least,* Marty consoled himself, *I won't have to worry about him leaving me for a while. It's a relief to have someone watching my back for a change. If we can just catch up to Hulett before the snows come to the mountains.*

Keller and Sheriff Lowrey walked down the wooden

sidewalk to a small building across the street from the
city courthouse. DR. RUFUS GIBSON, M.D. was painted in
white letters on a small sign tacked over the door of the
stucco building. Curtains covered the windows of a living area adjacent to the office. The doctor lived next to
his work. The door to the office was open, allowing flies
to buzz in and out of the cool interior. The waiting room
was empty and Sheriff Lowrey called out, "Hey, Doc
Rufus, where are ya, ya ole coot?"

The connecting door to a rear room opened and a wiz-
ened man bent with age stepped out. Behind gold-framed
bifocals perched on a red button nose, keen blue eyes
peered out from under cotton white eyebrows. He
frowned at the sheriff and snapped peevishly, "Quiet, you
noisy old fart. This here is a hospital and you're disturb-
ing my patients. What do you want?" He glanced at
Keller, with a twinkle in his eyes. "You shoot yourself in
the toe or something?"

Sheriff Lowrey sighed in mock exasperation. "See
what I have to put up with, dealing with this ole reprobate? I'll be gettin' outta here afore he tries to push some
of his horse liniment down my throat. Doc, this here is
Mr. Keller. He wants to gab some with Frank Tucker. Ya
let him, hear? It won't hurt Frank none. He's probably
ready to enjoy conversation with a reasonable human
being fer a change. Marty, come on by around six. We'll
have supper together, if ya like. You can buy since yer a
famous bounty hunter." The old sheriff jammed his hat on
his head, then stomped out of the office, making as much
noise as possible.

Marty turned back to the doctor and held out his hand,
which the older physician took gingerly in his. "Nice to
meet you, Doctor. I won't take long with Mr. Tucker, I
promise."

The old doctor chuckled. "No problem, Mr. Keller.

Frank's plenty able to jabber. Just don't get him to laughin'. His ribs are a mite sore, I reckon." The doctor led Marty to one of the occupied beds in his little hospital and introduced him to the wounded cowboy. Then he moved over to the other bed, where a young boy with a broken leg in a splint was lying, fussing with the bandages and splint. The old doctor was obviously going to listen to everything and that was that.

Marty shook hands with the bed-ridden cowman. "Nice to meet you, Mr. Tucker. Thanks for talking with me."

Frank Tucker looked hard at Marty. "You Keller, the famous bounty hunter? I've heerd of you, Mr. Keller. I got a cousin over to Amarillo who's in the Texas Rangers. He always spoke kindly of ya. What can I do fer ya?"

"I'm on the trail of the jasper who winged you. He's wanted for murder in Texas." Marty looked hard at Tucker. "I think he's the one who killed my family. Have any idea what his plans were?"

"Can't say that the skunk did any talkin' about his plans, Mr. Keller. He jus' played his cards and watched my buddies, waitin' fer them to get drunk enough to hornswaggle. I wish I'd been a mite faster on the draw." Tucker shifted to a more comfortable position in the narrow bed. "If he took the convoy to El Paso, most likely he's headed fer Mexico or the Big Bend country of West Texas. Wouldn't be no sense in headin' west from there. Too much Injun trouble west. He might head east, but what fer? He'd do better startin' from here if he was headed that away. Nope, I reckon it's Mexico or the Big Bend. With money in his pockets, I'd bet on Mexico. It goes a long way down there."

Tucker shifted again, discomfort showing on his homely face. "You watch the skunk if ya catch up with him, Mr. Keller. He's sneaky fast on the draw and he uses that black-bearded henchman of his to draw yer attention afore he draws. That's how he got me. Hell, it's almost like shootin' a fella in the back, don't ya think?"

Keller bobbed his head in agreement. "Thank you, Frank. I'll try and put a hole in him for you, once I catch up with him." Marty gently shook the man's hand again and nodded to the doctor. "Thanks, Doc. I'm ready to go now, I reckon."

Doc Gibson led Marty out of the room, speculating on what he had overheard. He wished that he could hear the whole story of the famous gunman. He figured it would be a story worth telling. At the front door, he nodded to Keller.

"Be mighty careful, son. I sure don't need no more practice in plugging holes and pullin' lead from a body's insides."

"Thanks, Doc. I'll watch my back, I promise."

Marty impatiently waited out the days until Monday morning. Every day, he rode out into the mesa north of town and practiced his marksmanship. Sheriff Lowrey usually joined him, never ceasing to show amazement at the bounty hunter's skill.

"I swear, Marty, I do believe yer the best all-around shot I ever saw. I suspect Wyatt Earp was a tad straighter and John Wesley Hardin was a mite faster, but nobody reaches you fer all-around shootin' ability."

Marty chuckled. "Thanks, Ben. I'll be sure to tell the next outlaw I meet what you said. He might just curl up and quit on the spot."

They laughed, knowing full well how little it mattered to a man desperate to fight for his freedom.

Saturday, Marty wrote another letter to Caroline and the girls before replenishing his supply of ammunition and food for the trail. JB spent all his free time with the Pima Indian scouts at the fort. He learned that the

Apaches watched every convoy south, but did not necessarily attack every one. They watched and waited for the troops to relax their guard, or for the civilian wagons to string out so far that the guards could not cover them all.

JB announced to Marty at supper on Saturday night, "JB ride with Injun scouts on trail. I watch for sign and come quick, tell Keller if trouble ahead."

On the morning of their departure, Marty and JB joined twenty other men and six wagons that gathered at the edge of town. Twelve black soldiers led by a young white officer galloped out of the fort and rode toward them.

Sheriff Lowrey introduced Marty to the young officer. "Lieutenant Wallace, this here is Marty Keller and his scout, John Black Crow. He's headed to El Paso on the trail of a trio of outlaws. You make sure he gets there, savvy? Marty, you be careful and good luck. Stop by on your way back and let me know how you finish up."

Marty traded a firm handshake with the sheriff, grateful for all his help and the unexpected friendship. "Thanks, Ben. I sure appreciate all your help and advice. I'll look forward to seeing you again."

The crusty lawman rode his horse back across the river toward Albuquerque. Marty smiled at the young officer. "Nice to meet you, Lieutenant Wallace. I hope we have a quick and uneventful journey together."

"My pleasure, Mr. Keller. Now, if you'll excuse me, I'll get this convoy started, else we'll still be sitting here come sundown." The officer rode off and shortly the small group of travelers was plodding down the road, kicking up plumes of fine dust.

JB and two Pima scouts rode out ahead of the column, leading the way beside the shallow and muddy Rio Grande River. It was a hot, cloudless day and Pacer was frisky, sidestepping as he worried the bit in his mouth.

The horse was happy to be on the trail again, away from the confines of the stable. Lieutenant Wallace finally straightened out the convoy to his satisfaction, then rode up to join Marty riding at the front of the column.

"Where's our first stop, Lieutenant?"

"We have a long ride this day, sir. We'll stop about eight this evening at the water station at Soda Springs. Tomorrow we have an easier time of it, if nothing happens, and should make Socorro about four in the afternoon."

The respectful young officer and Marty exchanged pleasantries for a time as the column wound its way south. "Were you in the late conflict, Mr. Keller?" The young officer paused. "The War of the Rebellion, I mean."

"Yep," Marty answered, with a wry grin. "Rode for nearly four years with General Forrest. Hope that doesn't put you on the outs with me."

Wallace shook his head. "Hell, sir, it's all behind us now. My pa was a staff officer with Sheridan. That's how I got my appointment to West Point in sixty-seven. I appreciate the chance to talk with someone who was in the Southern cavalry. You'll tell me some of the things you people did, won't you? I was in school in Ohio when Morgan made his raid there and got captured. Were you with him? It sure caused a bunch of excitement."

Marty laughed. "Nope. I was back in Jackson, recovering from a shrapnel wound. A good thing, too, since I didn't relish spending time in a jail cell."

By the end of the first day's ride, Marty and the young officer were friends. Marty felt free to offer his advice whenever Wallace asked for it. The twelve black troopers of the Tenth Buffalo Soldiers Cavalry Regiment were under the firm control of a grizzled NCO who had plenty of gray in his curly hair. The veteran sergeant kept a close eye on his charges and they responded with immediate dispatch to his orders. It was clear to Marty that the old soldier knew his business.

At the first night's camp, Marty walked the picket line with Lieutenant Wallace, inspecting the posted guards and talking about cavalry tactics during the war. They turned in when the senior sergeant relieved Wallace at midnight. The night was quiet and peaceful, as was the next. Socorro was left behind in their dust as they continued on toward El Paso, moving slowly, but continuously. They were two days out of Socorro when their luck turned sour.

Chapter 18

A Hint of Rain

Caballo Hacienda, a partially built way station degrading into ruins, was their destination that day. A steaming hot spring that trickled across slick rocks gave the place its name. The relentless Apache troubles had forced its abandonment earlier that spring, but it was a perfect camping place for the Albuquerque convoys. Lieutenant Wallace described it as a chance to clean up from the trail and sleep behind the protection of stout walls.

Just before noon, they met the escort from El Paso en route to Albuquerque. The two young officers in charge briefed each other on the country through which they had just passed. The El Paso group had seen plenty of sign, but no Apaches. The two groups shared a hot lunch, then passed from one another's sight.

It was not yet three o'clock when JB galloped up, sliding to a stop before Marty and Lieutenant Wallace. The officer held up his hand, halting the strung-out column of riders and wagons in the hot sun. The horses snorted and dropped their heads to the ground. They were tired and hot, anxious to get the loads off their sweaty backs.

"Trouble ahead, Keller. Apache wait to ambush Keller and soldiers when pass rocks there." He pointed back down the road toward a cluster of massive rocks where a sandstone mountain had broken apart many years earlier. "JB leave Pima scout Hannak to watch and come warn Keller and buffalo soldiers."

Marty shaded his eyes against the harsh afternoon sun. "How many Apaches, JB?"

"Maybe five hands with ponies and rifles," the old scout replied. "They very careless. Make no attempt to hide from JB and Pima scouts."

Marty scratched his chin, his fingernail rasping against his stiff beard. He looked at Lieutenant Wallace. "Twenty-five, hmm. That doesn't hardly seem like enough to take on an escort your size does it, Randy?"

Wallace looked worriedly behind him at the waiting people. "Sure don't. Mostly there's fifty or more before they start somethin'. Since we've got over thirty guns in this group, I wouldn't think the Apache would want to take on odds that bad."

"You're right, Randy. That's sound thinking. Also, I'm a little surprised that they'd be so careless as to let our scouts come on 'em like that. What say we turn off the road at the springs and ride up to the walled hacienda?"

"Yes, the rest stop is about a quarter mile off the main road. The old hacienda has a walled enclosure. Once inside we can defend the place against a hundred savages, easy."

"Let's talk this over a minute, Randy." Marty got off Pacer and motioned for Sergeant Jefferson to ride up. A civilian named Dickersen, red-faced from the sun, accompanied the senior sergeant. With everyone gathered around him, Keller related JB's report.

"I don't like it much," Marty explained. "If I was to guess, I reckon the Apache wanted us to see 'em setting up an ambush by those rocks. Then, we'd gallop past as hard as we could and ride into the protection of the old hacienda at the hot springs. If some Apaches were already inside waiting in ambush for us, we'd be caught between them with no place to hide." Marty looked around at the faces of the men. "At least that's my way of thinkin' this thing out."

Lieutenant Wallace furrowed his brow in thought. "It's as good a reason as any for what we know so far. The question is, what do we do now?"

Marty responded, "We're only a hard day's ride from the Las Cruces Mission, aren't we?"

"Yes, a very hard day."

"I suggest we stay here until night in a defensive circle. As soon as it gets dark, we ride straight through to the mission, skipping the hacienda. There's enough water in our canteens to get us there without too much hardship. The horses may suffer some, but they'll make it. The Indians don't like fightin' at night, and after Las Cruces, they'll be too close to the army post at El Paso to be much of a threat. If we can just stay ahead of them for one more day, we should be home free."

The red-faced Dickersen spoke up. "We'd have to push the teams pullin' the wagons awful hard. It's a tough pull to Las Cruces from here."

Lieutenant Wallace answered for Marty. "It beats losing your hair, though, doesn't it? Sergeant Jefferson will assign a soldier to ride with each wagon so you can tell us when the animals need a blow."

"Yes, sir." The sergeant bobbed his dark head in understanding.

Marty continued. "For sure we'll be a tired bunch of pilgrims, but if the Apaches do have us boxed in, this'll beat 'em at their game, so I think it's worth the risk."

Lieutenant Wallace spoke up. "I agree. We'll stay here

until dark. Sergeant Jefferson, put out pickets. Mr. Keller, tell your scout to watch the Apaches at the rocks. Let us know if they start to move against us. The scouts can rejoin us as we ride past, after dark."

Marty looked at JB. "Understand, old friend?"

"JB do." The old breed leaped on his pinto and trotted back to the Pima scout Hannak, who was keeping a wary eye on the waiting Apaches.

The men sweated out the rest of the day, the hot sun parching their cracked lips. The wagons were in a circled defensive position, while the travelers nervously waited for their ambushers, hidden in the jumbled rocks to their front, to stream out in a ferocious attack. Marty sat under Pacer, shading himself as much as possible from the brutal sun with the horse's body. Sweat trickled down his face, cutting tracks in the caked-on dust. His eyes remained fixed on the western sky. Dark billowing clouds were piling up over the hot desert hills. "There's rain coming our way," he muttered to Lieutenant Wallace.

"Might help us get past the hostiles," Wallace answered. "The rain could hide the noise of our passing."

"True, but it would also mean we'd be slowed down some, travelin' during the storm." In the distance, a wall of billowing, sandy dust blew across the brown landscape. "Looks like a sandstorm is coming, too. Get everyone mounted and ready to ride. When it hits, we best be off—less chance of losing a team or a horse than staying here."

The wind and blowing sand hit hard shortly thereafter. The boiling sand effectively blocked the afternoon sun, making the day as dark as any night. Lieutenant Wallace ordered the party under way, moving as fast as possible and closed up tight.

Marty pulled his bandanna over his nose and mouth. The gritty sand blew into his eyes until he could barely

see. An unhappy Pacer was equally distressed by the
blinding sand. Keller licked the grit from his teeth with
his tongue and patted reassurance to his faithful horse.
Off to the right, he sensed more than saw the jumbled
rock pile where JB had spotted the Apaches. Hopefully
the two Indian scouts would be able to evade the angry
Apaches when they realized their plan had gone awry.

Marty and Lieutenant Wallace pushed on, leading the
sand blown procession of riders and creaking wagons
south. Keller heard the faint sound of gunfire behind him.
Lieutenant Wallace wheeled to investigate. "Keep 'em
moving, Mr. Keller. I'll find out what that was." The
young officer galloped off to the rear, his head bowed
into the wind. He returned shortly, pulling his snorting
horse up beside Pacer. "Must have been spotted by some
of the hostiles. Nobody was hit, so they were shootin'
wild, hoping to bring down a team. By God, it's dark. I
reckon we're in for an old-fashioned downpour."

He had hardly finished when the heavens opened up
and rain fell in a drenching sheet of water, accompanied
by brilliant flashes of jagged lightning. The horses were
skittish and hard to control, snorting in fear and agitation,
but the men kept the tired animals moving on, past the
old hacienda, and through the dark, rainy night. The only
saving grace for the storm-whipped convoy was that they
had escaped from their pursuers.

It was a windy, wet, miserable night, with no relief for
the weary wagon train as the dawn arrived. Marty had not
experienced such a downpour since his days in Mississippi during the war. Red and yellow mud coated everything it splashed against. Men, horses, wagons—all
carried their share of the claylike mud. About midmorning, JB and Hannak rode past the string of men and wagons to the point, joining Marty and Lieutenant Wallace.

Mud covered the old scout, as did it to every man and animal in the convoy.

"Apaches gone" was the first thing out of JB's mouth. He pointed. "All go east, toward White Mountains."

Lieutenant Wallace held up his hand, stopped the convoy, and climbed down. The dark slicker he wore was splattered with water and mud, concealing the identity of the man inside. He slung his cape over his shoulder and scratched his chest through the damp woolen shirt. "Damn, does this shirt itch. Must be five pounds of mud and water on it. What do you mean, the Apaches are gone?" He lifted one dark boot out of a puddle and stepped to the side of the slimy road, where the ground was a little firmer.

JB pointed to the east. "Apaches go back into mountains. Too much water from rain. Wait until sun out for one week, to dry up shallow water holes agin. Pony soldiers have too much water if they follow Apache now. Wait till desert more dry before fight agin. We have no more trouble, I think. Hannak agree."

"Well, there's good in all things, I guess," Lieutenant Wallace observed. "What do you think, Mr. Keller? Shall we stop here and dry out, or keep on going?"

Marty looked to the west. The sky was finally starting to clear in that direction. "I'd vote to go on, Lieutenant, if you were to ask for one. We might as well get to the mission at Las Cruces before we stop. We can clean up and rest there for a while. We'll still only have a few hours' ride into El Paso. Of course, it's your decision."

The officer pursed his lips as he considered the options. Finally, he called back for everyone to take a five-minute break and then pushed his little command on. The only sounds heard were the plops of hooves in the mud, the occasional squeaks of wagon wheels, and the relentless rain drumming on the soaked earth or canvas wagon tops. The rain continued to fall, working its way under the oilskin slickers worn by the sodden travelers.

The downpour finally began slacking off around noon, then quit altogether an hour later. By the time the exhausted convoy reached the Las Cruces Mission, the late-afternoon sun had just about dried them out. A crust of mud remained on every man and animal. It was well after dark before all the horses had been cleaned, wiped, and fed. The filthy men fell out around the edge of the barn and collapsed into a deep sleep.

Only the raucous sound of men snoring or the shuffling of horses punctured the night silence. The unlucky sentries tried their best to stay awake. It took constant visits from Lieutenant Wallace, Keller, and Sergeant Jefferson to keep the guards even half alert. When Marty turned over his guard duty command to Sergeant Jefferson, he stumbled to an empty spot in the hayloft, where he slept without stirring until well after sunrise.

Marty awoke, thankful that JB's prediction had been right. "Hell," he laughingly grumbled to Wallace as they tried to brush the worst of yesterday's mud from their clothes and bodies. "If the Apaches had come durin' the night, I'da wakened up scalped, surprised at the knowledge."

The two men ambled over to the fire crackling in the center of the circled wagons and got tin cups filled with hot coffee. "How much longer till we reach El Paso?" Marty asked the officer.

"We'll be there before three this afternoon, unless a wagon breaks down or we can't get over the low ground at Canutilla," Wallace replied. "That is, if we can get these layabouts saddled and on the road before noon." He tossed the last of his cup on the hot coals, steam hissing in the morning calm. "Sergeant Jefferson, Boots and Sad-

dles. Let's get a move on. Everybody saddled and ready
to go in twenty minutes or get left. Let's move it now."

The convoy curled around the western side of the
Franklin Mountains, a steep outcrop of stark barren hills
north of El Paso. The town lay before them in the valley
of the Rio Grande River, a ribbon of green carving
through the brown landscape. In the shimmering afternoon light, the rolling waters of the river looked fearfully
swift. *Probably the rain,* Marty thought. Usually the Rio
Grande was a gentle stream, barely even three feet deep.

At the Army fort, located north of the town on a
plateau above the river, Marty took his leave of the men
who had accompanied him from Albuquerque. Bidding
farewell to the likable Lieutenant Wallace and capable
Sergeant Jefferson, he and JB rode toward the heart of the
town, built along the banks of the now rushing Rio
Grande.

After a hot bath, a shave, and a change to clean, dry
clothes, Marty started his search. It didn't take long to
discover that Hulett and the others might have been in El
Paso. The local blacksmith vaguely remembered fixing a
horse's shoe that might have belonged to Lute Payson.
Nobody recalled a tall, skinny, three-fingered man.

Marty had a letter of introduction from Sheriff Lowrey
to the El Paso sheriff, a stocky man named Wedemeyer.
Once again, he explained his reason for seeking the three
outlaws. Sheriff Wedemeyer promised to inquire about
Hulett as he made his evening rounds.

After a restful night's sleep, Marty returned to the
sheriff's office. "Nope, Mr. Keller. I can't give you much
encouragement. I've had my deputies ask all over town.
Nobody fittin' that description stayed in any of the hotels
or played cards in any of the saloons. 'Course, he coulda
stayed over in del Norte, across the river. Or he coulda
headed out fer Pecos or Alpine. I'll send out inquiries by

the afternoon stages. We'll know in three days if they passed through either town. Meanwhile you could go across the border if you want and see if anyone'll give you information about 'em."

For the next two days, Marty doggedly asked around the town about the three men, hoping for a lead and finding none. No citizen of the town knew or would talk, even for the money he flashed as inducement. When the stagecoaches returned with negative results from Sheriff Wedemeyer's inquiries, JB and Keller left the sheriff's office discouraged and glum. They ambled over to the walkway that paralleled the bank of the Rio Grande. The river had already receded to its normal shallow depth, flowing sluggishly from the north, southeast to the Gulf of Mexico.

"Well, John Black Crow, we've got to throw the dice. We're losin' time around here. Tomorrow, we cross over into Mexico and head south. Maybe we'll pick up a trail outside the town. Otherwise we just stay here and kick straw."

JB nodded his shaggy head, the worn top hat firmly positioned in place and its black crow feather bobbing. "Yep, we find. JB knows this. We find."

Chapter 19

South of the Border

The two manhunters rode across the Rio Grande at sunrise. The rippling brown water barely reached the bottom of Marty's stirrups. The raging water fed by the earlier rain had already washed past, on its way to the Gulf of Mexico. They rode through the dusty little town of del Norte, just over the river, down the pebble-strewn road past a weathered sign proclaiming CHIHUAHUA, 200 MILES.

Marty shifted in the saddle, settling in for the long day's ride. He was closing in on his quarry—he felt it in his bones. If he could only succeed, the haunting memory of Meg and Matthew's violent deaths might recede from the forefront of his mind. For so long their tragedy shared nearly every waking moment with him. Marty couldn't remember the last time he'd had a pleasant memory of his family. The bitter specter of their death was always with him.

The pain and anger that drove him would not allow him any peace. The long lonely trails always seem to lead toward the setting sun. Perhaps this trail would be his last so he could get on with the rest of his life or die in the attempt. But he would not even consider failure. He would find the men and kill them. He owed his family that much. Marty stroked Pacer's muscular neck, then sipped from his canteen. It was a long way to anywhere here in northern Mexico, and the trip had only begun.

John Black Crow rode easily beside his friend. The old scout rode silently, as was his want, but Marty knew that he had earned the half-breed's trust and loyalty. He showed Marty a side only a few white men had ever seen. As if reading Marty's thoughts, he suddenly spoke out loud. "We find killers and send to underworld with other evil spirits. I feel the Great Spirit is with us." JB grunted in satisfaction at his words, then plodded on in silence. Finally he spoke again. "It good time to ride and think."

Marty concentrated on putting miles beneath Pacers long legs. The hot, bleak country was a hostile place, and the sooner they reached some shelter the better. Just before dark, they rode into a small village and stopped for the night. Marty asked around until he found a young boy who spoke some English. "They were here," he told JB over their small campfire. "The kid said three men rode through last week, two gringos and one Mexican. We're on their trail, thank God." He barely slept, he was so anxious for the dawn.

It wasn't difficult to follow Hulett's trail all the way to Chihuahua, but there the sign vanished. After a week of tireless inquiry, nothing had been discovered about the three outlaws. They had disappeared like raindrops on the dry earth. Keller and JB rode a circle around the provincial capital, seeking any sign indicating which direction the outlaws might have gone, without success.

"It doesn't make sense," Keller complained to JB while they rode back from another fruitless search. "They lived high on the hog for a week and then just slipped away. Something happened. I know it. Something caused them to move on, hiding their trail. What was it?"

They stabled their horses and walked over to the local hotel, where they had rooms, just as Hulett and Payson had a week prior. Marty's mood was sour as he walked into the adjacent cantina for a beer. He instantly spotted a Yankee face, a fellow Texican, if he was any judge. The man sat casually in rumpled, travel-stained clothes. As Marty moved to the bar, he nodded courteously toward the stranger. The man motioned for Marty to join him at his table, so he picked up his glass of beer and walked over.

The man stuck out his hand in welcome. "Howdy, pard. Name's Hec Billows, from San Antonio, Texas. Down here on a cattle-buyin' trip. Have a seat."

"Martin Keller's my name. Glad to meet you. Just get into town?" Keller eased down on one of the chairs placed around the scarred wood table.

"Naw, been here fer three weeks or more. Just got back from a trip to one of the big ranchers in the area. Gonna buy some cattle next month and drive 'em over to Laredo, where my associates'll have a trail crew waitin' to drive 'em to Fort Worth and the railroad. The old codger raises good cows 'n' horses, but he makes it clear he don't cotton to us Yanks."

"You mean there's a rail line down to Fort Worth now?" Keller exclaimed. "What do you know? I'll bet that's livened up the old town a mite."

Billows nodded. "Yep, it's just like Dodge or Abilene a few years ago. More folks than ya can shake a stick at." The cattle buyer took a sip of his whiskey. "What brings you down this far into Mexico? You ain't on the run from the law, air ya?" He eyed Marty warily.

Marty smiled at his table companion. "Nope, just the

opposite. I'm lookin for three killers that ran down this way from El Paso."

"Ya don't say. Well, tell me about 'em," Billows commanded.

"A tall fellow named Hulett, only has three fingers on his left hand. Got a black-bearded sidekick with him and—"

"Has a mean-lookin' little Mex runnin' with him," Billows interrupted.

"That's right," Marty answered, excitement suddenly causing his blood to pound. "You've run into him?"

"Shore did," Billows replied. "Took the skinny one to a party with me and got left to walk home. I sorta figgered that he was a bad un."

Marty was all business, leaning forward in his chair, his face intense, his hands clenched together. "What sort of party? Did Hulett seem to be meeting anyone special? Did you see him after that?"

"Slow down, Keller. I'll tell ya all I know. What say we move over to the café and grab us some vittles. What little I know won't take long to tell."

Impatiently, Marty followed Billows out of the cantina and next door to the café. After they ordered two helpings of beans and tortillas filled with meat and hot peppers, along with two beers, Billows continued. "I wondered why Hulett was so interested in getting to that fiesta. He said he jus wanted to meet some of the local folks. Gave me a song 'n' dance about wantin' to buy some land down here. Pleaded to come as my guest. Got all duded up, too. Bought hisself a fancy Mex suit and new boots. He fancied hisself quite the fella."

Billows paused while the swarthy waiter delivered their food. Then he took a couple of bites before continuing. Marty just gritted his teeth and allowed the man his time. The old cattle buyer was enjoying telling his tale and seemed determined to drag it out for all it was worth.

"Anyways, we got there—to the governor's fiesta, that is—and Hulett makes a beeline to one of the big shots in this neck of the woods." Billows chuckled. "Got his comuppance a mite, I reckon.

"Seems friend Hulett makes to hold a powwow with Don José del Vargas, who is mighty big medicine around here. In fact, I jus' came from his ranch, back in the high mountains to the west. He's got thousands of acres, deeded to his family back when the Spaniards ran things here. Don José musta insulted Hulett somethin' awful, 'cause Hulett got all red in the face and stomped out, madder than a rattlesnake in a sack."

Marty nodded and wrapped some beans in a tortilla. "Do you think the don could have been doing business with Hulett?"

Billows shook his head vigorously. "Nary a chance. The whole Vargas family has a strong aversion to gringos. The don complained to me the whole time we was making our cattle deal that he'd rather do business with the devil than with us gringos. I jus' happen to catch him when he needed hard-cash money. Nope, I reckon if anything, Hulett tried to convince the old man to make some sort of deal and got his ears scorched."

"Mr. Billows, do you think you could write me an introduction to this del Vargas? I'm gonna ride over and talk with him. He's about the only lead I can think of to help me find out what Hulett is up to." Marty sipped his beer. "Those peppers were *hot*. My tongue feels like I've been licking a black rock at noontime."

Billows chuckled. "I've had hotter uns back in Texas." He paused. "I doubt if anything I say would mean much to the old don, Mr. Keller. However"—he looked at Marty with a twinkle in his light brown eyes—"the governor is another matter. He's most anxious to do me all the favors he can, since I'm hinting that he's in fer a big commission from my buying trips."

Hec Billows wiped his mouth with the red-and-white checked napkin tucked into his shirt collar and stood up. "I'll get ya a real fancy introduction letter tomorrow morning. Now how about you buyin' me a real drink and I'll give ya the directions to reach the Lago del Azul? That's where the don's got his hacienda. It's a beauty, fer a fact. You're gonna like yer visit. That is," Billows cackled, "if the stuffed-up old coot will even talk with ya."

Two days later, Marty and JB rode out of Chihuahua as the sun rose over the eastern badlands of northern Mexico. In his pocket Marty carried a letter from the governor introducing him to Don José del Vargas and a map drawn on butcher paper by Hec Billows.

As Marty and JB rode farther west, the harsh landscape softened. By the second day they were high into the Sierra Madre Mountains. The terrain received more abundant rain than the flat desert to the east. Strands of evergreen forests and broad meadows of green grass cut by gurgling streams spread before them.

Billows had them following a rutted road that cut through a pass between two high mountain peaks. On the afternoon of the third day, they rode out of a cut in the hills onto a grass-covered mesa. In the far distance a striking blue lake shimmered in the bright sunlight. Like a cluster of pearls, a complex of white stucco buildings graced a small knoll in the center of the valley. Brown specks of cattle peacefully grazed on the lush, emerald green grass.

"Whoa, JB!" Marty exclaimed. "Would you look at that? Billows was right. This is indeed some place to have a ranch. Come on, if we hurry, we'll get there about suppertime. That should make it doubly hard for Don José to throw us out."

They rode up to a magnificent complex of white-washed buildings surrounded by a whitewashed stucco wall six feet high. In the distance, Keller counted five barns, as well as numerous other small buildings.

Marty and JB rode through the massive wooden portals at the entrance to the enclosure, creating a stir among the many people inside the walls. For the second time in two weeks, they were witnessing the unusual sight of a gringo riding up to the don's hacienda. Several vaqueros sidled over, prepared to help throw the interlopers out if required. Mothers grabbed bare-bottomed youngsters running about and hurried them inside their small huts.

A vast three-story hacienda, whitewashed adobe with a veranda surrounding three sides, dominated the rear half of the enclosure. A rock-lined drive wound around a twinkling water fountain to the veranda steps at the front of the hacienda. Green ivy and hanging mandivilla flowers in yellow and pink snaked their way along the walls of the main house, framing the veranda. Still more grew in profusion around the bubbling fountain. Backed against the side walls of the compound were the small homes used by the laborers and vaqueros.

As Marty and JB pulled up at the hitching post next to the broad steps, which led up to the main entrance, a stooped, white-haired servant came out and courteously addressed the two men. "Senors," he spoke deliberately, "what is it that you wish?"

Marty took out the letter and handed it to the man. "For Senor del Vargas, *por favor.*"

The old servant took the letter and motioned with his hand toward the shade of the porch. "I will give it to Don José, senor. Wait here."

Marty heard the servant knock on a door and a different voice answer, *"Quién es?" Who is it?*

There followed a rapid flow of Spanish that he couldn't follow, then a period of silence. Keller and JB exchanged glances and watched the gathering people in the courtyard, who in turn stared at them. The gurgling fountain provided the only sound. Suddenly Marty realized that someone stood behind him in the open doorway.

Turning, his hat in his hand, he faced a tall, dignified man holding the governor's letter. Next to him stood a younger man, curiosity evident in his expression. Behind them stood a shorter man, assessing them with obvious distaste while stroking his black mustache. Beside the short man stood a woman, tall and regal, the older man's daughter for certain. Her pale green dress would have cost a cowpuncher his yearly salary, Keller concluded.

"Senor . . . ah . . ."—the man looked at the letter in his hand—"Keller. What is it you wish?"

Marty courteously addressed the don. "Senor del Vargas, I'm Martin Keller. My friend John Black Crow and I have ridden from Chihuahua to speak with you. I wish to talk with you about some outlaws I am tracking. They may be headed your way."

Struggling to be as cordial as the governor had requested, but reluctant to welcome an uninvited gringo in his home, the old man hesitated, then acquiesced. "Of course, please come in. Welcome to *mi casa*, Senor Keller."

The interior was magnificently finished in rich tones of walnut and painted stucco. Intricately woven rugs covered the terra-cotta tile of the hall. Paintings of family ancestors lined the walls. The don led the group down the cool entrance hall into a large library stocked with books, more portraits, and the mementos of a fighting man. Ri-

fles, pistols, swords, lances, Indian artifacts, and Spanish
military hardware were mounted on the walls. Handsome
horsehair couches and chairs surrounded a massive desk,
leather inlaid and burnished until it reflected the flickering candlelight.

The don reread the letter in his hand, then laid it on his
desk, carefully smoothing the folded paper flat. "It seems
the governor has requested that I show you every courtesy, Senor Keller. As it is almost dinnertime and soon
will be dark, may I offer you my hospitality for the
night?" A disgruntled noise from the short man drew a
quick glance of silent reproach.

"Thank you, Don José. It has been a long trip from
Chihuahua. I accept your kind offer. After we eat, I will
explain more completely why I have come to see you."
Keller smiled at the younger del Vargas and his striking
sister. They were the only friendly faces at the moment.

"Wonderful!" the woman exclaimed. "It's been too
long since we have had a visitor for dinner. Father, why
don't you allow the gentleman to freshen up before we
eat?" She smiled engagingly at Keller. "Anselmo, our
chief house servant, will show your friend where he can
stay while you are here."

Keller understood that no well-bred Mexican would
allow an Indian to stay in their home. JB understood as
well. The scout willingly followed the servant out of the
room. "Come," the woman commanded. "I'll show you
to your room. My name is Isobel del Vargas Fierro. This
is my husband, Diego and my brother, Ramon. My father,
Don José, is alone now, so I act as his hostess. My mother
passed on to God seven years ago."

Her husband, Diego, turned away from Keller, unwilling to acknowledge the intruder, but the younger del Vargas came to Keller and offered his hand. "I am pleased to
greet you, Senor Keller. Please forgive my poor English."

   The two led Keller out of the room, with Diego's smoldering look burning holes in his back. Even Don José looked decidedly uncomfortable with the dilemma posed by the unexpected sudden arrival of the strangers.

Chapter 20

Unexpected Favors

After a skillfully prepared meal worthy of the finest served in Chicago or St. Louis, Don José del Vargas led his guest back to the library. Don José took a seat in a tufted leather chair near the fireplace, motioning Keller to join him. Ramon and Diego pulled up smaller chairs and waited for Don José to open the conversation. Isobel poured and presented delicately stemmed crystal glasses of dark brandy to each of the men, then returned to stand behind her father's chair, leaning her arms on its back. She gazed with frank curiousity at the tall gringo sitting across from her father.

Isobel carefully noted the width of his shoulders, his lean build, and the sky blue eyes that seemed to shine with inner strength and intelligence. The man was not soft, in either his belly or his brain. He was dressed for the trail, unshaven, yet not unkempt, and his teeth gleamed white against the tanned skin of his cheeks. His hair was a delightful sandy brown, so different from the dark hair of the other men in her life. His face was not classically handsome, yet it was interesting to her.

Her reverie was interrupted by her father's question. "Why, Senor Keller, have you come to my ranchero?" He looked intently at the gringo gunman who had shown up so unexpectedly.

"I am hunting three men, Senor del Vargas: three killers from the United States who have escaped across the border to your country. I believe they are headed your way."

The don and his two children listened attentively, but his son-in-law, Diego, squirmed in his chair in poorly concealed impatience. His distaste for the uninvited gringo visitor was visible to everyone.

"I don't understand, Senor Keller," Ramon del Vargas interjected. "Are you a Texas Ranger? The country of Mexico will not allow you to seek an Americano bandito in our country."

"No, senor, I'm not a Ranger. I'm what my country calls a bounty hunter. But my search is more than a chase for money. I was once a Ranger, until the men I seek forced me to leave the law to hunt them down, no matter where they run. They may believe they are safe here in Mexico, but I'll not stop until I find them." Marty described with deep emotion and visible anguish his reasons for finding the outlaws. The story struck a sympathetic chord within Don José.

"Senor Keller, I share in your pain. When my dear wife, Inez, was taken from me, I too was drowning in sorrow. Only my children"—he paused and favored Isobel with a fatherly smile—"saved my sanity." Don José motioned for her to pour him more wine, then settled back into his chair. "How may we help you in this quest for justice?"

Marty sat back in his chair, crossing one long leg over the other. Now he would have the support of the family, if in fact Hulett did have some plan involving them.

"Senor del Vargas, may I inquire if John Black Crow is comfortable? He is my friend and a valuable tracker." Marty was all too aware how some people might look upon half-breed Indians.

Isobel spoke up. "Do not concern yourself, Senor Keller. He is being well cared for in our guesthouse. He has all the food and drink he desires and dependable servants to answer his every need."

Keller bowed his head at the striking Mexican woman, his eyes quickly caressing her trim figure. *She is certainly restful on the eyes,* he thought. He reluctantly swung his gaze back to her father.

"Thank you. Now, as to the men I seek, their names are Hulett, Payson, and Sanchez. Hulett spoke to you, Don José, at the governor's ball. Do you remember a tall man with only three fingers on his left hand?"

Don José slowly pursed his lips. "I do remember such a man. He forced his presence upon me and said he was new to this area. He wanted to buy some of my land. I'm afraid I was rather abrupt with him. I refused to even consider his preposterous offer. I turned away from him, and when I next looked, he was gone."

"Strange," Marty mused. "How would he know to buy property from you if he was new to this area? It doesn't make sense. He must have been here sometime before. I suppose he is looking to stop running and buy a place in Mexico, where he thinks he is free of capture by American law officers."

Marty sipped some wine before continuing. "Senor del Vargas, this man is a vicious killer, used to taking what he wants. We shouldn't underestimate the lengths he might go to get what he's after. I strongly suggest that no member of your family ride alone until I find these evil men."

Don José nodded thoughtfully. "I will see to it, although my family is well protected by my vaqueros, I assure you."

"Thank you, Don José. I am certain that you are safe inside your compound. However, extra care will be worth the effort if Hulett and his men do have some scheme in mind."

Diego snorted derisively. "We can handle any gringo pistoleros without your warning. Don José, why do we allow this Yankee killer to disgrace our hacienda?" He curled his lip in disdain.

Don José's face grew stern as he spoke firmly to his son-in-law. "Diego, this is my home and I will decide who is allowed to be a guest under my roof. If this displeases you, you may return to your family in Mexico City at any time—by yourself of course. Isobel will stay here as my hostess." The don's rapid Spanish was too fast for Marty to translate, but he could tell from the tone that Deigo was getting his fanny burned good.

Diego rose and bowed, his face red with embarrassment, his fists clenched tightly at his side. "As you wish, Don José. Please excuse me. I will retire for the evening. Isobel, you will accompany me." Diego bowed slightly to Don José and led his wife out of the room. Her disappointment at leaving was apparent to Keller, who stood as they left. He wasn't quite certain what had been said, but her expression revealed it hadn't been pleasant for her.

A brief silence enveloped the room as she left. Don José watched his daughter leave with her rude husband, his face grim. He regretted the day he had insisted that his only daughter marry the spoiled son of a wealthy Mexico City merchant. The inescapable fact that she was unhappy saddened the old man. His Isobel was a living link to his beloved wife, Inez. His own marriage had been such a joyous and satisfying one. He sighed and cursed himself for the bad fortune he had forced upon his daughter.

Marty observed the interchange among the del Vargas family. It looked to him as if the woman was trapped in an unhappy marriage. *For all her finery she's not a happy woman,* he surmised. *Too bad.* He sat back down and returned his attention to Don José.

"Sir, may I have your permission to look around your property for a while? I may come upon sign that Hulett is nosing around."

"Of course, Senor Keller. I hope you will use my hacienda as your headquarters. I will assign guides to show you the country."

"Father," young Ramon spoke up, "allow me to accompany Senor Keller. I know this land as well as any of the vaqueros. I think we should take part in protecting our land from banditos, don't you?"

The old don's eyes showed a flash of alarm, which he quickly hid. Marty saw it, but the younger del Vargas apparently did not.

"I will leave that to our guest. He is more skilled in these things. Do you need the help of my son, Senor Keller?"

"Please, Don José, call me Marty." He used the statement as a time to consider Ramon's request. He really did not want the young man's help, yet to refuse would bring shame on Ramon. Unless they were ambushed, he could send the young man away from any immediate danger.

"Yes, I believe I can, Don José. But I must insist that he understand that if we find our quarry, he is not invited to the showdown. That is for me and John Black Crow. Will that be satisfactory?"

Don José nodded in agreement, relieved, while young Ramon sputtered, trying to defend his ability with firearms.

"Be quiet, Ramon. Senor Keller is right. It is his fight, and you must allow him to accomplish it as he wishes."

The don smiled at Marty, gratitude in his dark brown eyes. "Your terms are acceptable, Senor. Now come with me to my desk. I will show you the map of my estate and the land around it. You and Ramon can decide on the route of your search." He took a rolled-up map from behind a cabinet and spread it over the massive desktop. Keller stifled a gasp as he saw the extent of the family's holdings. The ranch covered over a hundred square miles.

Keller and JB rode out the next morning, accompanied by Ramon and Chico, a hard-looking vaquero. The don apparently had assigned a bodyguard to his only son, a plan Keller thought most prudent.

For the next week they scoured the estate of Casa del Azure and beyond, without results. If Hulett was in the area, he was lying low. The mountains held many sheltered valleys where a small party could hide out, but there were no blackened campfires, tracks, killed game, or anything else that would indicate the presence of the men Keller sought. Marty's disappointment grew with every fruitless day.

Only during the nights at the main hacienda was his morale renewed. Don José and his two children were perfect hosts, ensuring that Marty and JB wanted for nothing. JB had become friends with several of the ranch children, who ran errands for him and sat around him in the evenings as he awed his young listeners with stories from his life. The old half-breed had a fair grasp of Spanish and was able to spin his yarns reasonably well for his young admirers.

During the quiet evenings following dinner with the del Vargas family, Keller told the family, less the usually absent Diego, of his days as a rancher in Texas and before, when he had ridden with General Forrest during the war. Don José eventually recalled the time he had fought the Yankee army at the gates of Monterrey when he was only eighteen. Within the bounds of proper Mexican society, the two developed a friendly respect for each other. Young Ramon was cocky and proud to be helping the former lawman find the enemies who threatened his family. Keller treated the young Ramon as a man with talent and worth. The youngster was grateful for the trust bestowed upon him and quickly regarded Keller as his personal hero.

Isobel had taken Marty's sad story to her heart, she strove to provide the lonely manhunter every social grace. She quickly warmed to his shy smile and politeness toward her. Only Diego never wavered in his dislike for the interloper from the north. He despised all gringos, especially this handsome pistolero who had arrived uninvited and become the focus of attention at the hacienda.

For months he had wanted to break with the don and the dreary, boring life on the ranch. He longed to move back to Mexico City. As soon as he could get Isobel with child, he was certain he could talk the old fool into letting her leave the ranch to go where doctors were close at hand. Once in Mexico City, safely surrounded by his prominent family, he would never return to the tedious ranchero.

On the morning of the fifth day of his search, Marty woke up with a rasping cough and slight fever. Isobel and Don José insisted that he stay behind while JB, Ramon, and Chico looked over some rough terrain to the southwest. Pacer needed new shoes put on his hooves anyway, so Keller relented. "Be sure to come for me if you find any sign," he implored before the three men rode away. Marty watched from his window until they were swallowed by the morning haze. Sighing at his human frailty, he allowed Isobel to force a foul-tasting concoction down his throat and then returned to his bed, to sleep most of the next twenty-four hours.

In two days he was feeling much better. He cleaned up, shaved, and went downstairs to join the don for breakfast. Isobel was there, while Diego was not to be seen. "Thanks to you, I'm feeling just fine. I think you cured whatever was ailing me."

She smiled warmly at the praise and turned to her father. "Papa, may I show Senor Keller the new horses we are breeding? I believe he is well enough to take a ride today."

"Isobel, the herd is at the west pasture—you know that. It would take you most of the day to get there and back."

"I know, Papa. We can take a luncheon basket and eat at the lake."

Diego walked in, glared at Marty, and poured himself a cup of steaming coffee. Isabel spoke carefully to her husband. "Diego, I am going to take Senor Keller to see the horse herd. Would you care to join us?"

The surly Diego shook his head. "No, and I don't like you going off, especially if as this Yankee says, there are banditos about. I have to work on the estate books today and doubt I will even have time to walk outside during siesta." Seeing the look on her face and knowing it was fruitless to argue with her, he yielded. "However, if you must go, take Jorge with you. He worships the ground you walk on and will protect you from anyone who gets near you." He glared at Keller to ensure the meaning of his words weren't lost on the gringo interloper.

Keller reassured both Don José and Isobel's husband, anger penetrating the tone of his voice. "If the lady wishes to ride with me, I'll ensure that no harm comes to her, believe me."

Done José seemed to make up his mind. "Isobel, show

our guest the horses. It will do you good to ride in the sun
again. I'll have Jorge ready whenever you are." He
smiled at his elated daughter, but his smile faded as he
glanced at Keller. The proprieties of allowing the Yankee
to escort his married daughter were questionable. Keller
nodded slightly at the old man. He understood the look.
The two men had arrived at a neutral, unspoken understanding.

Isobel quickly prepared herself for the little expedi-
tion. She did not try to hide the relief she felt knowing she
was going to spend time away from her husband. In less
than an hour, she rejoined her father and Keller on the veranda. A huge vaquero followed her, carrying a large picnic basket. Although dressed for riding, she was as lovely
as if in her finest evening gown. She moved beside the
men and kissed her father's cheek, bidding him goodbye.

Marty helped Isobel mount her sidesaddle and climbed
on Pacer. The muscular hulk Jorge rode a few lengths behind the pair, the large wicker basket securely tied to his
saddle. Waving to her father, Isobel led them out of the
main gate and turned her horse toward the lake.

Marty rode beside the beautiful woman, enjoying the
enthusiasm she exuded. She was a skilled rider and
seemed to be as comfortable on a horse as he. Marty con-
stantly glanced at her, relishing her presence. He listened
attentively as she recited a short history of the ranch and
her childhood growing up on it with her beloved mother
and father. When they reached the blue lake, which was
glittering in the bright sunlight as if it had been dusted
with stars, they turned west, following the curving shore-
line.

As they rode and talked, Marty began to tell Isobel
about Caroline and her little girls. Since leaving Colorado, he had thought of them often, but had not spoken
about them. Now the words tumbled from his mouth. He

described Caroline's ranch and how he hoped to return there someday. As they topped a small hill, Marty saw a sizable herd of horses grazing in a meadow before them. Several vaqueros were attending the herd, as it slowly worked its way toward a finger of the lake shimmering in the distance. The herd was a mixture of Thoroughbred Arabian, pinto, and spotted appaloosa.

"They look magnificent! You have a wonderful herd of horses here. My congratulations."

"Oh, Marty, please call me Isobel. Now let's ride closer and I'll show you my favorites."

The next hour they rode among the herd, evaluating individual horses. Isobel had several roped and brought to them so Marty could get off Pacer and put his hands on the animals, like any good horseman. It took him back to a happier time, when an important highlight of his world was the quality of a horse's breeding. The time passed in pleasant conversation about breeds and bloodlines and horsemanship.

Marty was listening to Isobel describe a point about breeding the Arabians to the Mexican pinto to improve the gait of the offspring, when she grew quiet. He glanced at his companion, but she was looking over at the herd. At the far side of the mass of horses, a great black stallion had mounted a black spotted appaloosa mare. The shrill screams of their mating cut through the warm morning air like a knife. Marty's face flamed, since genteel women were supposed to be embarrassed by procreation and such. Isobel, however, watched with calm detachment, not speaking until the primitive act of procreation was complete.

When the black stallion pulled away, Isobel turned to Marty, an impenetrable little smile on her face. She was not the least upset by what they had witnessed. "I'm getting hungry. Are you?"

At his nod, she wheeled around her chestnut-colored filly and called, "Jorge, set up our picnic in the pine grove by the lake. Come, Marty, we have a fine meal to enjoy on this finest of days." She led the way toward a bare rock outcropping pushing through the ground beside a sparse grove of pine trees.

When they arrived, Jorge already had a blanket spread for them, with cold chicken, honey, biscuits, goat cheese, and fresh fruit laid out upon it. A dusty bottle of red wine was wrapped in damp burlap, with two small silver cups tied to the neck by their handles.

Isobel settled on the blanket, smoothing her fawn-colored riding skirt over her beautifully hand-tooled boots. She removed her green leather bolero jacket, exposing a ruffled white blouse with oversized sleeves draped over tight cuffs. She spoke in rapid Spanish to Jorge, who nodded, then disappeared around the rock upthrust. Keller could hear his horse trotting away and then silence descended upon them, save for the piercing call of a circling hawk high overhead.

The tall outcropping furnished a pleasant and shady spot to eat their luncheon. Their conversation was light and inconsequential until the food and drink were eaten. Then Isobel moved slightly closer to Marty and plucked a burr from the sleeve of his shirt. As she flicked it off the blanket, she put her hand on his and smiled, moving her face close to his.

Marty's breath caught at the bright intensity of her dark eyes. Her eyes drew him, her naked need for affection so plain on her face. His lips parted to speak, when she turned her face up to his and kissed him softly, tentatively. Marty enfolded Isobel in his arms, drawing her tightly to him, kissing her long and deep. She drew him down, until they lay on the blanket, their lips still locked tightly together. Finally, they broke apart, shaken by their sudden passion. Then Isobel moved again into his embrace. With the lightness of a feather, Marty felt her fingers brush his groin.

He gasped. "Wait, wait, Isobel, hold on. We can't do this. We both know it. We should quit right now."

It was too late. She melted into his arms. Her embrace drew him into a whirlwind of passion. His response to her lead spoke the depth of his own desire.

Isobel cried, "Oh, Marty, don't think. Just love me. I'm so hungry for a man's love. You don't know. Take me now. Take me hard."

Their kisses grew more intense and before either realized it, they were naked in each other's embrace. The unfulfilled desire and loneliness of both partners drove them to incredible heights of sexual satisfaction. So great was their need that they continued on for a second helping of the blessed relief. Their spirited coupling was as intense as the mating of the stallion and mare. Finally, he raised himself on his elbows and looked into her face. She opened her dark eyes and smiled up at him, completely satisfied. Slowly, he pulled away from her sweat-drenched body and rolled on his side. He gently stroked her face, looping a wet strand of hair behind her ear. For a few precious moments, they lay quietly, savoring their encounter and each other's presence. He gently cleared his throat. She looked into his eyes, smiling again.

"Isobel, I'm . . . I mean, that was wonderful. I don't know whether to beg your forgiveness or shout in happiness. But won't this be a problem for you? I mean, will Jorge keep his mouth shut?"

She moved even closer to him, rubbing her firm breasts against his arm in soft, sensual teasing. "Oh, Marty, don't worry. Just love me. I've been so empty for too long. Do not concern yourself about Jorge. He is devoted to me. He'll never say anything." She pulled his

face to hers and kissed him. "Just say you will want me
again."

Marty gasped, as she nipped at his lower lip. "Hell, my
dear. I want you again already. I'll have a hard time sleeping in the same house with you from now on."

"That's all I ask." Pulling him down, she skillfully
wiggled herself beneath him. This time, their lovemaking
was slower, less frantic, but still powerful and satisfying.

Afterward, she rose to her feet, unashamed in her
nakedness, and took his hand. "Now, my Yankee stallion,
come to the lake with me. We shall swim naked, as if still
children, to wash the sweat from our bodies before returning to my father's house."

Laughing, the two lovers enjoyed the cool waters of
the lake until its chill sent them scurrying back to the rock
to lie in the sun while its warmth dried them. Without
warning, Isobel lowered her hungry mouth until she en-
gulfed him in her moist embrace. He was instantly
aroused. Smiling in satisfaction, Isobel released him and
clambered astride him, riding him like the expert horse-
woman she was. She dreamily watched his eyes, savoring
the look on his face as her movements grew more agi-
tated and his reaction more intense—faster, and faster
still, until Marty joined her in yet another crashing cli-
max, and for a few moments, time stood still for the two
of them.

"Once again, my darling Marty, you have given me
great joy." She kissed him long and deep. "And it was
wonderful. You are wonderful, my dearest."

She looked at him, longing evident in her dark eyes.
"I'll come to you tonight or whenever. Simply say you
want me to."

"Isobel, I do want you, but we can't. I would be guilty
of betraying your father's trust. You and I must not plan
something so wrong. I want to be with you. I want to love

you, but it's not right. I know this, and you do too. What seems right out here, would be doubly wrong later. Don't you see?" He pulled on his pants, afraid he could not resist another passionate assault.

Isobel sighed audibly, reaching for her blouse. "Oh, very well." Isobel started to dress. She was disappointed, but the bloodline she was born into told her this man was right. One more time she tried. "I will come if you ask, Marty. I will."

The emotions running through Marty were so strong he could not answer. He got to his feet and started gathering the remains of the picnic. Finally he spoke. "Isobel, you are a beautiful, desirable woman. I hope and pray you will find the happiness you deserve. Now come on. Let's ride on back to the hacienda. I don't want your father worried that we've been gone too long."

As he helped her on her horse, Marty took the back of her hand and kissed it. "Thank you for the honor, Isobel. I shall never forget the beautiful Mexican woman of the blue lake." Isobel smiled, her eyes shining bright and a strange, wistful look on her face. Keller could not read the meaning of her expression. *It's best I don't know,* he decided.

Chapter 21

A Surprise for Caroline

Caroline lifted a heavy cast-iron skillet from the washpan and started to wipe it dry. The kitchen still held the aroma of fried potatoes and ham. Humming absentmindedly as she performed the mundane chore, she was startled when Mary suddenly burst through the doorway. Mary and Rose usually waited for her on the porch after supper, while she cleaned up the kitchen. Ever since Martin Keller had left to seek out her husband's killer, Caroline set aside the last few moments of the day to watch the sun go down while she thought about him and what he was doing at that very moment. She knew it was melancholy, but she couldn't resist envisioning Marty riding in with his shy smile, which lit up his face, and softly saying, "I'm back, Caroline—back to stay."

Even if it were a foolish thing to do, relaxing in the stillness of evening with the girls playing beside her on the porch had become a ritual for the lonely widow. She rationalized that if she were doing the work of a man around the ranch plus taking care of the girls and the house, it was only fair that she be allowed some time for herself and her private dreams.

"Riders coming, Mama!" Mary exclaimed excitedly. "A wagon and some men with horses. Do you think it's Marty coming back?"

"No, darling, I doubt it. Go back outside with little Rose. I'll be there directly." As Mary scampered out the door, Caroline straightened her dress and hair. Visitors would be welcome, no matter who they were. The sudden uneasiness of a woman alone skittered across her mind and was just as quickly abandoned. With the fortitude Marty so admired, she stepped away from the porch. Shielding her eyes from the brilliance of the setting sun with her hand, she resolutely awaited her visitors.

Her visitors consisted of three men herding about twenty horses, followed by a patent medicine wagon. A young red-haired girl drove the twin mules while an older, gray-haired man sat imperiously on the seat beside her. Caroline watched in silence, the two girls shyly peeking out of the open doorway. The group rode through the front gate, the horses stirring up clouds of dust with their hooves. The wagon turned toward her while the riders pushed the horses toward the corral beside the barn.

The girl driving stopped her wagon by the side of the porch steps. Caroline took notice of the writing on the wagon's side as it approached her. PROFESSOR SEAN MC-NULTY and PATENT MEDICINE FOR SALE made a circle around a picture of a brown bottle. The young woman smiled brightly at her and the girls, who were now peeking up at the pair from behind Caroline's billowing skirt.

The man beside the driver spoke with a lively Irish brogue. "Mrs. Caroline Thompson?"

"That's right. Welcome to the Box T. Climb down and rest a spell. What can I do for you?"

"Thank you. May I introduce meself. I am Professor

Sean McNulty, inventor of the most perfect medicine known to man, the McNulty Elixir of Health. It will cure—" Caroline saw the young girl nudge the old man in the ribs, interrupting his spiel. "Umph, of course. This is my niece, Fionna. Mr. Martin Keller directed us to you. He sent those horses there to you, by way of us."

"Marty!" Caroline exclaimed, raising a hand to her mouth. "How is he? Where did you see him? Come in, come in, please. We want to hear all about it." Caroline held out her hand to help the girl from the seat, then led the two inside the house. The little girls bounced around the pair of women, peppering the young redhead with eager questions about Marty without waiting for answers.

Caroline barely had the two visitors seated and cups of coffee poured, when a knock on the door announced the three men who had accompanied the wagon.

"Horses put away, ma'am," the older man announced as they entered the room. The professor introduced his nephew, Patrick, and the two wranglers, Bob and Joe Layden. "I brung a couple a letters from Mr. Keller fer you Miz Thompson," Bob Layden said as soon as everyone had finished greeting one another. "Maybe it'll explain what all this here is about." He handed the two envelopes to Caroline. One was marked PERSONAL, so she opened the other. The first thing she saw was a bank draft for sixteen thousand dollars made out to her, then a second draft for three thousand made out to the girls.

Caroline sucked in her breath. She'd never seen so much money in her life. Swiftly, she read what Marty had carefully written in the letter. A quick summary of how he got the reward money and the reason for the horses. He concluded by saying that he'd hired the two Laydens on her behalf to work at the ranch. He touched on the affection he saw growing between Joe and Fionna, asking her to help their cause if possible. He concluded by saying that his personal letter went into more detail about what had happened since they last were together. She decided she would save reading it for later, when she was alone.

Caroline raised her eyes to the five people around her table. "My goodness, I don't know what to say. For certain, that Martin Keller does things in a big way, doesn't he?"

"Aye, lass, that he does," Sean McNulty agreed. "You see here five solid friends o' the man and he saved our lives to boot."

Joe Layden shyly glanced at the beaming Fionna. "For that, I'll always be especially grateful to him, Mrs. Thompson."

The love sparks that radiated from Joe and Fionna warmed the room. *Martin certainly called it right with them,* she thought.

Bob Layden spoke up. "He sent you some fine horses, Mrs. Thompson, and me 'n' Joe to work 'em if'n it's all right with you."

"Well, I can certainly use the help, Bob. I hope you will be as happy working here as I am to have you." Caroline paused, then blurted out what was filling her every thought. "Now, tell me, how is Martin and when did you see him last? Do you have any idea where he is, or how his search is going?"

The next two hours, her guests told all they knew about Keller, the gallant circumstance of their meeting, and what had occurred in Santa Fe. Caroline's breath quickened as the fight with the outlaws was detailed. She knew Keller had taken an awful risk, attacking twenty armed men with just JB to help him. She thrilled to hear how he and JB had destroyed the attacking Comancheros. Her heart leaped when Fionna told of Keller and JB finding and killing the man who had murdered her husband. Finally, she had her revenge, but she immediately realized it was a hollow victory without Marty to share the moment.

Finally, Caroline had to call a halt. Rose was asleep in her lap and Mary was nodding in exhaustion. Caroline invited Fionna to take the spare bedroom and showed the men to the bunkhouse, empty except for old Mose, who eyed the newcomers warily from beneath his covers.

Finally, Caroline was alone in her kitchen. She changed into her favorite nightgown and curled up in her favorite chair by the fireplace, tucking her legs under the folds. She tenderly opened the letter from Marty, touching the writing with the tips of her finger. The crackling of the burning wood was the only sound in the house. It was a good time to be alone with her memories and a new letter from Marty.

> *Dear Caroline and Mary and Princess Rose,*
> *I take pen in hand to write that I am well, as is JB. We had some excitement en route to Santa Fe, which is the direction the killer took after he left Durango.*

Marty described the ensuing fight with the Comancheros and his meeting with the McNultys and the Laydens.

> *I have sent you some of the reward money to hold for me until I return. You are to use any of it you need to maintain the ranch and pay the Laydens' wages. If young Joe and Fionna seem to have feelings for one another, and I think they have, please consider letting them have the line shack up at the north pasture. It would be a good place for newlyweds to start their life together.*

Caroline turned the page, wiggling her bare toes at the warm fire. It was like Marty to think of others while involved in the search for three killers. Settling deeper into the chair, she read on.

I have given much thought to our agreement, my dear Caroline, and I believe I took advantage of your frustration. Your offer was made in desperation. Therefore, while I will accept your offer to come back from time to time, the agreement stops there. Any promises beyond that are unnecessary. I am grateful I can help you and find that is reward enough.

JB and I leave in the morning for Albuquerque, believing that is the direction the three I seek have taken. Unbelievable as it seems, we have found their trail while finishing the job I promised you. I am now closer to them than I have ever been. I swear that they will not long ride free, or I'll die in the trying. I pray that you and the little ones are well and happy. I think of you often, as does JB. We spend a lot of time riding and talking about you all. Hug the girls for me and stay well, as will I. JB was so proud to send the girls his share of the reward. You would have been proud of him. He is a fine scout and companion.

With warm affection,
Martin

Caroline sighed and pressed the letter to her bosom. She became aware of the presence of another person. She looked up to see Fionna standing in the doorway to the small bedroom, watching her.

"My pardons, Mrs. Thompson. I came out to get a drink and I didn't want to disturb ye."

"That's all right, Fionna. Please call me Caroline."

"I will, thank ye kindly. He loves you, you know,"

Fionna replied. "I tried to make him interested in me but he would have none of it. You were already in his heart. For a while I was jealous of you, may the Saints forgive me." She sipped from the water cup. "Now I have me Joey, so I am happy. I do pray Marty comes home to ye soon."

Caroline rushed over and hugged Fionna. Looking down into her green eyes, the older woman responded. "Thank you for that. Now we must get Joe to make his mind up before your uncle decides it's time to move on."

"It doesn't matter what Uncle Sean decides," Fionna declared. "I'm staying here with Joe, no ifs, ands, or buts."

"Good for you, dear. Marty suggested that I offer you and Joe the line cabin in the north pasture. It's in a lovely spot, and we can make it a fine home in no time. I'll be happy to help you fix it all up proper. Now let's get to bed. We've a busy time in front of us tomorrow."

The next morning, Caroline showed the Laydens and Patrick around her ranch, pointing out the boundaries and the livestock. It was evening before they returned to find that old Mose had prepared a hearty supper for everyone. Fionna and Joe slipped away after dark while Caroline sat on the porch with Bob, Pat, and Sean, discussing ranching, horses, and Martin Keller. The two girls played among the adults, enjoying the visitors.

"I suppose we should be under way soon," the professor abruptly announced. "We are not making any money sitting around here, nice as it is."

In the quiet that followed, Patrick spoke up. "Uncle Sean, I'm stayin' here. I want to settle down and learn how to ranch. That is, if you'll have me, Mrs. Thompson." He looked back at his shocked uncle. "And Fionna won't be going either, I'm certain. 'Tis my bet that she comes back tonight engaged to marry Joe. I'm sorry

Uncle Sean, but I must say this for me, before you go any further."

Caroline spoke up over the blustering protests of the professor. "You are welcome to stay, Patrick, as long as you want. And, Sean, I agree with Patrick. It is certain that Fionna and Joe are soon to marry. It's apparent to anyone who looks at the two of them together."

"But what shall I do?" the old man exclaimed. "I don't want to go on alone. All of this was for my children."

"I've thought about that," Caroline answered him. "You're obviously well read and educated. Why don't you consider starting a school in Cimarron? We need one and the tuition should provide you a decent living. That way you could see Patrick and Fionna anytime you wanted, and they wouldn't have to worry about you getting waylaid on the trail by some outlaw." She paused and looked at the old man. "If you're interested, we could go into town tomorrow. I'll rent a place for you and guarantee your salary for the first term. That'll give you a chance to build up the attendance. What do you say?"

"My word," McNulty mused. "I never considered undertaking the profession of education again. I always planned on spending my years on the open road, bringing health to the sick and satisfaction to the thirsty. My word." Professor McNulty stuck out his hand. "Very well, Mrs. Thompson, let's go to town and survey the situation. I must say, meeting Marty Keller has certainly had an impact on the McNulty clan. Saints be praised."

Caroline rode into town the next day with the professor and Fionna. Mose kept the girls, to their disappointment. By the end of the day, Caroline had rented an empty building to use as a schoolhouse, found the professor a room at the widow Jenkins' boardinghouse, and put the money from Keller in the bank.

Within a couple of weeks, the ranch was running

smoothly again. Bob and the others had relieved Caroline of the hard work involved in branding and breaking the horses. She was able to devote more time to her daughters and the long ignored ranch business book.

The last Sunday in September, Fionna and Joe married in a simple ceremony at the ranch house and moved out to the little cabin on the north meadow, deliriously happy to be alone with each other. The professor's school proved to be a welcome success for him and the community of Cimarron. Young Patrick worked hard to learn the skills of a rancher and was quickly earning his pay.

Every evening, Caroline continued to watch the sun set from the porch, her children and new friends close by. Her memories of the man so far away grew warmer and more intimate. Every evening she prayed for his safe-keeping before surrendering to sleep. Things were working out so well Marty had to return safe and sound. She hoped somehow that he knew that someone was waiting for him and praying for the day when he would come back safe. She hoped her thoughts reached him at his lonely campfire. "Oh, Marty, wherever you are right now, I'm thinking of you."

Keller stirred in his bedroll. He opened his eyes and looked around. All was quiet. He turned on the hard ground and settled back. Better get his rest, tomorrow could be a long day. Still, what had he heard in the soft mutter of the wind? He twisted deeper into his bedroll and relaxed. Until he fell asleep, he thought about the woman back at the ranch in Colorado. Would he ever make it back to them?

Chapter 22

The General Dies

Alva Hulett was rapidly becoming more than a little impatient. The so-called general appeared to be in no hurry to take his band of cutthroats on another raid. He had returned from Monterrey hungover and disheveled from his hard drinking. Al anxiously waited for an opportunity to dispose of the fat drunkard. He realized it would have to come during a raid. Otherwise the odds that he would be caught were too great. There were still a few men who seemed loyal to the dirty, tequila-guzzling outlaw leader.

Al made the best of the free time in the outlaw's camp working to ensure that Sanchez would be the heir apparent when something did happen to Morales. He and Lute spread the word that Sanchez was a skilled outlaw who had been on many bank and train robberies. The men Hulett had trained formed the core of his converts. Hulett knew he could count on them to back his move when the time came. Sanchez and his two cousins made as many friends as they could among the men and undercut the current second-in-command in the eyes of the others whenever possible.

Since Morales held a viselike grip on his gang, it was easy to make his unfortunate subordinate, Captain Hernandez, seem to be a complete buffoon in the eyes of the hardened banditos. "He is spit in the eyes of most of the men," Sanchez assured Hulett more than once.

Finally, one evening, Morales called the men together. "Compadres, tomorrow we ride. Pack enough food for a week, as we go far to the west, to take the silver of a bank that has too much stored in its safe." Waving grandly in acknowledgment to the cheering mass of men, he strutted back into his small abode.

Hulett grunted his satisfaction at the news, slyly winking at Sanchez. As they drifted slowly back to the main campfire, he again reviewed his plan. At last an opportunity was about to present itself. It would take only one shot fired at them while General Morales was in his presence. Then Sanchez would have the command of the outlaws, and they could finish what he'd sworn to accomplish back in Chihuahua: the death of Don José del Vargas and the seizure of all the land the old grandee possessed.

Fifty-two men rode out of the camp early the next morning, leaving behind only ten men to guard the stronghold. Most of those left behind were either sick or still recovering from wounds received previously. The camp's slatternly women and children waved as the heavily armed outlaws rode past before returning to the mundane tasks of their miserable lives. Little thought was given to the idea that some riders might never return. Affection was a rare commodity in a bandito's life.

The outlaws rode for several days to the west, only Morales knowing where they were headed. When the general finally gave the command to bivouac near a small town called El Palmito many miles to the west of their camp, the men were tired and surly.

After a night's sleep, the band was up and away before dawn. The men gathered around Morales behind a small hill just to the east of the town, as the eastern sky turned pale pink with the coming sun. Scouts returned to report no indication that their presence was known to the sleeping village.

"Bueno," the outlaw chief grunted. "Senor Hulett, you and Sanchez will ride with me in the main party. Senor Lute will be here with the rear guards." He appointed several others to watch the back road for any federales who might come upon the outlaws while they were terrorizing and looting.

"Now follow me," the pistol-waving general cried, spurring his horse around the hill and down the road toward the little town, basking quietly in the early-morning sunshine.

The forty-five men hit the town like a whirlwind of death and destruction. Anyone caught outside was immediately shot down. As soon as the shouting outlaws had circled their horses around the small village square, they peeled off to preplanned targets. The main party went to the bank, where two men kicked in the wooden doors. Hulett took his band of dynamiters inside and quickly had the iron safe packed with explosives. As he lit the fuses and ran outside, Al saw several outlaws looting the general store, while still others robbed the adobe-walled church across the plaza from the bank.

A thundering explosion signaled the blasting open of the safe. The bandits ran back into the bank, scooping up the small sacks of silver into saddlebags. Al hastily grabbed a stack of paper pesos, stuffing them into his dustcoat before he ran out and climbed on his horse.

Morales' grin was like that of a hungry wolf at the sight of bulging bags of silver pesos. He sawed the reins of his white stallion around and shouted over the noise and chaos, "Come on. Let's ride! Our visit is over." Laughing like a crazed man, he led the way out of town to the north, shooting at hanging water gourds or at any face peering from the windows of the mud brick houses along the street.

Just as Hulett was afraid that nobody in the town would fire back, several gunshots rang out from a small cantina at the edge of town. In the haze of dust thrown up by the galloping horses, with gunshots ringing out around him, he quickly fired a slug into the fat back of the general riding just ahead.

The old bandit swayed in his saddle, desperately holding on to the silver-inlaid pommel horn, then fell from his white horse onto the dirt road. The dead bandit chief's body was run over by horses. Finally he flopped in the ditch.

A few men tried to stop to rescue their leader, but Sanchez, riding at the rear of the group, shouted shrilly, "Ride on. Don't stop. It must be federales."

The band of rattled outlaws stopped in the woods about a mile from the town. Captain Hernandez argued that they should return for Morales. Sanchez argued against it.

Hulett threw in his two cents worth. "I saw the leader fall. He was dead before he hit the ground. I say you should elect a new leader."

Hernandez looked around the circle of confused, uncertain outlaws. His eyes narrowed at the implication. "What do you mean, elect a new leader? I am the chief now. There'll be no election."

Sanchez moved out of the crowd to where he could be

seen. "No, Captain. I say there should be a vote. I say I am the one who should lead, not you."

Ignacio and Pepe both shouted agreement. "Yes, vote for Sanchez. He should be our leader."

Others who favored Hernandez shouted their disagreement. In an instant the group was snarling insults at one another, many gesturing in angry, animated discord.

"Quiet! Quiet!" Hernandez screamed above the noise until they grew still. "I say there will be no election." He slapped the gun holstered at his side. "Any who dispute my leadership will answer to me right here and now."

Across the circle of outlaws, Sanchez answered, "I say I am the leader, Hernandez. I will answer to you if you are so anxious to join the general."

The other men watched the little drama unfold with morbid interest. The circle widened until it had cleared a field of fire between the two men. Captain Hernandez glared at quiet Sanchez. The unshaven captain was nervous and unsure of himself in his new role. Among the circle of dark faces were men not loyal to him, including the two gringos. He was worried who else would betray him for the newcomer, Sanchez.

Suddenly, he heard or saw something to his right. His eyes left the menacing Sanchez and flickered to Hulett, who had noisily shifted his feet. It was a fatal mistake, one Hulett had used before. Sanchez had been well briefed and was waiting for such an opportunity. Immediately he drew his pistol, an evil leer on his swarthy face.

Hernandez groaned. Out of the corner of his eye, he glimpsed Sanchez making his move. The distraction of the gringo had suckered him. Cursing to himself, he drew and desperately tried to bring his gun to bear on the evil grinning face of his opponent, but it was too late. Sanchez waited until he saw that Hernandez had a grip on his pistol so nobody could accuse him of shooting an unarmed man. Calmly, he put three bullets into the chest of Captain Hernandez, driving him back against the trunk of a massive pine tree.

Sanchez stepped to the center of the ring of men, looking around at the mute outlaws, deadly menace in his eyes. "Now I am leader—even Captain Hernandez agrees. Does anyone else dispute my claim?"

Seeing the submission in their eyes, Sanchez holstered his smoking pistol. Waving at the dead captain, he remarked in a nonchalant manner, "Dispose of that trash, divide up his goods, and let's be off." Several men scurried to comply, as Hernandez had many items of worth, including a fine pair of boots.

Sanchez called for Morales' white horse, which had galloped on with the men after its rider had tumbled from the saddle. "I will now ride the general's horse, but I will just be your chief, not a general. Come, we have silver in our pockets and I have a thirst to quench." He leaped on his new mount and trotted out of the clearing to the road, turning north. The band of outlaws hurried after him, already accepting his word as law.

That afternoon, Sanchez ordered the gang to ride in the flow of a small creek, which they followed for several hours, hoping to confound any pursuers. One of the outlaws had grown up in the area and directed the band to a large town called Parral, three days' ride northwest of the raided village.

For several days after they arrived, Sanchez allowed his new followers to drink and enjoy themselves. The men ran wild, spending all the money they'd just stolen on drink, women, and gambling. When they rode out of Parral, they were as broke as when they'd left the mountain hideout with Morales, two weeks earlier. That was exactly what Hulett and Sanchez wanted.

That night, Sanchez gathered the men around his campfire and revealed his plan. "There is a grand ranchero north of here. It has much silver and gold, many women and plenty of food. There are no towns or federales close by. We shall take this place and replenish our fortune before we return to the hideout."

The bandits all voiced their agreement, excited at the prospect. Talking animatedly about the coming raid, they returned to their bedrolls.

"Bueno," Hulett praised Sanchez, as they walked together at the edge of the camp. "We'll clean out the del Vargas family and have the entire ranch for ourselves. Those men who don't fall taking the ranch, we'll send off with a new leader, maybe one of your cousins. Then we'll file a forged bill of sale with the governor and live the rest of our lives with willing women and plenty of money."

"Yeah," the bearded Lute chimed in. "We'll live like kings, right, boss?"

Hulett sneered in the dark. *You'll never see the day, my smelly friend,* he thought to himself. *Unfortunately, you'll be killed in the attack and left for buzzard meat, just like General Morales.*

The next morning, they awoke to a persistent rain. It slowed their travel, but increased the odds against their being followed. Hulett had Sanchez spread the men so the rain would wash away any sign of their passage.

The outlaw gang reached the back slope of the mountains that formed the eastern boundary of the del Vargas ranch two days later. Sanchez sent scouts around the ranch and surrounding territory, looking for any sign of potential reinforcements for the ranch once they besieged the hacienda.

Meanwhile, he led the main body of men into a bivouac deep in the hills, well away from any casual passerby. There was no hurry, so Sanchez instructed that the scouts take a thorough look around. Al wanted no surprises, and time was not a factor in the planned raid. Besides, after a couple of days lying around, the men became restless, thus better at the job of killing and looting. As the sun dipped below the horizon, two scouts drove in a small cow, so they feasted on fresh meat for supper.

What the scouts didn't say was that a vaquero from the ranch had caught them driving the cow away from the herd and they had shot him dead, leaving him where he fell. That had been a violation of their orders not to leave any sign they were close to the ranch. Both bandit scouts assumed the dead vaquero would not be missed before the attack began.

Sanchez and Hulett rode out late the next afternoon to make a final check of the ranch complex before deciding on the tactics they would use to carry the fight inside the six-foot-high walls that surrounded the main ranch complex.

From a little knoll a half mile away, Hulett pointed toward the low ground falling away from the side of the ranch toward the lake. "We'll send the men carryin' the dynamite that way, while the main body attacks from the east. If the vaqueros git the gates closed afore we git inside, swing wide and wait fer the blast to knock down the walls. Then bust in hard through the hole." Hulett paused. "I guess I'd better go with the blasters, to make sure they git the dynamite set right."

Sanchez looked hard at his boss. "I must ride with the main body or they will never rush the walls. I'll be a good target, riding the general's white horse."

"No problem." Hulett grinned conspiratorially. "Let

Pepe lead the charge on the white. You tell him it is an honor as the man who will become the new leader after the raid. You lead the second group into the compound when the gates go down. Tell Pepe you don't like the gait of the white, but would rather ride your old horse."

The two men smirked at each other, buoyed by the evil and cowardly perfection of their planning. They retired to their bedrolls, engrossed in their private thoughts of a grand future filled with wealth and leisure.

Chapter 23

Time to Ride

Riding back from another fruitless search on the far side of the lake, Marty glared at JB, frustration plain on his sun-bronzed face. In spite of their skills as trackers, neither man had cut a single sign of Hulett's gang. "Well, old friend, we may as well face the facts square. We're getting nowhere here. If Hulett has any designs on the del Vargas ranch, he's staying away for now."

He shifted his weight in the saddle, stretching tired muscles. "No matter how you slice it, we're at a dead end. We've hit a dry water hole this time," he groused.

"JB agree with Keller." The old scout squinted at the sinking sun. "They hide someplace else."

After dinner, walking the perimeter of the hacienda's adobe walls with Ramon del Vargas, Marty concluded that the best thing to do was return to Chihuahua and see if they could pick up Hulett's trail again.

"It's my own fault," Marty grumbled. "I should have known better'n to try and take a short cut. We've lost a couple of weeks just because I got too anxious."

Ramon shook his head in disagreement. "It was worth

your efforts, Senor Keller. The men you seek cannot van-
ish like smoke in the wind. They are too evil to go unnoticed. You will find their trail again, never fear. I am
grateful that you came here to warn us. We will be prepared if they show their faces on our land."

Appreciating the encouragement, but feeling whipped,
Marty walked inside the hacienda and informed Don José
of his intention to leave the next morning. Isobel and her
husband, Diego, were with the grandee in his library. Isobel showed momentary dismay at the statement, but she
quickly recovered. A malicious gleam of satisfaction
passed across the hostile Diego's eyes. He might not have
been so smug had he seen Isobel's disappointment as she
turned away from the men and busied herself pouring
some wine.

The old don was gracious as always. "As you wish,
Senor Keller. I hope we have satisfied your needs while
you were our guest. While originally we only honored the
request of the governor, we have come to admire and respect you. You will always be welcome at my hacienda."

"You have been more than kind, Don José. I am grateful that my fears were unfounded and Hulett is not a
threat to you and your family. JB and I will leave in the
morning for Chihuahua. We'll pick up the trail from
there, I'm certain. I thank you again for your hospitality,
Don José. I will cherish our friendship." Keller shook
hands with Don José and Ramon. He nodded politely to
Diego and put his lips to the hand Isobel offered, before
striding out of the room.

"Well." Diego smirked at his departure. "I must say
that I, for one, am happy to see the gringo pistolero leave
this hacienda. I found his presence here a stench to the
nostrils."

"Oh, Diego," Isobel cried out in frustration. "That is a
terrible thing to say. If you will excuse me, Papa, I am re-

tiring to my bedroom." Glaring at her husband, she continued. "I have a severe headache and do not wish to be disturbed."

She swirled around and stalked from the room, the stiff taffeta fabric of her evening gown rustling in the sudden quiet. Behind her, she heard Ramon arguing in Keller's defense. Diego's hateful remarks stirred anew her desperate hunger for the handsome gringo. She gritted her teeth, knowing she was trapped in a lifetime of hell with Diego. Her desire for the tall, handsome gringo rippled through her, making her hands tremble like those of an old lady.

Swiftly, she climbed the stairs and walked to Keller's door, which was just closing as she entered the long hallway. Looking behind her, she saw that Diego had not followed her up the stairs. Moving silently to Keller's room, she knocked softly on the door and whispered, "Marty, it is Isobel. May I talk to you a moment?"

Keller opened the door and looked past the waiting woman. There was nobody else in sight. "Isobel, I was just getting ready for bed."

Isobel brushed past him into the room. "I know, but I must speak with you, *por favor.*" Without waiting for him to reply, she hurried on with what she had prepared herself to say. "I wish to go with you tomorrow when you leave. My life with Diego is empty and bitter. I only married him because my father insisted. There never was any love between us, and now I despise him. Please, Marty, take me with you, I beg you."

Keller hesitated as he looked at the distraught woman. What he said to her in the next few minutes would remain with her for a lifetime. If he humiliated or embarrassed her, she would carry the wound next to her heart. "Isobel, don't ask such a thing. I care too much for you and your father. It would bring shame and disgrace upon him if you and I ran off together. You don't want that, do you?"

Tears welled in her dark eyes. "I am so unhappy, Marty. Diego disgraces me every day, just by his presence in my house. Do not make me stay here, please."

Keller took the trembling woman in his arms and whispered gently into her ear. The fresh smell of her hair was intoxicating to his senses. It was all he could do not to give in to the passion racing through his heated body. "You are the daughter of Don José del Vargas. Your family is one of the most respected families in Mexico. Think, Isobel. You don't want to be responsible for the pain that our running away together would bring. I cannot dishonor your father's hospitality and trust by stealing away in the night with his daughter."

Keller felt Isobel's body growing stiffer. She withdrew from his embrace with a sigh. "Perhaps you are right, Martin. Perhaps we cannot do this, even though I want it with all my heart." She stared up at him with a look of burning passion in her eyes. "It would almost be worth it, for even one night in your arms, my handsome gringo pistolero. I shall always dream of what might have been. Now look out your door and see if I can leave without being seen. I shall cry my goodbyes for you tonight." Reaching up, she drew his head down and kissed him lightly on the lips. "Godspeed, my dear."

She slipped from the room, leaving a shaken man behind. Marty cursed the lust that he had surrendered to on the picnic. Then he cursed the fate that drove him to leave Caroline and the refuge that she offered.

Burdened as he was with feelings of desire and loneliness, he couldn't even consider sleep until he'd written Caroline and the girls. He would mail the letter in Chihuahua as soon as he arrived. It was very late before he found sleep.

JB and Keller rode out of the twin gates of the enclosed ranch before the sun cleared the eastern horizon. Behind them the del Vargas family stood on the hacienda's veranda and watched the two men until they receded into the mist of early morning that hugged the low hills.

Keller looked back just before the two of them entered the treeline. He imagined he could still see the tiny figure of Isobel standing next to her father. Shaking his head, he turned to JB. "It was hard to leave, wasn't it, old friend?"

The old Indian scout grunted and settled into his saddle, his eyes never still on the ride up the trail toward the summit of the mountain. "No question plan of Great Spirit, Keller. Take each day as Great Spirit gives it to you. Laugh, rest in the sun, enjoy a woman. Let her cook and care for small ones and keep your back warm in winter. Not hard to do."

Marty laughed and spurred Pacer on. "You old reprobate. No wonder the gals back at the hacienda were all over you every time I looked your way." JB merely smiled and rode beside his friend.

Keller rode on, silent in his thoughts, breathing the fragrance of the pine-scented air. John Black Crow was silent as well, finalizing his plan to take the manhunter back with him to the ranch, for Thompson's women. Then he could watch over all of them until he joined Thompson across the river of the Great Spirit.

They arrived in Chihuahua three days later, without incident. Grateful to be back in a room, they cleaned up in the hotel before going to supper. Keller led the way into the hotel café. The first person Keller saw was Hec Billows, the cattle buyer, sitting alone at a table covered with food. The burly Texan waved for Keller to join him.

"Keller, by Gawd. Just the man I was hoping to run into afore I left town fer Laredo. Come join me fer some vittles. I got some good news I was hoping to pass on to ya afore I'm gone."

"Howdy, Mr. Billows," Keller greeted him as he and JB joined the cowman. "What's been happening with you?"

"Been on a buying trip to the south," Billows replied. "Anyways, I was down in a small town called Delicias, about a hunred miles south o' here. It's on the main road to Monterrey." He paused to shove a taco into his mouth. After chewing and taking a sip of his beer, he wiped his mouth with the back of his hand and continued. "Now where was I? Oh yeah, well, the big news down there was a raid some bandit gang made on the town's bank. Shot up the place and a post full of troops. Anyways, one of the local boys said that two white men was with the gang. I sort of wonder if maybe it wasn't the fellers you was a-chasin'."

"Maybe," Keller mused. "What makes you think so?"

Billows looked around conspiratorially. "The Mex you said was ridin' with Hulett, that's what. He might have been able to git Hulett into the gang. Normally, no Mex bandit is gonna take a gringo into his bunch, no matter how tough the fella is. But the Mex ridin' with Hulett could've spread the grease on the rails. I figgered you'd wanta look into it, anyways."

"Thanks, Hec, I will, first thing tomorrow. Me and JB will ease on over to this Delicias and ask around. Lord knows I'm sort of thrashing around right now, like a fish out of water. This might be fresh sign."

"Great," the gregarious Hec replied. "I'll be off to Texas, 'bout the same time. Now finish up so you can buy me a drink and tell me what you've been doing the last ten days. How did ya like the old don's spread. Some place, huh?"

Three days later, JB and Keller rode into the small village of Delicias. The signs of the raid were still visible. The barracks of the federales was a scattered pile of debris, lying where the force of the explosion had strewn it. Keller saw tents in place for the troops sent into the town after the fight. The village square was filled with men repairing broken windows and battered-down doors. The bullet holes in the bank's stucco walls and boarded-over windows gave grim reminders of the destruction.

Keller spoke to the senior officer of the federales, and then to the town's only schoolteacher. The teacher confirmed that two gringo bandits were part of the raid. Neither man had the faintest idea where the bandit gang's hideout was located.

"It must be in the mountains to the south and east, Senor Keller," the federale captain surmised. "The banditos rode in that direction until we lost their trail in a sandstorm the next day. There is talk of a bandito general named Morales who hides in the highlands and rides with one hundred men to raid as he so chooses. If it was him, then he is many miles south of here, somewhere between Monterrey and Torreron."

Keller nodded. "Thank you, Captain. I will go that way tomorrow and see if I can cut the trail of the bandits."

"If you will allow it, I would be happy to detail a corporal to accompany you. He can be your guide and interpreter. If you find the bandito hideout, you can send him for federales to support you."

"That would be helpful. Please have him here tomorrow at sunrise, ready for the trail." Keller shook hands with the young officer. "JB and I will camp by the trees to the south of town tonight. We will leave as soon as your corporal arrives in the morning." He took his leave of the soldier and rode with JB back to their camp.

For two weeks, the three men crisscrossed the wild

country south of the Monterrey road. They heard many stories of the bandit general and his gang of cutthroats, but found no sign of the bandit's hideout.

Keller was prepared to give up the search and go back to Chihuahua when he heard of a recent raid by a bandit gang on the town of El Palmito, many miles west of where they were searching. It was rumored that General Morales and his men were the outlaws. Keller turned to JB and the corporal.

"That's our man, sure as shootin'. Come on, let's hit the trail for El Palmito. Corporal, do you know the place?"

The soldier nodded and led them west. They rode hard, arriving two days later, just after dark. The town was still in shock from the raid. The corporal and Keller spoke with the local federale sergeant who was stationed in the town.

"He says that the banditos numbered at least fifty, Senor Keller. They rode in at sunrise, shooting and looting everything. As they left town, this soldier and a couple of vaqueros visiting their family nearby shot after them. One man fell dead and the others rode away. The dead bandito was the one called General Morales."

"Are they sure, Corporal?" Keller interjected. "Are they sure they killed the leader of the outlaws?"

"*Si,* Senor Keller. They say the dead man had papers in his pocket that identified him. They are quite proud of themselves."

JB came into the small cantina where Keller was conducting the interviews of the survivors. "JB find tracks. Many men ride north. We follow?"

"Yep, we follow for sure. Corporal, get all the extra grub these folks will sell you and be ready to ride in two hours. If Morales is dead, this may be the break we're looking for. My hearty congratulations to you and your soldiers, Sergeant. They have done a great thing, killing the bandito leader."

Marty and his party doggedly stayed on the outlaw's trail, even though the bandits had ridden several miles up a small creek trying to hide their tracks. They almost caught up with the bandits in Parral, where the fifty outlaws had spent three days drinking and carousing. The outlaws had left the morning of the day Keller and the others arrived shortly after sunset.

"Damn," Keller muttered when he learned out how close they were to his quarry. "We have to stop for the night, but we'll start at daybreak. We're close now." His smile would have chilled the devil. The relentless determination of his years hunting the murderers showed itself. Keller woke the others just as the first traces of pink tinged the eastern horizon.

By riding hard all day, they cut the lead of the bandits to only a few hours. However it was a dark and rainy evening, forcing the hunters to stop for the night. They would have to wait until daylight to pick up the trail. Keller cursed in frustration as, once again, his quest was delayed.

As they sat in front of the small fire Keller allowed, sipping their coffee and listening to the sizzle of raindrops on the hot coals, Keller thought out loud to JB. "You know, old friend, the direction these bastards are headed is right for the del Vargas ranch. We can't be more'n two or three days south of there now."

JB nodded in agreement. "Maybe they go now to raid, like you say."

"Damn it all," Keller muttered. "I sure hope not. We'd better be ready to ride hard again tomorrow. If that's what they're doing, we've got to get there first."

He rolled up in his poncho, a cold and uneasy fear replacing the fire of hate in his belly. As he lay there,

watching the flickering flames of the little campfire, he
worried about the del Vargas family. Without his realiz-
ing it, he suddenly thought of Caroline and the girls. He
hoped the Laydens and the horses had arrived safely. He
tried to imagine the smile on Caroline's face at the news
of the death of her husband's killer.

To his dismay, he had a hard time putting any distinctive features on his mental image of the woman. Her soft
brown hair, warm smile, and deep brown eyes were all he
could envision. "Hell," he muttered to himself. "I'm so
tuckered out I can't even remember what anyone looks
like. God, I hope I catch up with the bastards tomorrow.
JB wants to go back to his home and I want to rest.
Damn, damn, damn." He slipped into an uneasy and restless sleep, the sputtering of rain on the fire a soft accom-
paniment to his fitful breathing.

Chapter 24

A Fateful Reunion

All day a steady, misting rain fell upon the three hunters. They would not have had a prayer of staying on the outlaws' trail were it not for Marty's gut feeling as to where they were headed. The tracks had completely washed away in the rain. It took all of JB's considerable skill to find the occasional broken twig or overturned rock that marked the outlaws' trail.

Unfortunately, to Marty's growing uneasiness, every hour made it more certain that the gang was headed straight for the del Vargas ranch. Marty racked his brain, trying to fathom the reason, always returning to the same conclusion: Hulett was bent on attacking the ranch to achieve with a gun what he couldn't with stolen money.

As Marty and his two companions topped a small rise on the southern edge of the del Vargas land, the sun finally broke through the low, dark clouds. In the brilliant late-afternoon sun, they could see the cluster of buildings that formed the ranch headquarters gleaming white against the pristine blue of the lake behind it.

Marty halted his party. Pacer stretched his neck to the

ground, nibbling at some of the tender green grass growing in abundance around him. The bounty hunter glanced
around, his brow drawn in a worried frown. He was torn
between riding straight for the ranch to warn Don José of
the peril or scouting around the area to find sign of the
outlaws' passing. It would not do to rush in warning of
danger and upsetting the inhabitants, only to have the
gang ride on past the ranch, heading elsewhere.

"What do you think, JB? Do we assume the bandits are
bent on attacking the ranch or should we find them first
and be sure what they're up to?" Keller shifted uneasily
in his saddle, his eyes sweeping the wooded foothills that
lay to the east.

"Wait." JB was staring intently to the front. "Something there." He motioned with his hand. He urged his
pony toward the distant object.

As the men drew closer, the shapeless lump on the
ground revealed itself to be a body, huddled in death as if
thrown from a running horse. JB and the corporal leaped
from their mounts and rolled the corpse over. It was a
young vaquero, his body growing stiff, the shock of death
still conspicuous on his face.

JB inspected the tracks that led away from the dead
man, up toward the foothills. "Two men and a cow go
that way." He pointed with a forefinger.

Marty took off his hat, wiping his brow with the back
of his hand. "Those skunks wouldn't take just one cow if
they planned to keep moving, would they? They're
pushin' tonight's supper, more'n likely. Well, that caps it
tight. JB, you and the corporal ease up after 'em, while I
take this poor boy down to the ranch. Don't get too close.
I don't want that bunch of murdering bastards to know
anybody has 'em spotted. Get back to the ranch house
when you can, but be careful coming in as I'll have 'em
alerted and ready for war."

JB nodded and turned his pony toward the hills, a visibly nervous corporal close behind him. The two men were soon lost to sight as the ground dipped and sloped up toward the high mountains. Marty heaved the dead body facedown on the vaquero's horse and climbed into his saddle. He nudged Pacer toward the distant buildings, riding instinctively while considering how the ranch could possibly be defended against an attack from fifty men. This concentration broke only when he had to tug on the dead vaquero's horse's halter to get the skittish animal to keep up. The horse smelled the death odor on its back and kept trying to shy away.

The peons working inside the ranch compound quickly clustered around Marty as he walked Pacer into the open courtyard of the hacienda. A young woman with a small baby on her hip suddenly shrieked in anguish and rushed to the body flopping facedown on the saddle. "Pablo, Pablo," she cried, tears streaming down her face.

Other women rallied to her side, while two vaqueros eased the body off the horse and laid it on the ground in front of the veranda of the big house. Everyone turned to look up at Don José, who stepped through the doorway, a perplexed grimace on his lined face.

"Senor Keller, what is the meaning of this? What has happened?" The old man's stern voice demanded a quick response.

Ramon hurried from his father's side to kneel beside the body. "Papa, it is Pablo Gomez. He has been shot." The young man appealed to Keller. "Senor Marty, please, what has happened?"

Marty pointed toward the hills. "I found him up by the east hills a couple of hours ago. I'm afraid I bring news of grave danger. Believe me, Don José, I am certain your ranch is soon to be attacked."

"Come inside Senor Martin. You say we have a danger

to face." The don held the door, following Marty and Ramon into the house. Isobel was coming down the stairs with Diego as Don José led the way into the library. Her husband observed the delighted surprise on her face and scowled his displeasure.

Marty faced the anxious and inquisitive faces of his friends, ignoring Diego's jealous glare. "Don José, what I feared before is now happening, only on a much more deadly scale. The outlaw Hulett has fifty men up in the hills right now and I am afraid they plan to attack this ranch very soon. JB is looking for their camp along with a federale soldier who has been helping us track the outlaws."

"Are you certain they are planning to attack us, Senor Marty?" Ramon interrupted.

"No, not for certain. We'll know more when JB gets back tonight." Marty looked earnestly at the don. "Don José, you must start defensive preparations immediately. If I am wrong, you will have only wasted time. If I am right, every second is precious."

"Why do you think we should believe you, gringo?" Diego snarled. "This is the del Vargas ranch. No bandito would dare attack it."

"Diego," Isobel gasped in shock and mortification, "your rudeness shames us. We may be in mortal danger. We should be grateful Martin risks his life to help us."

"Quiet, Diego. Don't talk loco." Don José spoke as if addressing an unruly child. "Senor Keller, we will defend our home against anyone who dares to attempt such a crime. Ramon, how many men do we have to defend the walls?"

"If I can get word to the vaqueros working in the south pasture, we should number, uh, twelve, plus the male servants and the blacksmith and his helper. Sixteen plus us, Papa. Nineteen in all."

"And over twenty women," Isobel interjected.

Marty spoke up. "Of course, you will have JB and me at your side, Don José. Please send for the vaqueros immediately. And, Ramon, as soon as you return, please show me what sort of defensive plan you and your father have for the ranch."

At his father's nod of approval, Ramon rushed out to send a messenger for the needed vaqueros. Don José turned to Isobel. "Senor Keller brought in Pablo Gomez, shot dead. You should go to his wife now. Return shortly so that we can plan on how to protect the women if we are attacked."

Isobel turned to Marty, taking his hand in hers. "Thank you for caring about us, Marty." She rushed from the room.

Don José instructed Diego, who was sitting on a chair seething from Don José's rebuke. "Diego, you take an immediate inventory of the ammunition and medical supplies on hand. Also get the new rifles from the storeroom and bring them to the front porch. Pass them out to any man who needs one."

The sullen Diego left without a word. Don José shrugged his shoulders and shook his head in disappointment. "Forgive his bad manners, Martin. He is not the man I once thought he was, I am sorry to say."

"*Está bien,* Don José. The important thing now is to be prepared when the banditos attack. Where is the nearest company of federales?"

"In Yepachic, which is nearly two days' ride to the north. They would never arrive in time, I'm afraid." Don José shook his head. "No, we must defend ourselves."

Ramon rushed into the room. "I sent Jorge for the men. He knows where they are and will have them back here before midnight. Come, Marty. I'll show you our plan for defending the walls."

Marty and Ramon excused themselves and hurried from the room. Rapidly they walked to the front gate. It was a double-hung wooden barrier, four inches thick, five feet high, capable of stopping a bullet or a man when barred. The adobe wall was six feet high and two feet thick. Several rectangular openings flanked by thick wooden shutters were intermittently spaced along its length as firing ports. There were enough for forty riflemen, and because the enclosed courtyard was nearly two hundred feet square, it would take that many to defend it adequately.

"We sent thirty men on a cattle drive to Durango," Ramon explained when Keller pointed out that twenty men were not enough. "They won't be back for two weeks or more."

Marty examined the long walls and the adobe houses that backed up to the inside of the square. He sighed and with his finger drew the outline of the ranch enclosure in the dust. "We'll put four men on each wall and keep the rest here at the main gate. When we see what direction the outlaws attack from, you can reinforce that wall." Marty looked over the ground beyond the walls. "They'll probably not come from the north or west—the lake gets in the way."

He paused. "However, be sure you instruct the men on those walls that they must not leave their post without a direct order. The bandits may attack from those directions because such an attack is unexpected."

Ramon gazed at the drawing, stroking his chin with his fingers. "I understand, Senor Martin. From where will you fight?"

Marty faced the main house, which towered over all the other buildings inside the adobe square. "I will start on the roof of the hacienda. My rifle shoots much farther than these outlaws would ever imagine. I hope to drop a bunch of them before they ever get close to the ranch. JB'll stay with me—maybe two or three other vaqueros as well. We'll be your reserve. We'll counterattack if they breach the front gate. It is the weak point in the wall. You and Diego must each take one of the two most dangerous approaches, the gate and south wall.

"I will obey, Senor Martin. We will do our duty, have no fear. Now let us go and tell Father of our plans."

Don José agreed to the defensive plan. Ten women would be brought to the main house, where they would tend to the wounded men carried in from the fighting positions at the walls. The rest would stay beside their husbands, to reload their empty rifles. Isobel argued that she should fight beside the men. "You know, Papa, that I can shoot as well as any man."

The don shook his head firmly. "You will supervise the women as they care for the wounded as I have instructed you, my dear. That will be work enough for you."

Ramon and Marty climbed the stairs to the flat roof on the three-story main house. A four-foot-high parapet provided him protection and cover as he moved from side to side. His view in all directions was adequate for his plan, which was to use his sniper rifle at targets long before they got in saddle rifle range of the house. Unfortunately, he only had thirty rounds, not enough to stop them all even if every shot found its mark.

Marty brought his sniper rifle and Winchester to the roof, leaving them in the custody of a young boy assigned by Ramon as lookout. The youngster swore with pride that he would guard the weapons and watch for any sign of approaching riders.

Marty suggested that each man be given a water jug, some tortillas, and bandages. "We want them to stay at their post, as long as possible," he explained. "Fortunately, you have plenty of weapons, ammunition, and water. They won't be able to wait us out."

The sun was setting by the time the preparations were completed. The women had cooked beans for everyone. After they had eaten, there was nothing to do but wait for dark and the return of JB. Keller still hoped the old scout would bring news that the outlaws were not intending to attack the ranch.

The sun slipped below the horizon before the youngster on the roof whistled an alert. He pointed. "Riders coming on the road toward the house, Senor Keller."

Marty and Ramon hurried to the front gate. It was JB and the corporal, riding fast. Quickly, the two massive doors were swung open for the men to gallop through, sweat from their tired mounts flying with every step.

"Did you find them?" Marty asked JB while handing him a tin cup of water.

JB nodded. "We find. They attack soon. All are cleaning weapons and making boast of what they do with women. White man in charge. He send out men to watch. We hide close by and hear. They know only few men at ranch."

"Mother of God, did we not almost have them sitting in our laps," the corporal interrupted. "For an hour, they were so close to us, I could count the fingers on the hands of one of them. He had only three on this one." Carlos held up his left hand.

"I know him well," Marty replied. "He's the man I'm looking for. They'll come at first light, I reckon." He turned to Ramon. "I think we should send the corporal to the federales, even if it will take two days. Would you give him your best horse?"

"Of course," Ramon answered. He took the worried federale to the small stable at the rear of the compound. Soon the corporal was on his way, grateful to be out of the coming battle. The odds were a little long for his liking.

Just before midnight, the summoned vaqueros quietly entered the compound and were assigned their posts. *Our chances just improved a mite,* Marty thought to himself. *They can't know we got the reinforcements. Still, they know something about fighting. Do these vaqueros?*

He went inside. The women were gathered in the dining room, rolling bandages cut from old sheets. Don José and Ramon were in the library discussing their plan of defense. Marty didn't see Diego, but he ran into Isobel coming out of the dining room. He lightly held her arm. "I'll be close by if you need me," he told the dark-eyed beauty. "Don't be frightened."

"I'm not, Martin," she answered regally. Careful to attract no attention, she placed her hand in his and held it firmly. "You take care of yourself. I pray that we will prevail and you will not be harmed. May God hold you safe in his grace, as I do in my heart."

"*Gracias,* Isobel," Marty replied, trying hard to keep his voice from showing the tension he felt inside. "I've waited too long for this day to worry about that. Just know that I'll be here if you need me. For now, get some rest." He gently squeezed her hand and watched her climb the steps toward the bedrooms. Then he entered the library, where Ramon and Don Jose anxiously awaited the dawn.

Chapter 25

Diego's Deadly Decision

Keller awoke with a start. Isobel had just opened the door to the library, carrying a tray with cups of steaming hot coffee. Keller rubbed his eyes with the heel of his palms and looked around. Don José was gone, and Ramon was still asleep in the other wingback chair.

"What time is it?" he softly asked. "I must have fallen asleep."

"It's nearly four in the morning. Papa said it was all right for you to get some rest. He is outside on guard at the front gate. He says there has been no sign of the banditos. Now drink your coffee and come to breakfast. It may be the only food you'll get today."

Ramon lifted his head and growled, "How can a person get any sleep, my sister? What time is it, anyway?"

Keller and Isobel chuckled. In a few minutes, both men were at the table eating a hearty breakfast of eggs and ham steaks. Before the sun rose, they had joined Don José at the front gate.

"It is all quiet, Senor Keller," Don José reported. "There has been no sign of anyone all night."

Marty looked over the wooden gate. A morning mist

draped feathery tentacles of white across the fields beyond. "I hope they're not using the morning fog to sneak up. I suppose I'd better get up on the roof," Marty remarked. "If they come with the sunrise, it won't be long now."

He sent for JB, and together the two men walked back to the main house. Marty stopped to speak with three vaqueros building a barricade on the front porch. One of them tipped his wide-brimmed hat in respect.

"Senor Keller," he spoke carefully, his sweat-stained sombrero in his callused brown hand. "I am Felipe Martinez, this is Jésus Gomez, and that is Jorge Gonzales. Don José says we are to fight with you if the banditos come past the walls."

Marty nodded. "I will call for you if needed, Felipe. Until then, protect the hacienda and the women inside from here on the porch. JB and I will be on the roof."

"We understand, senor. We will fight at this spot until death if necessary or until you call for us."

Marty gripped the courageous vaquero on the shoulder. "I have no doubt, Felipe. The women's lives are in your hands." He turned to his companion. "Well, John Black Crow, it's almost dawn. We'd best get on the roof."

JB merely grunted before heading to the front door of the hacienda. Marty suppressed a wry smile. The war blood was rising up in the old-timer. JB and Keller made their way up to the flat roof, joining the young sentry José, who was still on alert for any sign of trouble.

"See anything yet, José?" Keller asked as he moved from one side of the roof to the other with JB looking for any movement in the morning's gray mist. The damp ground was covered with a heavy fog swirling in the cool night air. "Just what we need," he groused to JB. "It'll be the devil to pay if they rush us before it burns off."

"No, senor," the young boy answered. "It is still as before, with no sign of the evil ones." José rubbed his dark eyes and stared out into the darkness.

Keller squinted, seeking to pierce the veil of fog. He leaned his sniper rifle against the roof wall and squatted down. "Everyone stay low, just in case the bandits are watching. Maybe we can surprise them."

The sun slowly exposed the mountains in front of them. With every second the day brightened, the mist dissipated, but still the attack didn't come.

JB swept the countryside with his binoculars and remarked softly, "No sign, Keller." He looked on all four sides of the tiled roof with the same result. "No sign."

"I don't understand it," Marty whispered. "Why don't they attack?"

By midmorning, Marty announced the obvious. "Come on, we might as well go down and face Don José. I feel like a nervous fool, upsetting them unnecessarily."

Just as he turned to climb down the ladder to the floor below, JB spoke. "Three riders come down road."

Marty hurried to the east wall of the roof. Sure enough, far down the road, three tiny figures could be seen trotting in the direction of the main gate. Swiftly, he scanned the area on either side of the distant riders. He caught sight of several men easing their mounts into a fold of the undulating land. "Come on," he said as he hurried to the trap door on the roof. "We've got scouts coming for a closer look. We have to warn Ramon and Don José not to let them inside the compound."

The younger del Vargas was walking up to the front porch when Keller led JB out of the house. "Ah, Marty, I'm afraid all we got ourselves prepared for was—what do you call it—a wild-duck chase."

"Goose, amigo, goose. But don't let your guard down yet. Three men are riding toward the house right now. And I saw others out to the east hiding in a fold in the ground. Talk to 'em, but don't let them inside the compound. Don't even let them see past the gates. JB and I will cover you. Felipe, you go with him."

The four men quickly mounted the tethered horses and rode to the front gate. "Open the gate and let us out," the younger del Vargas commanded of his men. "Then shut it behind us. Don't let the strangers riding toward us inside, no matter what."

The four waited silently just outside the barred main gate. As the riders drew nearer, their appearance clearly marked them as outlaws. They all wore crossed bandoleers with cartridges reflecting the bright morning sun, high-topped boots, and wide sombreros. Each had a colorful bandanna around his dirty neck. The coarse, unshaven faces with cruel black eyes wore exaggerated smiles.

Ramon confronted the three a few yards in front of the closed gate. He greeted them in Spanish, and soon a rapid dialogue ensued between the outlaw leader, who rode a pure white horse, and the younger del Vargas.

Marty studied the three outlaws closely, his face grim, deadly, his hand hovering close to the butt of his pistol. While the leader spoke with Ramon, the two accompanying riders scanned the walls of the compound, straining to see over the white stucco walls. They looked at Keller's weapons, and one looked hard into his face before hastily glancing away. The spokesman on the white horse squirmed under Marty's dark glare, while listening to the rapid replies from Ramon.

Suddenly, shouting a string of rapid Spanish, the leader grew red-faced and wheeled his horse around. The other two men took one last look around and followed their leader's galloping retreat. As the four defenders reentered the compound, Marty spoke to JB. "Get back to the roof and see where they drop off the road. Ramon, what did they say?"

Ramon held up his hand and rode to the porch, where Don José and Diego waited for them. As soon as Ramon got to his father's side he relayed his report.

"The one on the white horse said he was the leader of twenty-some vaqueros returning from a long cattle drive. He wanted to come inside with his men to buy some food and grain for his horses. I told him we were unable to entertain guests at the moment because a band of cowardly banditos had surrounded the ranch. I offered to let him take cover with us if he would give up his guns. I also said any of his men who wanted to take refuge inside our walls would have to surrender their guns as well." Ramon laughed and continued. "The leader, who called himself Sanchez, didn't like that at all."

Keller interrupted. "Did you say the one on the white horse called himself Sanchez?"

"*Sí,* that is what he said. Do you think it is one of those you are seeking?"

"Might be," Keller answered. "I'm surprised he was able to get control of the outlaw gang so quickly, but it must be him. He is a dangerous enemy, Don José."

The old man nodded his head in agreement. "What next, my son?"

Ramon continued. "Then the one who called himself Sanchez grew angry when I called him a common thief and told him he would get nothing from the del Vargas ranch. He threatened to take the compound by force and take whatever he wanted. I told him he would die in the dirt by our front gate if he tried. Then he threatened us again and rode away. He gave us until sundown to open the gates or face destruction."

Marty spoke up. "There you have it, Don José. Hulett and Sanchez will stop at nothing to take your ranch away from you. I'm afraid our worst fears have been confirmed."

Don José nodded. "*Sí*, but we have more strength than some poor village. This they will find out if they attack. For now, I suggest we continue to prepare our defenses and rest. The night ahead will be long and tomorrow even more so."

JB joined the men on the porch. "They go where the others wait, Keller." He pointed out to the east and south. "I see men all around the hacienda, watching."

Hulett hurried to Sanchez as soon as the three advance scouts ducked into the slight fold of ground that hid them from view of anyone at the ranch compound. "How did it go, amigo?"

"They know. Somehow they know. I was not able to even see inside the compound walls. They met us beyond the gates and called me a common bandito. And"—he paused and looked back in the direction of the ranch— "there is a gringo there. A man who hunts men—you could see it in his eyes. He stared at me as if his gaze would roast the heart inside my body. It is a bad sign, I tell you."

Hulett felt a chilling uneasiness. "Did he look familiar? We ever cross paths with him?"

Sanchez shook his head. "No, I never saw him before. But he looked at me like he knew me. My blood ran cold for a moment."

Hulett shrugged off the news. "It don't matter none. We'll hit 'em tomorrow at sunrise if they don't open the gates for us by dark. I can't figger out how they found out about us, but with the men we have, it don't matter. This time tomorrow, we'll be the new owners of the del Vargas ranch. Come rest and have some tequila." Al led the way to a campsite under a towering pine. Al looked nervously back toward the ranch. *Who is that gringo? What does he want?*

Inside the compound, the vaqueros hurried to strengthen their fighting positions. Don José placed two men on the roof of the main house. They scanned the rolling landscape for any movement of the outlaws, who now surrounded them. Aside from a few fleeting sightings of bandit lookouts, nobody moved toward the compound.

Keller walked around the inside of the yard with Isobel. He began telling the alluring Mexican woman about Caroline and her daughters. "I'm not sure how she did it. Her husband's death forced her to assume an enormous responsibility, and she took it on, showing the courage in her soul. She's been running the ranch by herself, without much help, while raising two daughters. You should meet her, Isobel. You remind me of Caroline. You're proud and strong, just like her."

He smiled at his companion. "The two of you would soon be the best of friends. And her daughters—why, there's not a soul alive who couldn't help but love 'em." Keller looked out over the vine-covered wall, but his vision was a long way from where he stood.

Isobel understood more completely why this exciting man had resisted her offer of clandestine love. He was in love with the gringo widow and didn't even realize it. She sighed, fighting to keep the pain from her voice and her eyes dry.

"Oh, Martin, you foolish man," she interrupted peevishly. "Can't you see? You love this widow and her children. They are in your heart to stay. Go to them when this is done. Just remember that if there is not a place for you with them, you will always have one here at this ranch, with my family and me." She put her hand on his chest and gently pushed him away. "Now, Senor Keller, return to your duty. Save my father's ranch and my life. God sent you here for that, you know." She blinked away her tears and hurried to the main house. There were always more bandages to roll and food to cook. She could not stay with Marty one second longer.

Their stroll had not gone unnoticed. As Isobel fled the tall gringo, Diego watched from the window of his second-floor office, his heart burning with jealousy and hate. *Damn the gringo pig,* he thought. If the Yankee pistolero had never come there, Isobel and he would have been able to return to Mexico City. Now he wasn't sure she would even share a bed with him again. The Yankee had become an obstacle between him and the del Vargas fortune.

A crafty look flashed across his face. Maybe there was some way he could strike a deal with the banditos outside—offer them money in exchange for sparing his and Isobel's lives. He had his family's money, and when it was combined with the inheritance she would receive should Don José and Ramon be killed, the total would be substantial. Then he wouldn't care what she did. She could spend her days in the chapel, praying her dead gringo would return from the grave for all he cared.

He would wait until dark. If the night were black enough, he would slip over the wall behind the blacksmith shop and make his way to the banditos before they attacked the compound. Diego nodded to himself. Yes, it was a good plan and might be the only way to survive the coming battle.

Later, as the crescent moon slipped behind dark clouds, Diego crouched behind the rear of the ranch's blacksmith shop. Peeking around the corner of the building and seeing no observers, he hastily scaled the wall and dropped to the ground. Stealthily, Diego darted through the shadows until he was well out onto the grassy meadow that lay south of the ranch. He scurried toward a small gully that ran just beyond rifle range of the walls.

His mouth was dry, while his breath was ragged and hoarse. Fear and exertion made him sweat. A terrible thought ran through his head. *What if some bandit shoots first before I can speak?* Diego forced himself not to think of it. He breathed more easily when he reached the cover of the gully. He was certain to find the bandito camp before dawn. Quietly, he moved toward the north, praying nobody from the ranch had seen him desert. No one must know he had fled the compound. After the battle, he would reenter the compound and pretend he had participated in its defense.

Tomas Villano had been a bandit with General Morales for five years. He'd killed more people than he could count and, quite frankly, enjoyed his life. The thought of returning to the village where he had grown up as the oldest son of a peon was abhorrent. He remembered the bone-tiring work his peasant father had done to support his family. Farming a tiny patch of rocky ground was not for Tomas.

Tomas heard the scuttling sounds of the intruder long before he saw the stranger. The man was either careless or very inept. He was creeping down the center of the gully, not even trying to be quiet. Tomas pulled out the sharp knife he had taken from a wealthy gringo prospector he'd killed several months earlier. He licked his lips in anticipation of the surprise he was about to spring on the noisy intruder.

As the panting man passed the slight mound of earth where Tomas lay watching the ranch, Tomas leaped down on his exposed back. A single swift thrust of the deadly blade and a quiet moan marked the end of Diego's grand plan to outwit his fate. The unconcerned bandit robbed the dead body of everything of value, then returned to his post. He would not even mention the encounter among the other outlaws. That way, he'd get to keep the fine silver watch and gold ring the luckless deserter had so generously brought to him.

The bloodthirsty outlaw watched the compound with greedy eyes. If the stupid man was any indication, tomorrow would be a fine day with much booty.

Chapter 26

Gunsmoke in the Mist

It was well past midnight. After another hasty check of the guards positioned along the outer walls, Keller gratefully eased himself into one of the overstuffed chairs in the library. He desperately needed sleep. After two frantic hours of people searching for Isobel's missing husband, the house was finally quiet. The people of the ranch had searched the compound thoroughly, but to no avail.

Don José had shaken his white-haired head in exasperation. "He must have left the protection of our walls, for what reason I cannot imagine. It is pointless to look any further. We shall have to find him after we deal with the coming attack. For now everyone get some rest."

He watched his distraught daughter climb the stairs; then he wearily turned to his son and Keller, who were standing beside him in the foyer. "If he still lives, after all this is over, I'll cast him from my lands. Damn the day I ever allowed him to marry Isobel."

Ramon agreed. "Yes, Papa. That and more, may God forgive him." He turned and motioned to Keller. "Come,

Martin, you need to sleep. It won't be long before the dawn breaks."

Marty wearily laid his head against the leather covering of his chair. He tried to think of anything he had missed, but quickly fell fast asleep. Ramon awakened him before dawn, and the two of them went into the dining room. Isobel was serving breakfast to JB and several of the vaqueros. She brought Marty a cup of hot coffee, but said nothing. Aside from slightly swollen eyelids, she gave no indication of the distress she was suffering over Diego's unexplained absence.

Marty took the hot cup. "Thank you. I need this. Are you all right?"

She responded with a curt nod, before turning back to the work at hand. He shrugged. Hopefully there would be time later, after the attack, to comfort her. After bolting down their hasty breakfast, Ramon and Marty checked the perimeter of the compound one last time. The vaqueros were at their posts, alert for any movement in the early-morning dimness, weapons at the ready.

"Well, amigo," Ramon said as they returned to the veranda of the main house, "it's time I took my position. May God watch over you." He held out his hand and Marty shook it.

"The same for you, Ramon. And your father and sister as well. I'll go to the roof now. Good luck to you."

Marty spoke to the three men guarding the porch. "Felipe, Jésus, and Jorge, are you ready for the coming fight?"

"*Sí*, Senor Keller," they answered in unison, white teeth gleaming against their sun-browned faces.

"Good," Marty answered. "Protect the house and the women. I'll join you if the bandits get over the walls." Slapping the friendly Felipe on the shoulder, Marty entered the house. He looked around for Isobel, but couldn't find her. Resolutely, he headed for the roof, where he found JB and young José waiting. Carefully, they all peered over the wall into the rising white mist of daybreak.

The thick mist would provide cover for the bandits, enabling them to get closer than Marty had anticipated before he would be able to fire at them. "Nothing ever goes like you plan," he grumbled to JB. "Keep your ears open, old friend. Maybe you can hear them before we see 'em."

JB settled in, his rifle beside him, his eyes never ceasing their careful scan. In the calm, they watched and waited. The next move would be up to Hulett and his gang of murderers. As Marty waited, a simple melody Mary and Rose had taught him ran continuously through his mind. The pervasive unease of the impending battle penetrated his mind, forcing out hope, charity, humanity. A burning in the pit of his stomach, as if he had gulped hot, bitter coffee too quickly, reminded him of the nerves he wanted to ignore. Stoically, he did his best to repress his nervousness and waited for the dawn to grow lighter.

Hulett and Sanchez stood on the road, about a quarter mile in front of the gate, talking softly. The fifty men in their band of cutthroats sat on horseback behind them, silent, menacing, impatiently anticipating the command to attack. They too hated waiting, even more than the prospect of death that would hang over them once the raid started.

"This morning fog is perfect," Al chortled. "I'll take ten men and come up from the north, while you send half of the others straight at the front gate on horseback. Take the rest and come in on foot. The riders'll make enough of a ruckus that we'll be able to git to the wall without bein' seen. When I blow the dynamite, you send the foot

soldiers in after us. Have the men on foot open the gate
for the horsemen. Now git Pepe up here and tell 'im the
news."

Pepe crept forward. "Pepe," Sanchez whispered, "I'm
gonna lead half the men on foot against the ranch. You attack the front gate with the rest on horseback."

"*Sí,* my cousin," the bandit replied. "I will take the
men straight up the road and then swing south. We'll circle and return the way we came, down the road."

"Fine." Al patted young Pepe on the shoulder. "Since
you're the leader, take the white horse as yours."

"You mean it? I can ride the general's horse!" exclaimed Pepe, his eyes wide with excitement and pride.

Sanchez slapped Pepe on the back. "You'll be the
leader of the army as soon as this business is done, my
cousin. You may as well start riding the leader's horse
right now." Both men hid cruel grins as the unsuspecting
Pepe hurried to the white stallion and scrambled onto its
back.

Hulett motioned for his dynamiters to pull away from
the main group. Silently they disappeared in the swirling
fog as they circled the shrouded compound somewhere to
their front. "I'll start in as soon as I hear your guns," Al
told his Mexican accomplice. "Keep up steady fire until
you hear the explosion. Then come on the run." Hulett
and his detail faded into the mist, the noise of their horses
muffled by the dew-laden grass.

Sanchez waited a few minutes before motioning for
his men to advance. He glanced over his right shoulder.
The sun was just peeking over the mountaintops behind
him. He thought, *the sun will be in their eyes.* At his
wave, the riders moved down the road, while the dismounted bandits eased off to the left and right until they
were strung out in a long skirmish line. The men on foot

would fire at the gun ports cut into the wall as soon as they could make out their targets.

JB's attention suddenly focused toward the front of the ranch. He had not seen anything yet, but he did hear ever so faintly the jingle of bridles and the clip-clop of many horses' hooves. After a few tense seconds, Marty saw the riders emerging like wraiths from the mist, not two hundred yards in front of the main gate. He doubted if the defenders at the front gate had yet seen the bandits through the white shroud.

Cursing for the valuable minutes he had lost to the fog, Marty brought the .52 caliber Spencer rifle to his shoulder. The crosshairs of his scope settled on a black-bearded man, probably the same one who had ridden with Hulett, Marty thought to himself in merciless satisfaction. Gently he squeezed the twin triggers of the deadly weapon.

The massive *boom* of the rifle shattered the morning calm. Unlucky Lute Payson flipped backward out of his saddle, his legs up in the air. He was stone dead before he hit the ground. It was the signal for the attack to begin. With a rush, the screaming riders charged the walls, firing at anything in their sight. Marty and JB calmly chose their targets, dropping several men before the vaqueros at the walls even saw an opportunity to fire. Soon, however, their gunfire added to the din.

The dismounted bandits under Sanchez' command charged forward until they were close enough to see the wall of the ranch, then dropped to the ground. They added their covering fire to the melee. As the horsemen reached the front wall, they turned and raced south toward the inviting cover of the fog. Several more fell from Marty's and JB's deadly rifle fire as well as that from Ramon's defenders. As the riders galloped into the mist,

Marty dropped one last man with a shot that sent his sombrero sailing through the air. Tomas Villano never knew what hit him.

Three vaqueros were down, hit by the fire from the dismounted bandits to the front. Marty scanned the battleground, hoping to catch sight of the hidden shooters. He saw the dim outline of one outlaw, his red kerchief a beacon through the filmy mist. His big rifle boomed again and then again as the morning sun burned off more of the filmy white cover.

The riders came thundering back out of the fog, the renewed hammering of gunfire again shattered the still morning air. Three men ran to the front wall from their positions at the north wall. Marty wanted to shout for them to return to their positions, but he was too busy firing at the moving targets, and his call would not have been heard above the noise of the fight. As the riders thundered out of the cover of the mist, Marty saw the distinctive white horse the bandits' leader had ridden yesterday. Just as the outlaw leader galloped into the cover of fog, Marty centered the crosshairs on the man and blew him out of the saddle. *One less bandit general to worry about,* he thought.

The warm sun continued to burn away the morning mist, revealing more of the dismounted attackers. Marty methodically went about his grisly business. He shot twenty-six times in the first few minutes of the fight, felling twenty-four men. Added to those downed by JB and Ramon's vaqueros, only a few outlaw riders were left alive, and not many more dismounted outlaws. The ones who were left had discovered Marty's location; they began firing at him as well as at the front wall. The whine of ricochets and the thump of bullets hitting the plaster-covered bricks of the roof parapet showed just how precarious his position was. Marty's ability to fire decreased as the outlaw's shots at him caused him to duck. Carefully aimed shots suddenly became much more difficult to do.

Keller laid aside the Spencer, saving his last four bullets, and took up his Winchester repeater. The men were close enough for him to use the weapon effectively. The air crackled with gunfire as men inside and outside the walls blazed away at one another.

Hulett slipped up to the north wall, the roof of a small house hiding him from Marty's view. Neither saw the other, but Hulett heard the massive *boom* of Keller's rifle and knew someone was probably taking a fearsome toll on the bandits to the front. From the sound, he knew the unseen rifleman was on the roof of the main house. It had to be the strange white man who had spooked Sanchez.

Hulett signaled for his men to light the fuses on their wrapped sticks of dynamite. He crouched behind a small tree at the north side of the compound, safely away from the front wall where all the fighting was occurring. One of his men squirmed around the corner of the compound and threw his explosives at the front gate. That exposed him to JB's aim, and the Indian scout promptly drilled a bullet hole above the bandit's left ear. Hulett's other man refused to expose himself, so he threw a charge against the north wall, then scurried to cover behind Hulett.

Marty spotted the arcing flight of the dynamite bundle and vainly shouted a warning just before it exploded. The twin explosions overwhelmed the gunfire, throwing up two great clouds of dust and debris. The bodies of two vaqueros fighting along the east wall flew up and back like mule-kicked dogs. They lay motionless in the front of the courtyard, stunned or killed by the blast. Marty could not tell if Ramon was among them.

In the momentary cover of the blast, Hulett slipped through the jagged rent in the wall with his men. He hoped Sanchez would lead the charge through the gaping hole where the wooden gate once stood. Peering around the corner of a small building, he saw all the defenders were firing at the shattered front gate as the remaining outlaws burst into the compound. The men along the south and west walls ran toward the front, firing as they did, adding their fire to the last of Ramon's defenders. The few outlaws who managed to get through the heavy fire fanned out for cover among the buildings, engaging in a ferocious firefight with the desperate defenders.

Hulett and his men slipped around the building. He and his men were almost to the side of the main house before anyone noticed their approach. Suddenly, Felipe spotted them and shot down the man next to Al. Hulett and his men rapidly returned fire at Don José and three vaqueros on the porch. At a cost of four men, Hulett silenced the defenders on the porch, then raced up the steps and into the house.

On the roof, Marty and JB could hear the sound of gunfire below them. "They're inside the house," he shouted at JB. "You stay up here and I'll go help."

JB nodded and continued to fire at the bandits scattered along the front of the compound. Marty raced down the ladder from the roof. Drawing his twin six-guns, he eased down the stairs to the second-floor hallway. Quickly he moved toward the staircase, his back against the wall.

At the top of the stairs, he could see the open doors of the dining room off to the right and the library off to his left. As he gingerly descended on the first step, two men ran out of the library, guns drawn, looking wildly around. He shot them with two bullets, fired almost as one. Three men, pushing women in front of them, burst through the doorway to the dining room. Marty shot the first in the head and dropped to the floor as the other two fired up at him. Shots also came at him from the library doorway.

Splinters of wood clipped from the banister stung his face as Marty steeled himself to rise up and return the fire. The women screamed in terror, twisting in their captors' arms. Just as Marty made his move, Don José dripping blood, dragged himself across the threshold and shot one of the intruders in the back. The distraction caused the third outlaw to look away from Keller. The deadly bark of the manhunter's guns made the move a fatal error.

Marty raced down the stairs and threw himself through the door of the library. He hit the floor, guns blazing, dropping a shadowy figure by the window. The deadly assault was too much for the other man in the room. The intruder emptied his gun without hitting Keller, then dove through the glass window to the courtyard. Marty scrambled to his feet and ran to the shattered window. A lanky figure was just rounding the corner of the small building by the wall. Marty fired both guns, sending up a shower of dust from the adobe plaster, but failed to score a hit.

He turned and ran out of the library. Don José was propped on one elbow, just inside the main door, a stream of bright blood trailing down his white shirt. Marty looked at his ashen face and turned. "Isobel, where are you?" he shouted.

The tall woman stepped from the kitchen, a large butcher knife in her hand. "Here I am, Marty. Is it safe now?"

"Come quick. Your father's hurt. I must go and help Ramon."

He heard her shouting rapid instructions in Spanish as he ran through the front door. The three vaqueros lay where they had fallen. Keller leaped over them, sprinting to the cover behind the rock wall of the courtyard fountain. A single vaquero shared his cover, exchanging gunfire with bandits shooting from their hiding places inside the wall. Keller looked toward the rooftop. JB was gazing down at him.

"Cover me," he shouted. "I'm headed over there." He pointed to a building off to the right.

JB immediately pushed his rifle over the wall. As soon as the old Indian started pumping bullets at the bandits, Keller ran as fast as he could to a vaquero's small house. Reaching cover beside it, he peeked through a small window, shattered by bullets. A lone bandit, defined by his crossed cartridge belt, was peering out of the door. Another dead outlaw lay on the packed-dirt floor, red blood pooling at the standing man's feet. Only JB's barrage of covering fire saved Keller from certain death.

Without hesitation, Keller shot the bandit from his place at the window and then crawled through it into the house. The dirt floor was slick with blood. Marty pushed the dead outlaw away and glanced out the door. From his vantage point, he had a clear shot at several bandits. He immediately fired with both pistols, dropping all in his sight.

His six-guns were empty when he ducked back inside the doorway. The few outlaws left alive had had enough. Some inside the walls ran for the hole blasted in the wall or tried to scramble over the wall, while others held up their empty hands in surrender. JB and the remaining defenders took the opportunity to shoot several of those fleeing before they got out of range.

Only six terrified men joined Sanchez and his cousin, Ignacio, kneeling behind a slight fold in the ground. Neither had even tried to enter the compound. The two had wisely waited outside while others faced the deadly work of fighting in the close quarters of the courtyard.

Hulett galloped up, his eyes wild. He screamed in

anger and frustration, "Let's git outta here! The bastards were waiting on us. It all fell apart, damn 'em."

The outlaws grabbed the nearest horse and rode hard toward the beckoning foothills, two miles to the east. Hulett cursed and sputtered the entire way. Sanchez kept looking warily behind him. The one who hunted men would be coming—he felt it. He knew the damned gringo had been a bad sign. Now all he wanted to do was get back to the hideout. Survival was their only concern. They could always get more recruits for the gang. He thought briefly about the magnificent white horse. He sure hated to lose it.

At the hacienda, the subsequent silence was as unnerving as the chaos of the battle. Marty ran to the front gate and fired at the retreating forms until they disappeared into the lingering morning mist. Even after the range was too great, he continued to fire, just to hasten their departure. The fight had taken twenty minutes, at the most. The nervous release of tension caused his hands to quiver as he finally turned away from the retreating enemy and holstered his smoking pistols.

He found Ramon near the front gate, struggling to his feet, disoriented from the explosion. The young del Vargas had a bloody scratch oozing on his cheek. Wiping the blood away with a casual swipe of his hand, he asked, "Did we stop them? Is it over? What of my father and Isobel?"

"They're back at the house. Come on, we've got to repair the wall and post guards, in case they return."

Once the ranch's security was firmly reestablished, Marty accompanied Ramon to the house. Isobel came running down the stairs as they walked in. "Ramon, thank God, you are safe. Papa's shot. He is in his bedroom. He is asking for you."

Ramon hurried up the stairs. Isobel moved to Marty's

side. "Are you all right?" she worriedly inquired. She gently put her hand on his arm.

"Yes," he answered. "How are you? What of the others?"

Isobel smiled into his dust- and grime-stained face. "I am fine. As for the rest, so far as I know, six were killed and eleven hurt. One is very bad, I fear. One of the women is badly hurt. A bandito struck her head with his pistol."

JB came down the stairs pointed toward the east. "They ride toward hills. We follow right quick?"

"Damn," Keller replied. "I was sure I hit the leader on his white horse. Yes, we'll follow them. Just give me a few minutes to see that everything is secure here. Isobel, would you please pack food for JB and me? We're going after the rest of them."

"And for me, my sister," Ramon spoke from the top of the stairs. "I believe Papa will recover. Meanwhile, I will go with you, Senor Martin. The ones who did this to our family must be punished."

"That's for sure, my friend," Keller answered. "They forfeited their right to live a long time ago. It's time for them to pay up the account. Hell's waitin' for them."

Chapter 27

Desperate Flight

Marty stood on the veranda, surveying the compound. A slowly dispersing cloud of dust and acid gunsmoke marked the magnitude of the recent fight. "JB," he said to the old scout, "take a couple of vaqueros and check on the bodies outside. Bring inside the compound any who are still alive. Stack the dead by the front gate. The federales will want some of the wounded for interrogation, I reckon." He looked back at Isobel, standing next to her brother. "Isobel, if there are survivors, you'll have to guard them carefully after you tend their wounds. They're vicious people and wouldn't hesitate to slit your throat."

She nodded. "I understand, Martin. Now pardon me while I see that you are properly provisioned for the trail. Carmella, come with me." Isobel hurried away, followed by a frightened servant girl.

Keller wearily sank onto the wooden rocker next to the door. "Damn. I'm bushed and the day's just started."

Ramon reached into his vest pocket, taking out a small silver flask. "Here, this may revive you," he said, passing it to Marty. The fiery taste of fine tequila burned its way down his gullet. Soon, he felt like he was capable of walking across the room.

Marty accompanied Ramon on a tour of the compound. The remaining defenders rushed from one place to another, treating wounded men or repairing the breached wall and front gate. Keller was gratified to see men with rifles alert at every corner. Even young José was still at his post on the roof, watching for danger.

The morning haze evaporated as if it had never existed. Beyond the walls, JB and two companions turned over still forms. *One must still be alive,* Keller decided, as a vaquero scooped a limp body up in his arms and dumped it in the back of a small wagon. JB and the other vaquero entered a small depression to the south and were lost from view.

Presently, they returned, several bodies draped in the wagon's bed. As they approached the porch, where Marty stood, he recognized a fancy white shirt with a bloodstain on its back. Marty nodded at the corpse. "Diego?"

JB slid off the seat of the wagon and rolled the body faceup. "We find him. Knifed in back."

Marty called inside for Ramon. When the younger del Vargas saw the bloody corpse, he knelt beside it, making the sign of the cross; then he looked up at Marty, a question in his eyes.

"JB found him over in a ravine, knifed in the back," Marty responded.

Ramon swiftly rattled off some instruction in Spanish to a nearby vaquero, who ran toward the house, probably for Isobel.

"He must have gone out to scout the enemy and got ambushed," Marty graciously offered to his young friend.

"*Gracias*, Marty. That is what I will tell Isobel. Perhaps it will make it a bit easier for her. You and I know that was never so. Diego got a just reward for trying to run away from the danger we faced."

Marty left Ramon waiting for his sister. What was coming was a family affair. He walked outside the front gate to inspect the growing line of bodies from the decimated bandit gang. Black-bearded Lute Payson lay among his comrades in death, a snarl of disbelief on his face. Keller gazed dispassionately upon the dead man. "One down," he spoke softly. "Two more to go—if only I can finish it now."

Felipe limped over to him, his left arm heavily wrapped and in a sling. "Ah, Senor Keller. We have done a great thing here today. Thirty-four dead and ten wounded banditos for the federales to hang."

"Yes," Marty responded, "but the price was too high. Will you be all right?"

"*Sí*, I have but small scratches, which I shall show my grandchildren someday, when I tell them of the fight and the fearless gringo lawman who helped me save our ranchero."

Marty laughed with the irrepressible Felipe. A body just couldn't stay glum with him around. "You do that, Felipe. I reckon you'll always be young, dodging the Almighty's lightning bolts thrown at you for bulling such lies."

"As God is my witness," Felipe protested, "all I say is the truth."

Marty laughed again. "Well, just wait until I've put some distance between us before you start your tall tales, amigo." He started back toward the house. It was time they got going. The outlaws would be pushing hard, as long as their horses held out. No sense in falling too far behind.

JB and Ramon met him at the steps to the veranda.

"Are we ready?" Marty asked. Both men nodded and checked their saddle cinches one last time.

Isobel brought out a couple bags of provisions, which JB tied to the packhorse. She kissed Ramon and whispered something to him. Then she turned to Marty and kissed him on the cheek. Her red-rimmed eyes and tight lips revealed the grief she was struggling to contain. Husky tremors affected her voice as she spoke to Marty. "Take care of yourself and my brother. I'm here for you when you return." Then she hugged the startled JB and ducked back inside the hacienda.

JB led them through the front gates and down the road toward the grassy hills rising up to the east. Hulett's tracks were fresh and easy to follow. "Six or seven," JB announced.

"More than I'd hoped," Marty muttered. "JB, you'd best get out ahead a ways. They might be of a mind to set up an ambush. Ramon, keep your eyes peeled. If they do, we won't have but one chance to fight our way out of trouble."

JB trotted on ahead, until he was about one hundred yards in front. Marty made it a point to keep him in sight, a difficult thing to do since the trees grew more dense as they climbed toward the summit of the mountains. By nightfall, they had hardly closed the gap. The outlaws were riding hard, pushing their horses to exhaustion, trying to distance themselves from the place where they had suffered such a resounding defeat.

The day passed, twilight fell, and still Marty pushed them on. "We quit for night," JB rode up and announced. "Cannot see tracks and many turnoffs in trail."

Marty hated to stop so close to his elusive quarry, but the old scout was right. The bandits would also eventually have to stop and rest their horses. If he insisted on

riding at night, they might ride past the outlaws or miss a
turnoff. "All right," he agreed. "Let's get some hot grub
and coffee made. Tomorrow, we'll get moving as soon as
it's light enough to see their trail."

Later, Marty checked the perimeter of their campsite
one last time before he woke Ramon for the young man's
turn at guard duty. Then Marty lay exhausted in his
bedroll, but sleep eluded him. He tried to conjure up Caroline's image, but all he saw were disconnected remnants
of her. He could visualize her slender hands quite clearly,
but not her face. *What does it mean?* he wondered. Was
fate preparing him for some destiny? Isobel awaited his
return—he knew that. She was his if he wanted her. Did
he? He had to decide. Did he want her? The allure of the
proud, beautiful Mexican woman seemed to stand between Caroline and him.

The three men were under way before sunrise the next
morning, and as the fiery orb cleared the mountaintops,
they came upon the outlaws' camp. A tiny curl of smoke
still snaked upward from their abandoned campfire. The
gap was closing. The outlaws were slowing down; perhaps their horses were giving out from the previous day's
hard riding.

They reached the summit of the mountain range well
before noon, having closed to within a few miles of
Hulett. Marty took his Army-issue binoculars and surveyed the land falling away before him. This side of the
mountain range was less rain-blessed and had far fewer
trees. The harsh landscape was undisturbed by any
human presence, as far as he could see.

"Senor Marty, may I look?" Ramon asked.

"Sure thing," Marty replied as he handed the binoculars to him. "Just be careful."

But it was too late, the exuberant Ramon had placed
the glasses to his eyes and swept across the view to his

front. Marty groaned to himself. If anybody below had been watching, they might have seen the sunlight reflect off the lens.

Somebody was. All night, Alva Hulett had battled against his private nightmare. He was beside himself with agitation. The dark stranger once again shadowed him, and had ruined his plan to take the del Vargas ranch. All morning he cursed his rotten luck and his worthless companions. Two of the horses were almost completely broken down. They'd been ridden too hard the day before. The outlaws had stopped to give the tired animals a quick rest before entering a treeless, rocky canyon. "Damn it, Sanchez," he snarled to his partner. "Those two boys'll git us kilt, goin' so slow. We got to leave 'em and git back to the hideout." He shifted in his saddle, anxious to get moving.

He looked back toward the mountain, retracing the trail they had just traversed. "Good Gawd," he whispered. "There's someone up there spyin' on us with a telescope glass. I jus' seen the sun reflectin' off it." He spurred his horse toward the last six remaining members of the gang.

Hulett stopped the group and pointed at four of them, including the two with bad mounts. "You four, stay here and watch our backs fer a while. Set up a little surprise fer anyone who might be trailin' us. The rest of us'll move on ahead. We'll stop fer the night at the far end of this canyon. You kin catch up with us."

Sanchez nodded his agreement, since his cousin was not among those to be sacrificed as rear guards. "Sí, that is a good idea. Pedro, you will be in charge. From now on, you are Captain Pedro."

The gullible Pedro, grinning from ear to ear at his promotion, led his fellow guards toward a cluster of bushes and rocks that overlooked the narrow animal trail they had just followed down from the top of the mountain. As they rode away, Hulett looked back at the men being left as sacrifices. Except for Pedro, their expressions were glum. Hulett had little confidence in their ability, although they might get lucky and ambush their pursuers. He could only hope they killed the man who was following him so doggedly.

JB sensed danger as he approached the rocks where the four ambushers waited. His years scouting for the Army and for Sheriff Thompson had honed his reflexes for trouble. The last few weeks with Keller had restored his innate gift for tracking, which had been unused while working at the ranch. The eerie silence and the raised ears of his horse immediately alerted him to the presence of the hidden killers.

He slowed his pony to a walk, easing off to the left, away from the perceived danger. Behind a huge boulder, he waited for Keller to come into view. When he saw the tall rider, he motioned with his rifle to the right. Marty stopped and drew his Winchester from the saddle scabbard under his right leg. He had to save the four bullets he had left for the big Spencer, in case of emergencies. Marty eased off Pacer, motioning wide-eyed Ramon to dismount.

"What is it?" Ramon whispered.

"JB's spotted something ahead—off to the right, since he's drifting to the left. Walk beside your horse and keep to the left." They slowly started on down the trail, their horses acting as shields. In a few moments, JB was gone, and Marty and Ramon were alone on the trail.

They emerged from a small gully and saw the cluster of rocks and brush to their right front. The morning was quiet, the air still. His guts churning, Marty led the way on down the trail, resisting the impulse to stare at the suspected menace on his right.

From their hidden positions, Pedro and his three brother killers looked with disappointment at the approaching men. As much as Pedro hated to kill a good horse, it would be almost as good as shooting the man. At least their pursuers would be afoot and maybe would try to run away. Then they could be easy targets, like scared rabbits. Grinning, he rose slightly to get a clear shot at the big gray horse in front.

Suddenly, JB's bullet tore through Pedro's cruel heart, then slammed into the ground in front of the newly promoted, but now very dead, bandit captain. The old scout had quietly worked his way around the ambush site and come up from the rear of the surprised men. The three remaining bandits quickly sought cover to protect themselves from the new threat behind them. When they looked back, the two men and the horses to the front were back in the gully, out of sight.

A lull fell over the ambush site. Marty and Ramon lay against the wall of the gully, their rifles pointed at the cluster of rocks and bushes. "Do you see them, Senor Marty?" Ramon whispered.

Marty merely shook his head and watched the rocks. A skitter of pebbles fell from beside one of the bigger boulders. Marty aimed at the mass of dried brush growing there and released half a breath. The parched bush moved, ever so slightly, but there was no wind. He pumped six quick shots at the target, and Ramon cut loose beside him, aiming wildly. Marty's target flopped out, drilled in three places, sliding down the rocky slope to the flat trail below. The two remaining bandits had had enough. They tried to scramble to their horses, but one of them fell to JB's rifle. The last outlaw galloped away as fast as his tired horse would carry him, riding toward the hellish desert of central Mexico.

Ramon leaped to his feet and fired in vain at the fleeing bandit. Marty considered getting out his sniper rifle and shooting the panicked outlaw, but decided against doing so. *Only two more,* he swore to himself, *and then never again—that is, if God wills it.*

JB rode out of the cover of the boulders he had been hiding in. "Think Hulett know plan not work?" he asked.

"Most likely, I reckon," Keller answered. "There were too many shots to figure the ambush worked. Check those fellows out and let's get going. We've lost time we can't afford because of 'em." Marty looked down the mountain. "Hulett, you bastard, it didn't work. I'm still coming—you hear me, killer?"

Not surprisingly, Hulett did not hear anything. He, Sanchez, Ignacio, and another outlaw were in a deep canyon. The sounds of the skirmish passed over the fleeing men. Their horses' clattering hoofbeats against the loose rocks of the canyon floor drowned out any sound.

As the four of them trotted on, Hulett listened for gunfire, praying the unknown hunter had fallen prey to his trap. *"Who is he anyway?"* his mind kept asking as he rode. The sun had reached its zenith and begun its downward slide toward the night. Still no sound. *"What the hell is going on?"* the rattled outlaw thought for the hundredth time. *"What the hell is going on?"*

Chapter 28

Death Delivered

Ramon threw up his hand and slid his panting horse to a stop. The three men had just reached a tangled jumble of rocks and twisted pinon trees. Some tracks led directly into the red walls of a twisting sandstone canyon. "Senor Marty, I have been here before. Climb down and let me show you how this canyon comes out."

Grabbing a stick, Ramon drew in the powdery dust. "As I remember, the canyon goes for nearly twenty miles and then splits very much like a Y. Once you ride into it, you can only escape by climbing the walls and leaving your horses. This the banditos would not do, I think." He paused and pointed at the top of the Y he had drawn. "The right fork goes many miles to the south. The left one exits shortly thereafter onto the flatlands to the east."

Ramon wiped the sweat from his upper lip with the back of his hand, looking at the entrance to the canyon. "If you think they will continue east, I can show you another trail that will cut five miles off the journey. We can get in front of them very easily."

It was the break Marty had been waiting for. "By gum,

at least it's worth a try. JB, you stay on their trail. If they turn south, fire three shots and follow 'em. Ramon and I will light out after you. We'll catch up as soon as we can. You just stay on their trail." He paused, considering the options. "If they head our way, you can cut off any retreat."

JB nodded. "I go. You save one for JB to scalp." A wry grin softened his weather-seamed face.

Marty watched the old scout trot his pinto into the winding canyon. He whispered low, "Good luck, old-timer. Take care of yourself." Tightening Pacer's cinch strap, he looked at Ramon. "Amigo, lead the way and ride hard. I want to be in front of the bastards when we see 'em next."

They did ride hard for the next two hours. Ramon's shortcut led them out of the winding maze of rock and gullies and onto flatter ground. They galloped toward the gaping exit, which opened out of the stark mountainside. The land had been tortured by the harsh winds and driving rains for centuries. It was scarred by eroded ravines and slabs of broken rock. As they approached the exit to the canyon that hopefully contained their quarry, Marty looked for sign that riders had passed that way before them. "Ramon, my young amigo," he chortled, "I think we did it. If they're coming this way, we're ahead of 'em."

He led his horse onto a plateau with a clear view of the rugged terrain below and about two hundred yards from the mouth of the canyon. "Ramon, you take up a spot here," Marty instructed. "I'm moving over there behind that rock. We should have 'em bracketed between us unless they leave the trail once they're out of the canyon. Don't fire until I do, but then let 'em have it with all you've got."

"*Sí*, Senor Marty. I pray we are successful. As for me,

I am ready. Let the sons of Satan come." He settled down behind a small boulder, his rifle poking at the barren ground before him.

Marty wrapped Pacer's reins around a small shrub nearby, then carried his two rifles to a jutting rock slab, where he made himself a firing position in the shade. He settled himself and started the mental sequence that would take him to a killing frame of mind. He should be able to knock down all the riders coming out of the mouth of the canyon before they got close enough to present any threat to Ramon. He didn't want to tell Isobel that she had lost a brother, as well as her husband.

This was the moment he'd been waiting for all the long years since that awful day he'd ridden into his front yard. He saw again the two fresh graves beside the old cottonwood and the grief-stricken faces of his friends. Marty examined his feelings. So far he felt no different from any of the other times he'd sat waiting for some outlaw to come within range. This time, however, he'd shoot first and damn the stain on his conscience.

He allowed his mind to wander, confident that he would quickly react at the first sign of the outlaws. He pictured Meg, and his boy. The images would not quite come to him, yet there was enough to trigger the pain. Without effort, the faces of Caroline's two daughters worked their way into his thoughts, and then came Caroline followed by the regal image of Isobel. He had been a man who connected to no one only four months ago; now he had four females floating around his brain. *Get your mind on the business at hand, bub,* he reminded himself.

Still, his thoughts wandered. Isobel was free. He could stay in Mexico with her, maybe build a new spread somewhere near the blue lake. He believed Caroline was sincere when she said he could return to her, but had her desire to use his skills overwhelmed her good sense?

Still, he argued to himself, he had felt the unspoken promise of her desire for him before he left. He could go back to Texas, to his old home range, and start again, free of the demons that had dogged him for so long.

Abruptly, a desert grouse flew up, right about where Hulett's band should have been exiting the canyon. Marty glanced over at Ramon. The young Mexican was watching the gap. He'd seen the spooked bird as well.

There they were: four of them riding sweat-stained horses with heads held low. Marty sighted them through the scope of the Spencer rifle. Sure enough, a white man was in the lead. It had to be Hulett sitting warily in the saddle, his eyes darting from side to side—the man who had brutally murdered Keller's family. Beside him had to be Sanchez, slouched in the saddle. Behind them rode two others, both oblivious to any threat, as if capture was the last thing on their minds.

Marty wiped a sheen of sweat from his brow. He looked back into the optics of the sniper scope. The men framed in the scope shimmered from the heat waves as they rode toward him. Marty waited. *Shoot,* his brain commanded. His finger tightened on the double trigger of the gun. The soft *click* of the safety releasing alerted him to the immediacy of the gun's firing. *Shoot!* he commanded himself. *Shoot!*

Still he waited, sweat dripping off the angle of his jaw. It was no use. He couldn't kill these men without warning. Of all the outlaws he had ever chased, these deserved the least amount of mercy, yet he couldn't find it within himself to kill them without a warning. Praying that his weakness wouldn't bring harm to Ramon, he let the outlaws ride closer and closer.

He could see the little puffs of yellow-brown dust kicked up by the hooves of the horses. A man's body completely filled the round circle of the scope. It was time. Rising to one knee, he shouted down at the riders, "Hulett! Sanchez! You're covered. Throw down your guns and get off your horses with your hands up."

The loud shout reverberated around the quiet landscape. Hulett jerked his eyes up, looking for the source. His back had been twitching for the last hour. He had sensed something bad was about to happen. Reacting faster than he ever had in his murderous life, the lanky killer drew and fired his pistol at the kneeling man covering him from up on the little bluff.

The range was too far for a pistol, and the round hit in front of Marty. The grit kicked up by its impact caused the tension-stressed Texan to flinch as he pulled the rifle's trigger the rest of the way. The heavy 450-grain bullet, instead of smacking into Hulett's chest, hit his unfortunate horse right between the forelegs, instantly killing the poor animal, dropping it into the dusty trail. Hulett flopped over the head of his dead mount and rolled to his feet, shooting as fast as he could pull the trigger while running toward the bluff where Marty stood.

Marty struggled with the ejection mechanism of his rifle. "Damn it," he muttered. "What a time to jam on me." He dropped the Spencer and levered a round into his Winchester. He looked up just in time to see Hulett running behind a fractured sandstone rock, ducking into the safety of a ravine that opened under the overhang. As soon as Hulett reached it, he was free of detection from above. The scared outlaw moved around the hillside toward what he hoped was cover and a place to fight from when Marty came down after him.

Marty glanced toward the outlaws riding behind Hulett. Hulett had not even bothered to look to see what had happened to them before hightailing it down the ravine.

At the sound of Marty's voice, Sanchez savagely

sawed his reins, spurring his tired horse back into the canyon they had just exited. He would find cover, then consider his next move. Looking back over his shoulder, he saw no one was pursuing him. With a wicked grin, Sanchez rode away from his comrades, unconcerned as to their fate.

Ignacio and his comrade broke hard to the left, drawing their pistols and firing blindly at the bluff. Their path took them behind another rock outcropping, which shielded them from the hidden Ramon. Cursing in frustration, the young Mexican slid down the backside of the bluff and leaped on his horse. Gigging his spurs in the animal's flanks, he quickly had the animal at a dead run. Gun in hand, he galloped after the two bandits.

Ignacio realized that the person after them was gaining fast. Seeing a broad expanse of open ground to their front, he shouted to his comrade over the noise of the running horses, "Turn right and close on the one chasing us. I'll turn left, and we'll have him trapped. Kill him!" He swung wide and turned back toward the single rider galloping after him. He saw the other outlaw swing right as instructed. Ramon had suddenly become the hunted instead of the hunter.

Ramon slid his horse to a halt and fired at the man on the right, knocking him out of the saddle. He turned to the bandito on the left, but too late. He saw the flash of red as the gun fired, and he felt a burning sensation slash against his left side. He suddenly realized he was on the ground, fighting to get a breath into his body. Sharp pain radiated from his side and his left arm. When he tried to move it, nothing happened. *It must have broken when I fell,* he thought to himself. *Madre de Dios, if they come for me, what will I do?*

Motionless, Ramon carefully glanced through slitted eyes and saw his assailant sitting on his horse thirty yards in front of him, watching for signs of life. When Ramon didn't move, the confident bandit cautiously spurred his tired horse forward.

Ignacio wanted the downed man's horse and would look for booty while he rested a minute. The bandit was certain he had killed the young man lying in front of him. He had seen the bullet strike, heard the grunt of pain, and seen the man fall hard.

Ramon lay quiet, scarcely breathing, as Ignacio approached to only a few yards from him. As the outlaw slid from his saddle, Ramon twisted until his right arm and his pistol were free. The excruciating pain left him breathless, but he was able to rapidly fire two killing shots into the stunned Ignacio. That proved to be the easy part. Now he had to get out of the dry dust and return to Martin and JB. Groaning in agony, he painfully, slowly, pulled himself into the saddle of his patient horse. Slowly he urged it back toward the mouth of the canyon, struggling to stay in the saddle.

Ramon held his broken arm tightly against his side and took shallow breaths to minimize the pain. He surprised himself by making the trip without passing out. Sliding off his horse, the wounded del Vargas held on to his animal's reins and lay against a large boulder, waiting for someone to return. Friend or foe, it didn't matter. He was out of the fight now.

Meanwhile, Sanchez rode hard for a few hundred yards into the twisting canyon. Warily he slowed, looking over his shoulder for sign of pursuit. Gradually he relaxed and started to mull over his options. His horse cantered around a bend in the trail. A hundred yards in front of him sat a silent figure on a pinto pony, a rifle cradled in his arms. Surprised, Sanchez looked around. Just one man. *Well, too bad for him,* the bandit thought. Spurring his tired horse viciously, he charged the intruder, drawing his pistol.

With a fluid movement, John Black Crow raised his rifle and shot the charging Sanchez right under the brim of his floppy sombrero. The dead bandito fell backward off his horse and lay faceup, spread eagle in the sandy soil of the trail, his sightless eyes staring into the hot afternoon sun.

JB rode up to the body and dismounted. Pulling his knife, he slashed the forearm of the dead man and muttered, "For my friend Keller, dog dung." He started to remount, then paused and slashed the other arm. "And for me."

Satisfied, he grabbed the reins of the departed Sanchez' horse and trotted toward the gunfire he heard to the east. *Maybe more fight,* he thought, flushed with the heat of battle.

In the meantime, Marty peered over the side of the overhang. The others had fled, leaving just Hulett and him. The outlaw had disappeared behind some rocks to the side of the bluff. Marty slid down the dirt embankment beneath his ledge and hurried after the fleeing killer. Cursing himself with every step for not killing Hulett when he had the chance, he followed the footprints left by the one man he had wanted most to face for the past seven years.

The ground was broken and rugged. A deep ravine, with more than a sixty-foot drop, angled out of the foothills to his front. Hulett would have to bear right or risk tumbling down the steep, slippery sandstone walls. As Marty reached the edge, he saw that from this point on the drop was too steep for any escape. Hulett had to be hidden in the jumbled boulders along the edge of the precipice. Slowly, Marty moved into the maze of yellow sandstone boulders. He stayed close to the edge of the high cliffs that formed the right side of the trail. A deadly drop to the left and a steep rock face to the right. His foe was trapped. The only sure way out was past him.

Hulett darted from boulder to boulder, trying to stay concealed and still searching desperately for an exit. He sensed someone closing in on him, but so far the panicked killer had seen no one. He stopped behind a ten-foot-high rock that had crashed to the trail years before. His fingers shaking, Al punched out the empty shells from his pistol and thumbed in six fresh rounds. His breath was rasping in and out, his mouth was as dry as cotton, yet while sweat dripped off his forehead, stinging his eyes.

Al took a hasty peek around the rock. He spotted his pursuer, steadily moving from cover to cover, coming straight toward him. His first shot chipped shards from a boulder next to the oncoming stranger.

Marty dropped behind the rock, where the bullet hit, and returned three shots in the general direction of Hulett. Then he ran hard to another boulder and peered around it, looking for his unseen target.

The panicky Hulett couldn't wait; he didn't know who else might be joining the man after him. He darted toward another rock, farther into the ravine. Marty snapped a quick shot at the movement, just missing. Then he moved in closer, using a boulder between him and Hulett as cover.

The sting of grit from the near miss rattled Hulett. He made a disastrous mistake and ran toward the edge of the ravine. The sheerness of the drop stopped him in his tracks. He tried to angle toward the high wall of the ravine, but Marty had moved forward and cut him off. They traded shots, the whine of ricocheting bullets and blasting six-guns filling the air. Marty moved again and now was only a few paces from Hulett, who crouched be-

hind the last rock available as cover and nervously reloaded his pistols.

Marty took off his hat and waited. As soon as he saw
Hulett's head appear around the stone, he flipped the hat
toward him, then dove to the right. Hitting the hard
ground with a grunt, he rolled and emptied the pistol he
held in his left hand. Only one bullet hit its mark, but it
was a telling strike. The .44 slug slammed into Hulett's
right shoulder, shattering the socket and breaking the collar bone. Hulett dropped his pistol and staggered back,
off the sharp edge of the cliff.

Marty got to his feet and cautiously moved to the edge
of the dropoff. A few feet below, Hulett held on to a root
with his left hand, his right hand dangling uselessly and
both feet desperately scrambling, trying to get a purchase
on the shear rock. The outlaw looked up at his nemesis.

Hulett whimpered, "Help me. Help me, damn ya. I
cain't hold on much longer." He sought a ledge with his
toes, seeking any crack or crevice to get a foothold in the
smooth, hard shale.

At long last Martin Keller faced the murderer of his
family, unable and unwilling to move a muscle on
Hulett's behalf. For seven long years he had worked and
prayed for this moment. His tormentor now begged for
mercy, probably much as Margaret had on that awful day,
back in Texas. Marty stared coldly at the anguished face
of the killer he had hunted for so long.

Gasping in fear and agony, Hulett struggled to pull
himself up with his one good arm. "Damn ya. Who are ya
anyway?"

Marty spoke in a calm voice. "I'm death, Hulett, and
I've been hunting you for seven long years."

To Alva Hulett, it did not seem as if he was falling, but
rather that the dark stranger was rising away from him,
receding faster and faster into the blue sky. The babbling

killer didn't even feel the impact of his body against the jagged rocks at the bottom of the gorge.

His face impassive, devoid of any emotion, Marty looked down at the broken body and whispered his final goodbye to his family. "Meg, darlin' Meg, and my little son who'll never be a man—it's all over now. God bless you and rest in peace."

At his feet, he saw the pistol Hulett had dropped. It was a .44 Smith & Wesson, with gold coins inlayed into the polished wooden grips. *Sheriff Thompson's pistol,* he thought. *I'll take it back to Caroline. Maybe it'll close the book for her as well.* He picked it up and shoved it into the waistband of his pants. Now he had to find out if JB and Ramon were alive. As he made his way off the narrow pathway, he never looked back.

Chapter 29

Homecoming

Isobel rode out of the front gate to meet the men while they were still a quarter of a mile from the ranch. It was a pleasure to see the beautiful woman, gracefully mounted sidesaddle on a brown Thoroughbred, riding toward them. She rounded her horse to join them, speaking in a rush, her eyes sweeping over Marty's face.

"Oh, Martin," she gushed, "we saw you ride out of the trees. I couldn't wait any longer." She looked down at the travois bouncing along behind Ramon's horse. "Is my brother . . . ?"

Marty shook his head. "No, he's just weak from shock and loss of blood. He has a broken arm and a bullet bounced off a rib. Maybe it's broken too. I don't know. A little time in bed and he'll be fine. How is your father?"

"Papa is recovering," she answered. Looking at him with serious eyes, she asked the question foremost in her mind, now that everyone was safe. "Did you catch them?"

Marty jerked his thumb at the string of horses trailing

along behind JB. "Yes, we got 'em all, Isobel. Your family will never again have to fear them." He slapped the saddlebags behind his saddle. "Hulett had near six thousand in gold on him. You'll be able to fix up your ranch and have plenty left over."

Isobel didn't seem to even hear what Keller said. She jumped off her horse, her black mourning dress catching on the saddle, momentarily showing a long expanse of slim leg. Marty stopped his horse so she could speak to Ramon.

Isobel bent over the quiet form wrapped in the blankets of the travois. "Ramon, my brother, are you all right?"

Ramon blinked his eyes open. "Yes, I'm fine. I'm just very tired. How is Father?"

"Father is going to be all right." She laughed and grabbed his free hand in hers. "And the federales came two days after you left. They were very, very surprised. They expected to find a smoking ruin. Their captain was truely impressed when he saw the number of banditos we had killed or captured. He took the wounded ones back with him. He said not to worry. They would not be coming this way again, ever."

Isobel walked the rest of the way to the ranch beside her brother, asking questions about the fight at the canyon and telling Ramon of the activities at the ranch. By the time they had put Ramon to bed and eaten their supper, it was well after dark.

Marty sat on the porch with Isobel. He told her about the chase and the final gun battle. "Ramon took on two bandits by himself and got both even though they had wounded him. He was very brave, Isobel. You and Don José can be proud of him."

She took Marty's hand and looked up into his eyes. "And you, Martin Keller. Is it over for you now?"

"It has to be," he replied. He paused, collecting his thoughts, then continued. "I'm surprised to say that I feel sort of empty. I thought I'd feel satisfaction. Instead, all I know is that I'm empty inside. Whatever was there, it's gone now, thank God. What I feel is empty and tired." Marty looked down at Isobel. "I need to be with others, to fill up the hole inside me with people, laughter, something besides the stench of death."

She moved closer to him, running her hand up his arm to his cheek. "Then this is the place for you, my dearest. I am free now. Diego's death has given me another chance at happiness. You can live here with me. We will raise fine horses, and one day you will be the grand jefe with me at you side. My father will let you do as you please while he enjoys his last years in peace."

"Whoa, Isobel," Marty interjected. "What about Ramon? He's gonna want to call the shots in a few years, I reckon."

"Oh, Marty, Ramon loves you as I do. He'll be happy too. You both can work together."

"Beside," Marty continued, as he gestured aimlessly in the darkness, "I sort of wanted to make my own mark in the world, not stand in the shadows of what some other man has built. Would you be interested in taking off with me and starting from scratch. Maybe building up a small spread into a bigger one?"

"Dear Marty, that's not necessary—don't you see? We have it all here, right now, without having to start over. Besides, I cannot leave my father's hacienda. He needs me near to take care of him."

Marty could only nod his head in understanding. "Your father needs you and I need to make my own way. That's why I must go, even though I wish I could stay."

Isobel started to say something, then stopped. They remained silent for a moment. Then a servant called Isobel to her father's bedside. "Excuse me, dear Marty. I must go." She hurried off into the house.

Marty ambled to the repaired front gate of the compound. An armed vaquero greeted him, smiling warmly in the bright moonlight. *"Buenos noches."*

"Buenos noches." Marty walked aimlessly up the road, breathing the fragrance of the evening. It would be easy to stay here and not have to face the prospect of returning to Colorado only to find that Caroline had changed her mind about him. It would be unfair to demand that she honor her offer. She might have met someone else, these last two months. As uncertain as he was, he knew he had to go back to find out for himself. He walked for a long time, thinking about Colorado.

The next morning, he met with the injured Don José and Ramon. Both were doing well, and it was obvious that Isobel didn't need Marty's help running the ranch for her father. The activity of the ranch was back to normal and repairs had been completed. He did what he could to help, but he could see his effort was unnecessary.

That night, he and Isobel sat alone at the dinner table, liveried servants standing by to replenish their plates. "Isobel, I suppose I'd best be getting on back to Colorado. You've got things under control here, and John Black Crow is anxious to get home before the snows come."

Isobel dropped her eyes to her plate. After a long pause, she raised her head and looked at him, her eyes shiny with tears. "As you wish, Martin. You are welcome to stay. If you think you must go, then . . ." She stopped, fighting to keep her face composed.

Marty was quiet. He did not know what to say or do. Presently, Isobel left the table, saying her father needed her. He was a little disappointed, yet also relieved he didn't have to be alone with her. He felt a strong attraction for the elegant Mexican woman, and the desire that coursed through him when she got near made him very uncomfortable.

The next morning, Ramon sent for him. Marty entered the bedroom of his young friend to find him propped up with pillows, smiling brightly. "Ah, you are ready to leave us?"

"Yep, I reckon JB and I had better get on back before it gets too cold in the high country."

"Martin, my friend, will you come see us again when you can?"

"I can think of nothing I'd like better, Ramon. You can count on it."

Ramon flashed a bright smile. "Good. Now listen. You said your rancho breeds horses, *sí*? Well, we breed fine horses too. Come down in the spring, bring some of your best. We'll trade and sell horses to each other." He nodded knowingly at his friend. "If you are lucky in love, bring her too. If not, come alone. By then Isobel will be through her mourning period, and you know—"

Marty shook the outstretched hand. "Partner, it's a deal. I'll be seeing you when the desert flowers bloom. It's a promise. In the meantime you get well."

Marty left the room and went out to the veranda. Isobel and Don José were waiting for him, the old man supported by a sturdy vaquero. JB was already mounted, holding a halter tied to the magnificent white stallion once ridden by General Morales and four black fillies, all beautiful Spanish-Arabian purebreds. Marty looked questionably at Don José.

"The white is yours, by right of combat," the old man replied to the unasked question. "And the mares are from my best stock. Add them to your herd in Colorado. They

should give you many fine colts to raise. It is but little reward for the help you have given me. You saved my
ranch and family and helped Ramon prove himself to be
the man I had hoped he would be. My son has asked you
to come back. I add my invitation as well. We hope you
will honor this house with your presence again. Farewell,
my brave amigo."

Don José gripped Marty's hand, then limped into the
house. Marty was left with Isobel. Her dark eyes were
shiny with glistening tears. "Farewell, my brave Martin.
Come back to us." She brushed her lips against his cheek
and looked up at him with tear-filled eyes. "My brave
Yankee, you leave your Isobel with a gift of our love."
She rushed into the house, her head held high. Keller
swung into the saddle, wishing there was something
he could have said, but he was momentarily speechless.
He paused. *What does she mean by a gift of their love?
She can't be . . . ? Naw, she's just upset. That's what it has
to be.*

The two men rode away from the ranch to waves of
farewell and shouts of good fortune, heading toward the
mountains once again. Keller stopped just before they entered the treeline. The white ranch and walled compound
sat serenely in the morning sun. *A jewel on an emerald
carpet*, he thought. *From here a person would never
know that a battle raged here such a short time ago*. The
view etched itself in Keller's memory.

That night he found three thousand in gold buried in
the sacks of food and gifts given him by the del Vargas
family. He and JB considered returning the money, but finally agreed it was their hosts' decision. "We'll just have
to bring down the best horses we have when next we
visit, old friend."

JB nodded in satisfaction. He had made a special

friend of one of the female members of the household staff. He looked forward to renewing the acquaintance.

It was nearly sundown when Caroline finished cleaning up the remains of supper and bathing the girls. She was tired, but satisfied. They'd finished cutting the hay for winter feed today, and it was all stacked in the high meadow, by the stream where she had picnicked with Martin last spring. The help of Joe and Bob Layden had made all the difference in completing the task. Since Joe had married Fionna McNulty, the two hands had become woven into the fabric of the ranch.

As they did every day, her thoughts drifted to Martin Keller, the man she now knew she loved. She wondered where he was and if he was safe. She whispered a little prayer for him and JB, visualizing the picture of him that she carried in her mind: tall and strong, standing in front of the porch, his blue eyes crinkled in a smile, his hair blowing in the wind.

The evenings were getting cooler now, autumn reigned supreme. The gold leaves of the aspen trees covered the mountains, shimmering in the evening breeze. A long flock of honking geese flew high overhead, probably headed for the fresh-mown field of oats in the high meadow. She listened to them honk their support for one another as they beat their way through the thin mountain air. Breathing deeply, she felt in her pocket for the latest letter from Martin.

Caroline caught movement out of the corner of her eye, then spied riders headed up the road from the cutoff. She watched for a few minutes and suddenly her heart began to beat faster. *It looks like him. Pray God it is him. That has to be JB behind him.*

"Thank you, God," she whispered. Nervously, she worked some loose strands of hair into place. Her heart thumping in her chest, she stepped off the porch and waited by the hitching post for the men to ride up.

Marty pulled up at the hitching post and threw his leg over the pommel of his saddle, sliding off to stand beside his horse. "Hello, Caroline. We're back."

She looked at him. He was lean and worn, with a tired look on his face, but otherwise much as she remembered him. "You're both well?" she asked.

"We're fine. How are you and the girls?"

"They're fine. So am I."

For a moment there was silence. Then the old scout spoke up. "Thompson's woman, I see you."

"I see you, John Black Crow," she solemnly replied.

"Thompson can sleep with his fathers. He is avenged. It is good." He handed the dead sheriff's pistol to Caroline. With majestic grandeur, he pointed toward Marty. "I return Keller to you, safe and well. Now I take horses to corral. Then JB rest."

Caroline watched the old scout lead the horses away, and then turned back to Marty, still standing beside Pacer. "We're lucky to have that fine old man with us." She looked at him. "What about you, Martin Keller? You going to stay awhile or what?"

Keller smiled at the woman, his blue eyes crinkling. "I'm going to stay just as long as you'll let me, Caroline. And then you may have to run me off with a whip"—he paused and looked at her shyly—"if that's all right with you." His eyes never left her face as he awaited her answer.

Her smile reflected the joy her heart was feeling. She stepped toward him, opening her arms to hold him. "Well then, Martin Keller, welcome home. We missed you." As she felt his strong arms enfold her, she shouted toward the house, "Mary, Rose, come here and see who just rode up."

The red sun of day's end slipped behind the western horizon, reflecting a warm crimson glow against the low-lying clouds. Two little girls, squealing in happiness, wrapped themselves around Marty's long legs. The peace of evening descended upon the family, as they held tight to one another.